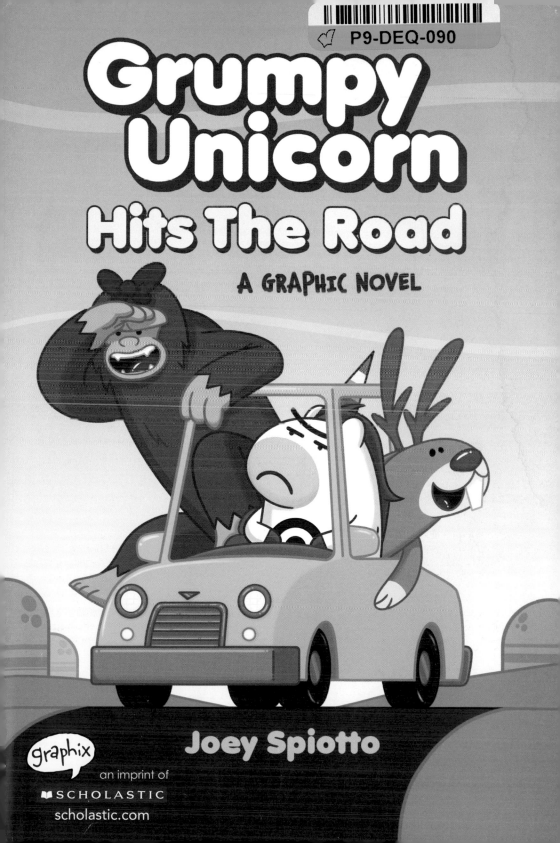

# Grumpy Unicorn
## Hits The Road
### A GRAPHIC NOVEL

**Joey Spiotto**

graphix

an imprint of

**SCHOLASTIC**

scholastic.com

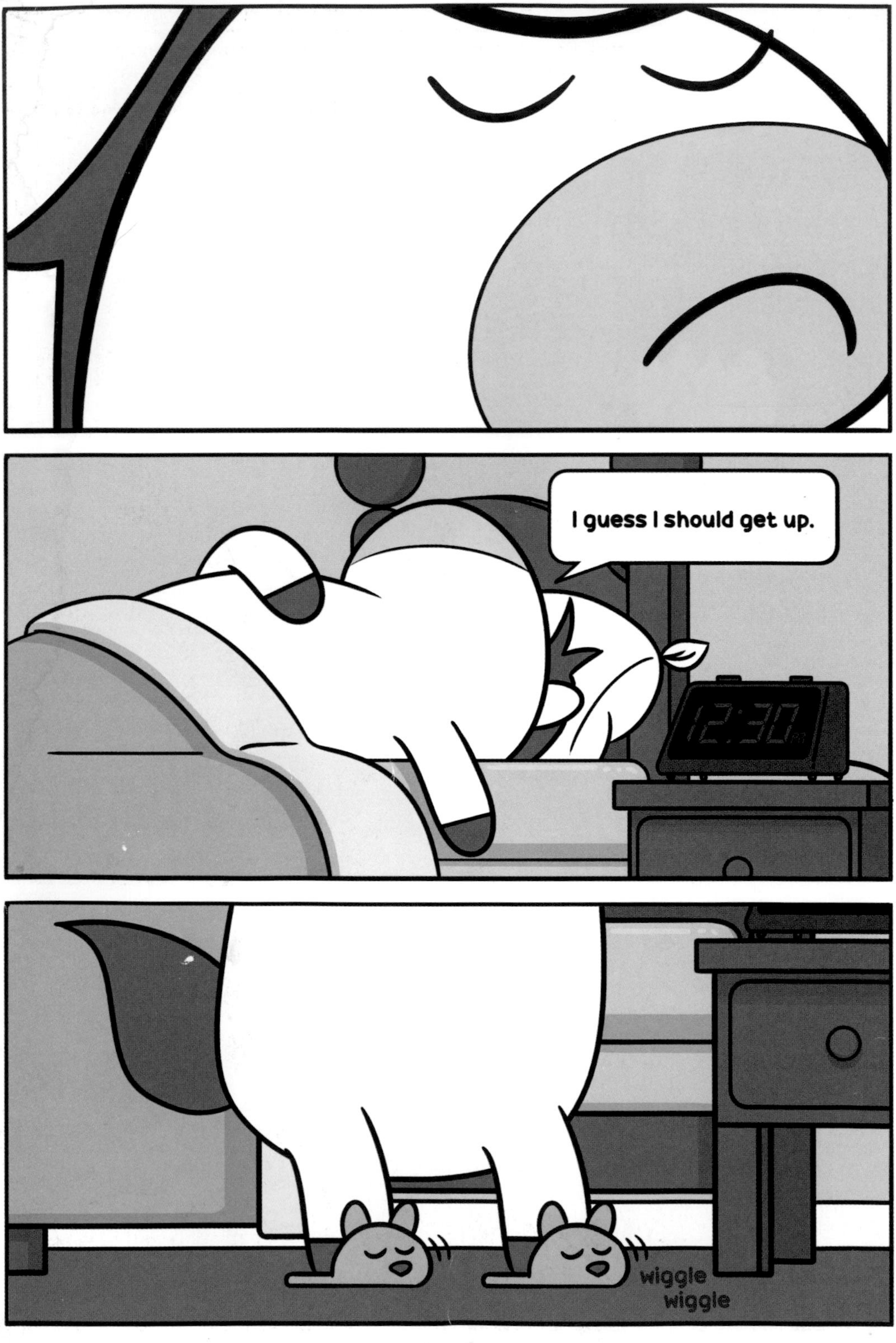
I guess I should get up.
12:30
wiggle
wiggle

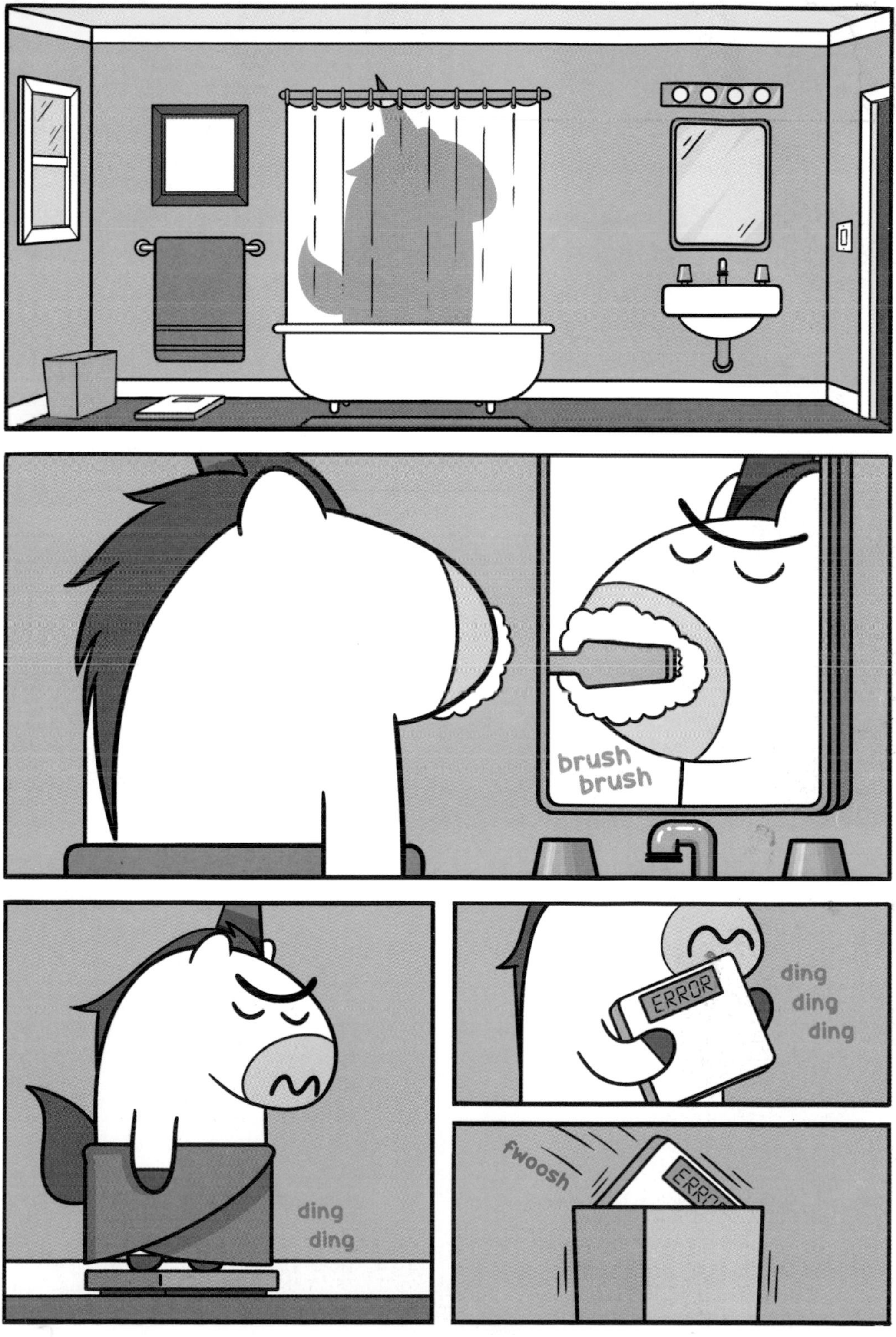
brush
brush
ding
ding
ERROR
ding
ding
ding
fwoosh

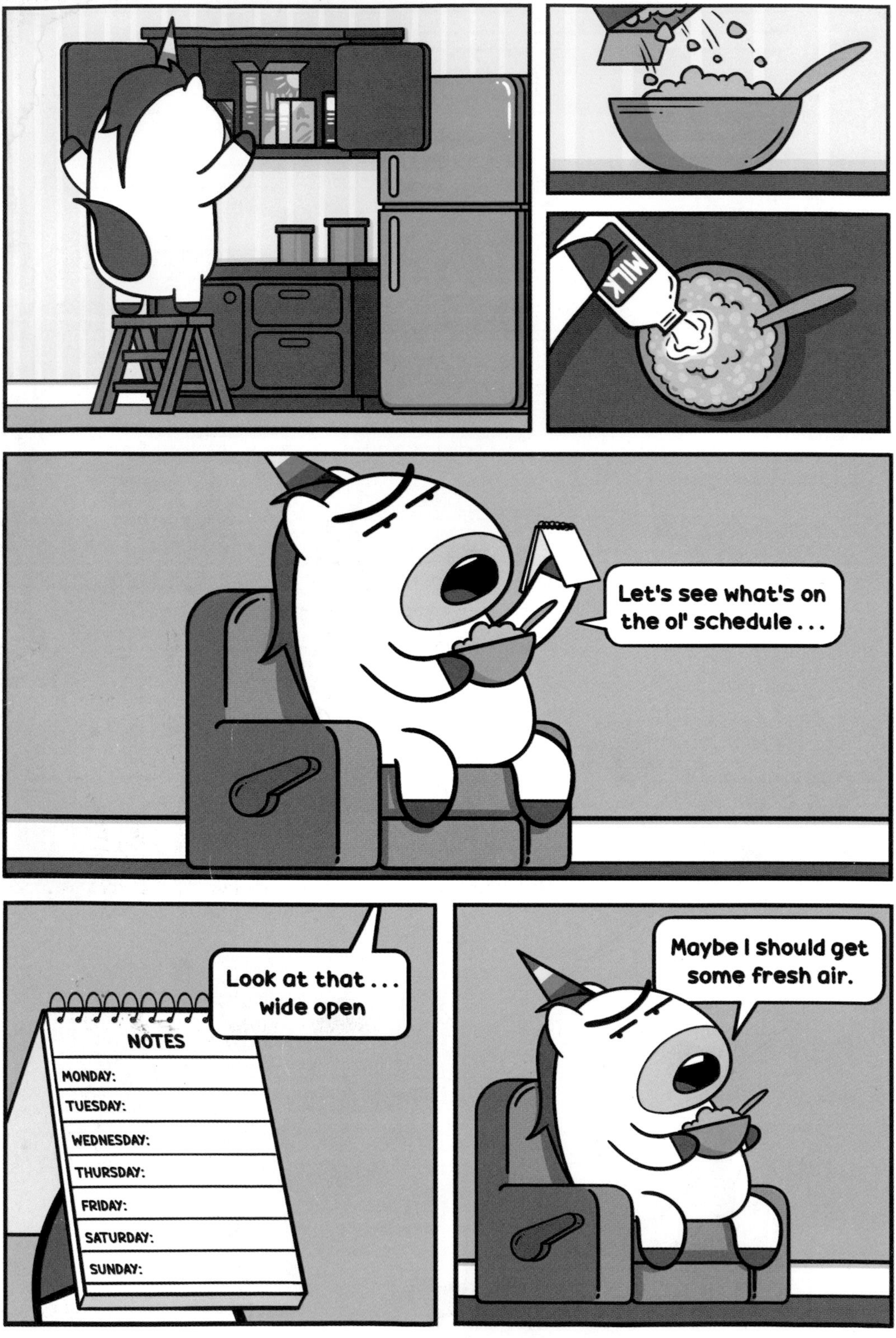
MILK
Let's see what's on the ol' schedule . . .
Look at that . . . wide open
NOTES
MONDAY:
TUESDAY:
WEDNESDAY:
THURSDAY:
FRIDAY:
SATURDAY:
SUNDAY:
Maybe I should get some fresh air.

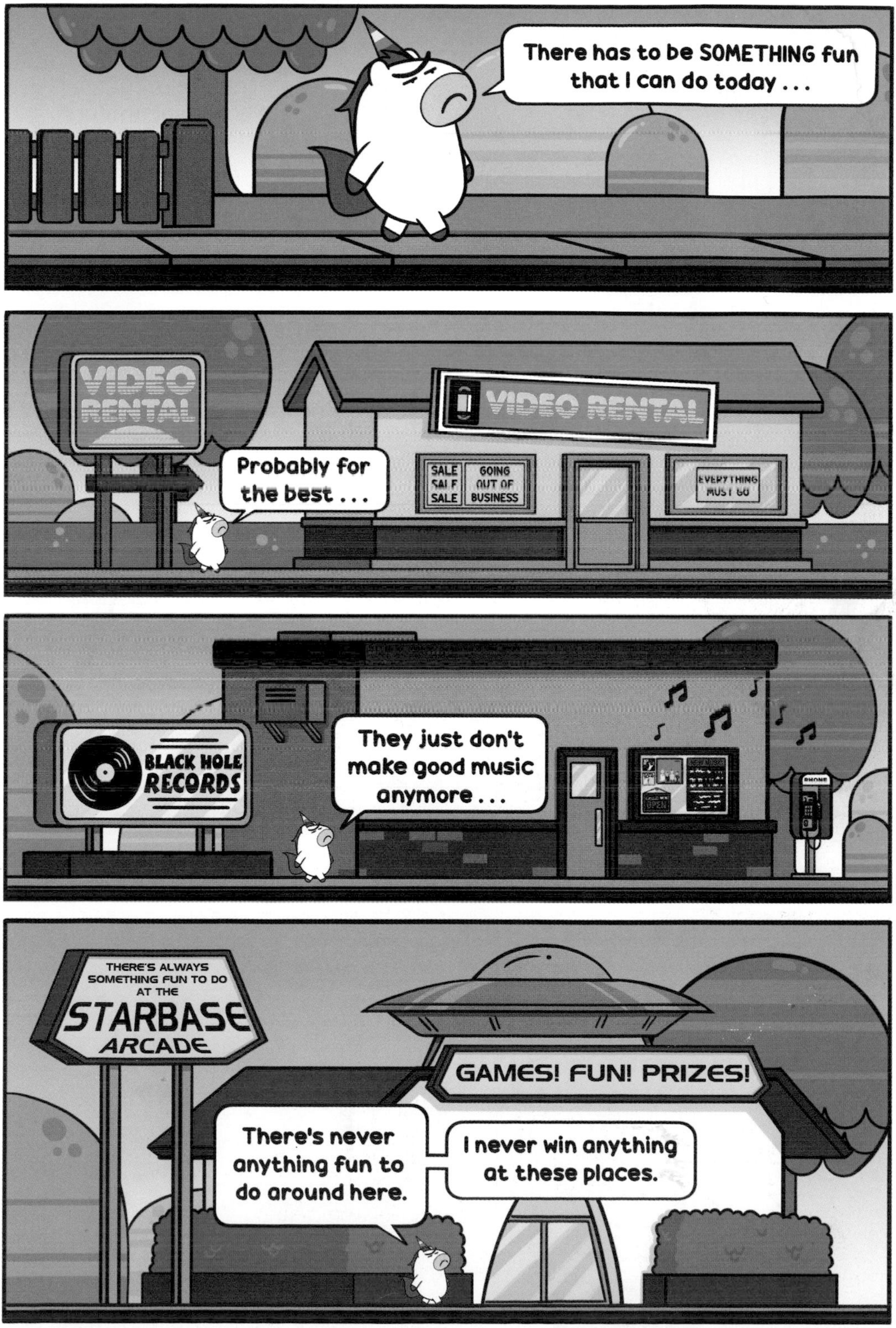
There has to be SOMETHING fun that I can do today . . .
VIDEO RENTAL
VIDEO RENTAL
SALE SALE SALE
GOING OUT OF BUSINESS
EVERYTHING MUST GO
Probably for the best . . .
BLACK HOLE RECORDS
They just don't make good music anymore . . .
PHONE
THERE'S ALWAYS SOMETHING FUN TO DO AT THE STARBASE ARCADE
GAMES! FUN! PRIZES!
There's never anything fun to do around here.
I never win anything at these places.

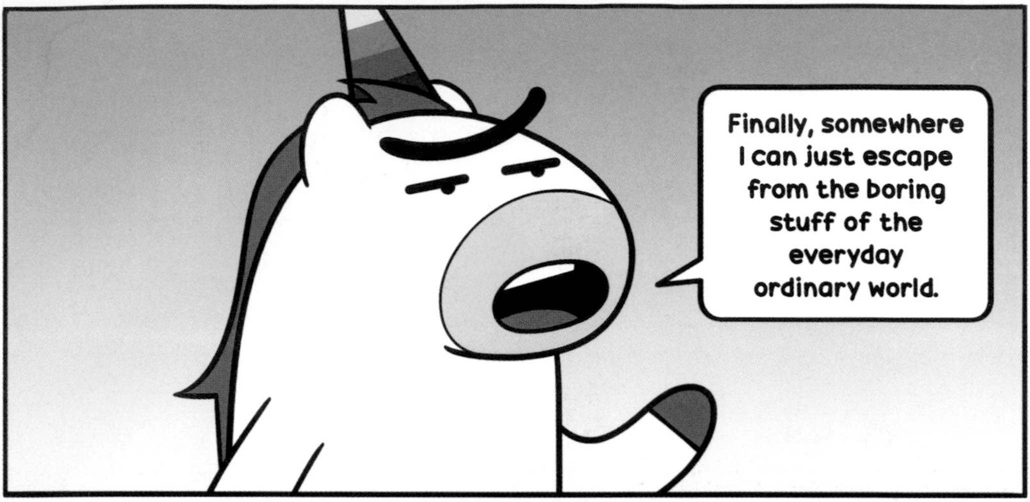
Finally, somewhere I can just escape from the boring stuff of the everyday ordinary world.

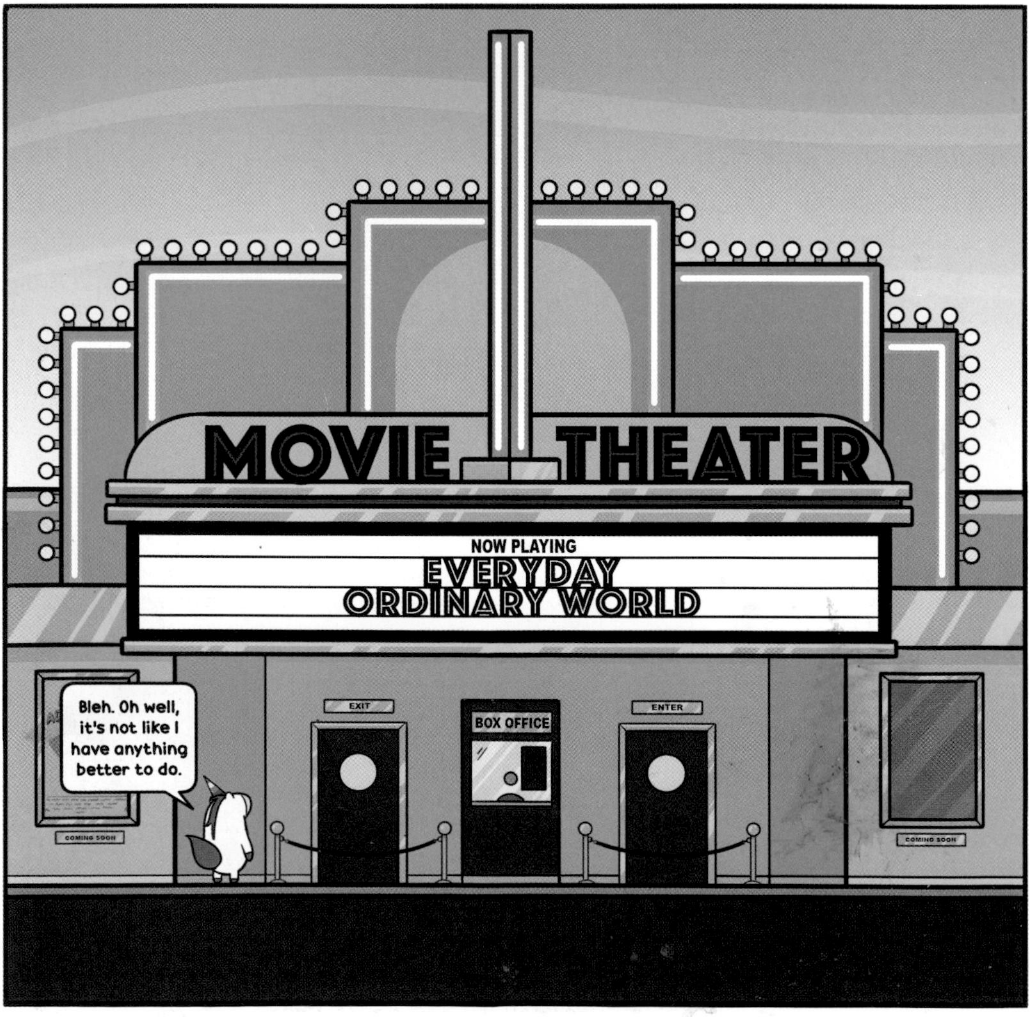
MOVIE THEATER
NOW PLAYING
EVERYDAY
ORDINARY WORLD
EXIT
BOX OFFICE
ENTER
COMING SOON
COMING SOON
Bleh. Oh well, it's not like I have anything better to do.

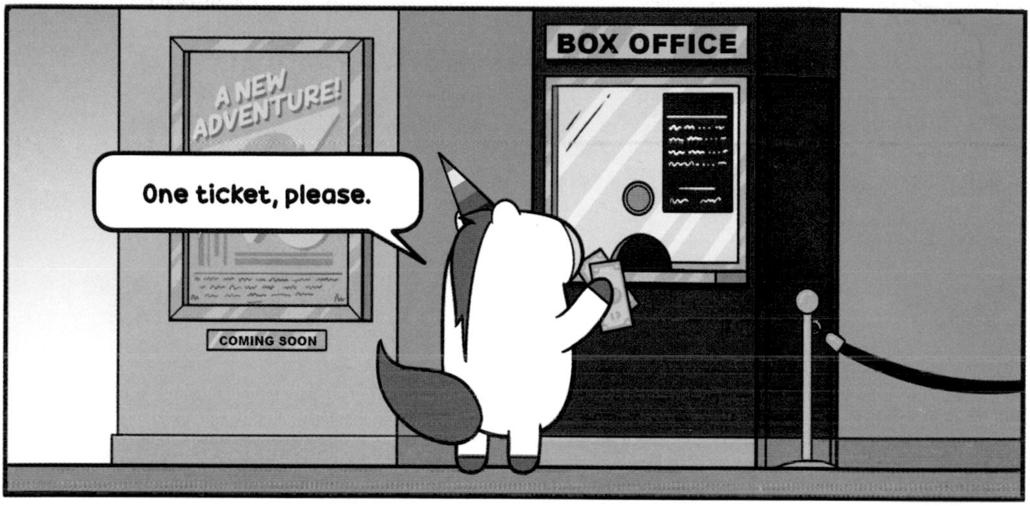
BOX OFFICE
A NEW ADVENTURE!
COMING SOON
One ticket, please.

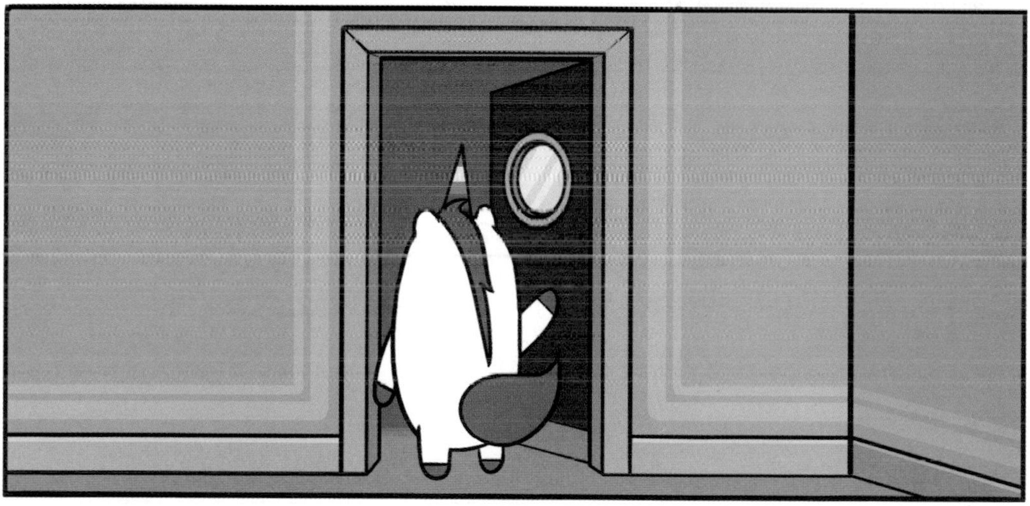

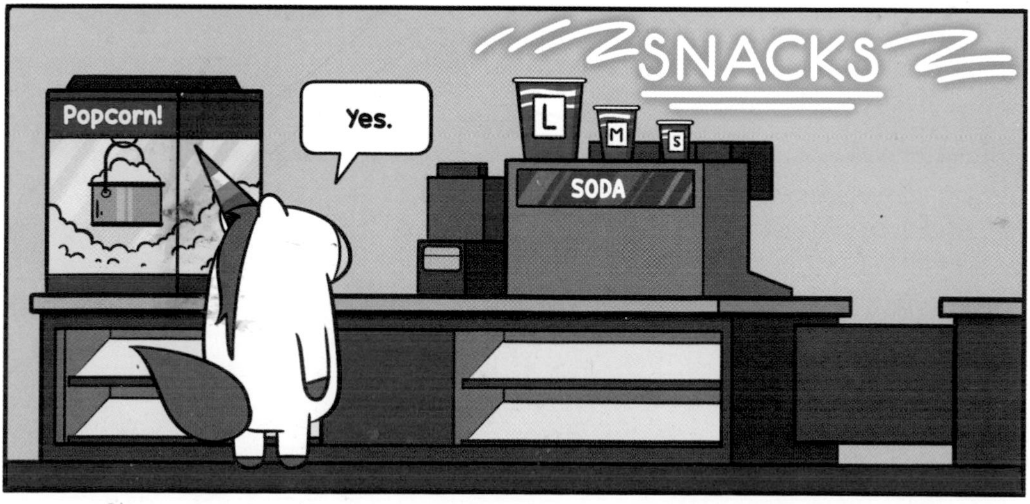
SNACKS
Popcorn!
Yes.
L
M
S
SODA

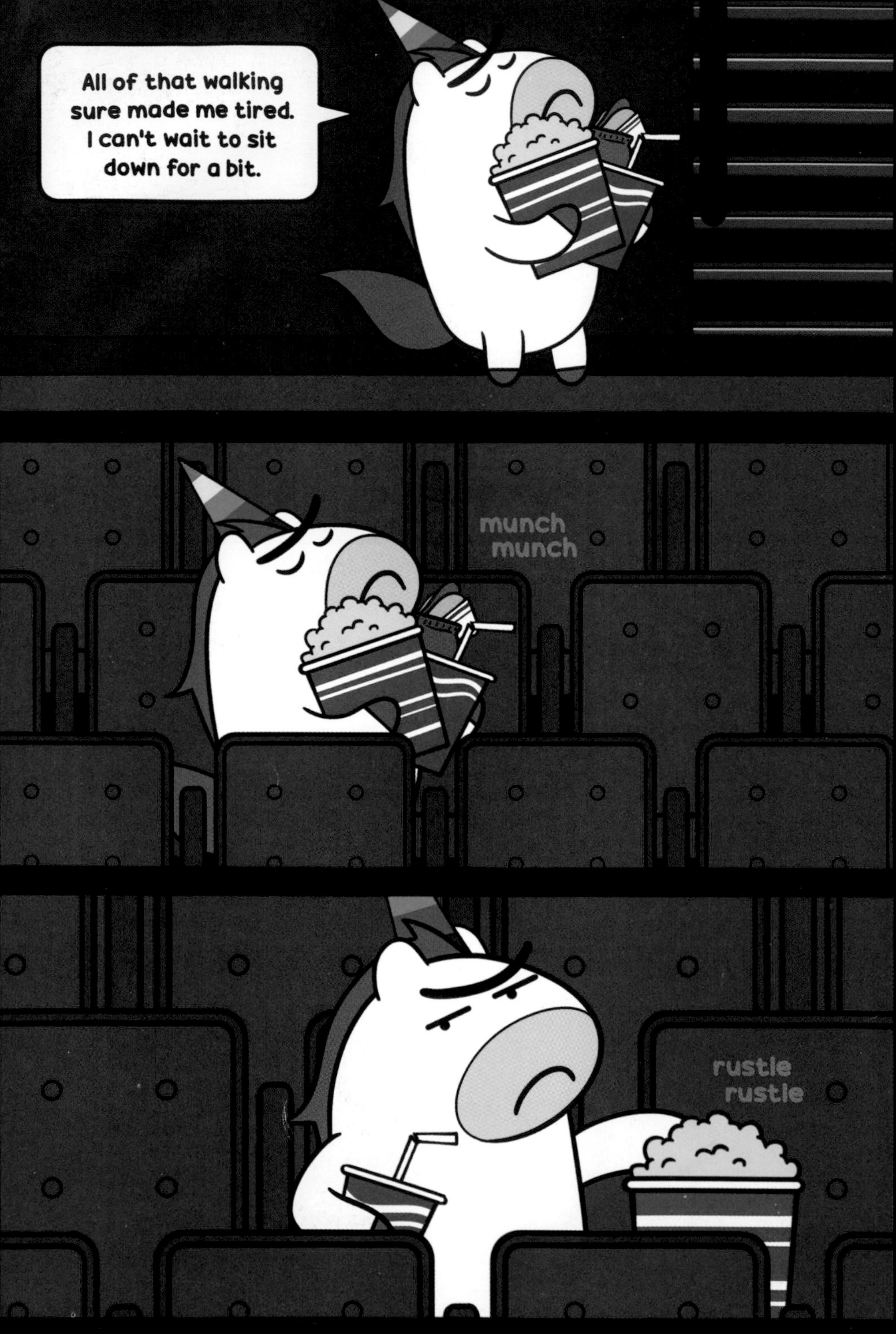
All of that walking sure made me tired. I can't wait to sit down for a bit.
munch munch
rustle rustle

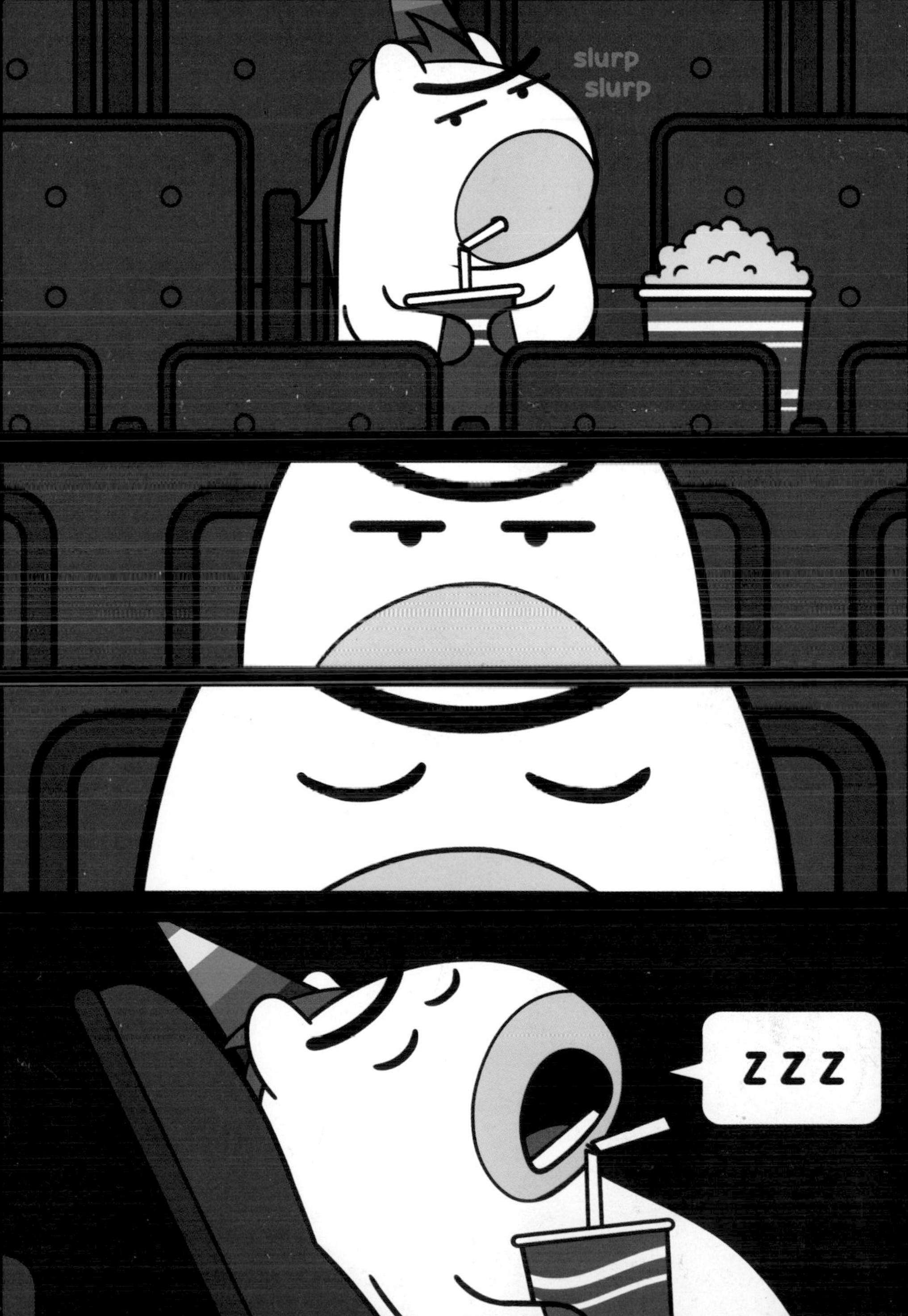
slurp
slurp
ZZZ

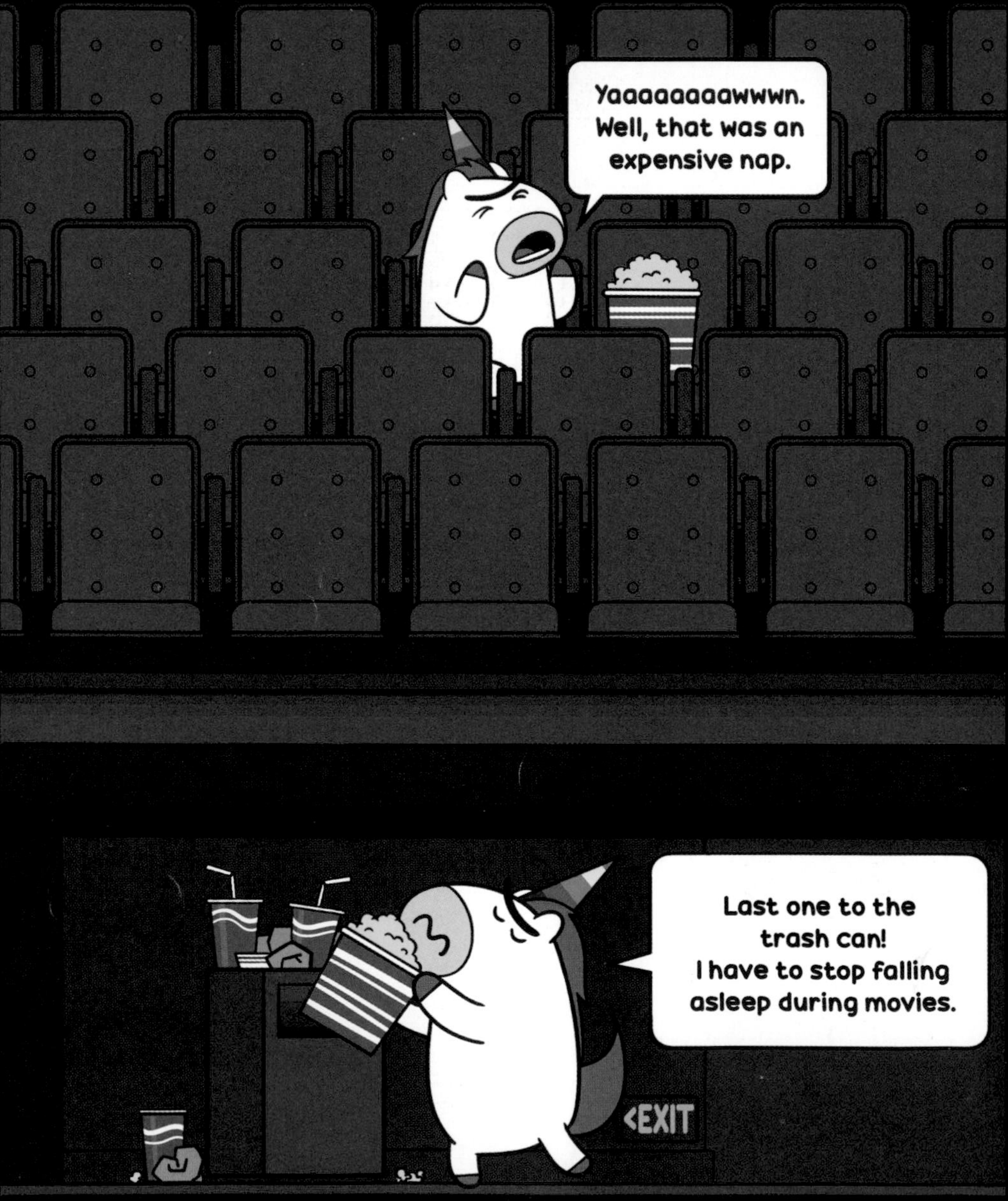
Yaaaaaaawwwn.
Well, that was an expensive nap.
Last one to the trash can!
I have to stop falling asleep during movies.
<EXIT

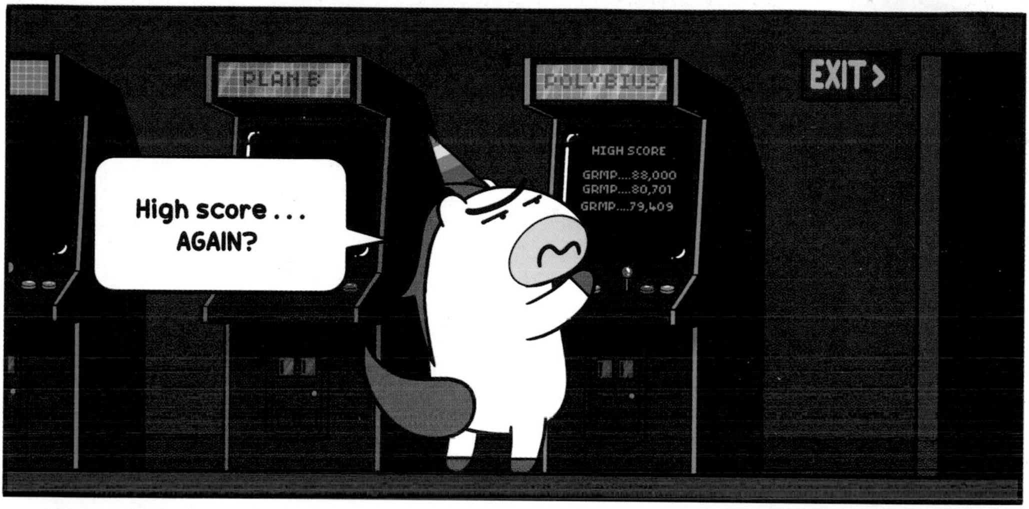
PLAN B
POLYBIUS
EXIT >
HIGH SCORE
GRMP....88,000
GRMP....80,701
GRMP....79,409
High score . . . AGAIN?

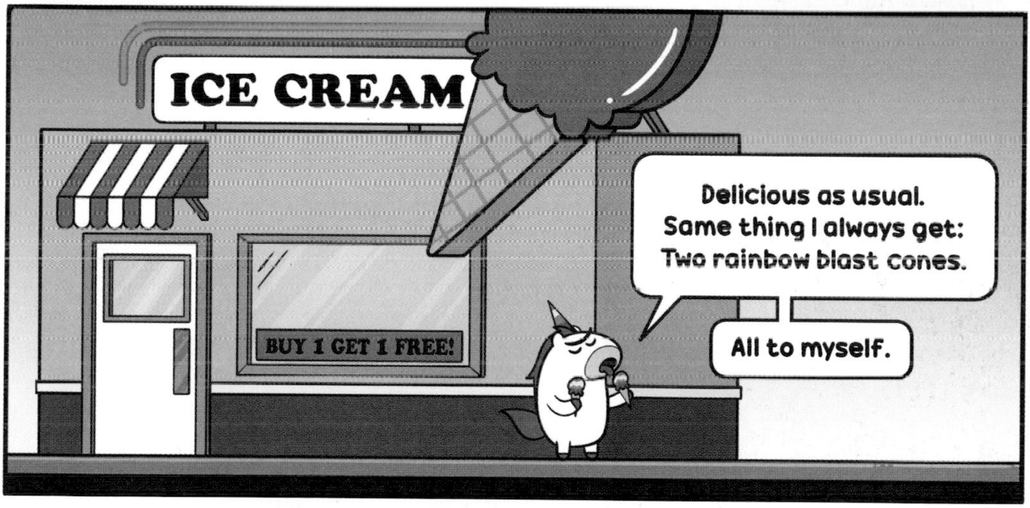
ICE CREAM
BUY 1 GET 1 FREE!
Delicious as usual. Same thing I always get: Two rainbow blast cones.
All to myself.

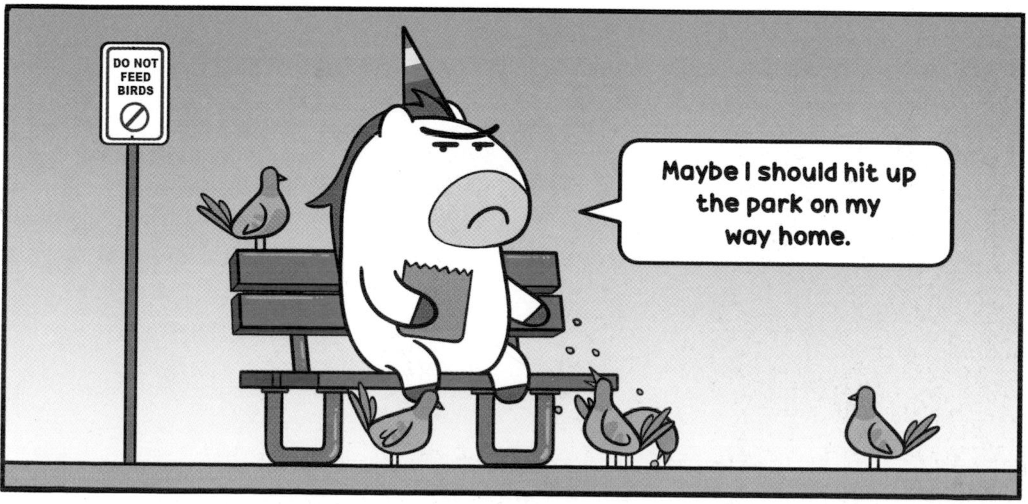
DO NOT FEED BIRDS
Maybe I should hit up the park on my way home.

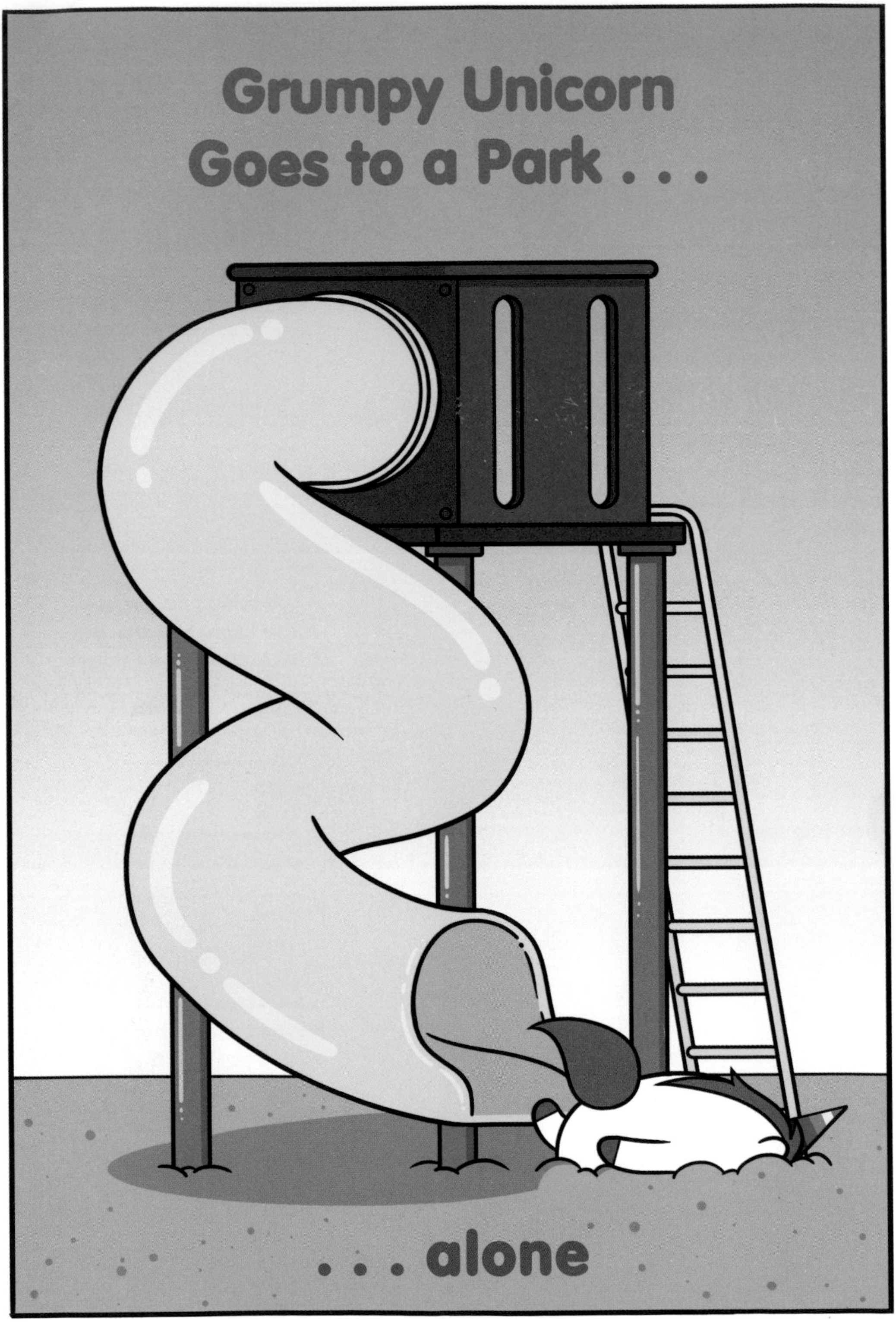
Grumpy Unicorn
Goes to a Park . . .
. . . alone

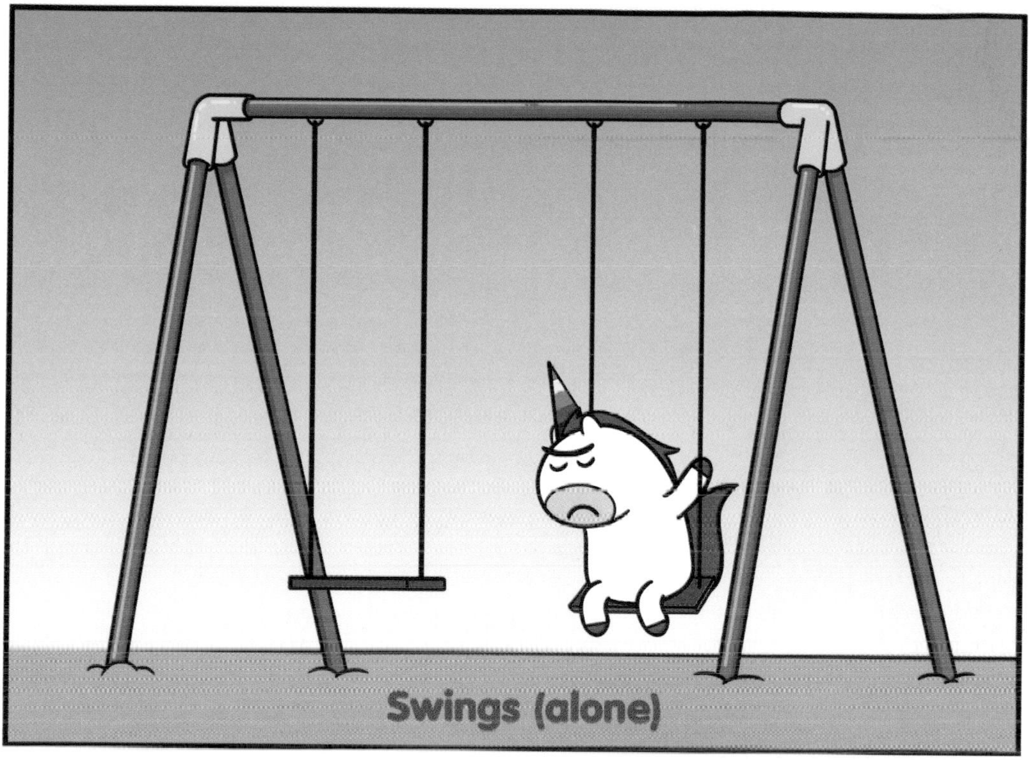
Swings (alone)

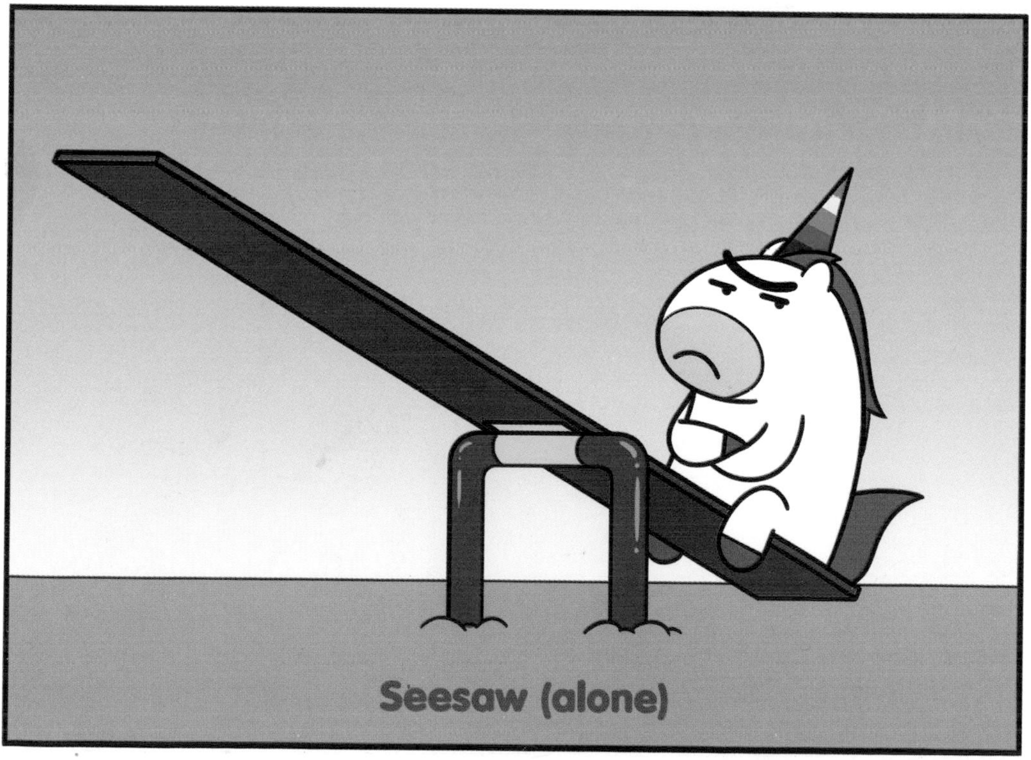
Seesaw (alone)

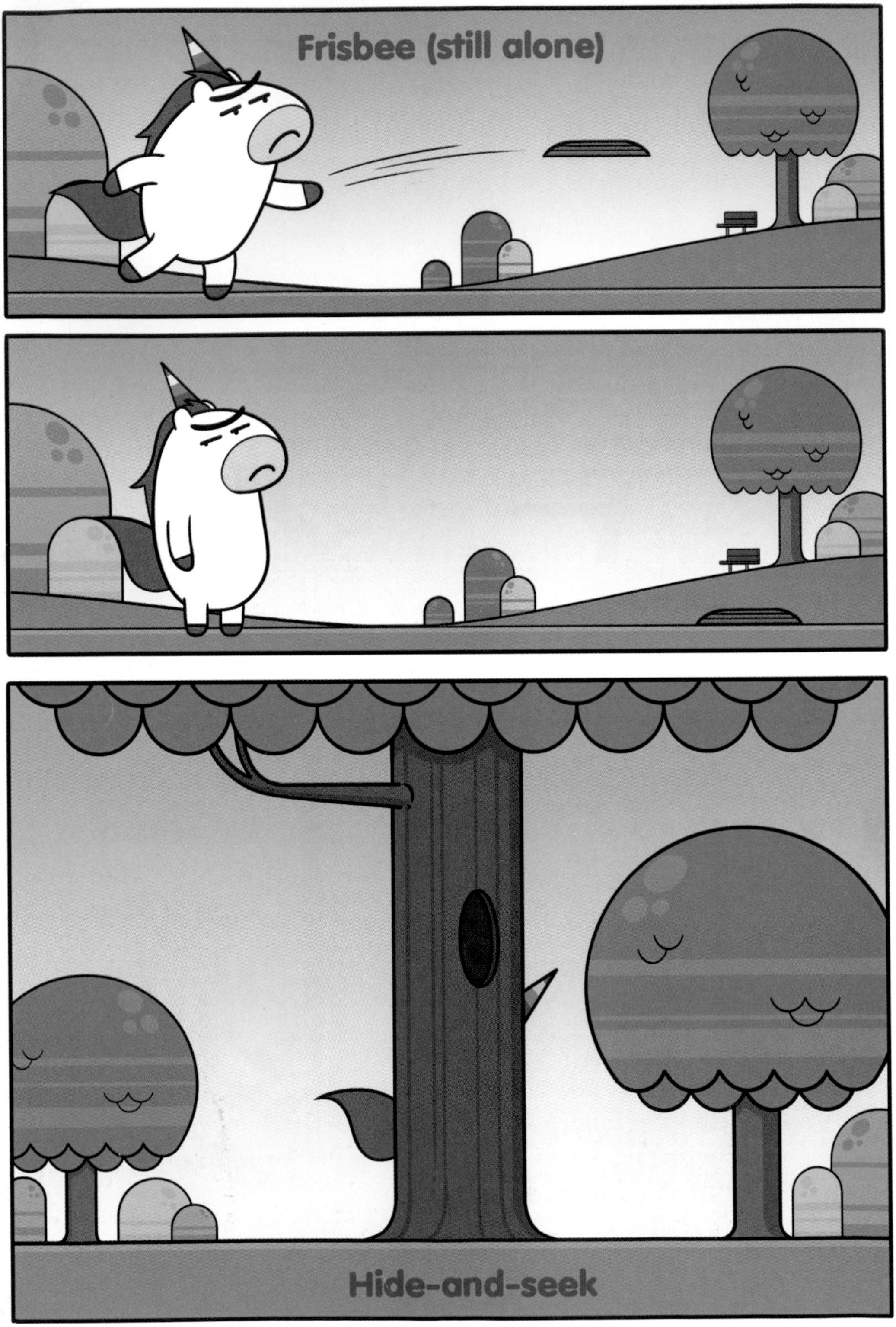

Frisbee (still alone)
Hide-and-seek

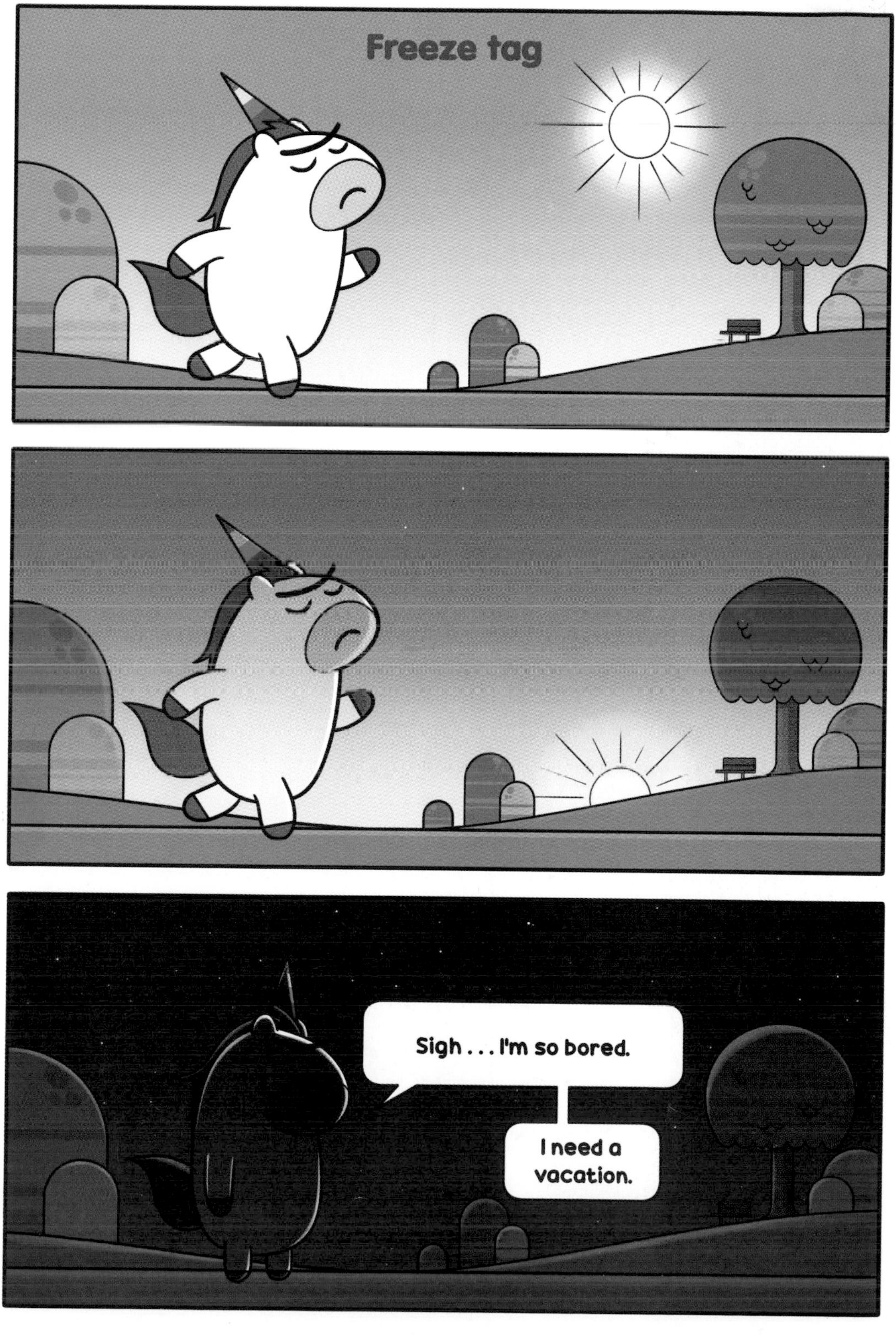
Freeze tag
Sigh . . . I'm so bored.
I need a vacation.

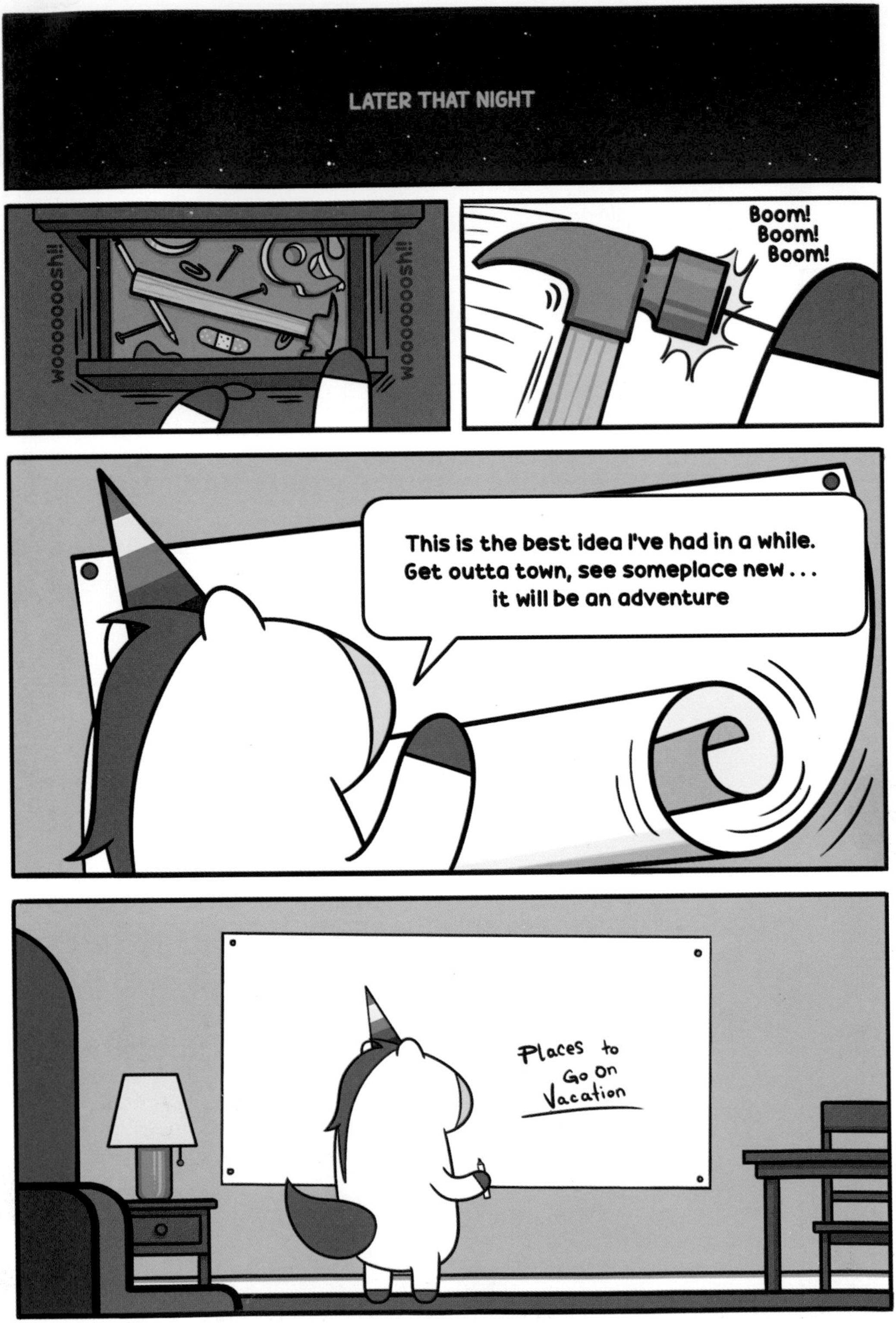
LATER THAT NIGHT
WOOOOOOOOSH!!
WOOOOOOOOSH!!
Boom! Boom! Boom!
This is the best idea I've had in a while. Get outta town, see someplace new . . . it will be an adventure
Places to Go On Vacation

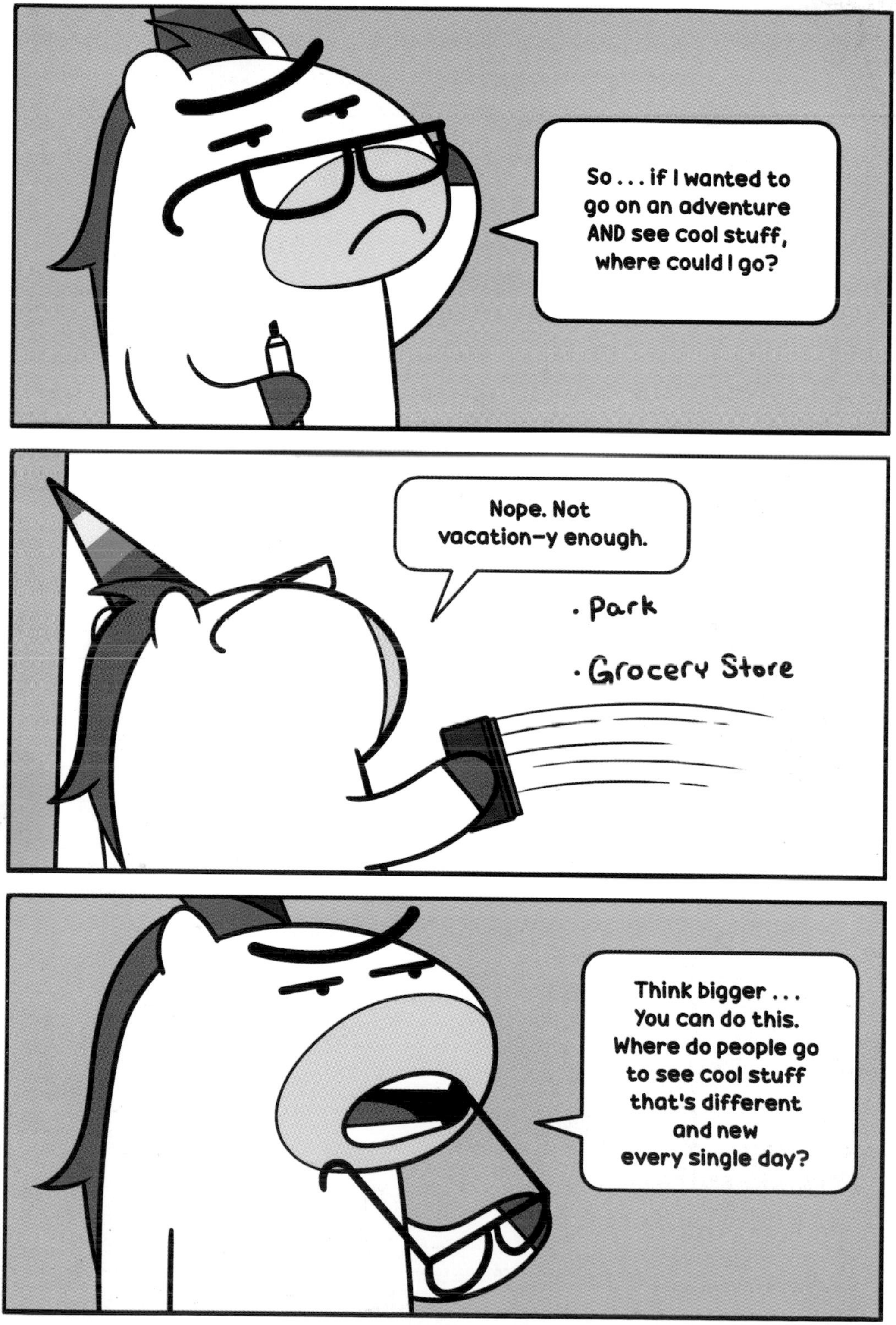
So . . . if I wanted to go on an adventure AND see cool stuff, where could I go?
Nope. Not vacation-y enough.
• Park
• Grocery Store
Think bigger . . . You can do this. Where do people go to see cool stuff that's different and new every single day?

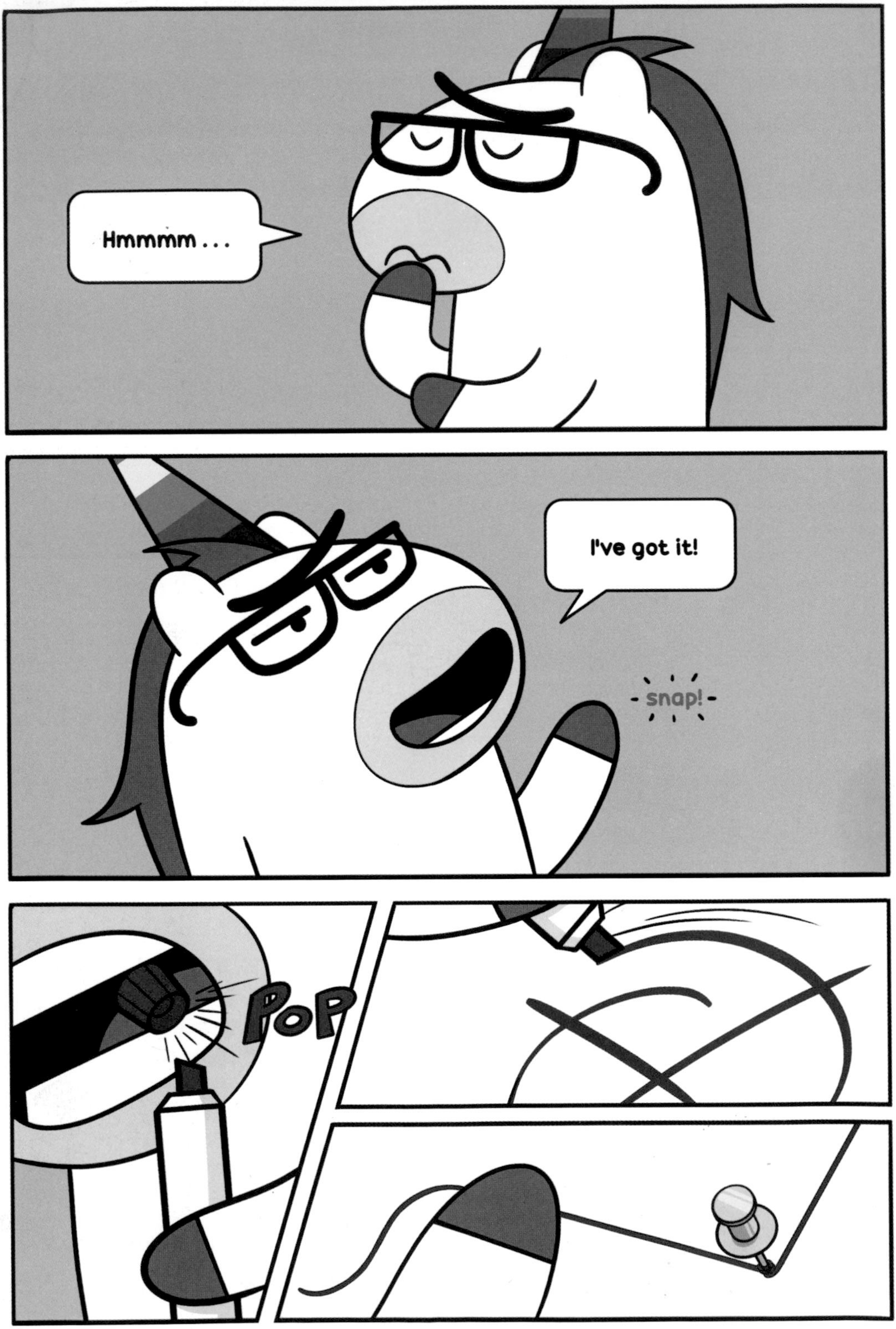
Hmmmm . . .
I've got it!
snap!
POP

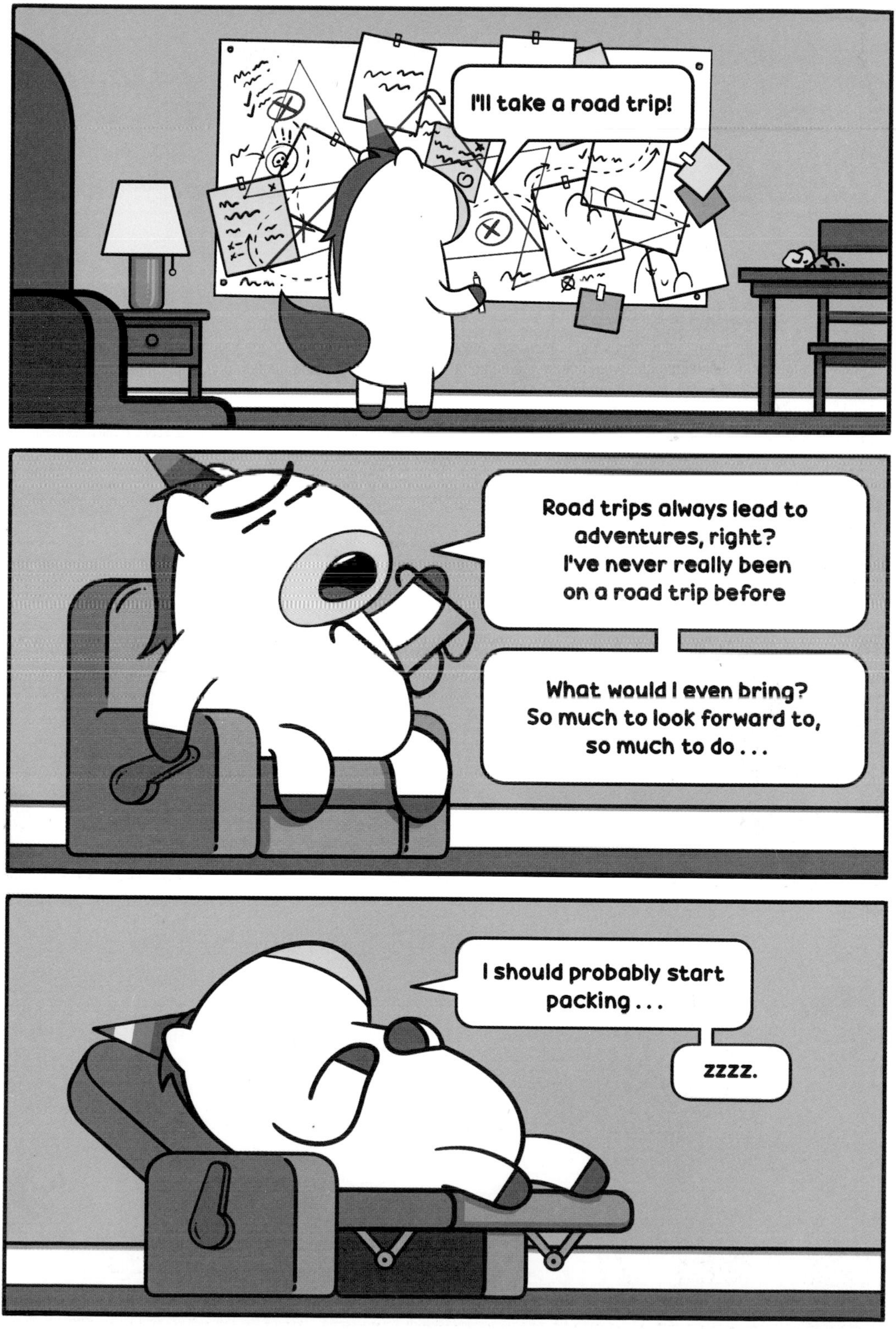
I'll take a road trip!
Road trips always lead to adventures, right? I've never really been on a road trip before
What would I even bring? So much to look forward to, so much to do . . .
I should probably start packing . . .
zzzz.

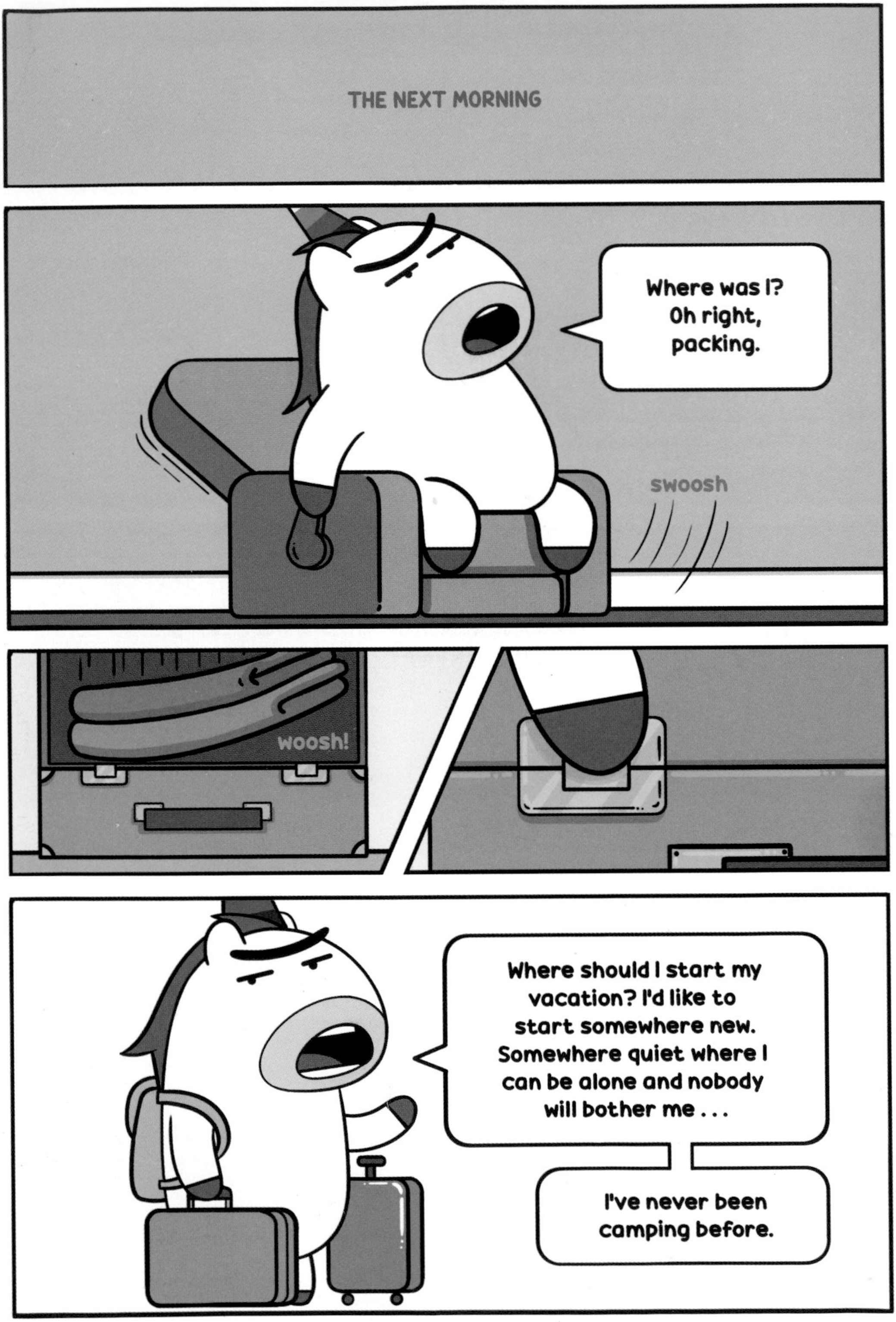
THE NEXT MORNING
Where was I? Oh right, packing.
swoosh
woosh!
Where should I start my vacation? I'd like to start somewhere new. Somewhere quiet where I can be alone and nobody will bother me . . .
I've never been camping before.

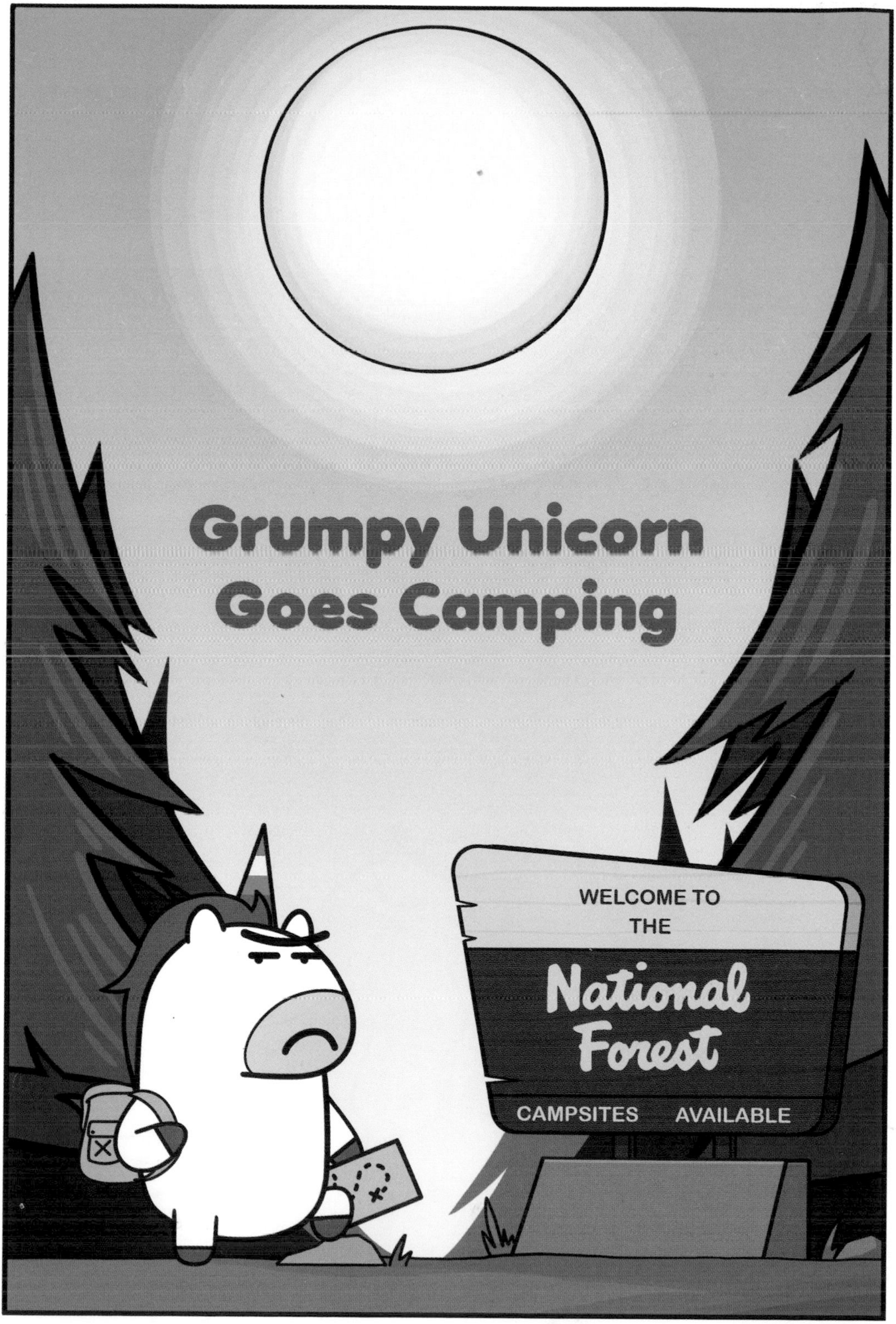
Grumpy Unicorn
Goes Camping
WELCOME TO
THE
National
Forest
CAMPSITES AVAILABLE

# How to Go Camping:

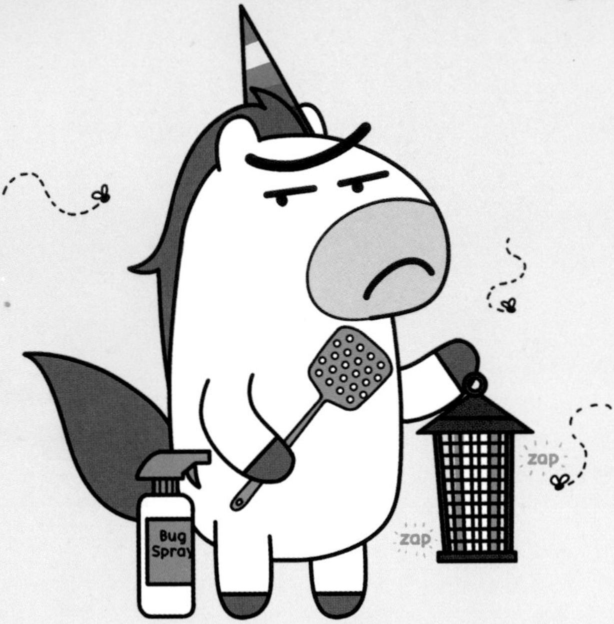

zap
zap
Bug Spray


1. Go outside.

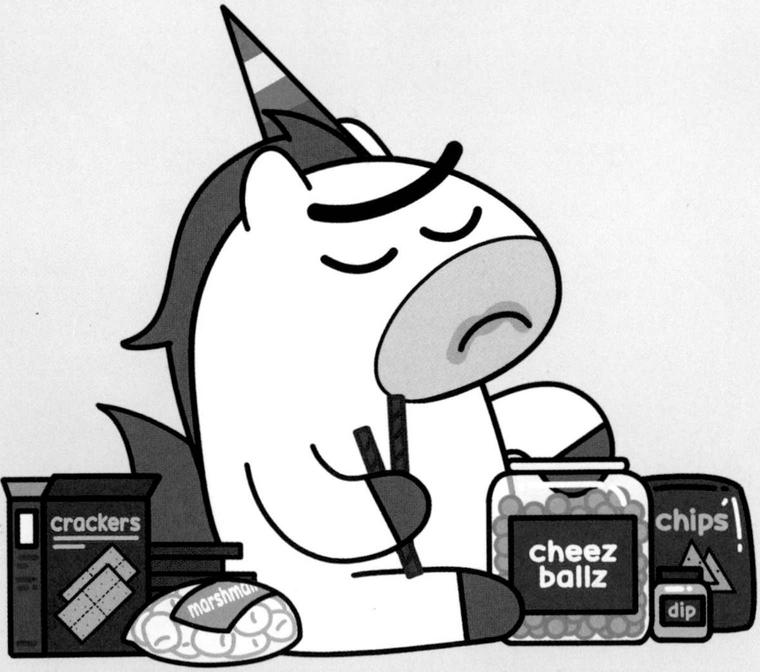

crackers
cheez ballz
chips
dip


2. Bring plenty of snacks.

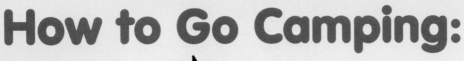

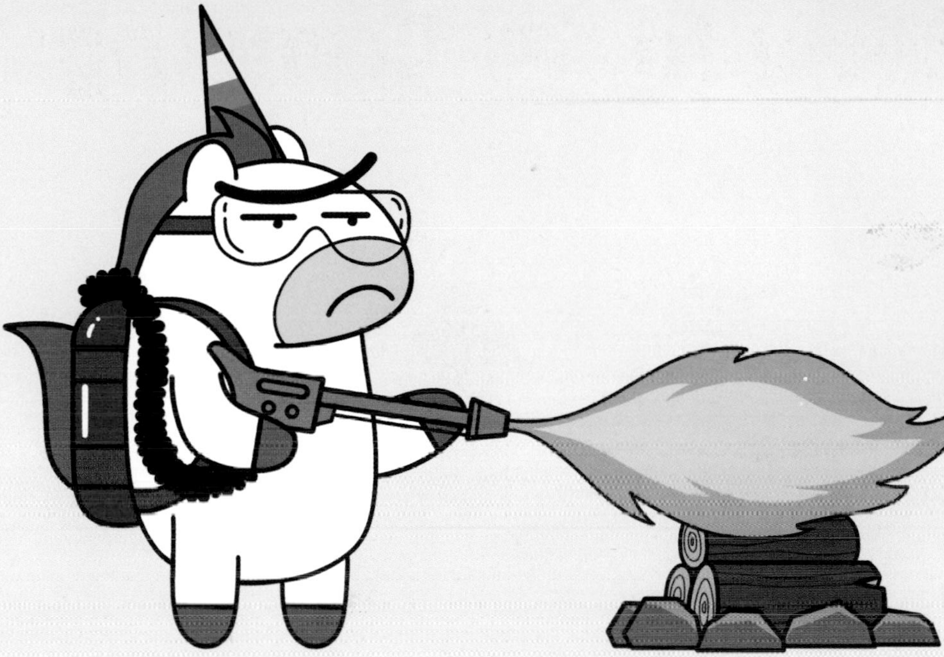

3. Build a fire (safely).

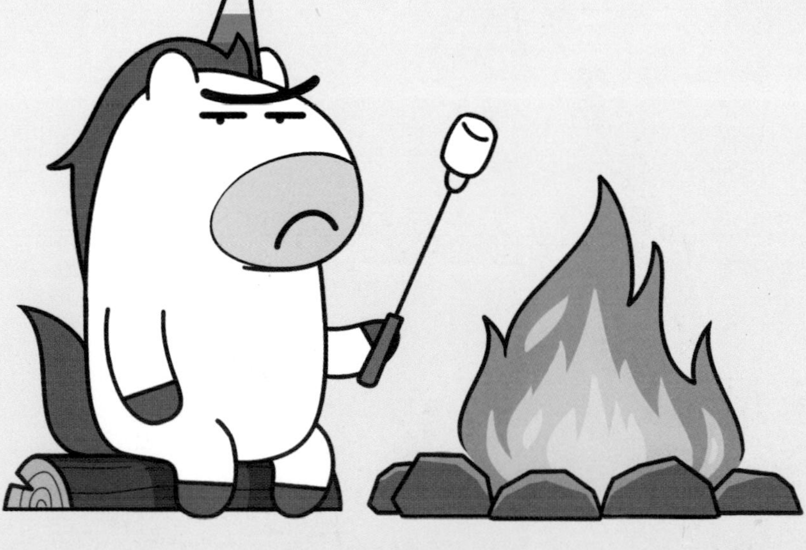

4. Now you're ready for camping.

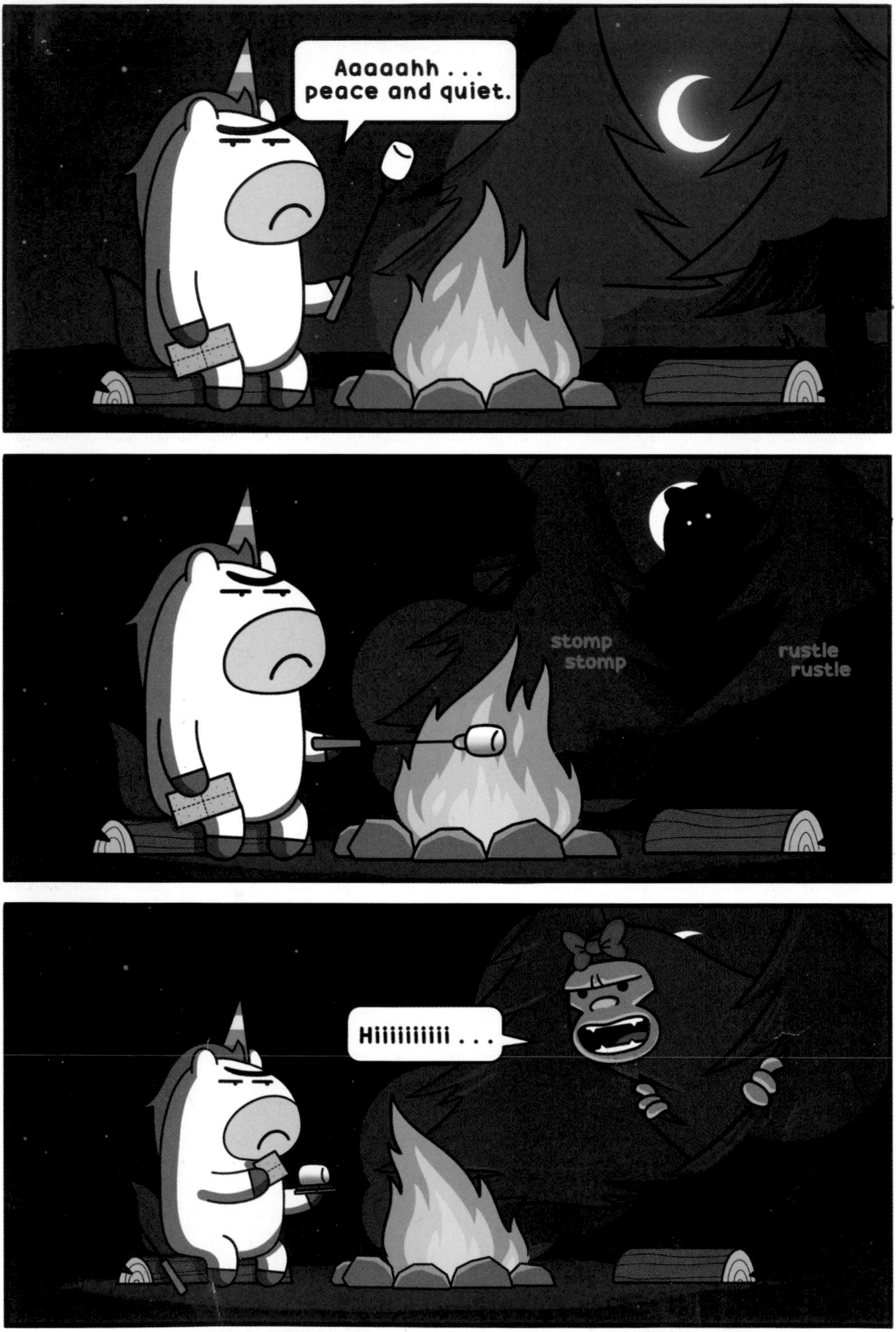
Aaaaahh . . .
peace and quiet.
stomp
stomp
rustle
rustle
Hiiiiiiiiii . . .

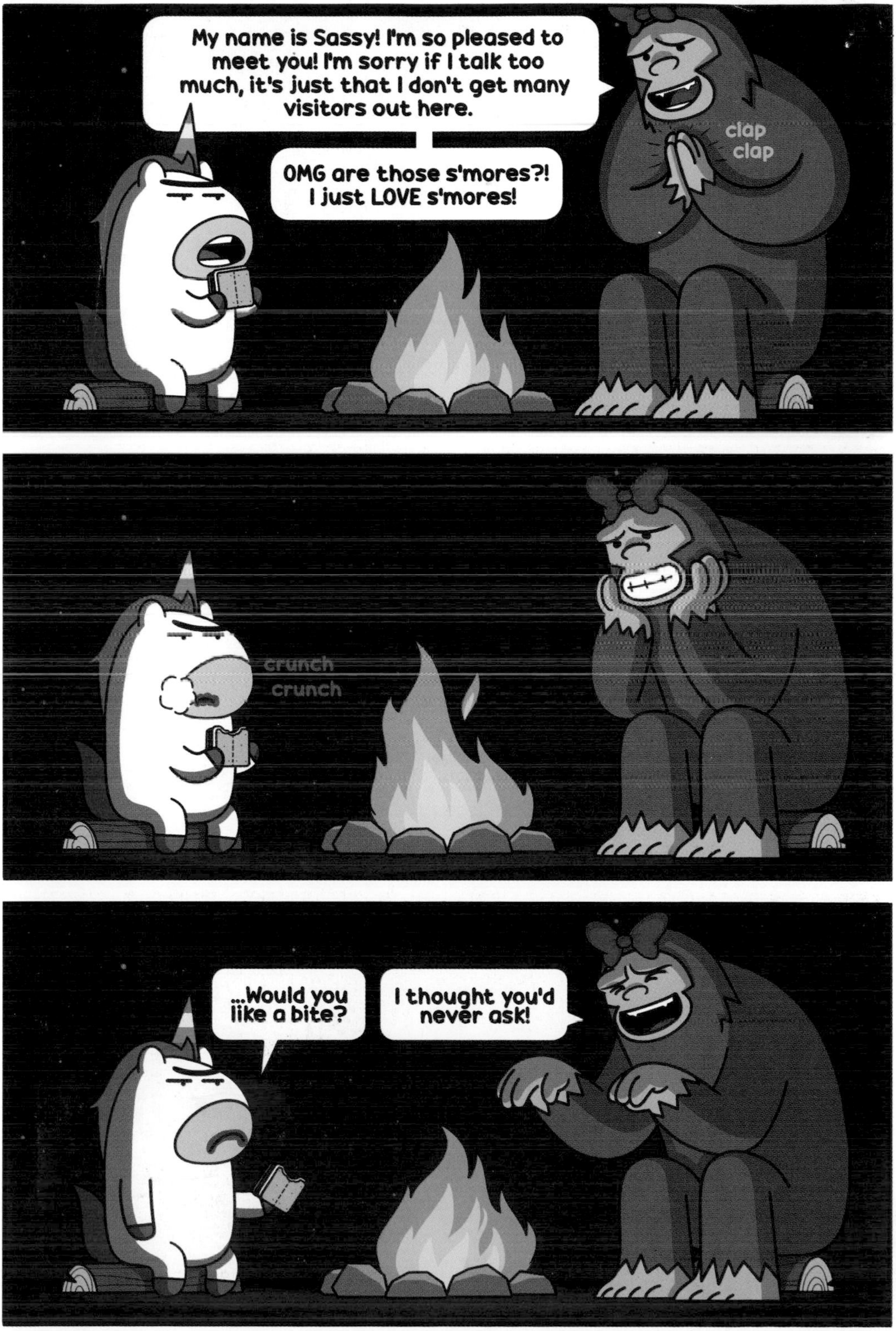
My name is Sassy! I'm so pleased to meet you! I'm sorry if I talk too much, it's just that I don't get many visitors out here.
OMG are those s'mores?! I just LOVE s'mores!
clap
clap
crunch
crunch
...Would you like a bite?
I thought you'd never ask!

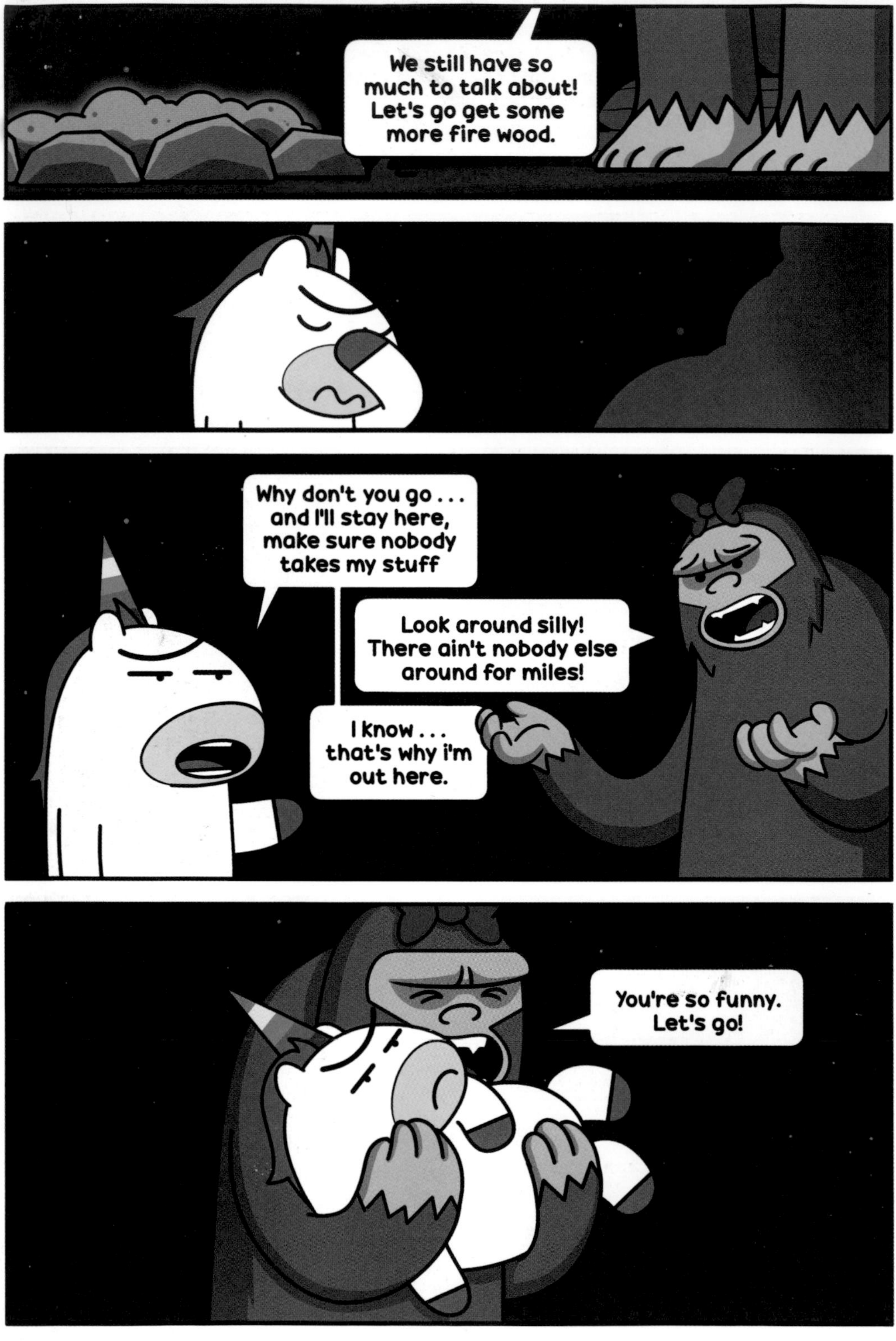
We still have so much to talk about! Let's go get some more fire wood.
Why don't you go . . . and I'll stay here, make sure nobody takes my stuff
Look around silly! There ain't nobody else around for miles!
I know . . . that's why i'm out here.
You're so funny. Let's go!

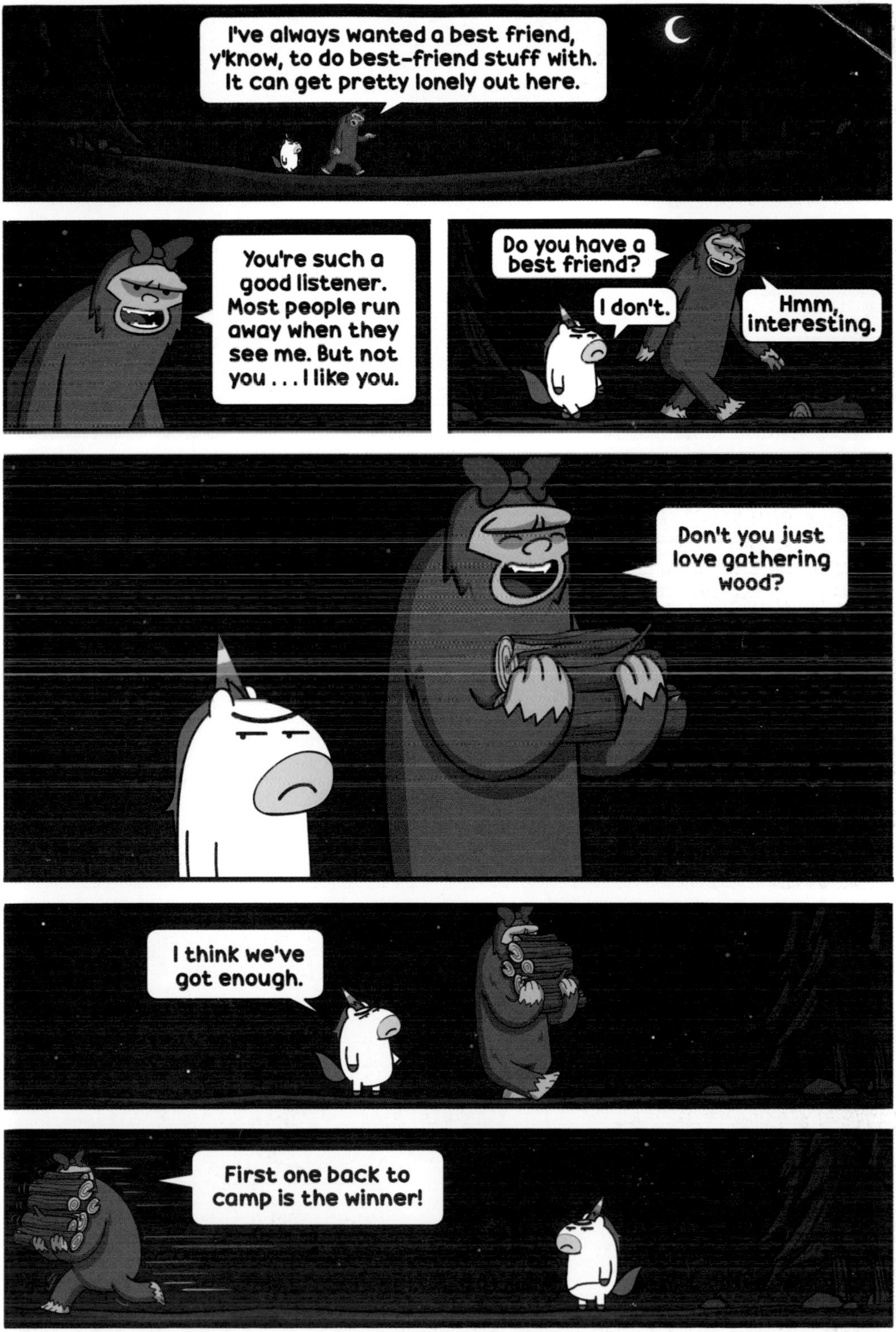
I've always wanted a best friend, y'know, to do best-friend stuff with. It can get pretty lonely out here.
You're such a good listener. Most people run away when they see me. But not you . . . I like you.
Do you have a best friend?
I don't.
Hmm, interesting.
Don't you just love gathering wood?
I think we've got enough.
First one back to camp is the winner!

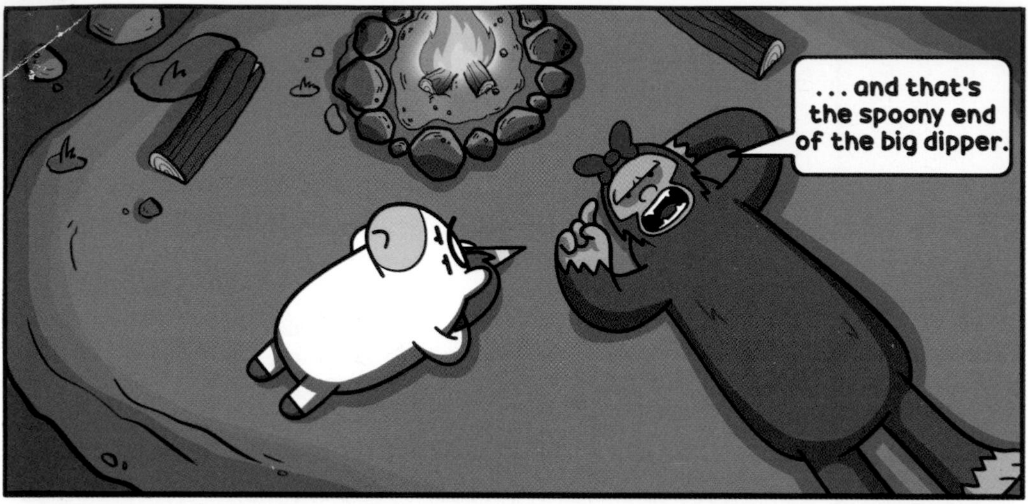
. . . and that's the spoony end of the big dipper.

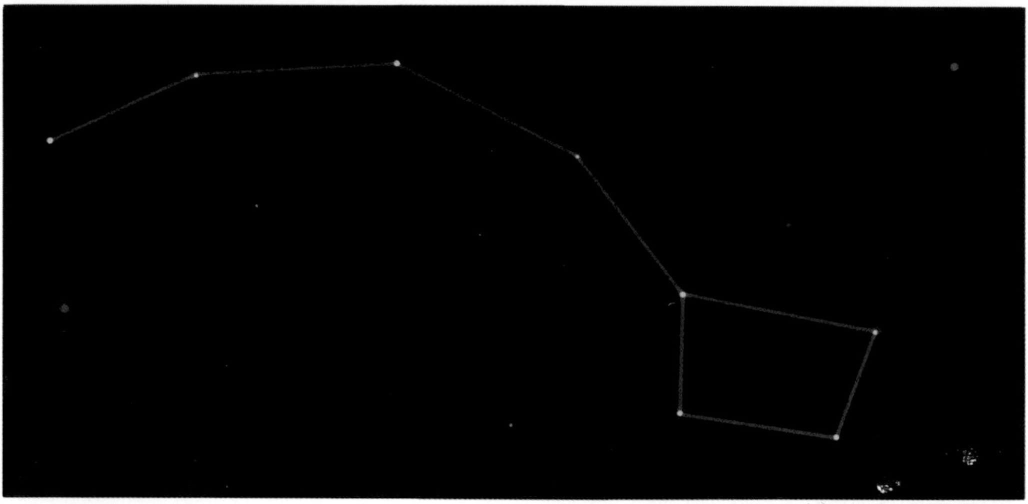

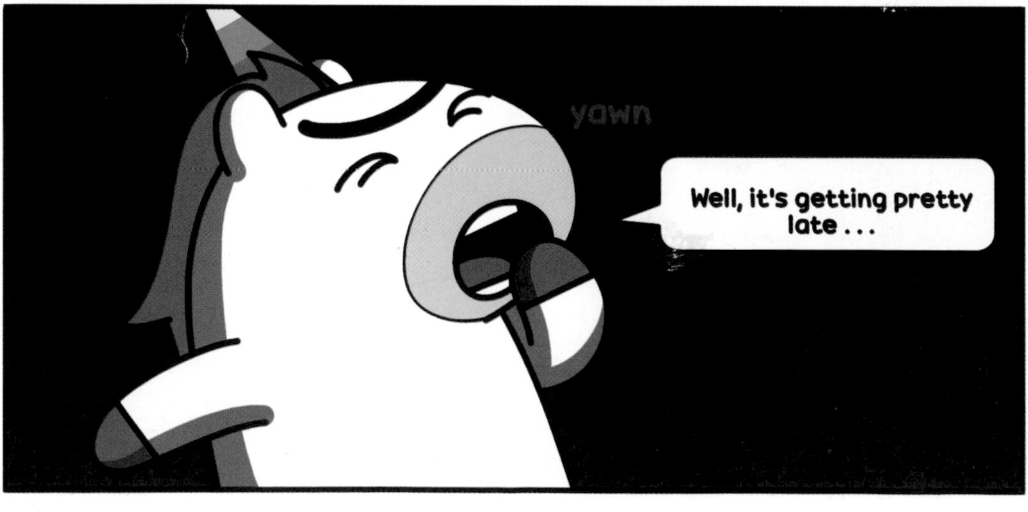
yawn
Well, it's getting pretty late . . .

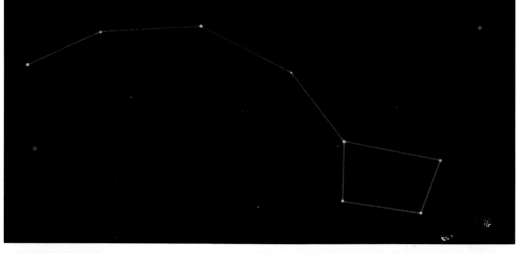

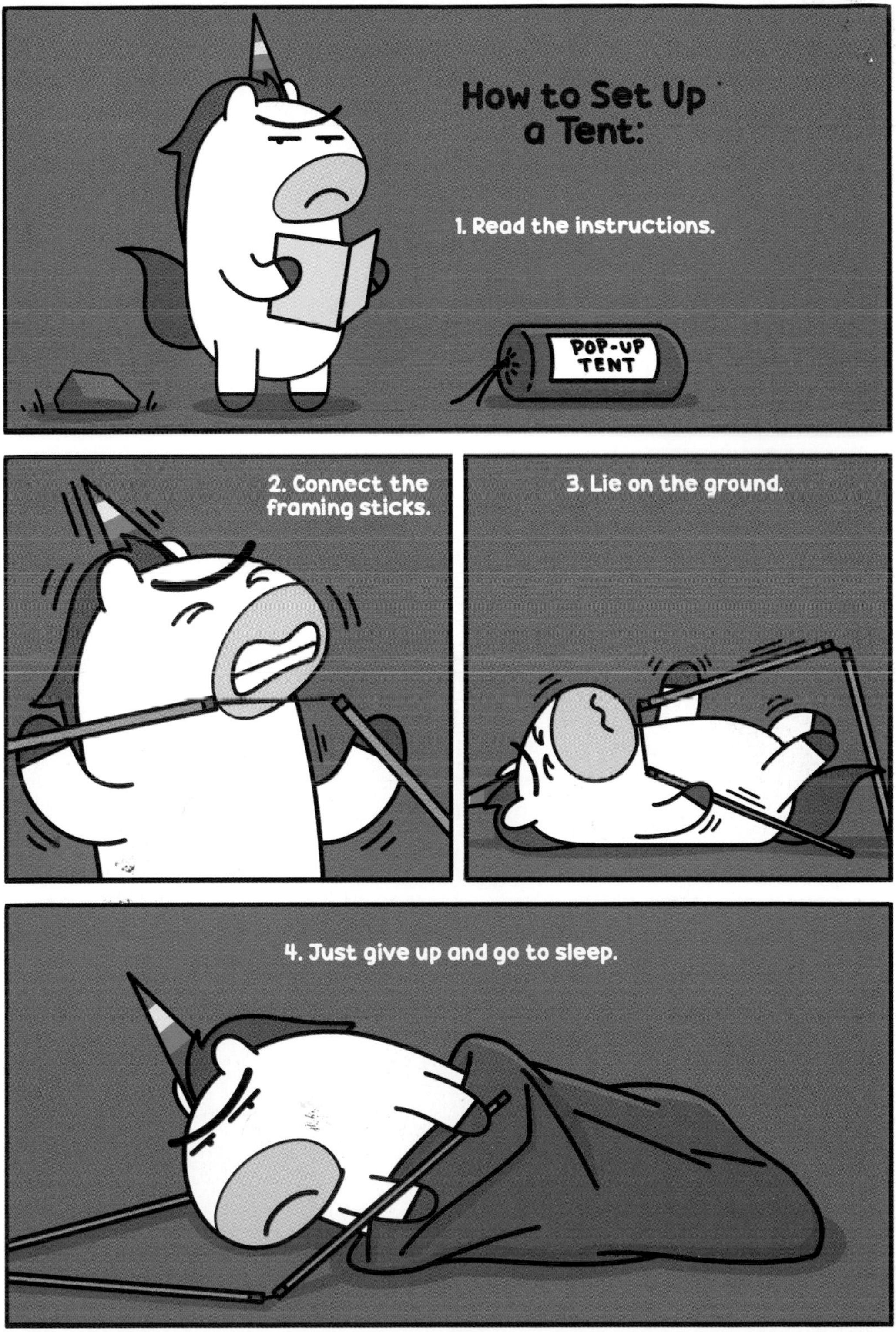

How to Set Up a Tent:
1. Read the instructions.
POP-UP TENT
2. Connect the framing sticks.
3. Lie on the ground.
4. Just give up and go to sleep.

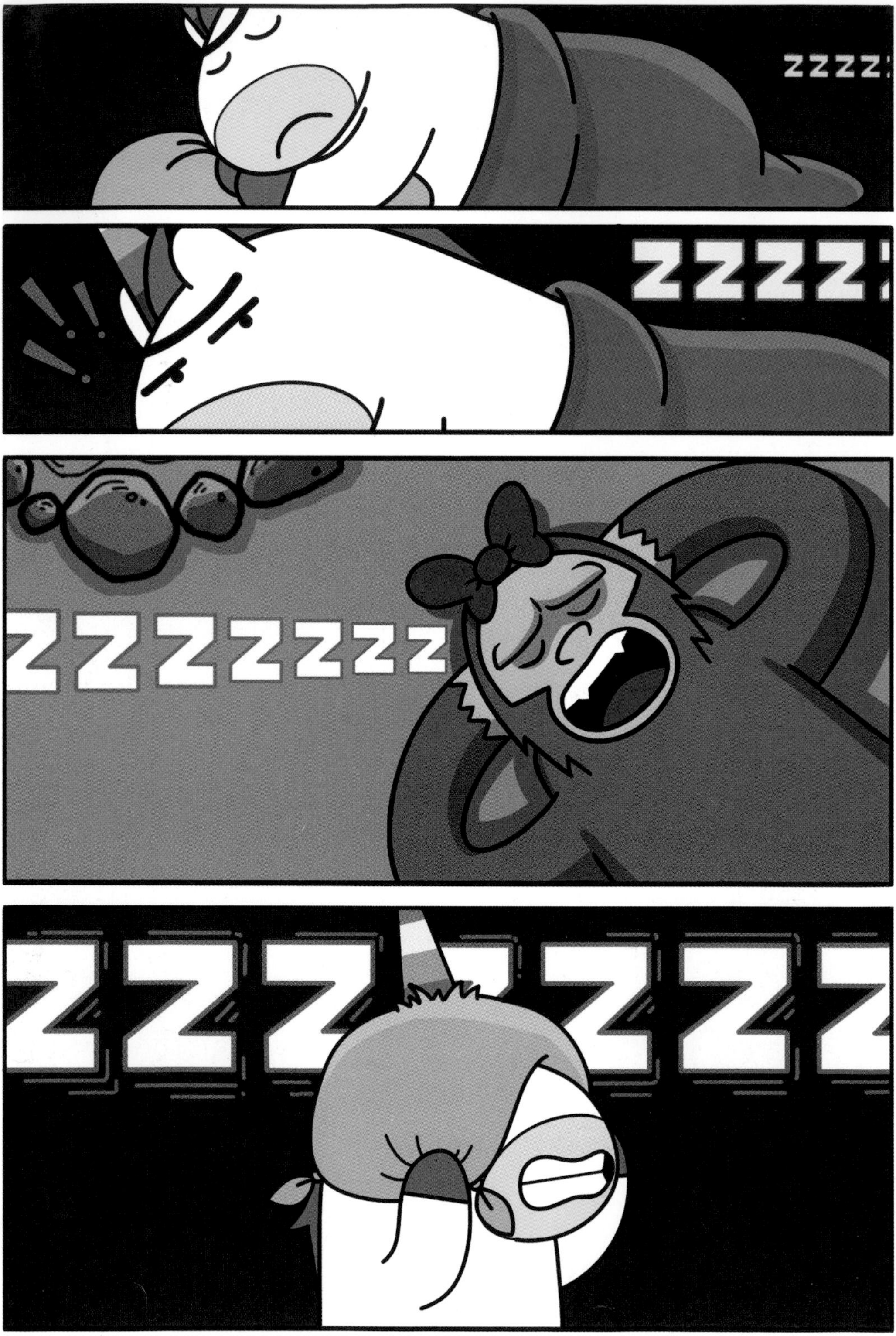
ZZZZ
ZZZZ
ZZZZZZZ
ZZZ
ZZZ

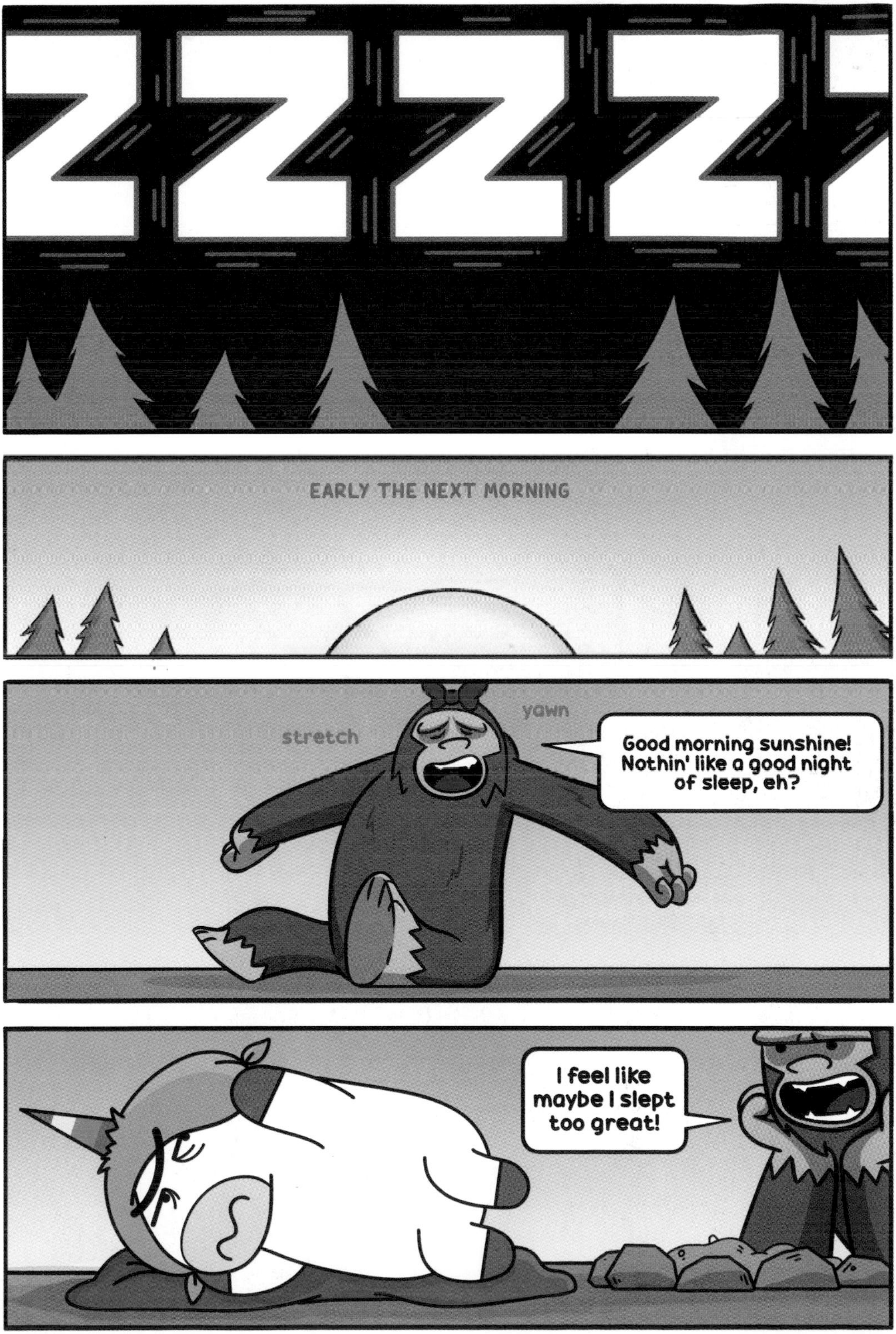
ZZZZZ
EARLY THE NEXT MORNING
stretch
yawn
Good morning sunshine! Nothin' like a good night of sleep, eh?
I feel like maybe I slept too great!

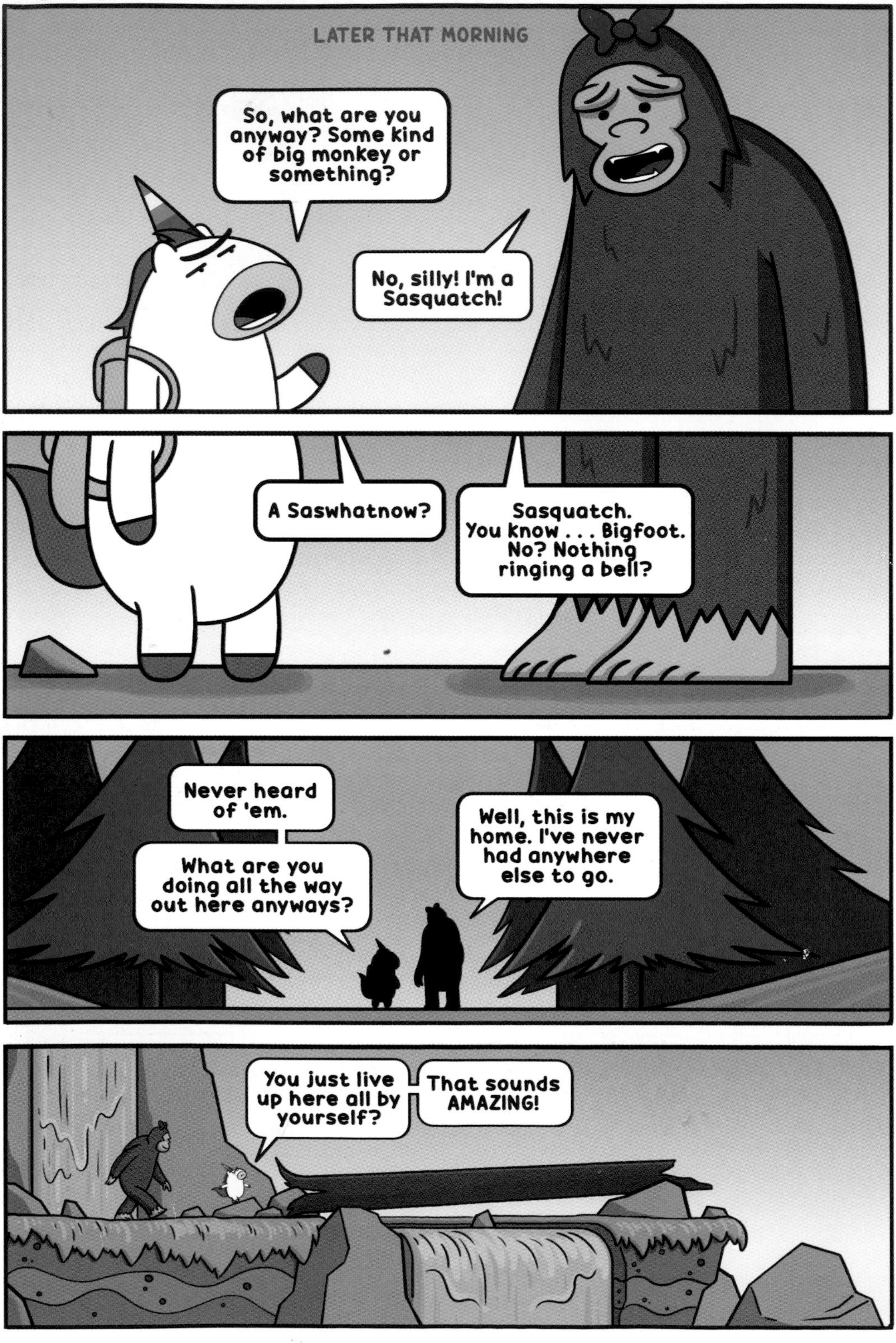
LATER THAT MORNING
So, what are you anyway? Some kind of big monkey or something?
No, silly! I'm a Sasquatch!
A Saswhatnow?
Sasquatch. You know . . . Bigfoot. No? Nothing ringing a bell?
Never heard of 'em.
What are you doing all the way out here anyways?
Well, this is my home. I've never had anywhere else to go.
You just live up here all by yourself?
That sounds AMAZING!

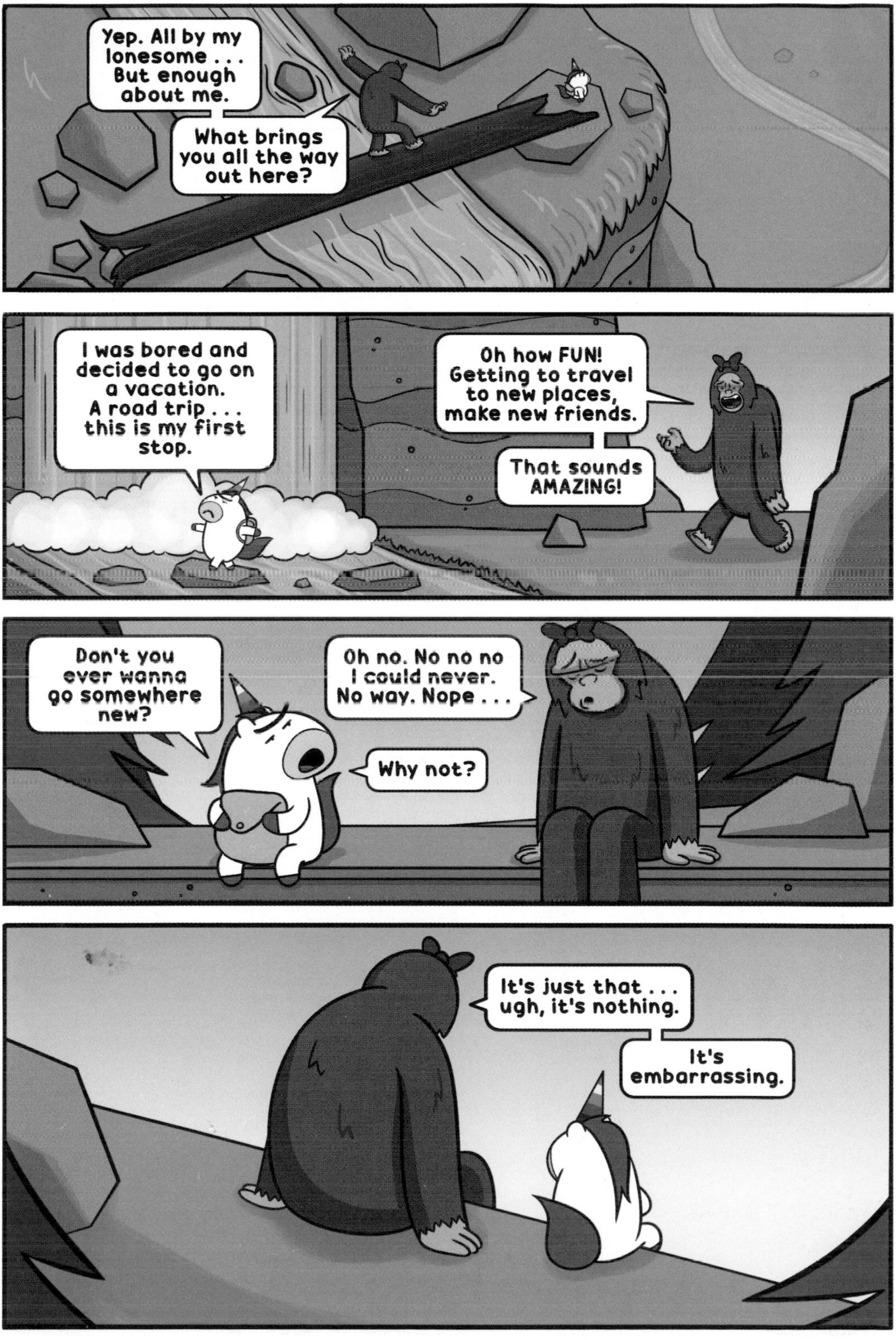

Yep. All by my lonesome . . . But enough about me.
What brings you all the way out here?
I was bored and decided to go on a vacation. A road trip . . . this is my first stop.
Oh how FUN! Getting to travel to new places, make new friends.
That sounds AMAZING!
Don't you ever wanna go somewhere new?
Oh no. No no no I could never. No way. Nope . . .
Why not?
It's just that . . . ugh, it's nothing.
It's embarrassing.

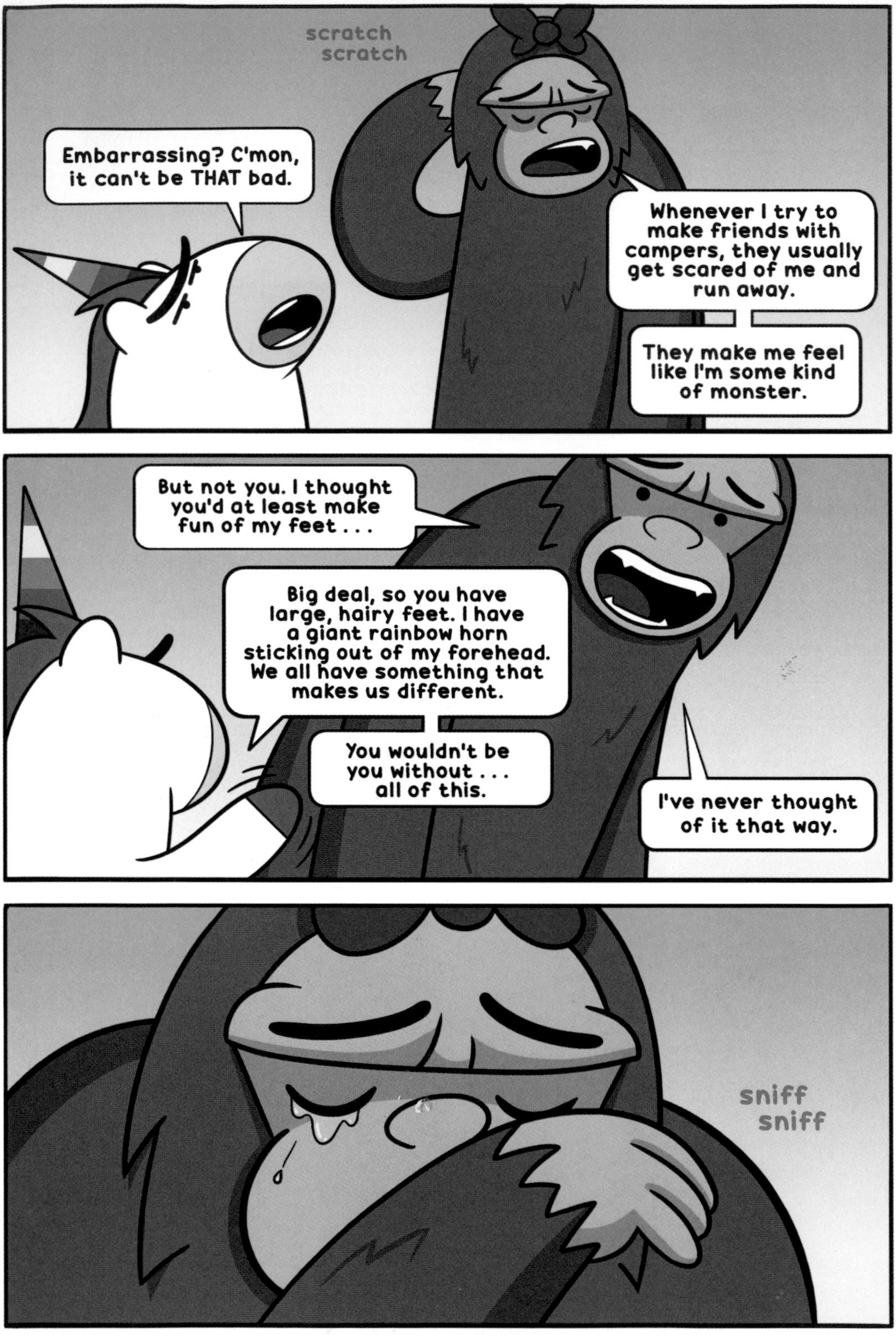
scratch scratch
Embarrassing? C'mon, it can't be THAT bad.
Whenever I try to make friends with campers, they usually get scared of me and run away.
They make me feel like I'm some kind of monster.
But not you. I thought you'd at least make fun of my feet . . .
Big deal, so you have large, hairy feet. I have a giant rainbow horn sticking out of my forehead. We all have something that makes us different.
You wouldn't be you without . . . all of this.
I've never thought of it that way.
sniff sniff

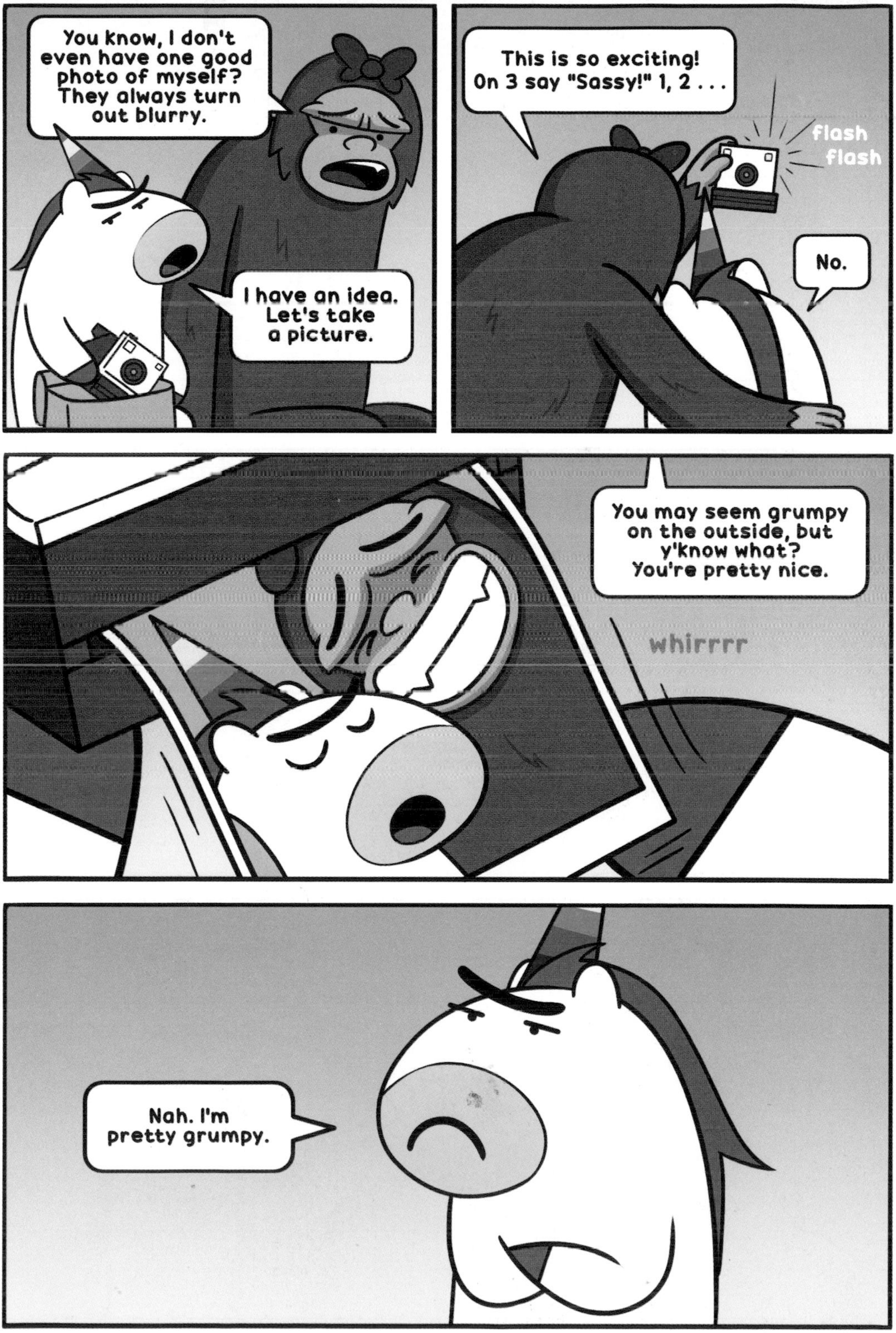
You know, I don't even have one good photo of myself? They always turn out blurry.
I have an idea. Let's take a picture.
This is so exciting! On 3 say "Sassy!" 1, 2 . . .
flash
flash
No.
You may seem grumpy on the outside, but y'know what? You're pretty nice.
whirrrr
Nah. I'm pretty grumpy.

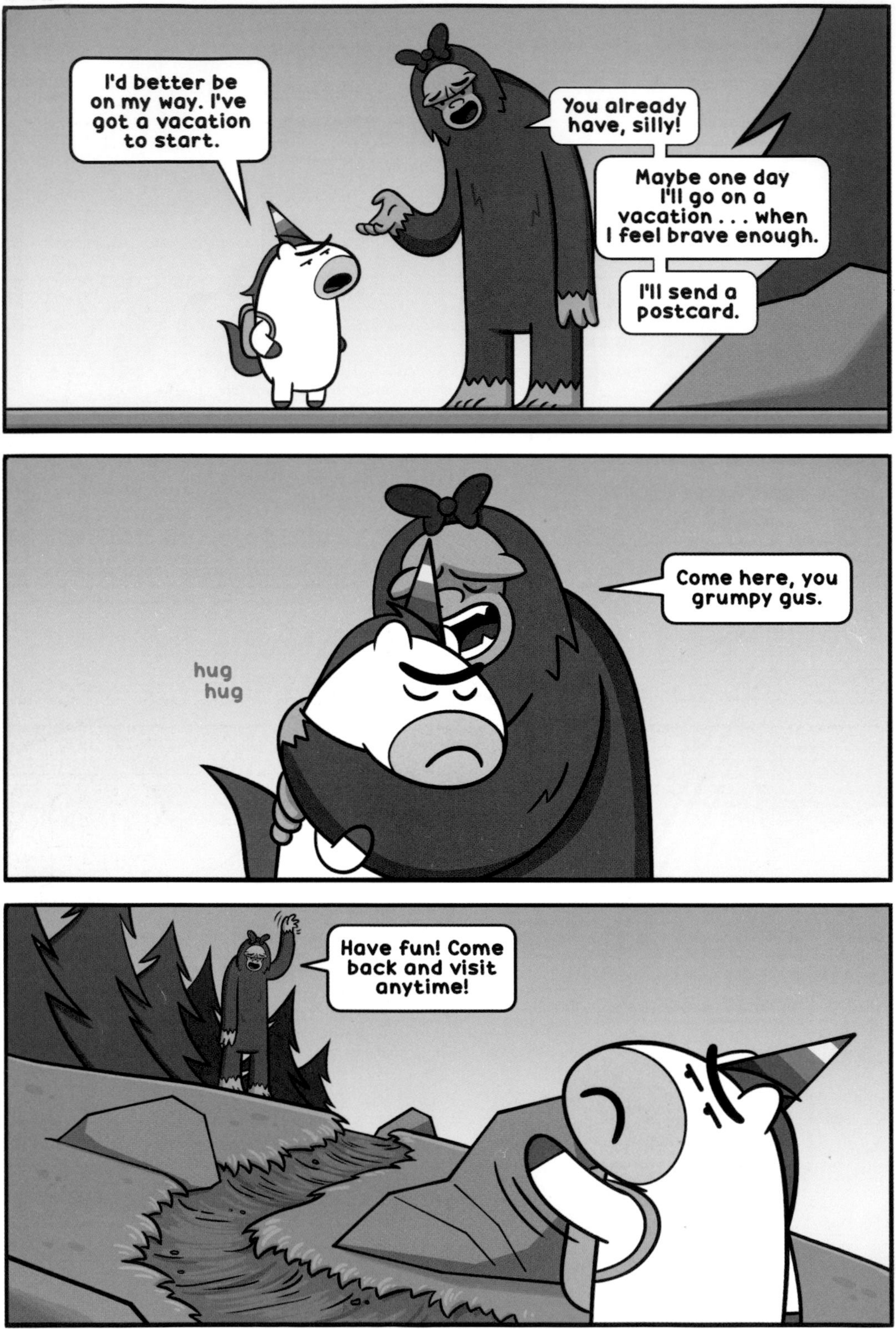
I'd better be on my way. I've got a vacation to start.
You already have, silly!
Maybe one day I'll go on a vacation . . . when I feel brave enough.
I'll send a postcard.
Come here, you grumpy gus.
hug hug
Have fun! Come back and visit anytime!

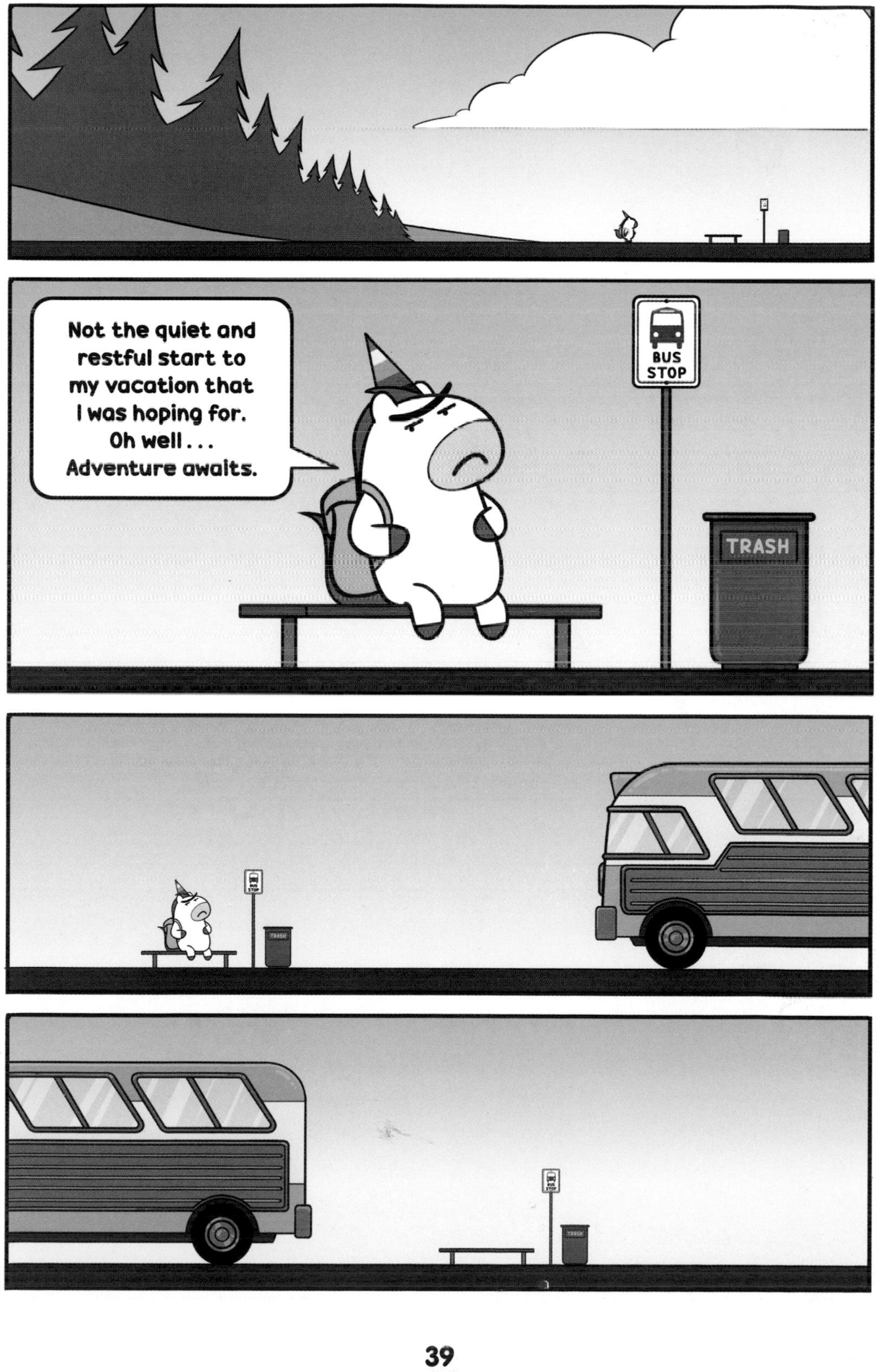
Not the quiet and restful start to my vacation that I was hoping for. Oh well . . . Adventure awaits.
BUS STOP
TRASH

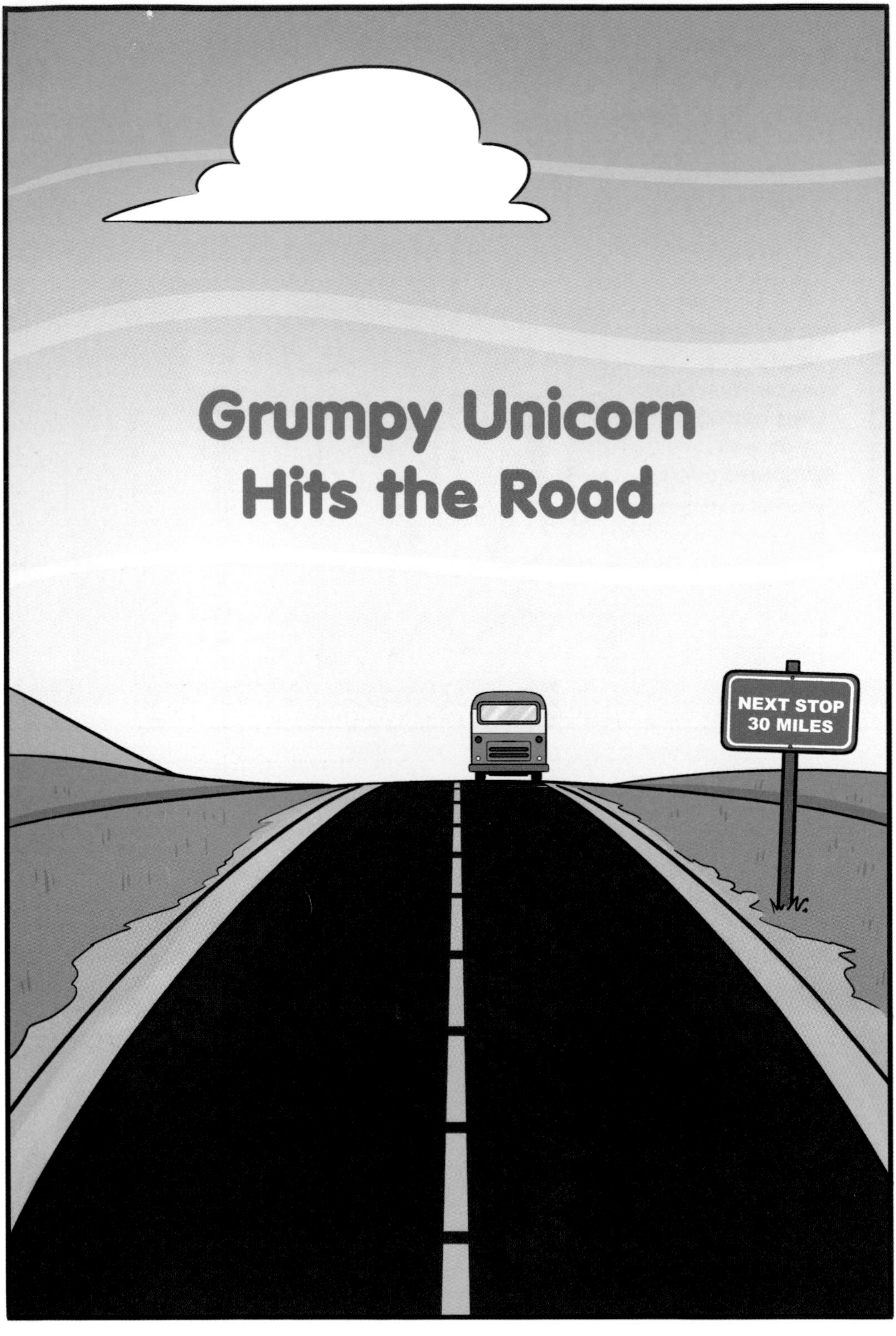
Grumpy Unicorn
Hits the Road
NEXT STOP
30 MILES

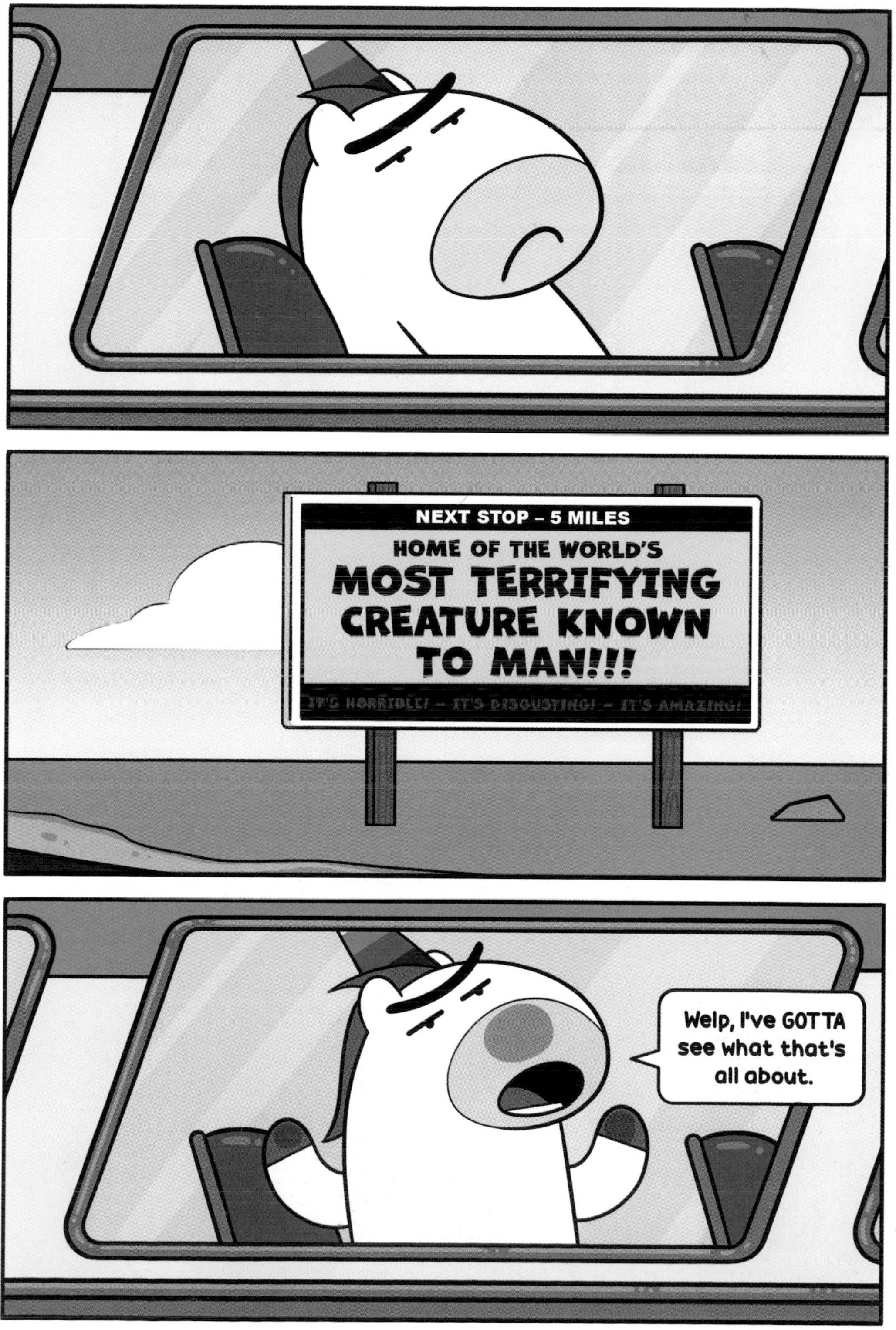
NEXT STOP – 5 MILES
HOME OF THE WORLD'S
MOST TERRIFYING CREATURE KNOWN TO MAN!!!
IT'S HORRIBLE! – IT'S DISGUSTING! – IT'S AMAZING!
Welp, I've GOTTA see what that's all about.

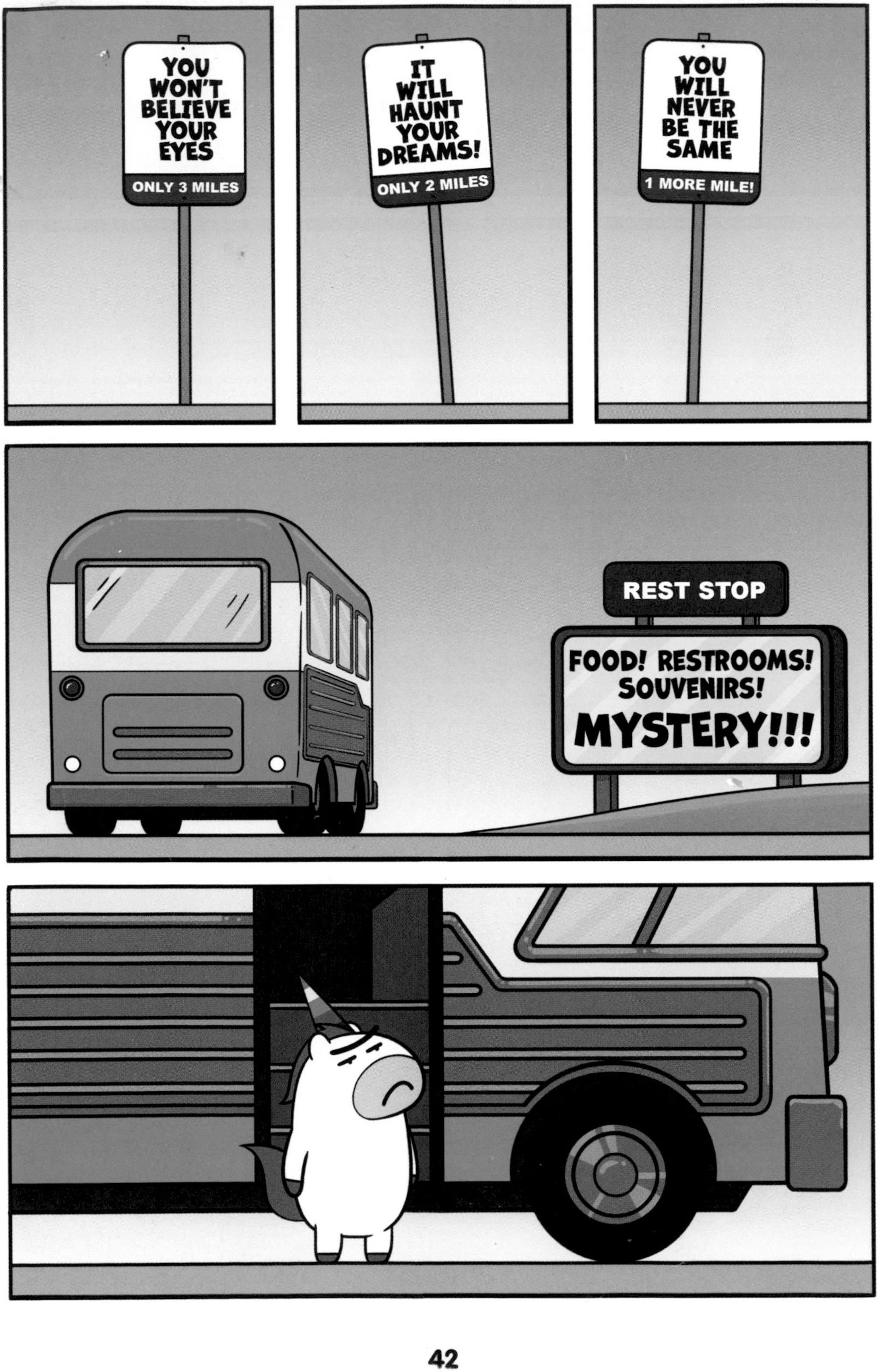
YOU WON'T BELIEVE YOUR EYES
ONLY 3 MILES
IT WILL HAUNT YOUR DREAMS!
ONLY 2 MILES
YOU WILL NEVER BE THE SAME
1 MORE MILE!
REST STOP
FOOD! RESTROOMS! SOUVENIRS!
MYSTERY!!!

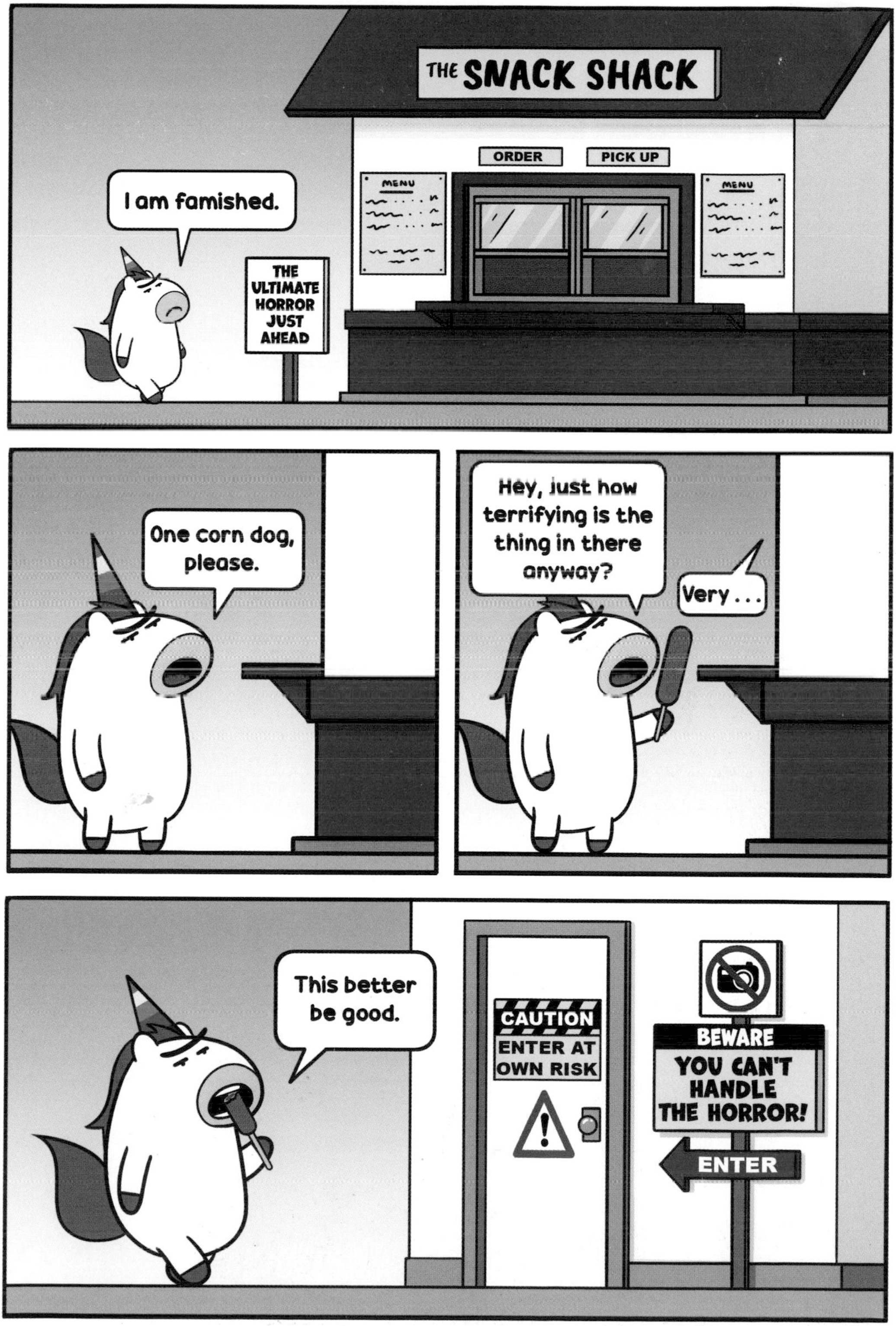
THE SNACK SHACK
ORDER
PICK UP
MENU
MENU
I am famished.
THE ULTIMATE HORROR JUST AHEAD
One corn dog, please.
Hey, just how terrifying is the thing in there anyway?
Very . . .
This better be good.
CAUTION
ENTER AT OWN RISK
BEWARE
YOU CAN'T HANDLE THE HORROR!
ENTER

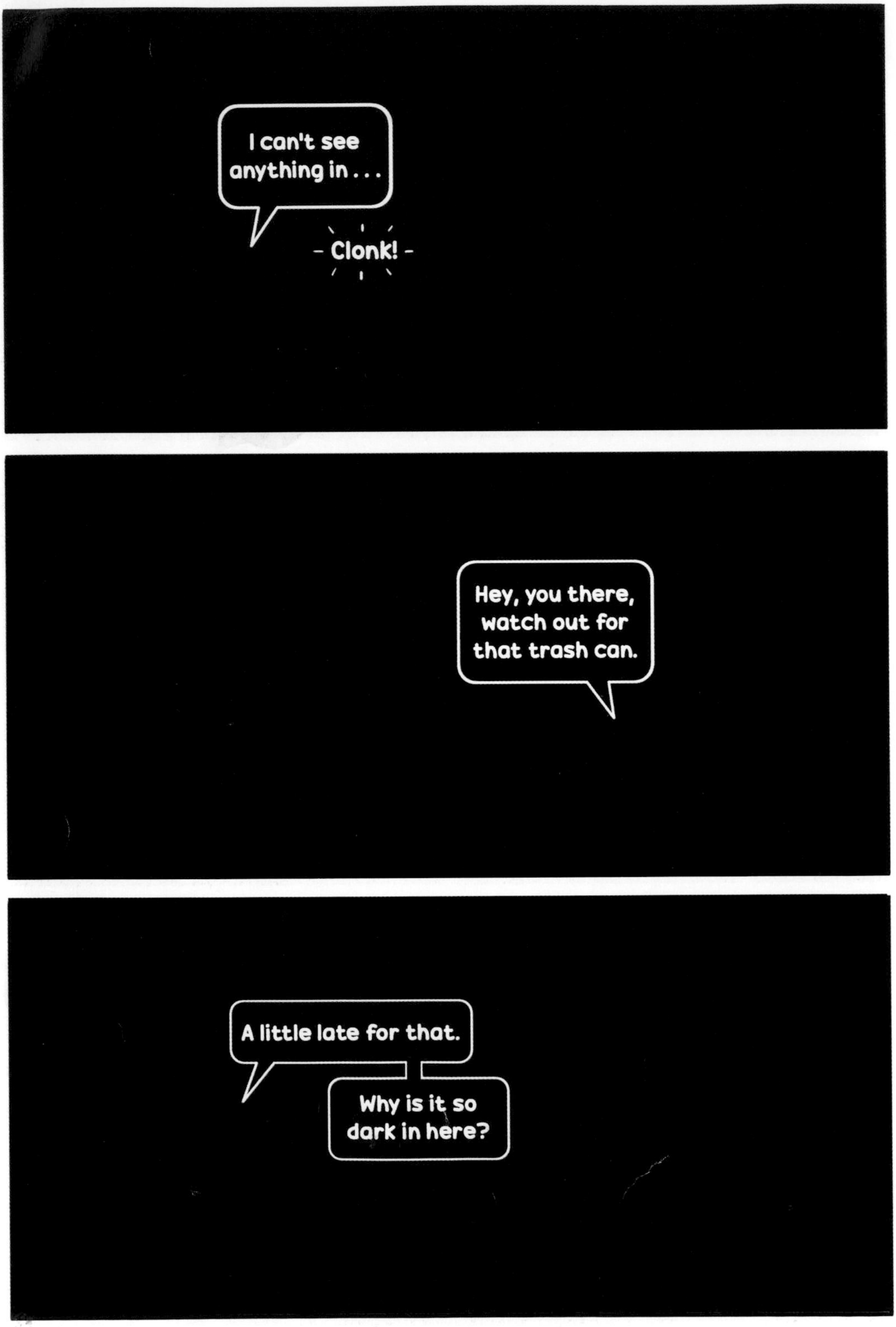
I can't see anything in . . .
- Clonk! -
Hey, you there, watch out for that trash can.
A little late for that.
Why is it so dark in here?

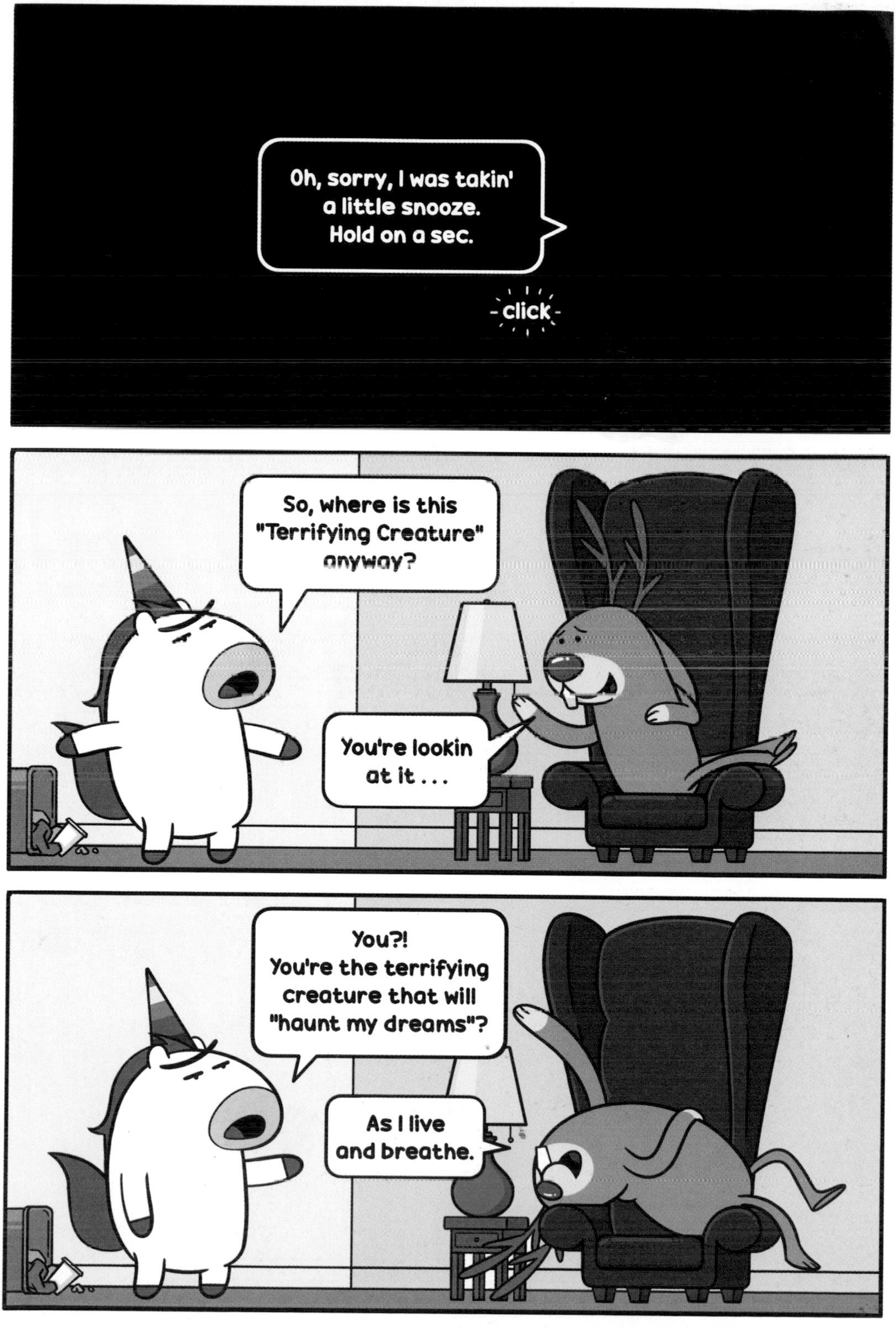
Oh, sorry, I was takin' a little snooze. Hold on a sec.
click
So, where is this "Terrifying Creature" anyway?
You're lookin at it . . .
You?! You're the terrifying creature that will "haunt my dreams"?
As I live and breathe.

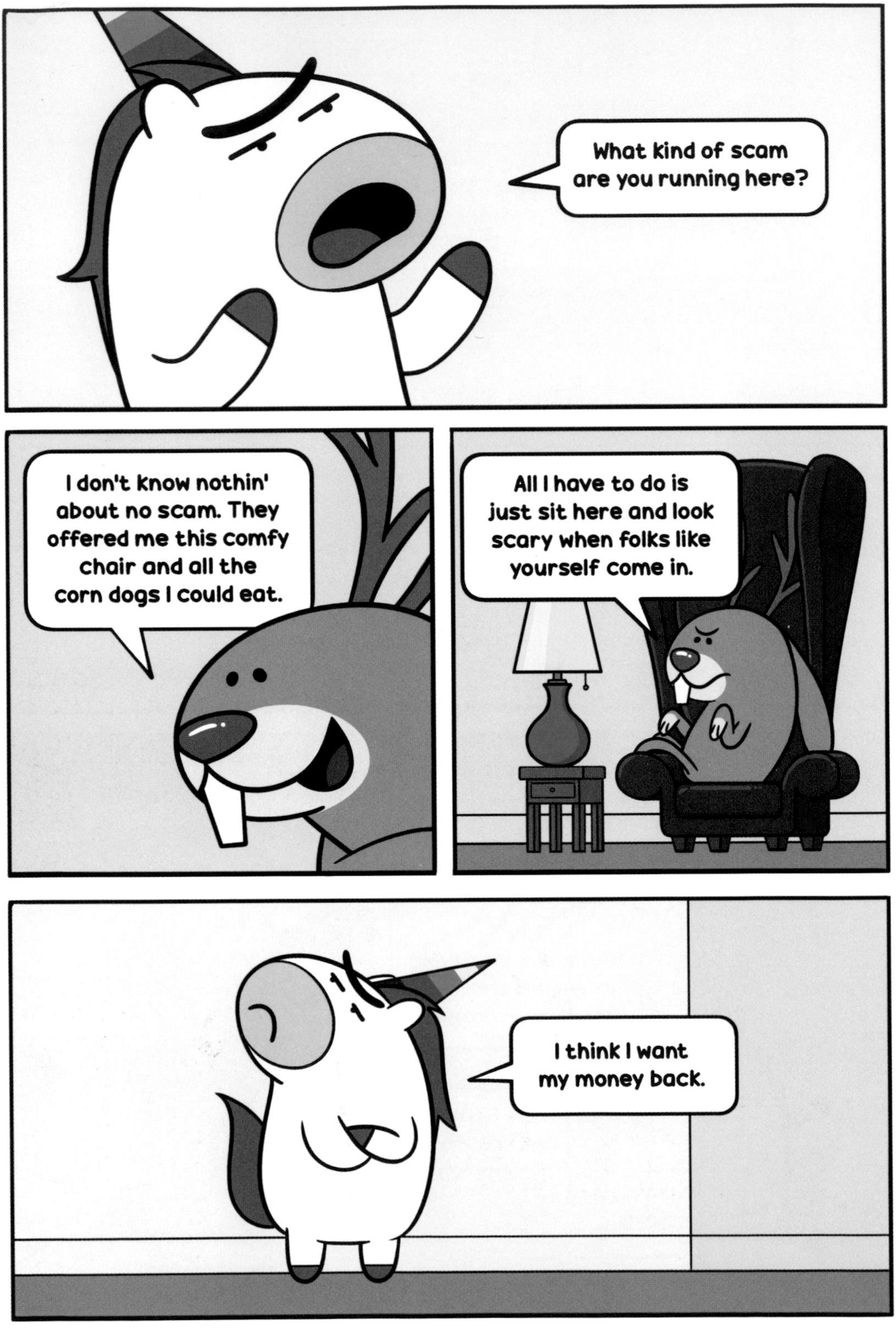
What kind of scam are you running here?
I don't know nothin' about no scam. They offered me this comfy chair and all the corn dogs I could eat.
All I have to do is just sit here and look scary when folks like yourself come in.
I think I want my money back.

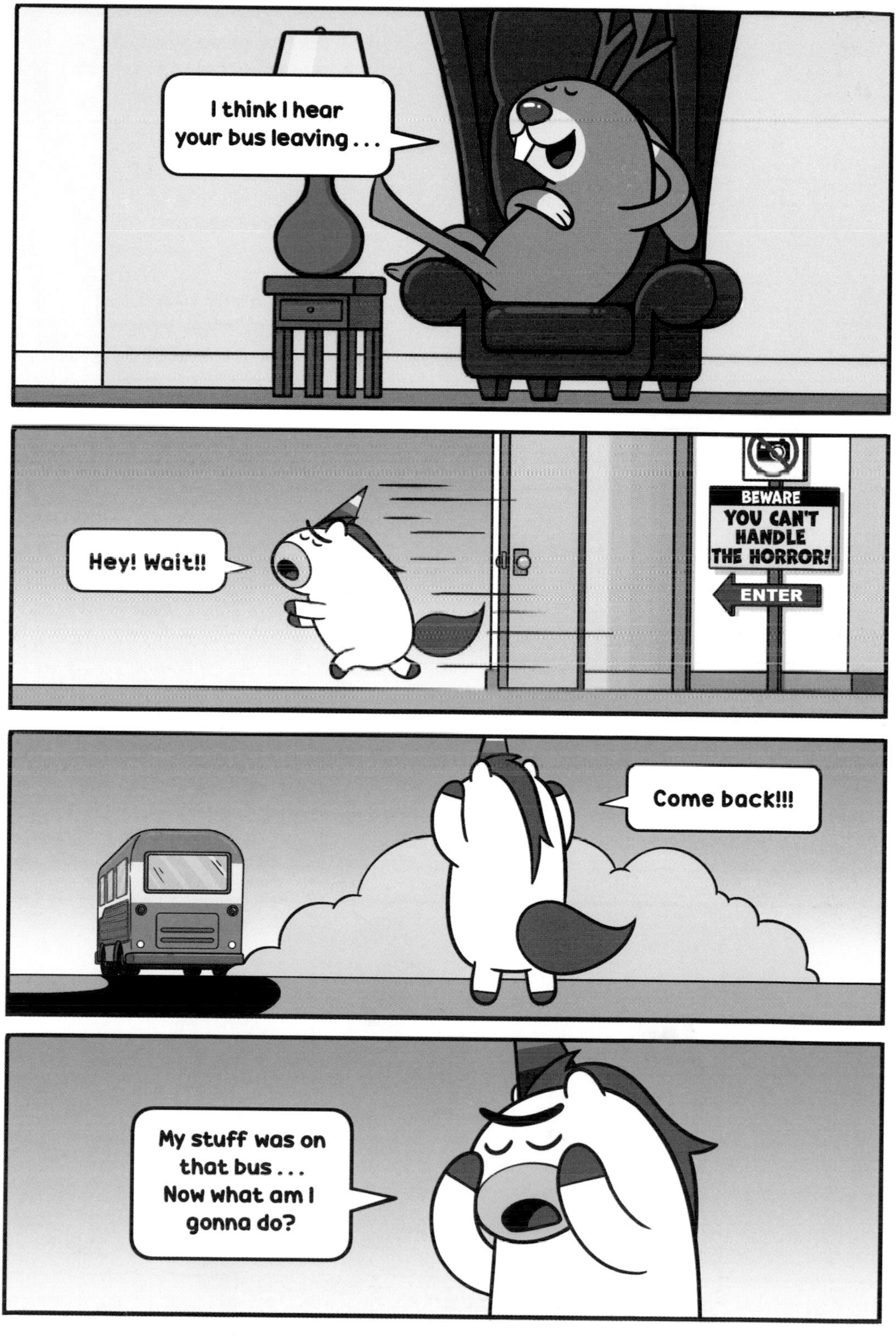
I think I hear your bus leaving . . .
Hey! Wait!!
BEWARE
YOU CAN'T HANDLE THE HORROR!
ENTER
Come back!!!
My stuff was on that bus . . . Now what am I gonna do?

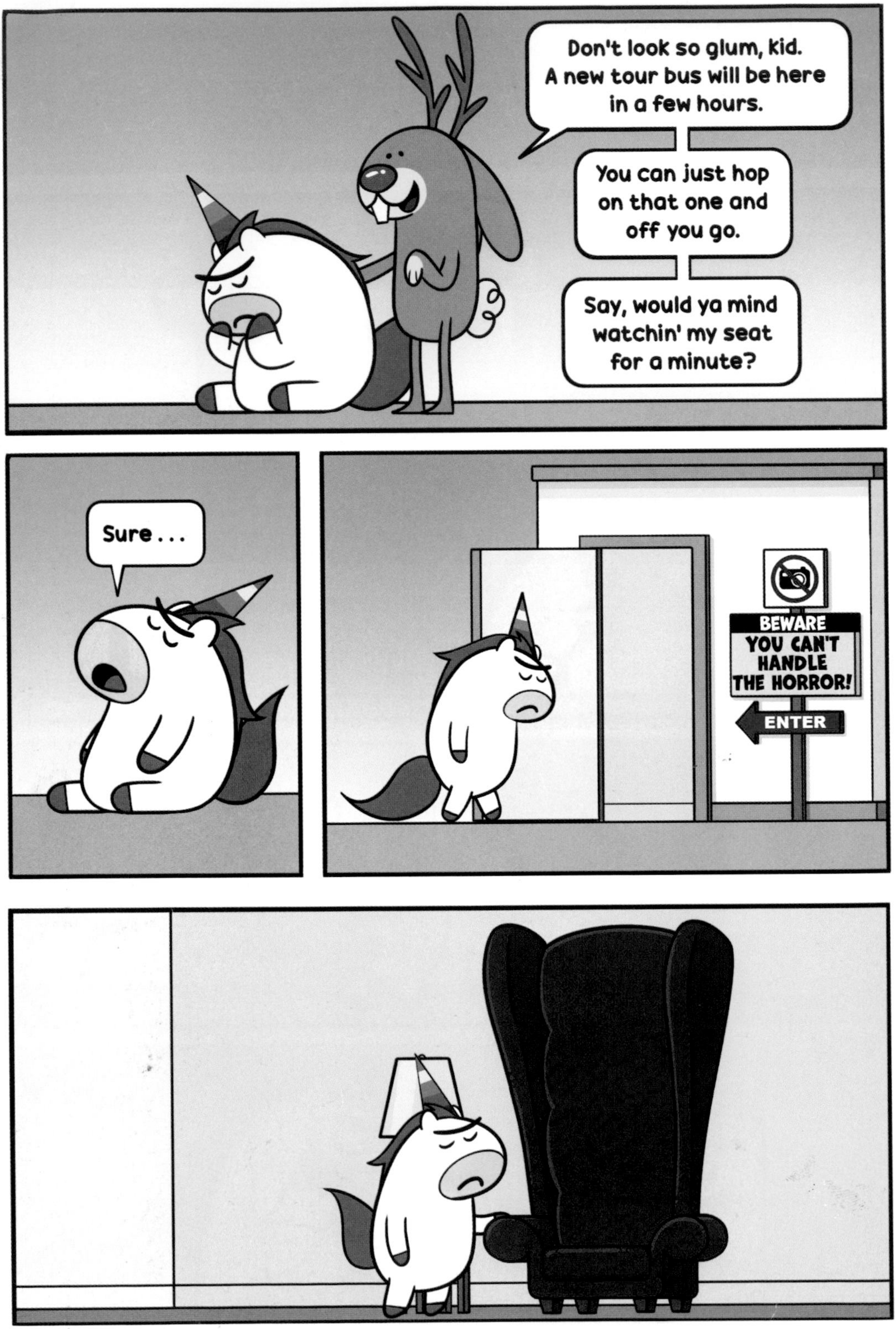

Don't look so glum, kid. A new tour bus will be here in a few hours.
You can just hop on that one and off you go.
Say, would ya mind watchin' my seat for a minute?
Sure . . .
BEWARE
YOU CAN'T HANDLE THE HORROR!
ENTER

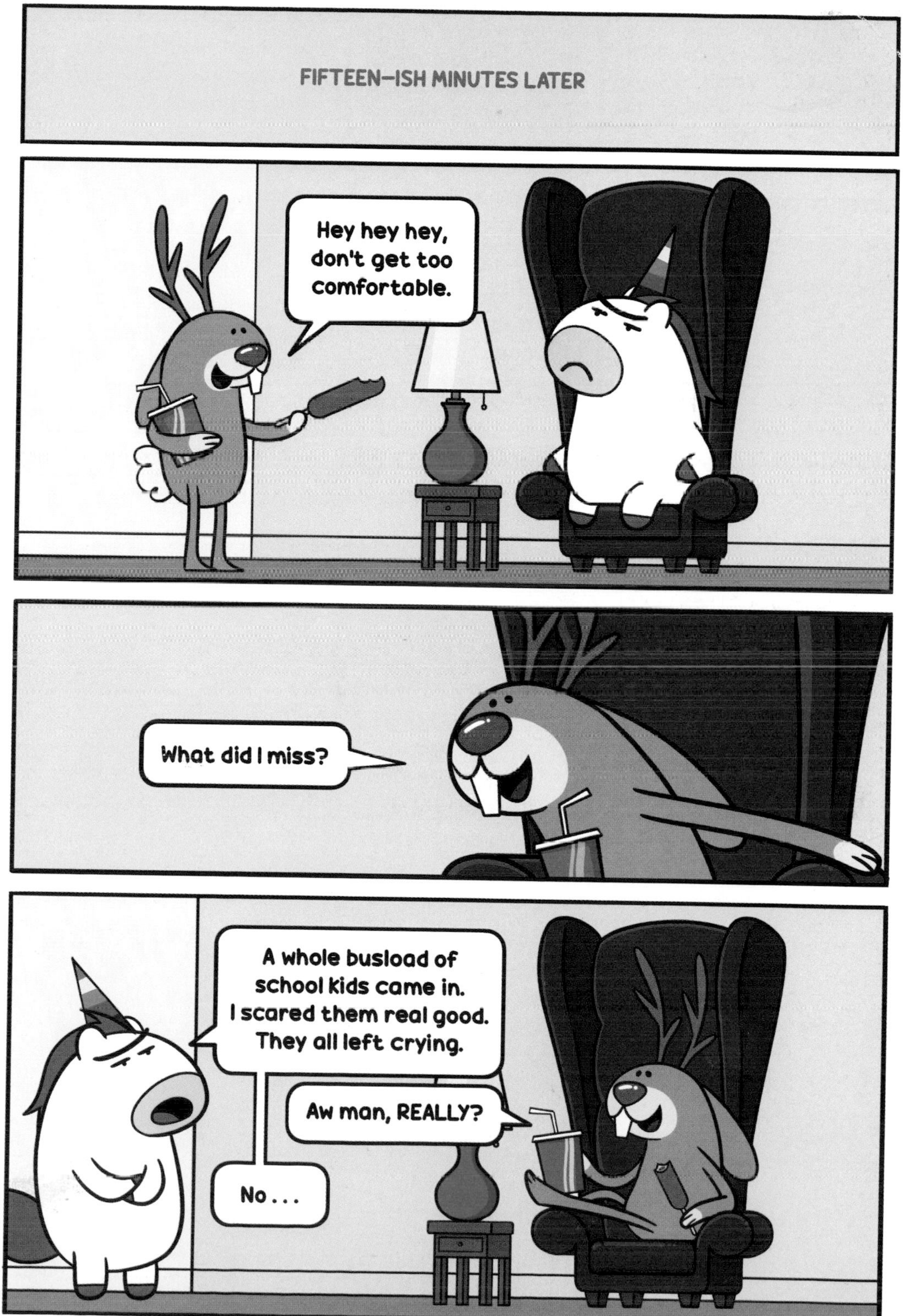
FIFTEEN—ISH MINUTES LATER
Hey hey hey, don't get too comfortable.
What did I miss?
A whole busload of school kids came in. I scared them real good. They all left crying.
Aw man, REALLY?
No . . .

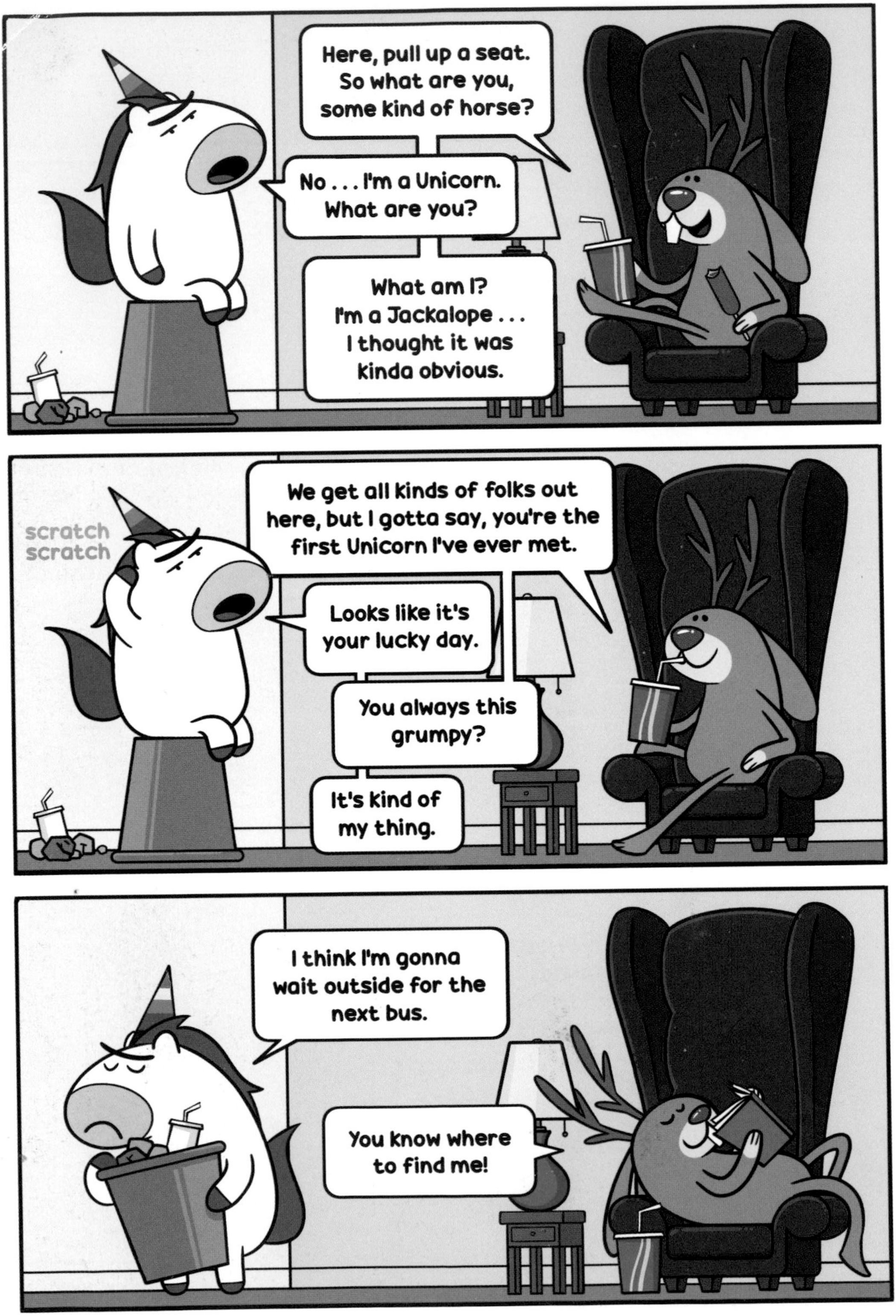
Here, pull up a seat. So what are you, some kind of horse?
No . . . I'm a Unicorn. What are you?
What am I? I'm a Jackalope . . . I thought it was kinda obvious.
scratch scratch
We get all kinds of folks out here, but I gotta say, you're the first Unicorn I've ever met.
Looks like it's your lucky day.
You always this grumpy?
It's kind of my thing.
I think I'm gonna wait outside for the next bus.
You know where to find me!

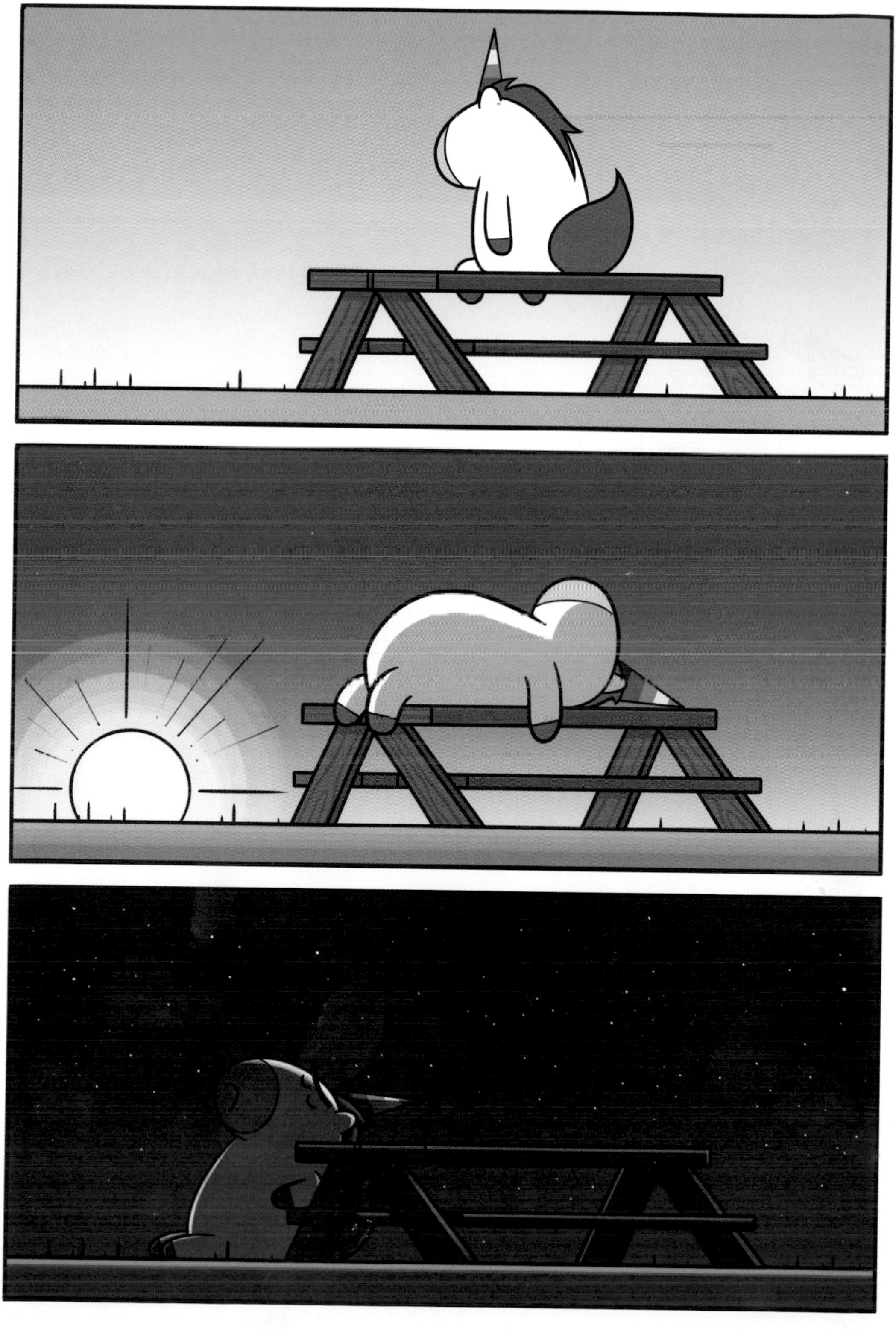

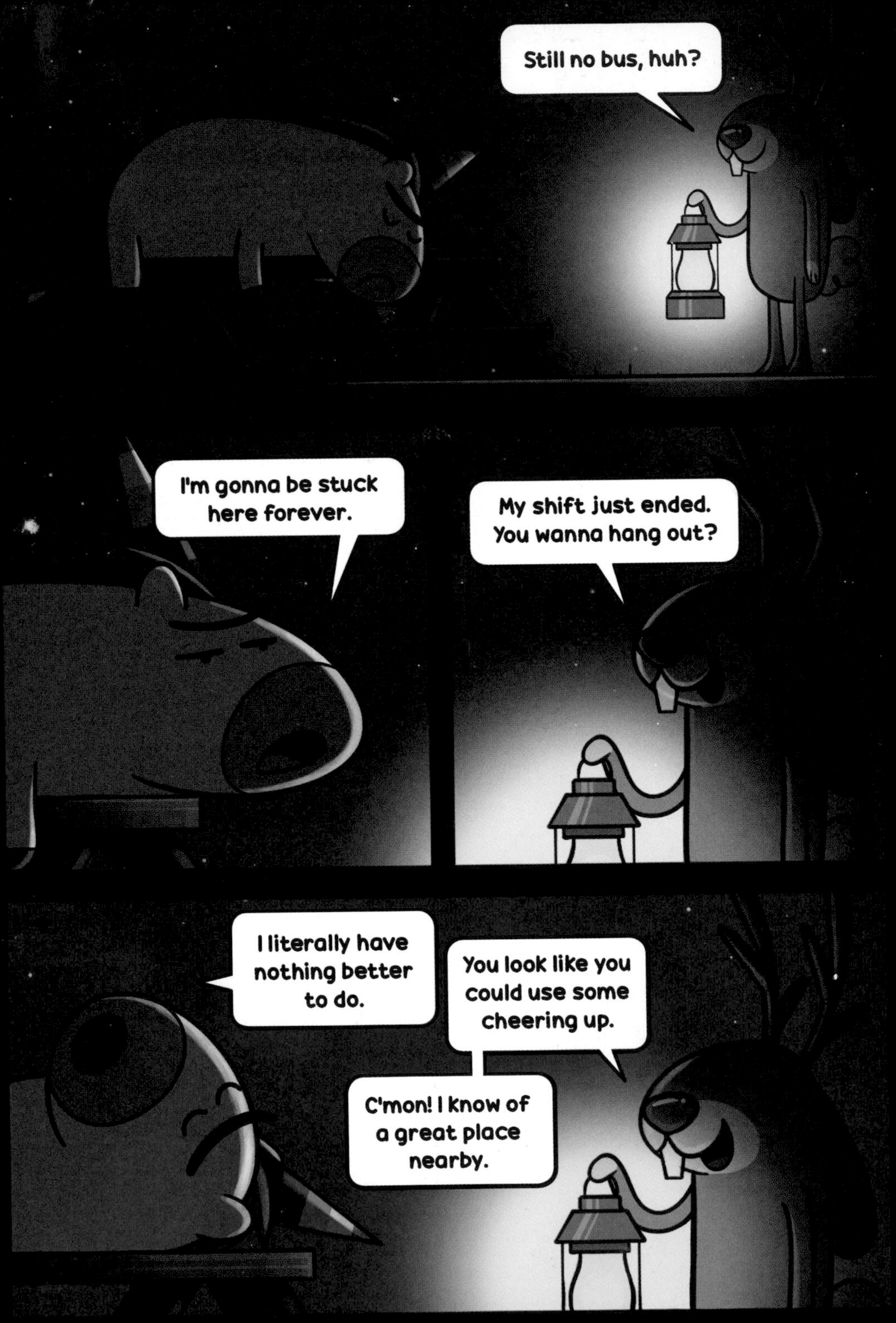
Still no bus, huh?
I'm gonna be stuck here forever.
My shift just ended. You wanna hang out?
I literally have nothing better to do.
You look like you could use some cheering up.
C'mon! I know of a great place nearby.

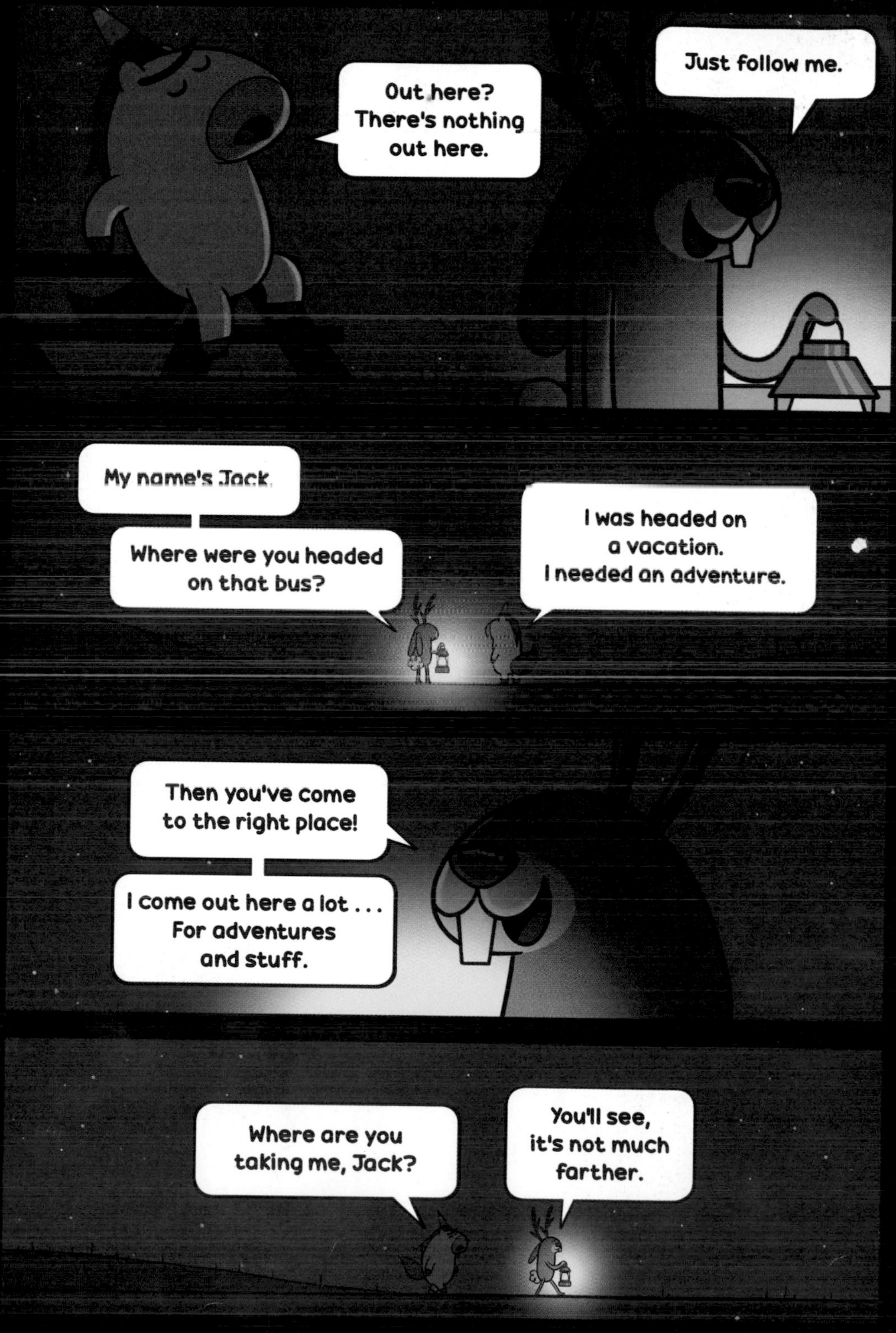
Out here? There's nothing out here.
Just follow me.
My name's Jack.
Where were you headed on that bus?
I was headed on a vacation. I needed an adventure.
Then you've come to the right place!
I come out here a lot . . . For adventures and stuff.
Where are you taking me, Jack?
You'll see, it's not much farther.

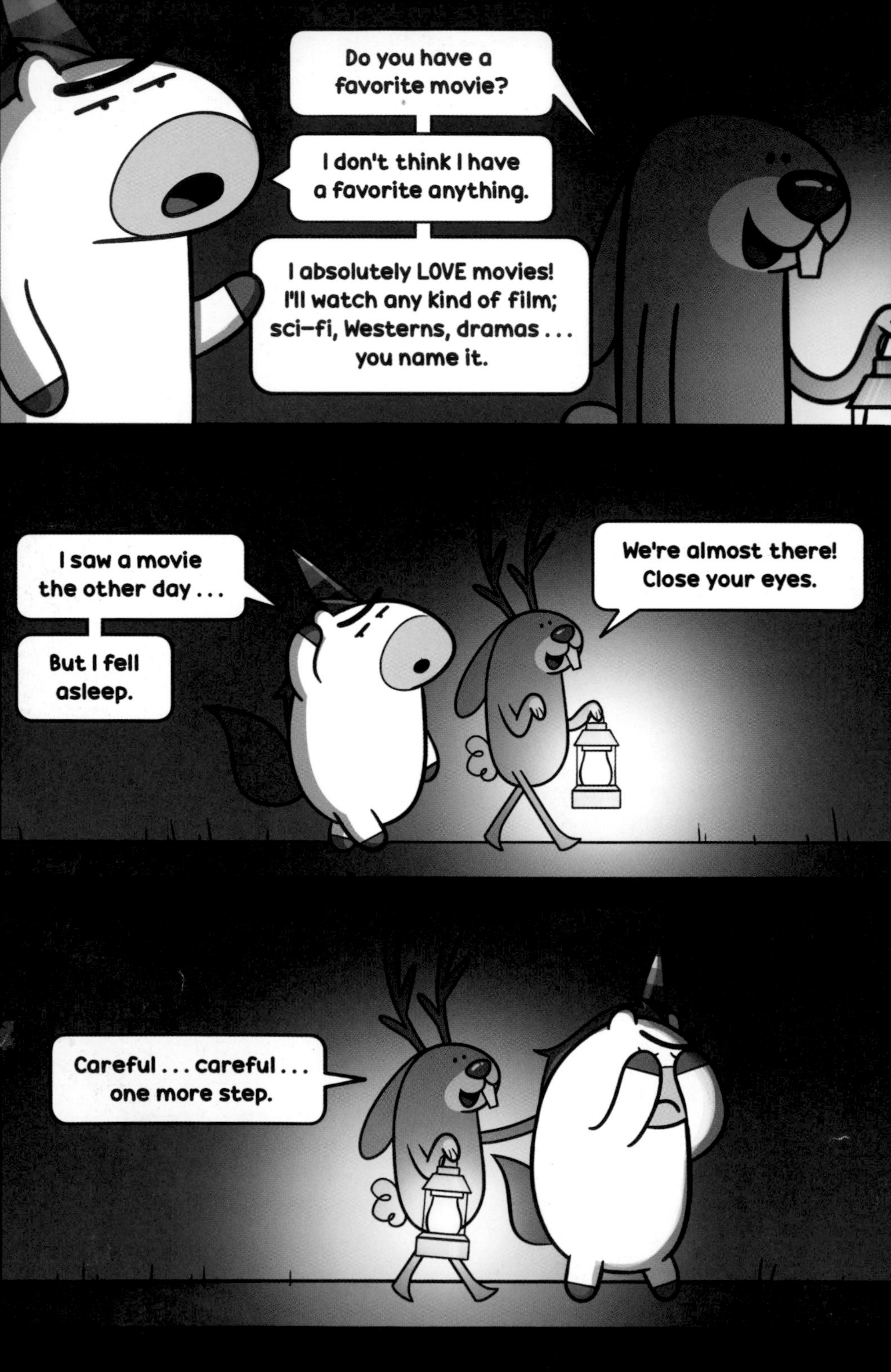
Do you have a favorite movie?
I don't think I have a favorite anything.
I absolutely LOVE movies! I'll watch any kind of film; sci-fi, Westerns, dramas . . . you name it.
I saw a movie the other day . . .
But I fell asleep.
We're almost there! Close your eyes.
Careful . . . careful . . . one more step.

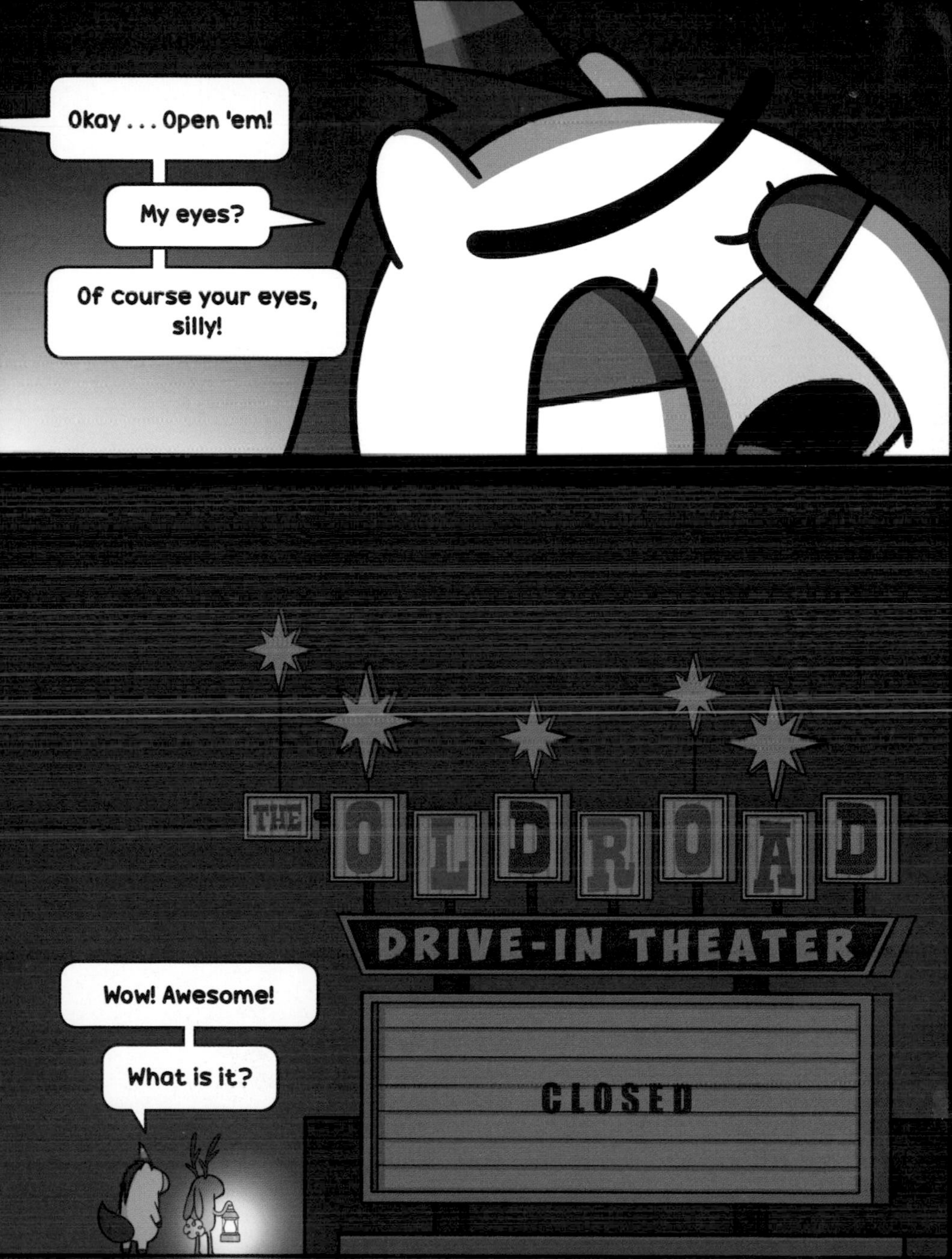
Okay . . . Open 'em!
My eyes?
Of course your eyes, silly!
THE OLD ROAD
DRIVE-IN THEATER
Wow! Awesome!
What is it?
CLOSED

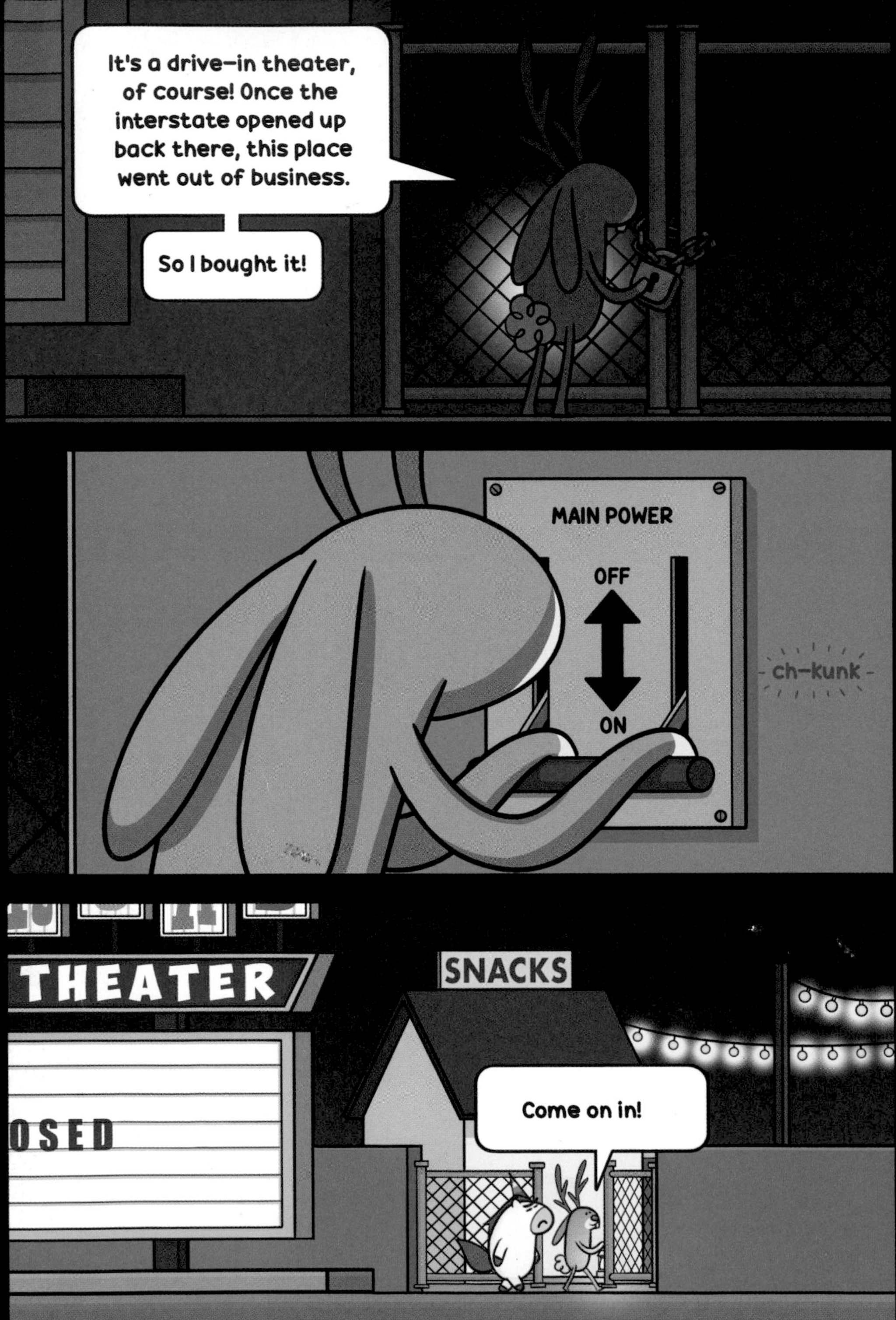

It's a drive-in theater, of course! Once the interstate opened up back there, this place went out of business.
So I bought it!
MAIN POWER
OFF
ON
ch-kunk
THEATER
SNACKS
OSED
Come on in!

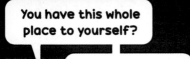

**You have this whole place to yourself?**

**That sounds amazing!**

**It's fun, but it can get pretty lonely. I'm happy you're here!**

**I'll pick a movie for us to watch. Head over there and take a seat. I'll be right there.**

**Wow!**

**This is awesome!**

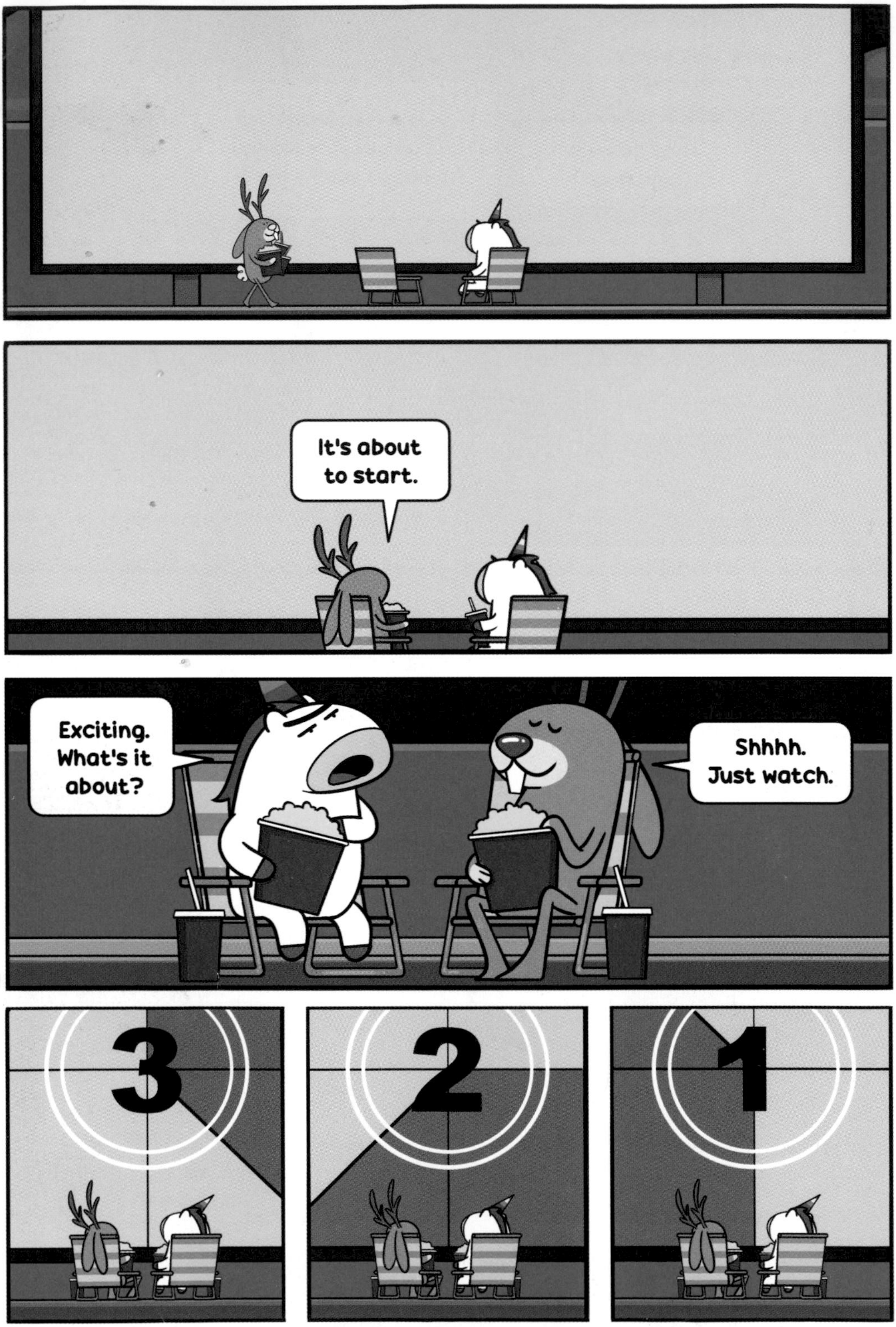
It's about to start.
Exciting. What's it about?
Shhhh. Just watch.
3
2
1

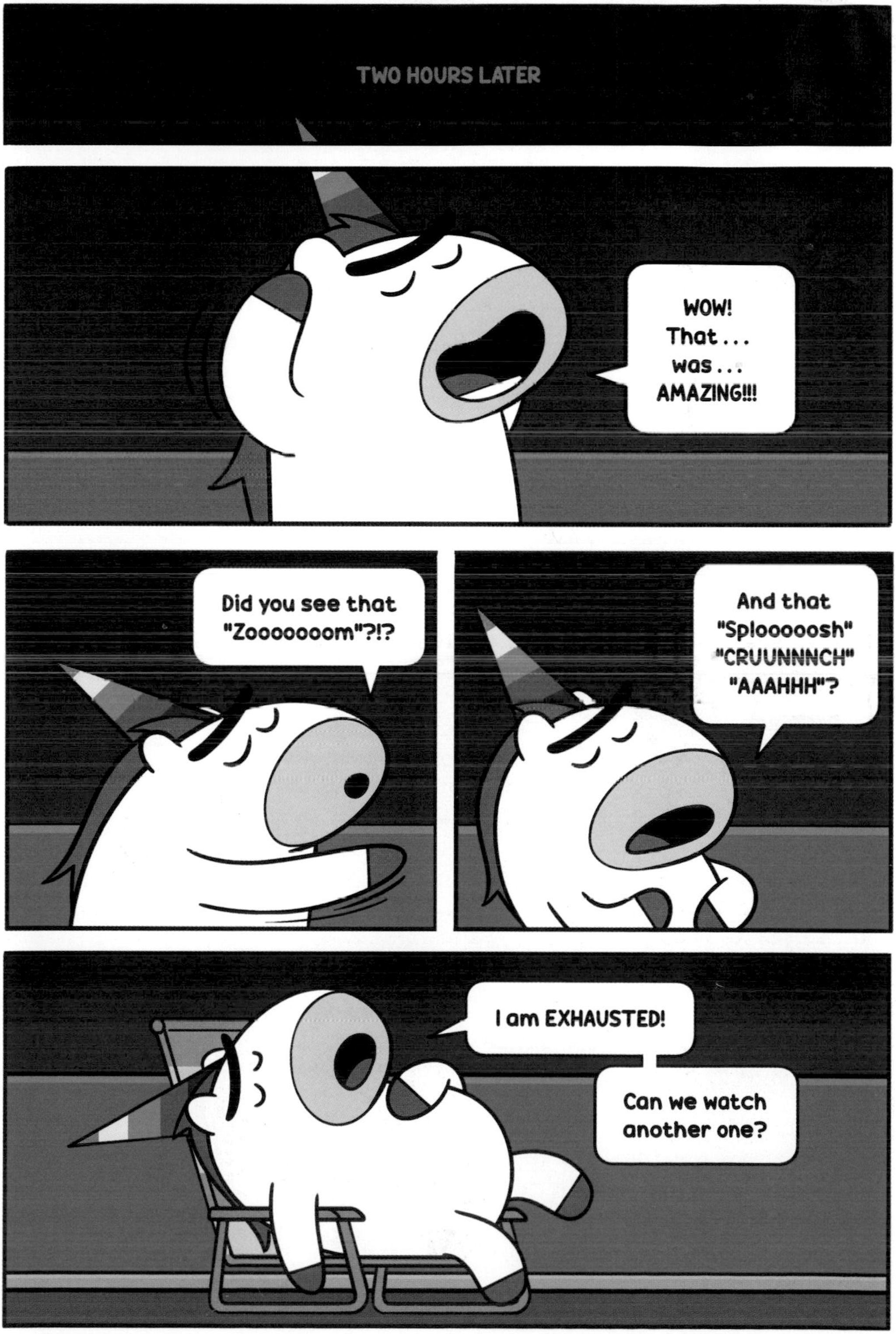
TWO HOURS LATER
WOW! That . . . was . . . AMAZING!!!
Did you see that "Zoooooom"?!?
And that "Splooooosh" "CRUUNNNCH" "AAAHHH"?
I am EXHAUSTED!
Can we watch another one?

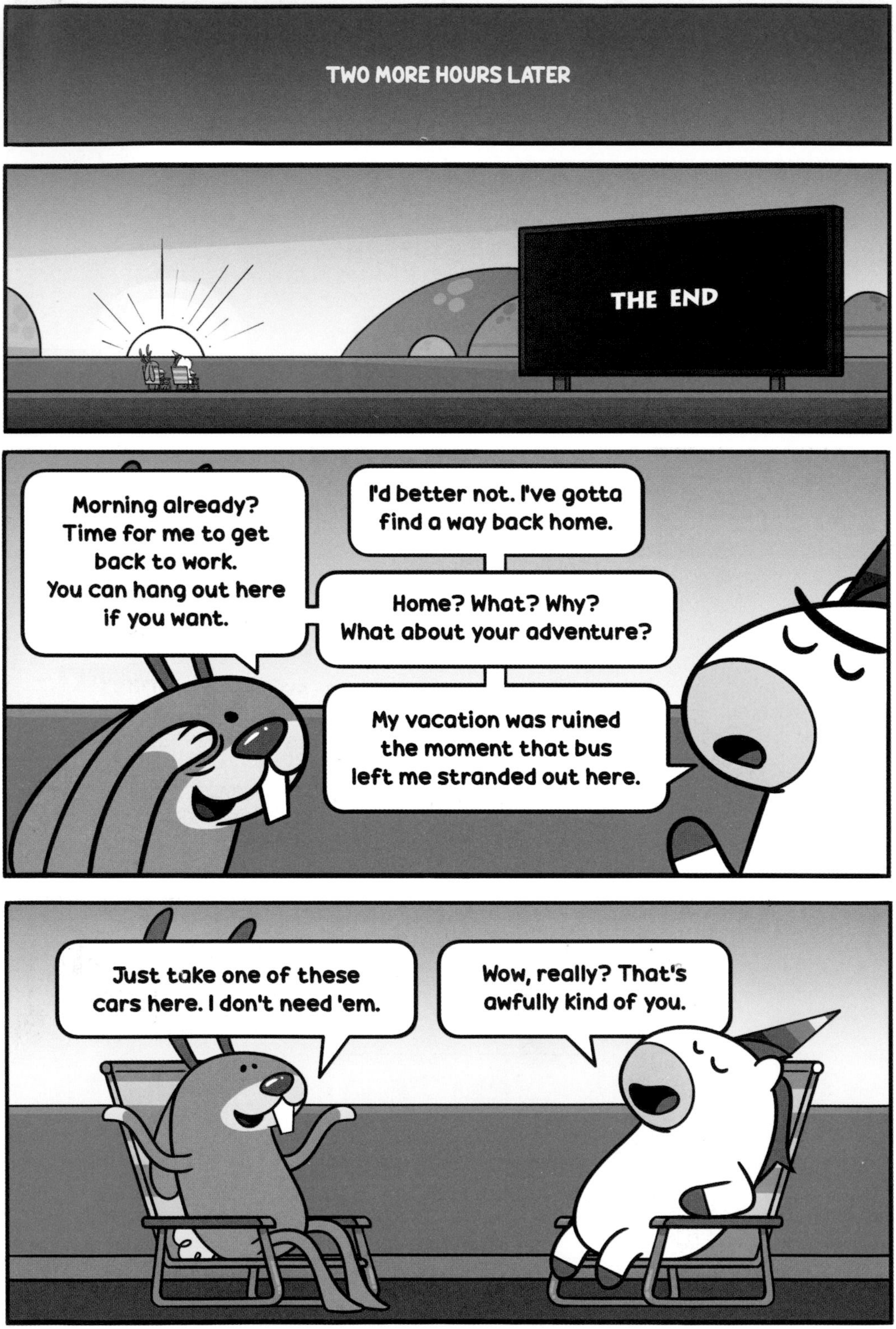
TWO MORE HOURS LATER
THE END
Morning already? Time for me to get back to work. You can hang out here if you want.
I'd better not. I've gotta find a way back home.
Home? What? Why? What about your adventure?
My vacation was ruined the moment that bus left me stranded out here.
Just take one of these cars here. I don't need 'em.
Wow, really? That's awfully kind of you.

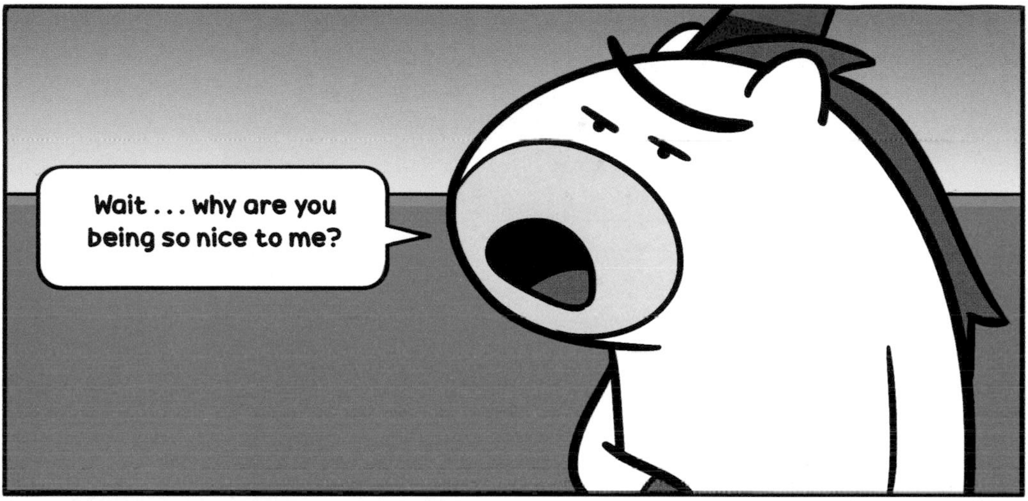
Wait . . . why are you being so nice to me?

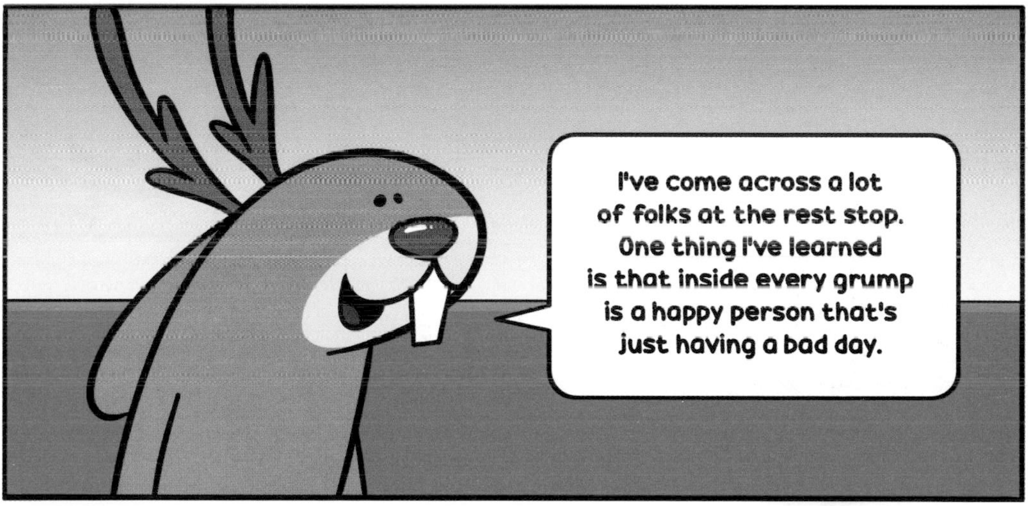
I've come across a lot of folks at the rest stop. One thing I've learned is that inside every grump is a happy person that's just having a bad day.

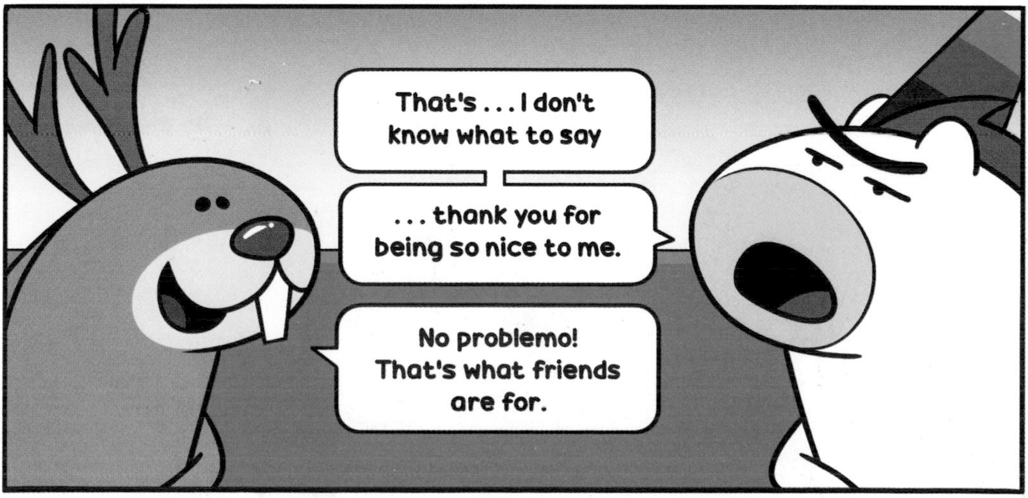
That's . . . I don't know what to say
. . . thank you for being so nice to me.
No problemo! That's what friends are for.

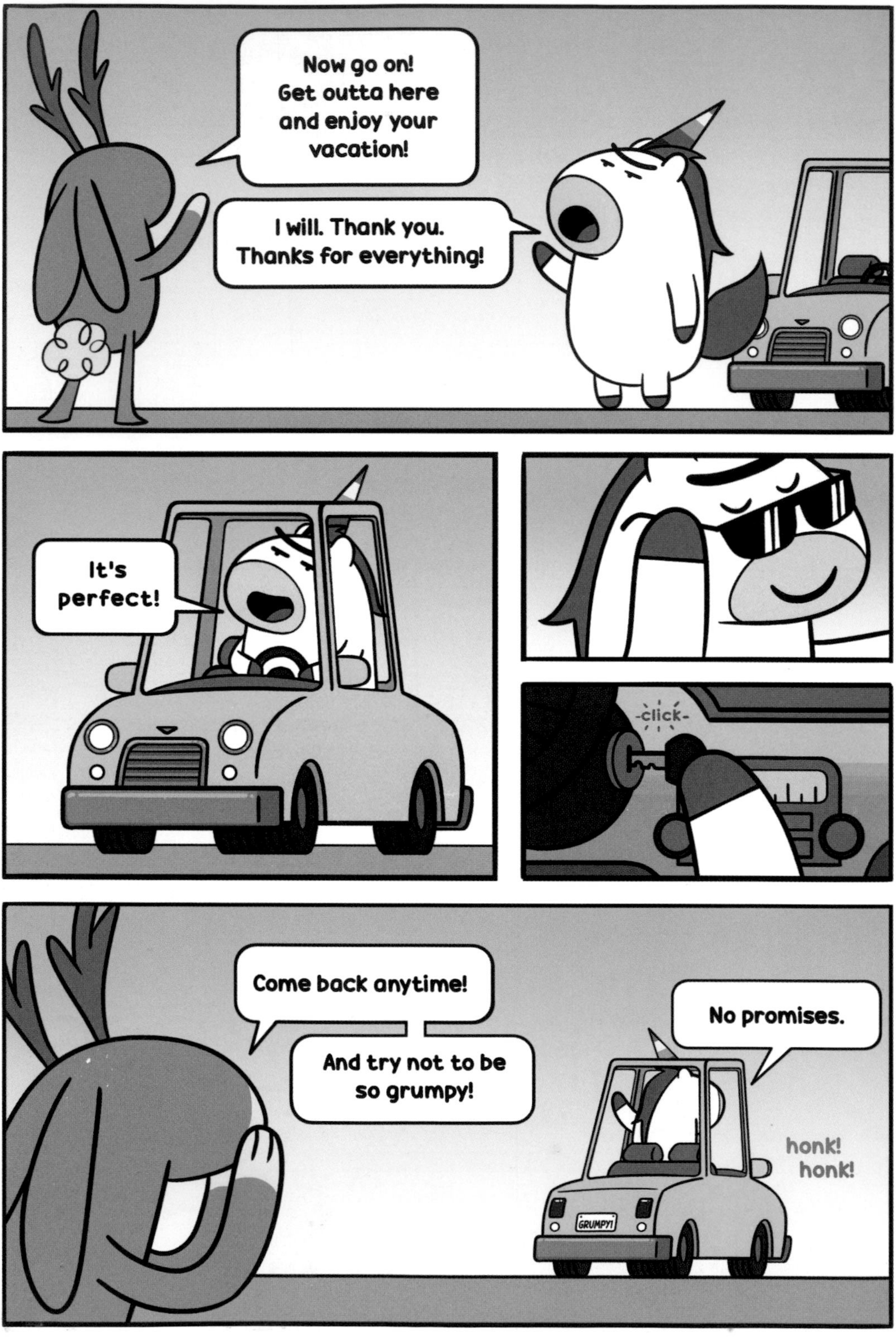
Now go on! Get outta here and enjoy your vacation!
I will. Thank you. Thanks for everything!
It's perfect!
-click-
Come back anytime!
And try not to be so grumpy!
No promises.
GRUMPY1
honk! honk!

# Grumpy Unicorn Hits the Road

## (again, for real this time)

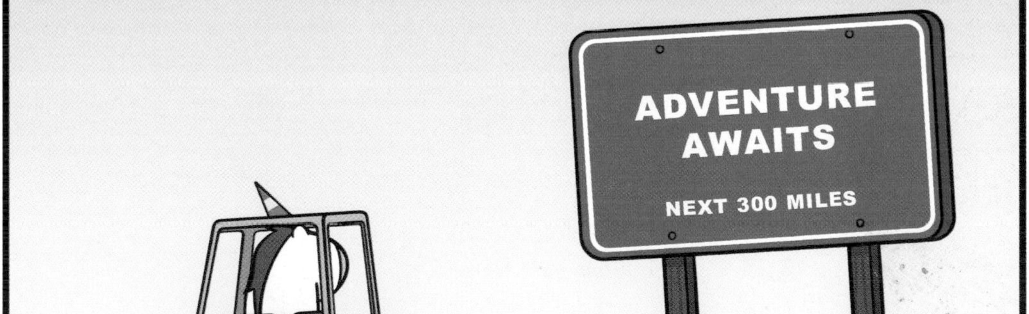
ADVENTURE AWAITS
NEXT 300 MILES
GRUMPY1

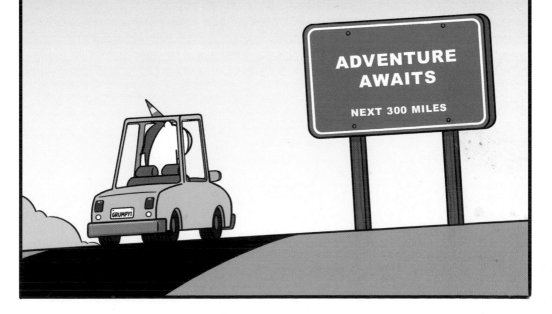

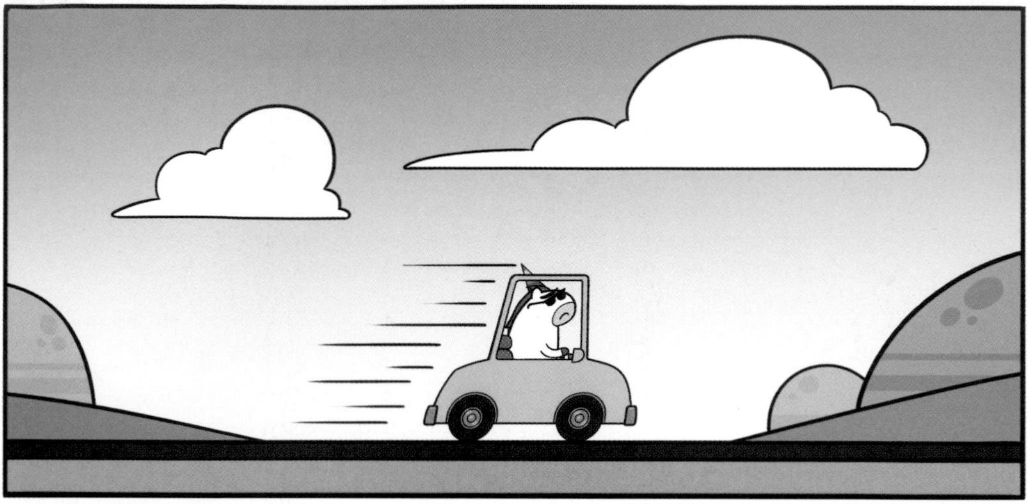
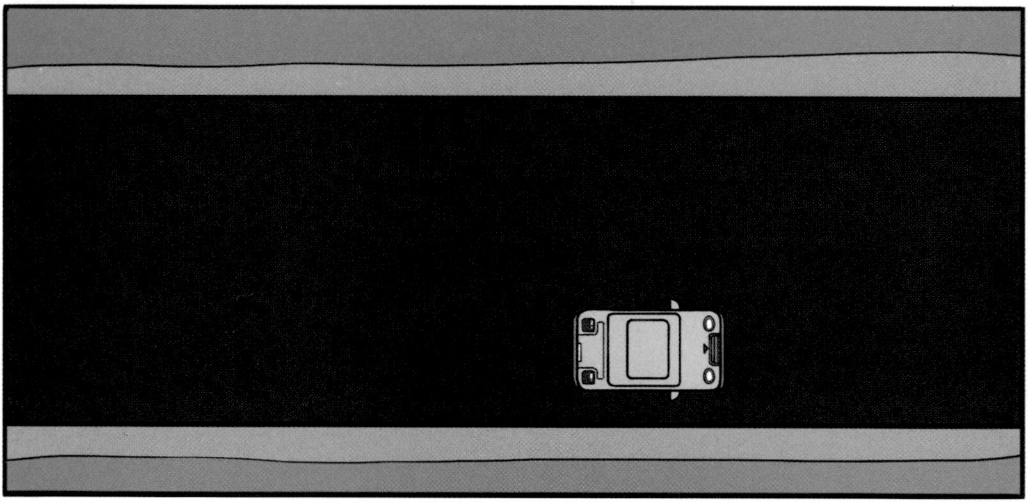
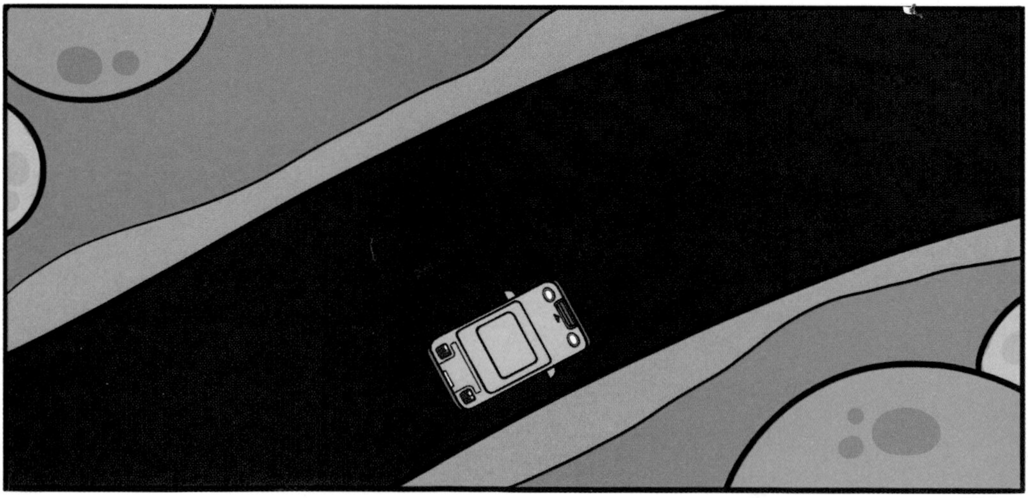

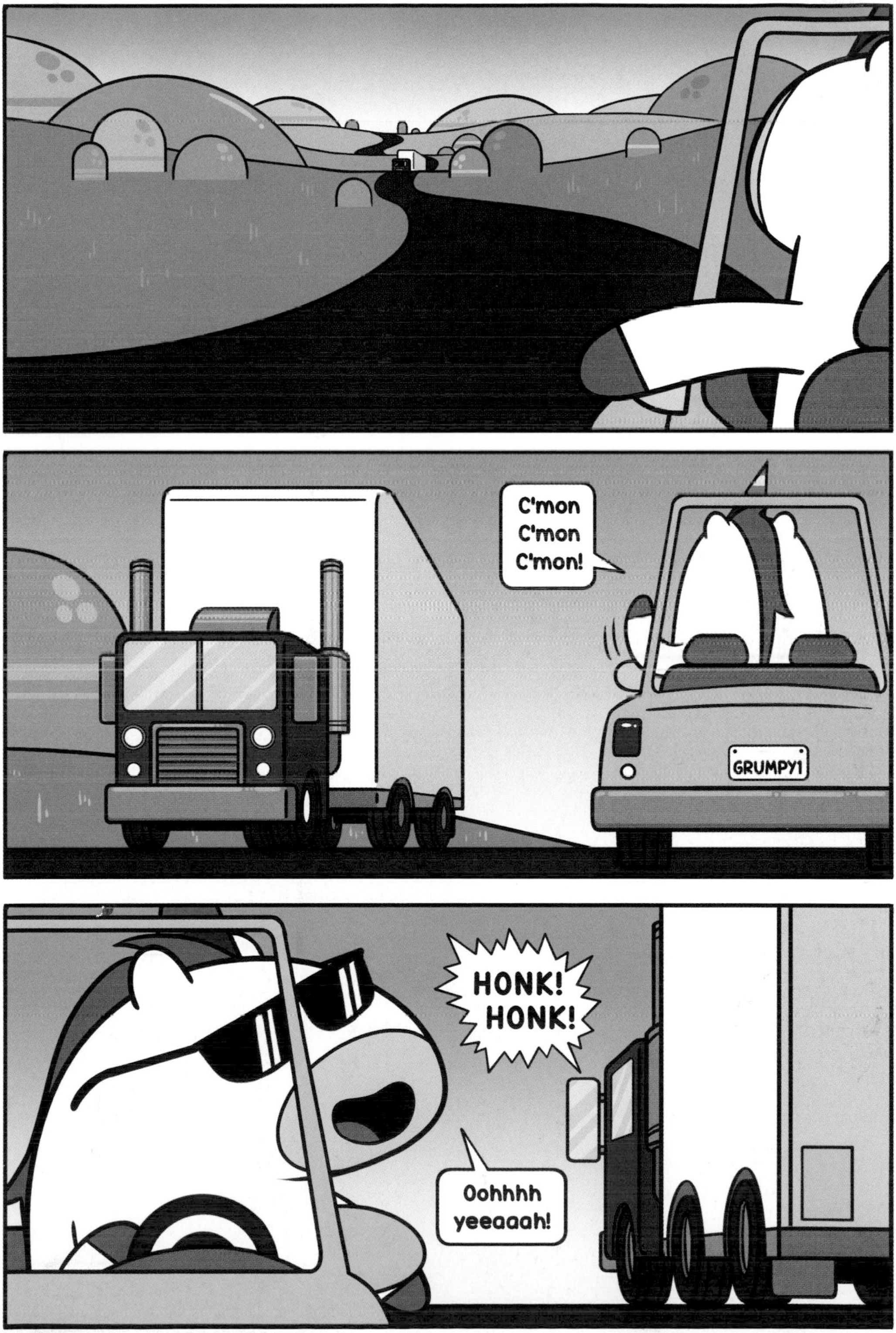
C'mon
C'mon
C'mon!
GRUMPY1
HONK!
HONK!
Oohhhh
yeeaaah!

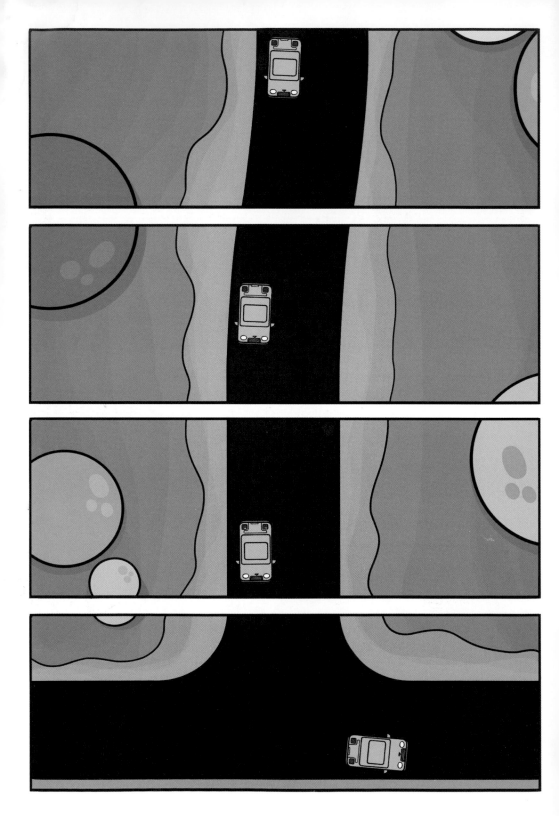

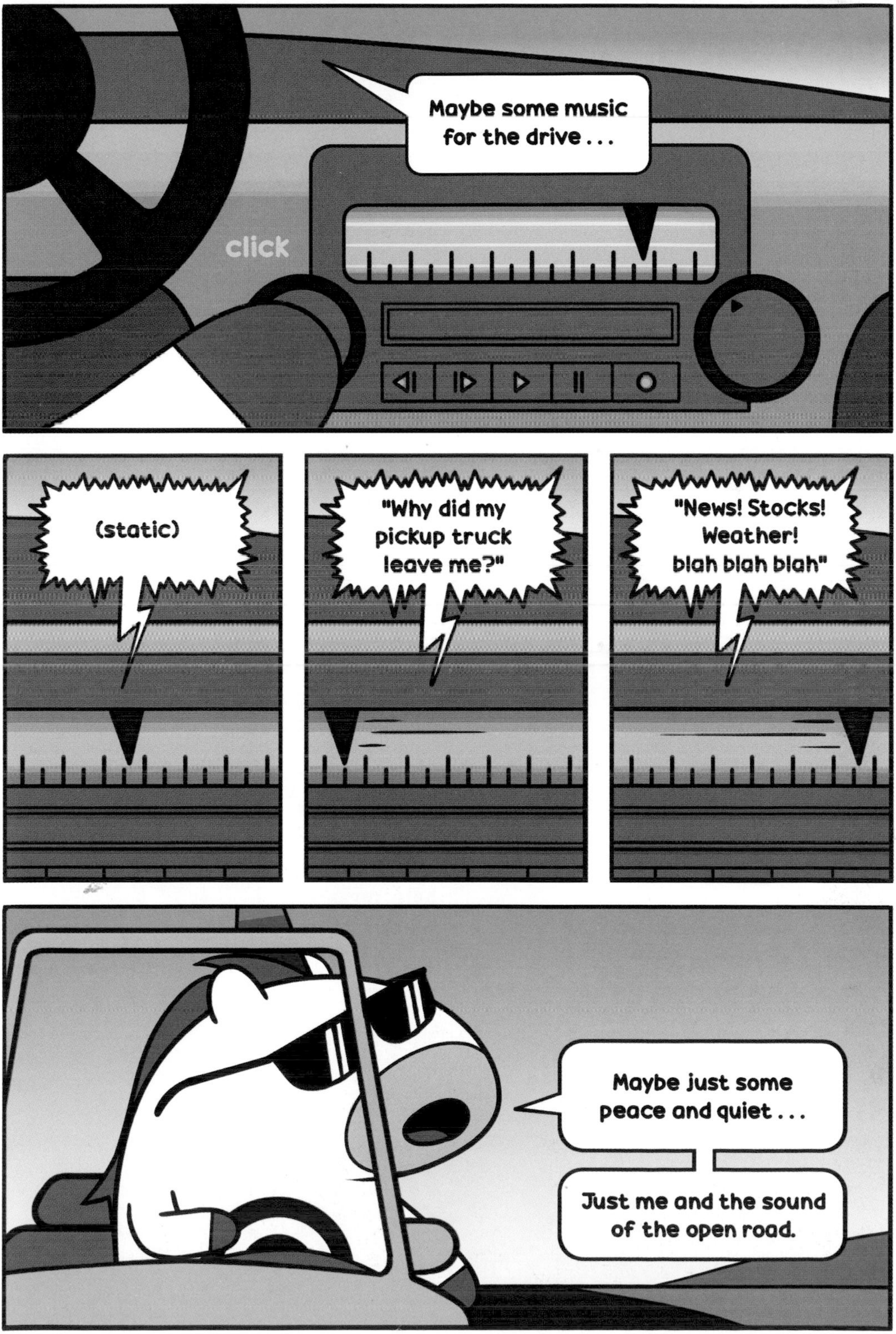
Maybe some music for the drive . . .
click
(static)
"Why did my pickup truck leave me?"
"News! Stocks! Weather! blah blah blah"
Maybe just some peace and quiet . . .
Just me and the sound of the open road.

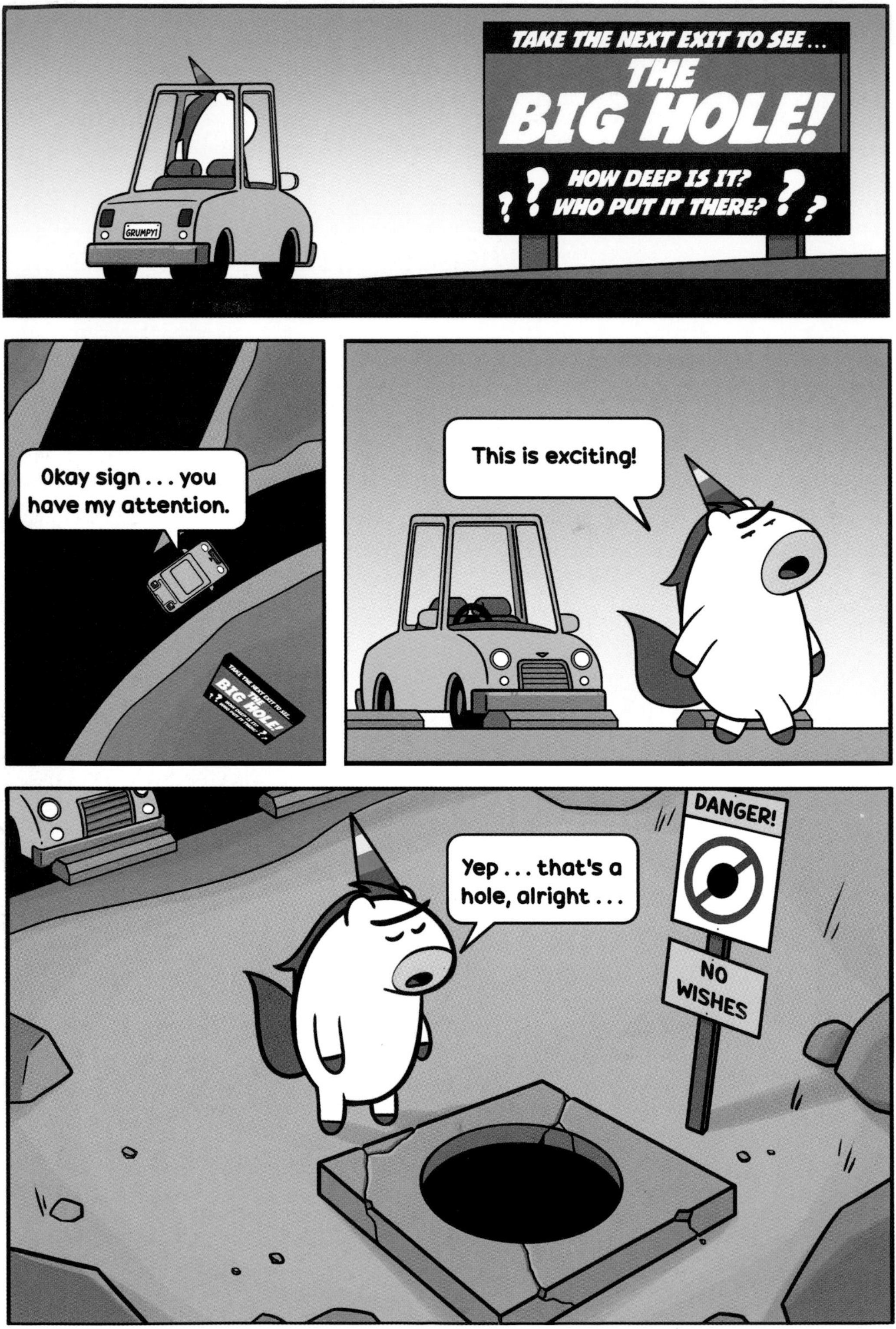
TAKE THE NEXT EXIT TO SEE...
THE BIG HOLE!
HOW DEEP IS IT?
WHO PUT IT THERE?
GRUMPY1
Okay sign . . . you have my attention.
This is exciting!
Yep . . . that's a hole, alright . . .
DANGER!
NO WISHES

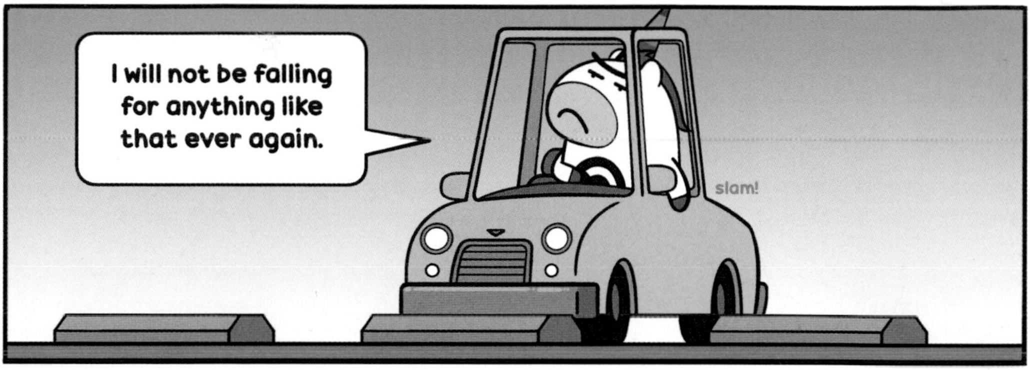
I will not be falling for anything like that ever again.
slam!

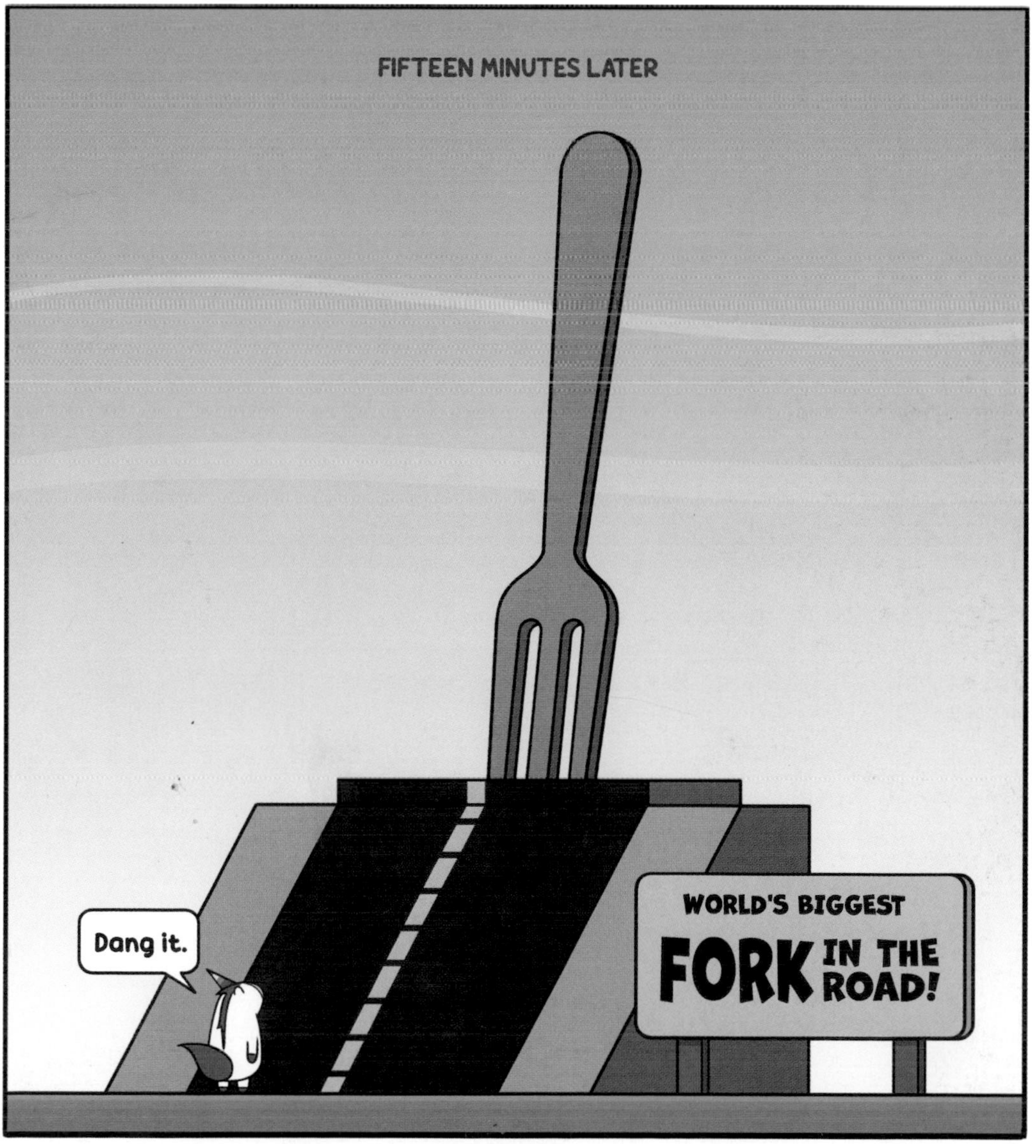
FIFTEEN MINUTES LATER
Dang it.
WORLD'S BIGGEST FORK IN THE ROAD!

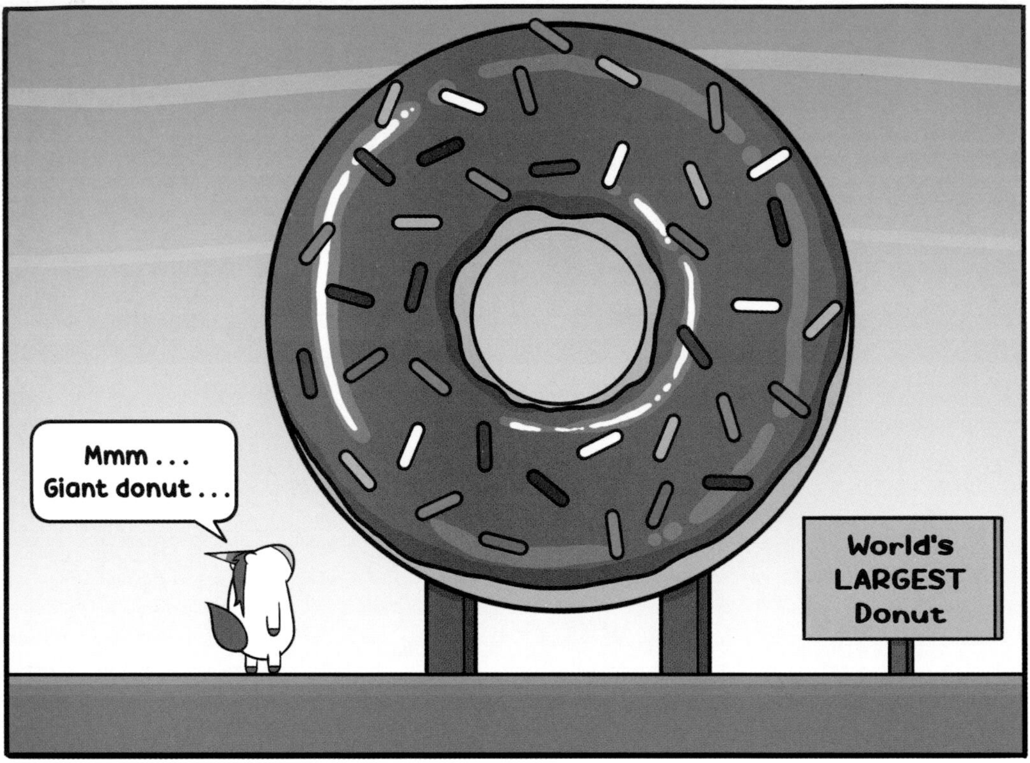
Mmm . . .
Giant donut . . .
World's
LARGEST
Donut

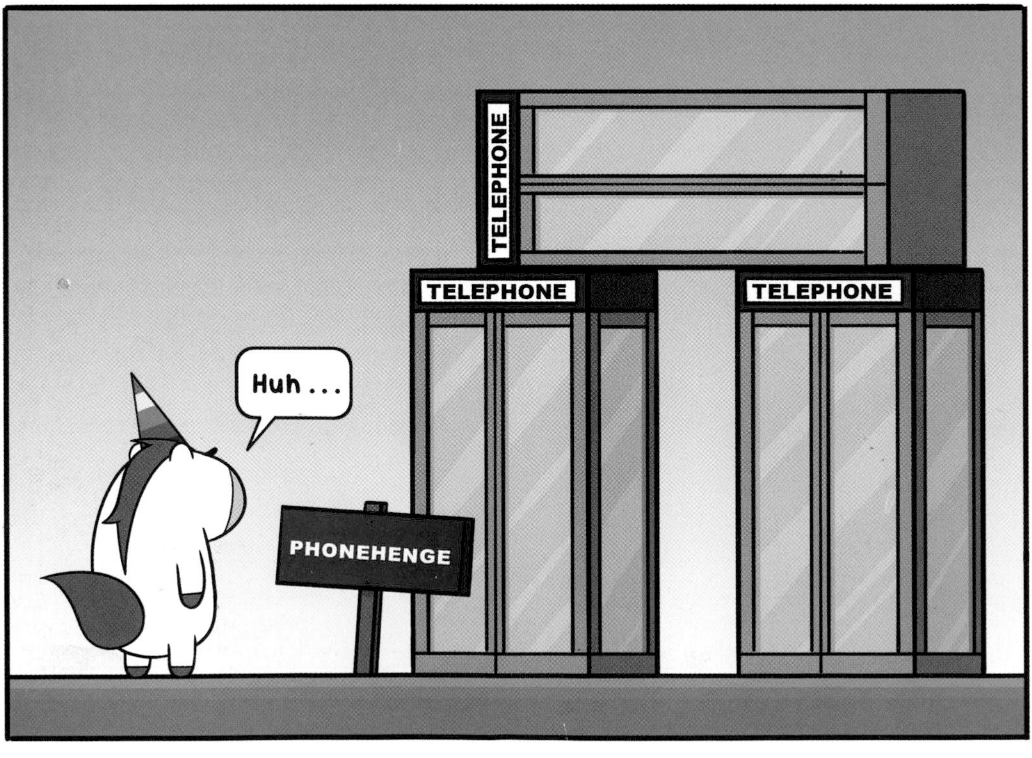
TELEPHONE
TELEPHONE
TELEPHONE
Huh . . .
PHONEHENGE

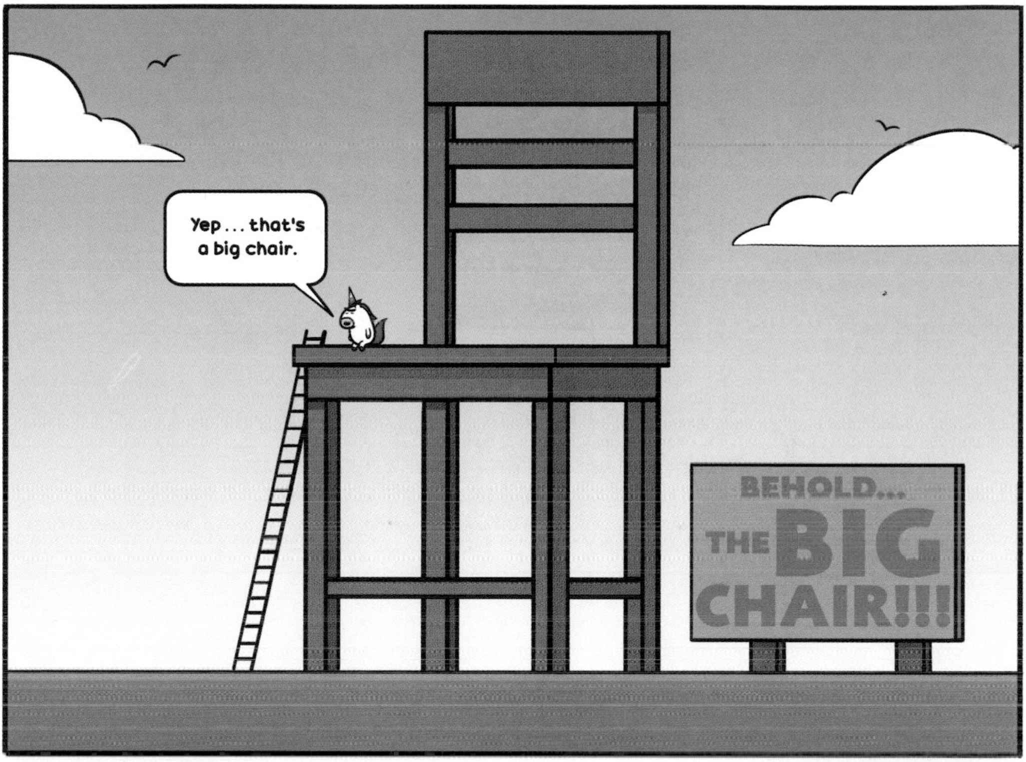
Yep . . . that's a big chair.
BEHOLD... THE BIG CHAIR!!!

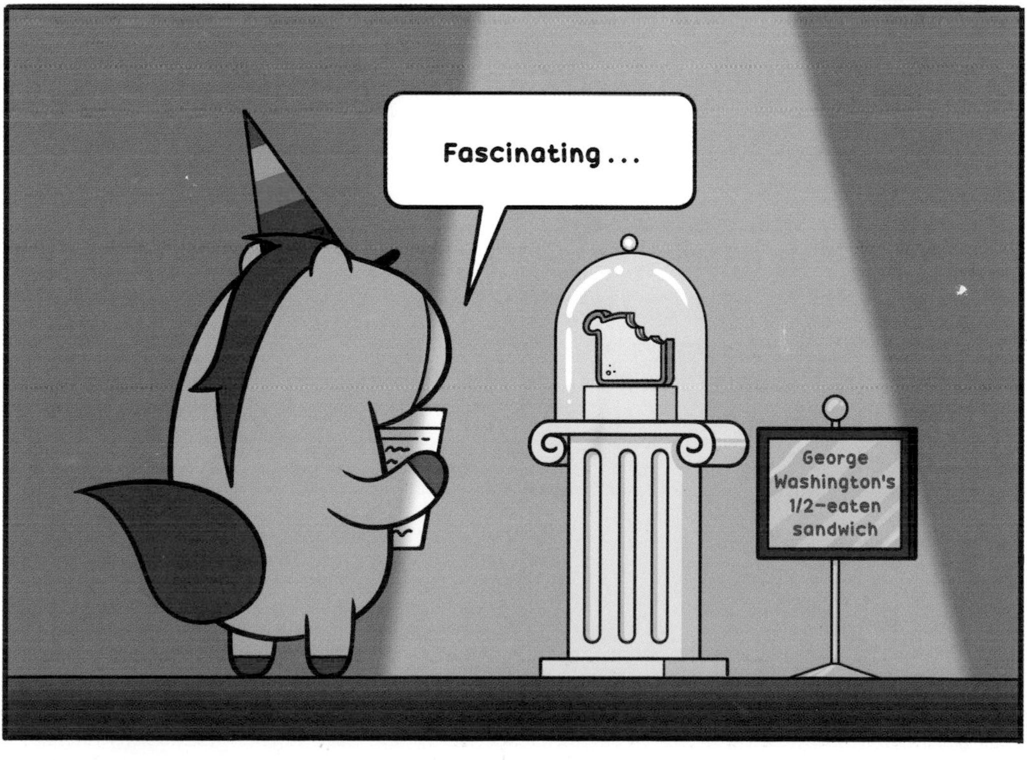
Fascinating . . .
George Washington's 1/2-eaten sandwich

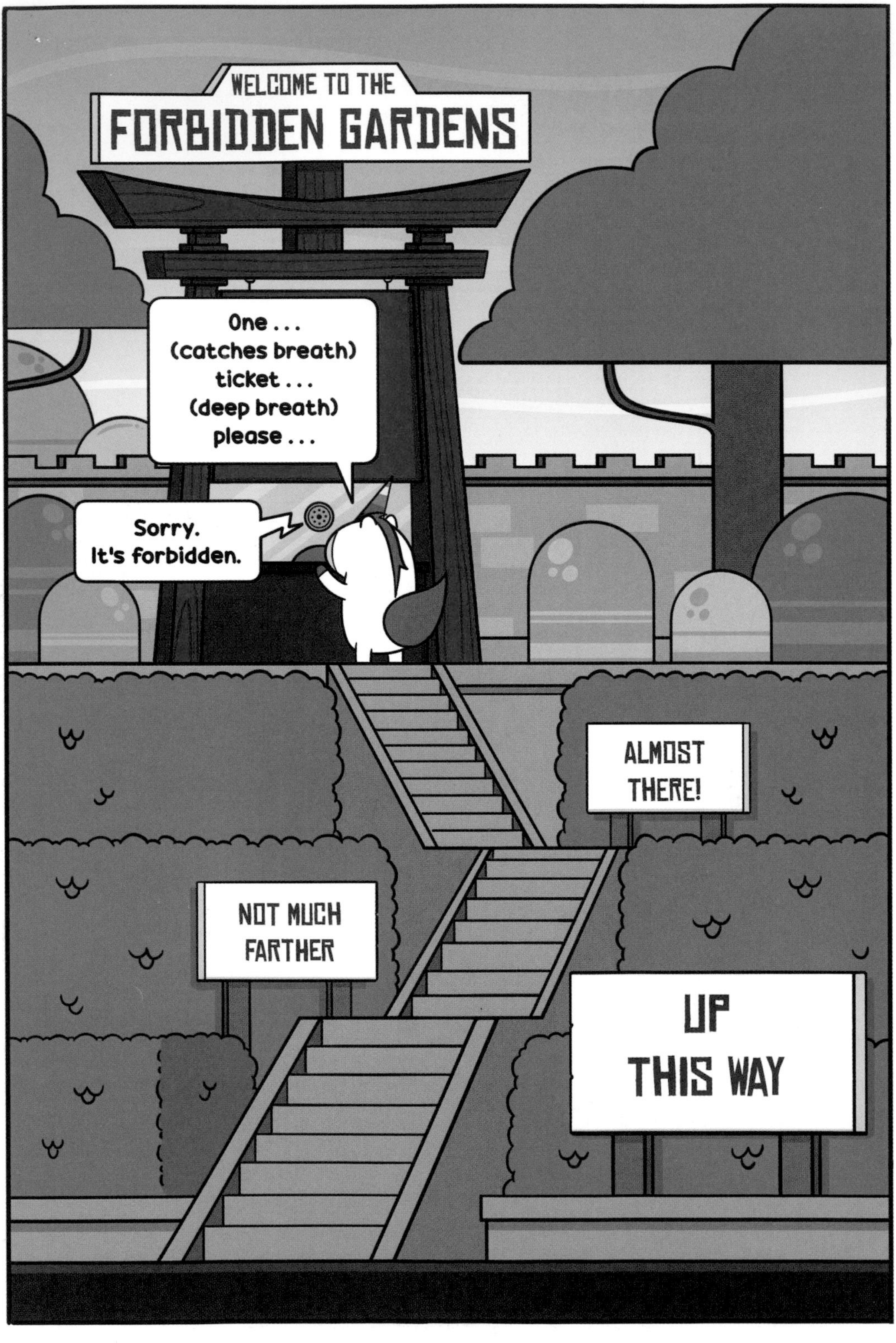
WELCOME TO THE
FORBIDDEN GARDENS
One . . . (catches breath) ticket . . . (deep breath) please . . .
Sorry. It's forbidden.
ALMOST THERE!
NOT MUCH FARTHER
UP THIS WAY

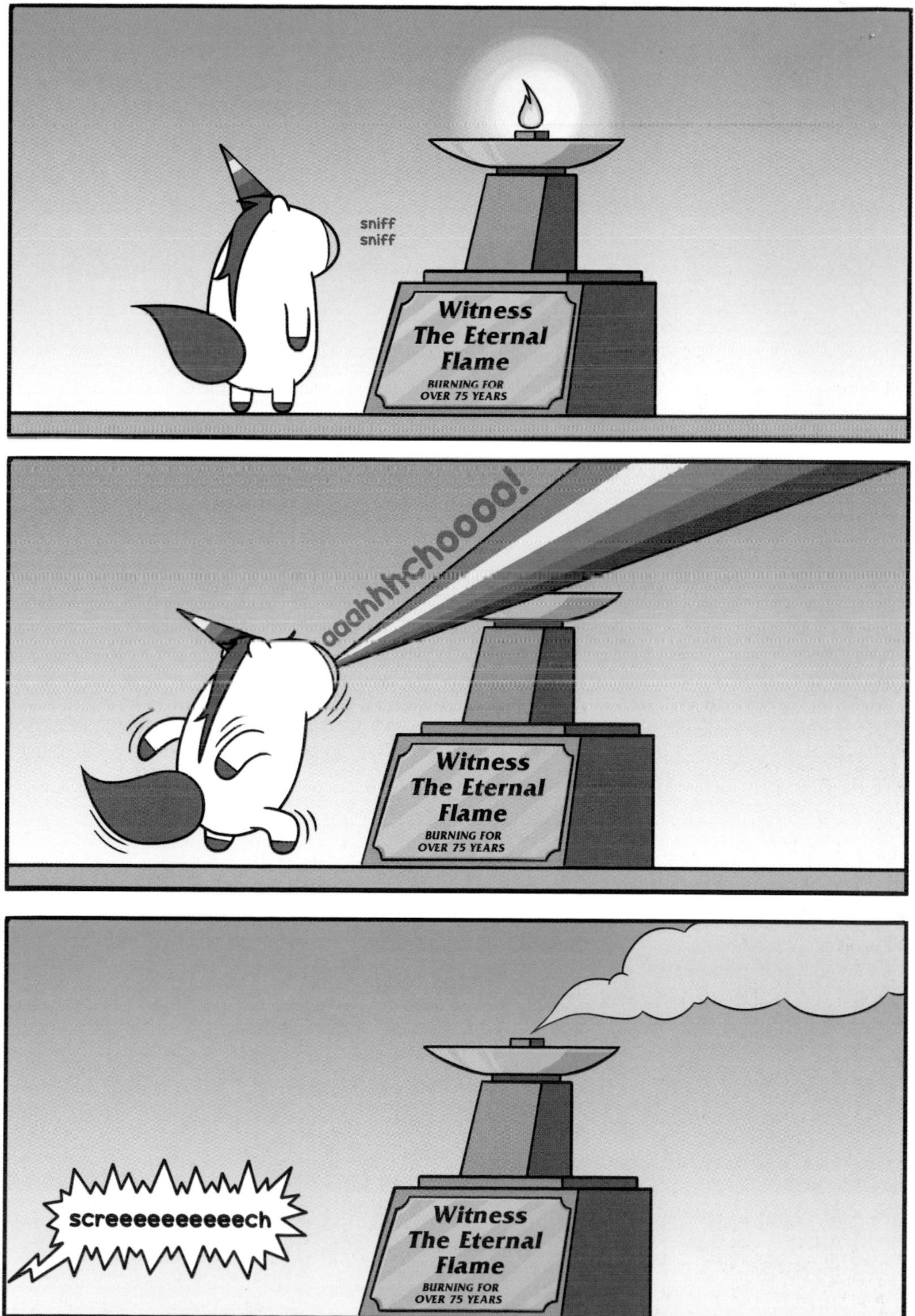
sniff
sniff
Witness The Eternal Flame
BURNING FOR OVER 75 YEARS
aaahhhchoooo!
Witness The Eternal Flame
BURNING FOR OVER 75 YEARS
screeeeeeeeeeech
Witness The Eternal Flame
BURNING FOR OVER 75 YEARS

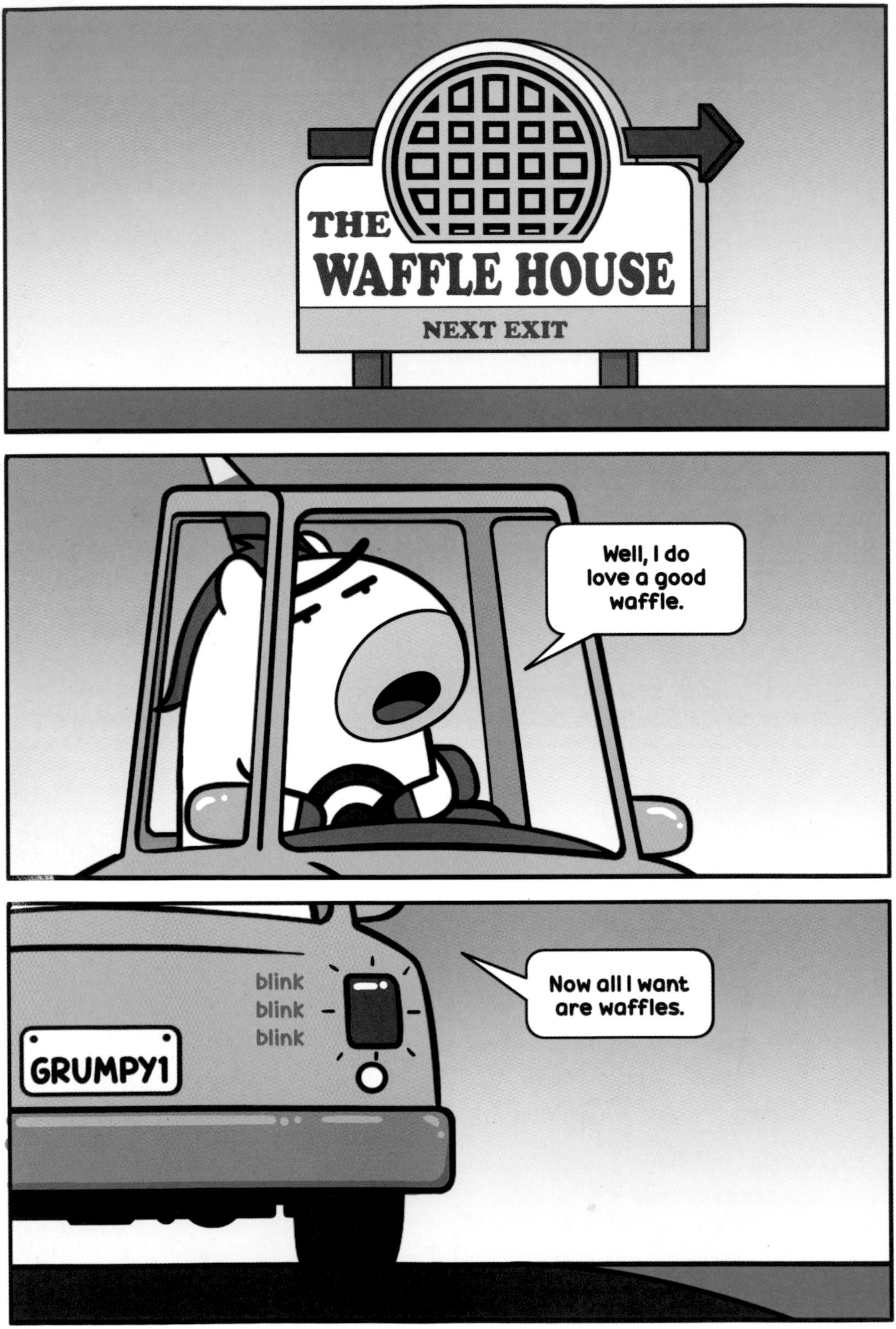
THE
WAFFLE HOUSE
NEXT EXIT
Well, I do love a good waffle.
blink
blink
blink
GRUMPY1
Now all I want are waffles.

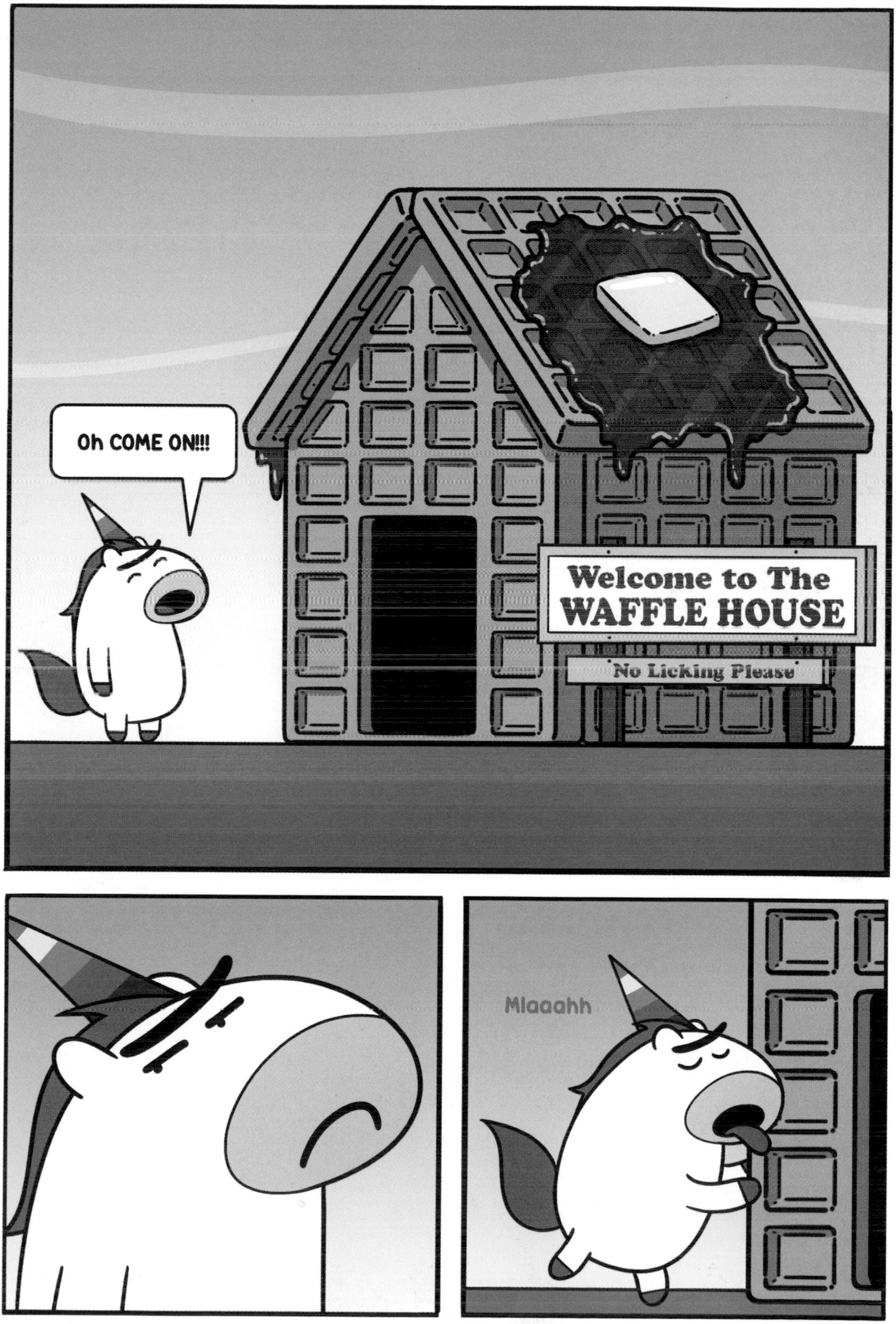
Oh COME ON!!!
Welcome to The WAFFLE HOUSE
No Licking Please
Mlaaahh

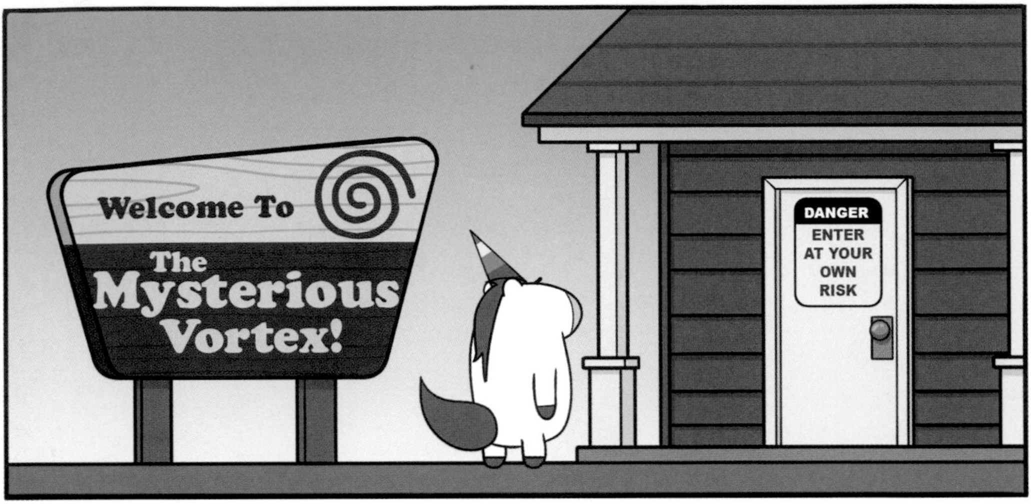
Welcome To
The Mysterious Vortex!
DANGER
ENTER AT YOUR OWN RISK

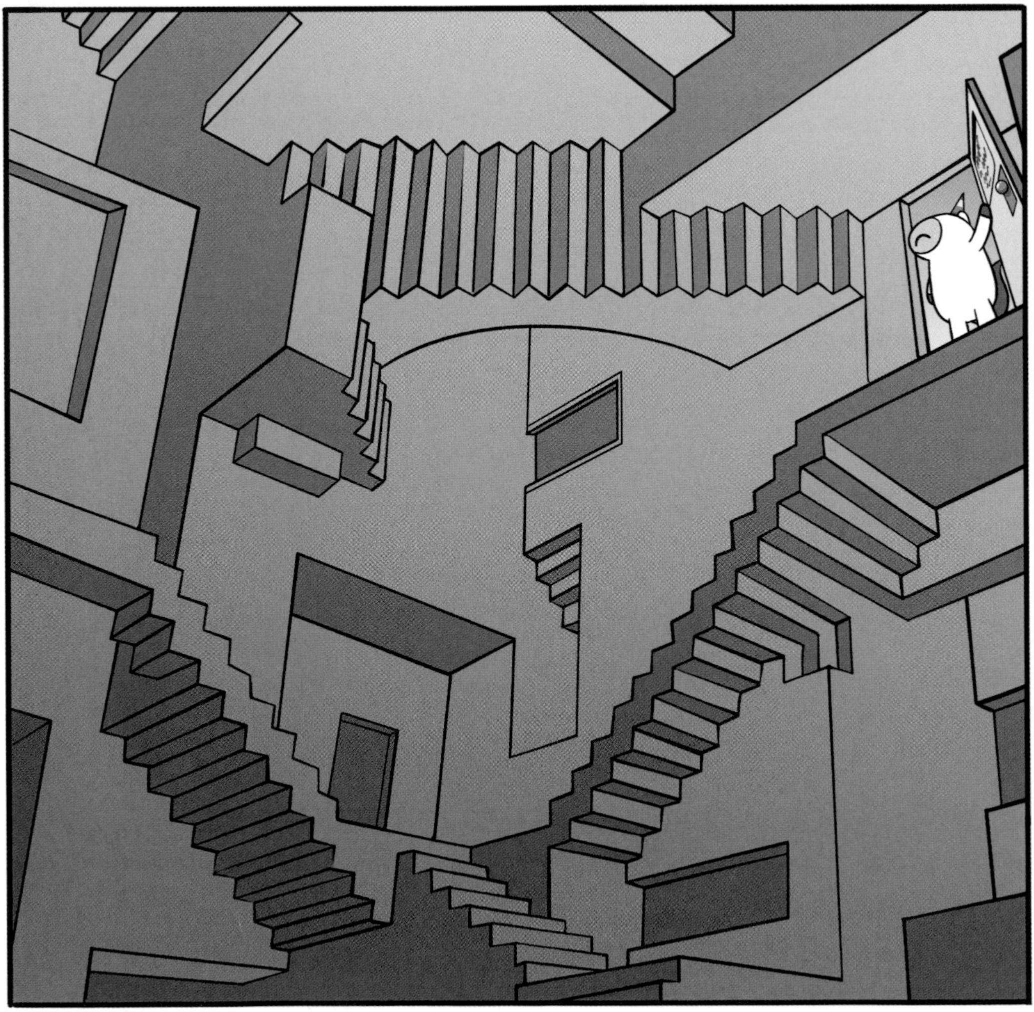

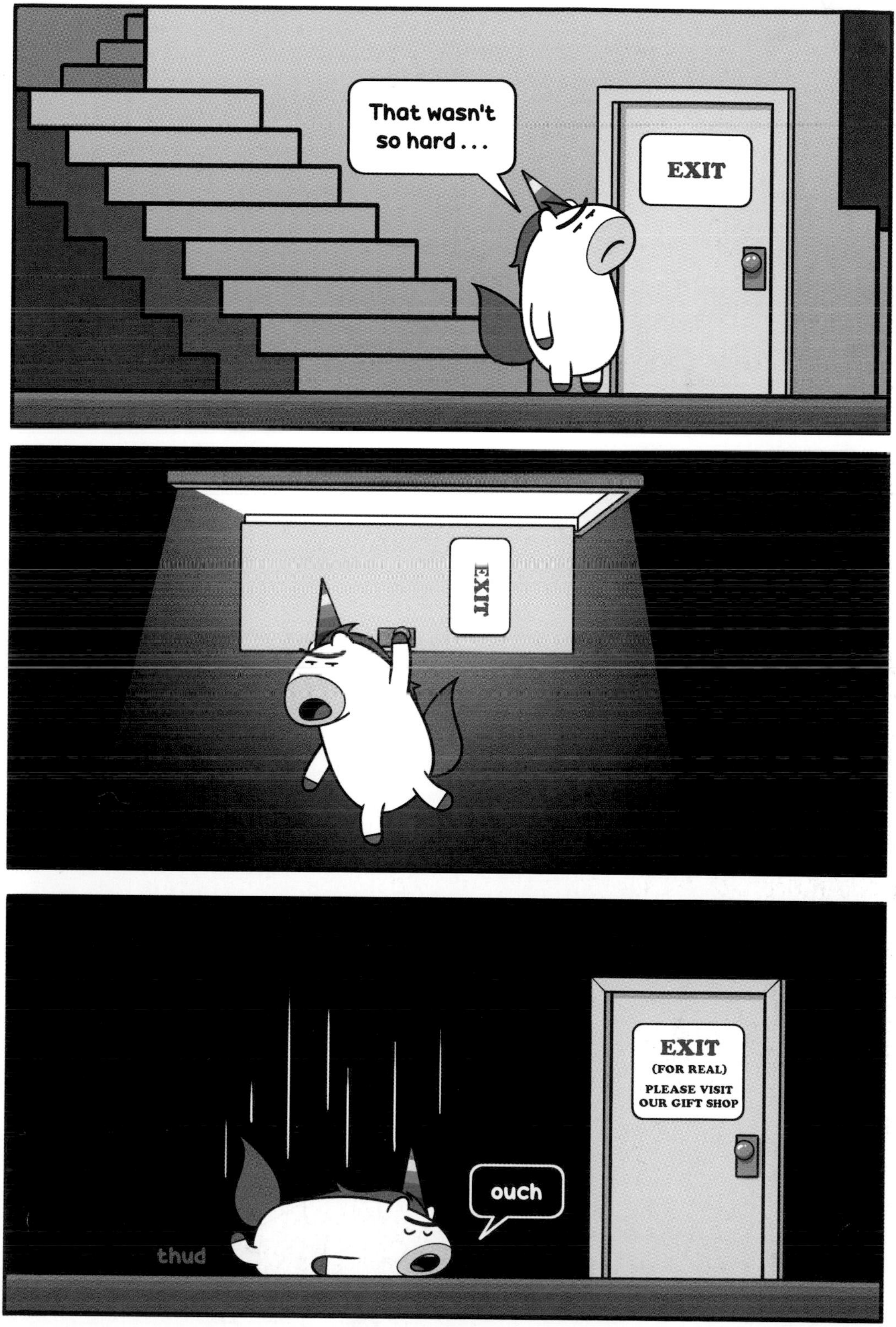
That wasn't so hard . . .
EXIT
EXIT
EXIT
(FOR REAL)
PLEASE VISIT OUR GIFT SHOP
ouch
thud

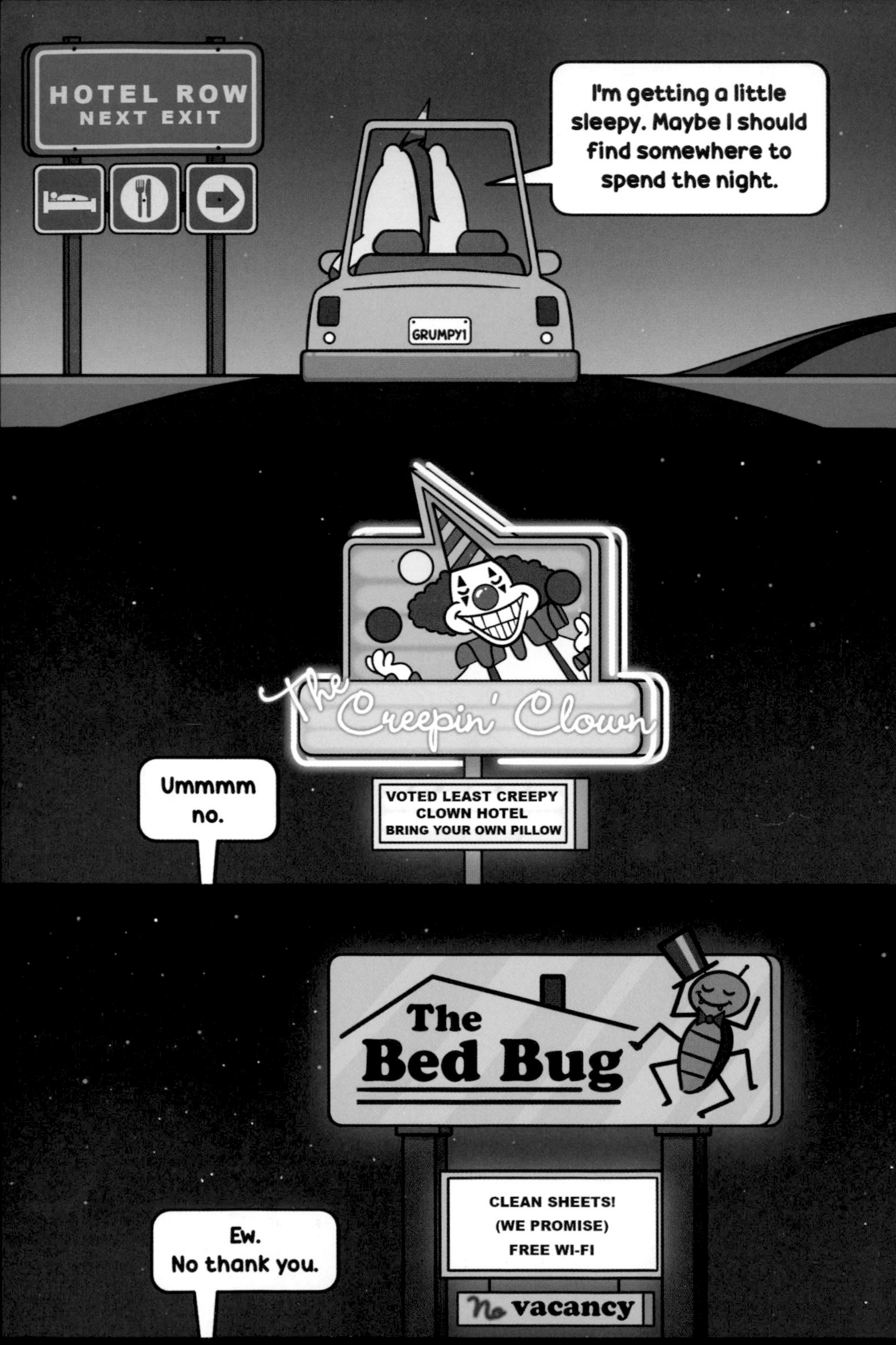
HOTEL ROW
NEXT EXIT
I'm getting a little sleepy. Maybe I should find somewhere to spend the night.
GRUMPY1
The Creepin' Clown
VOTED LEAST CREEPY CLOWN HOTEL
BRING YOUR OWN PILLOW
Ummmm no.
The Bed Bug
CLEAN SHEETS!
(WE PROMISE)
FREE WI-FI
No vacancy
Ew.
No thank you.

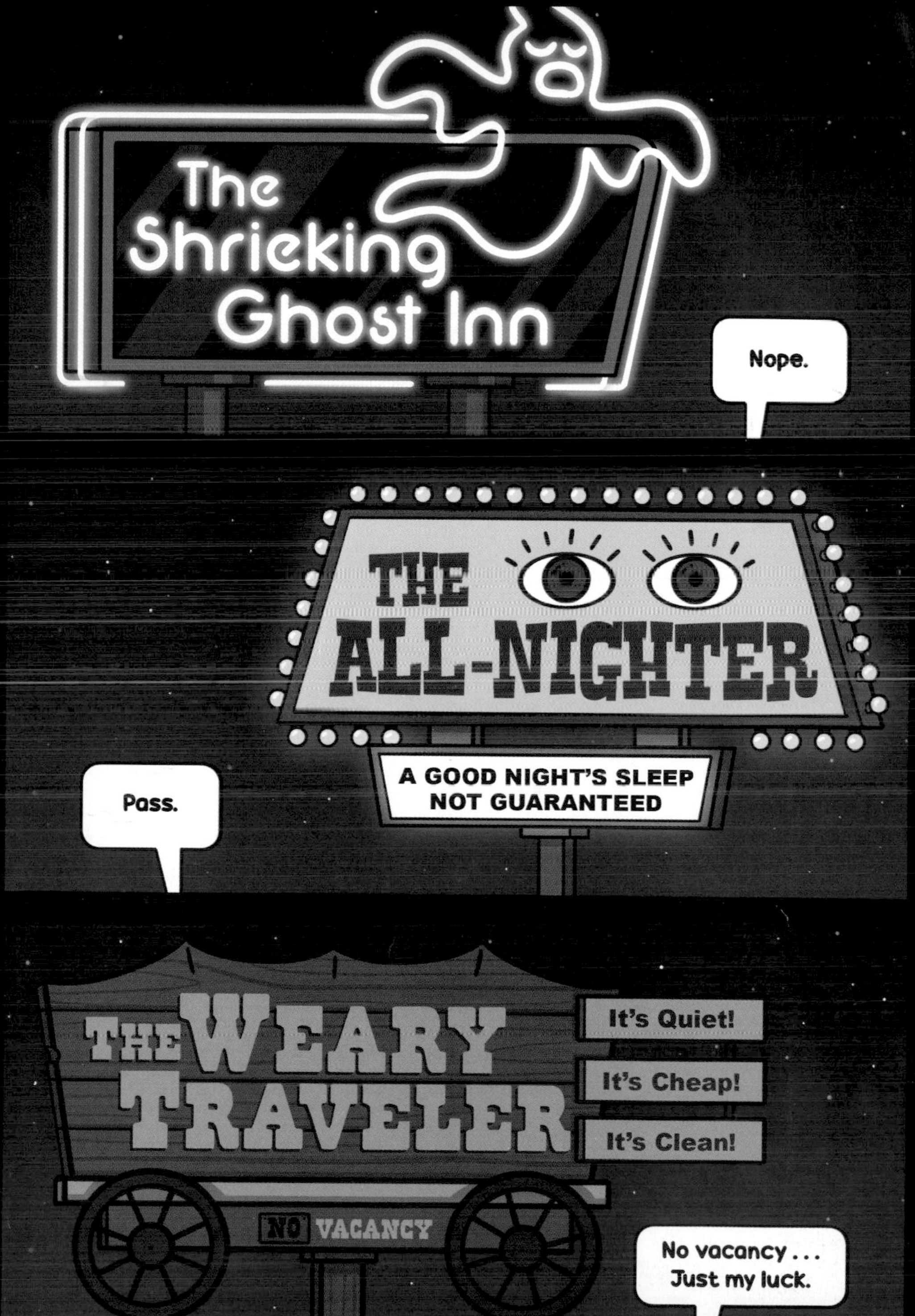
The Shrieking Ghost Inn
Nope.
THE ALL-NIGHTER
A GOOD NIGHT'S SLEEP NOT GUARANTEED
Pass.
THE WEARY TRAVELER
It's Quiet!
It's Cheap!
It's Clean!
NO VACANCY
No vacancy . . . Just my luck.

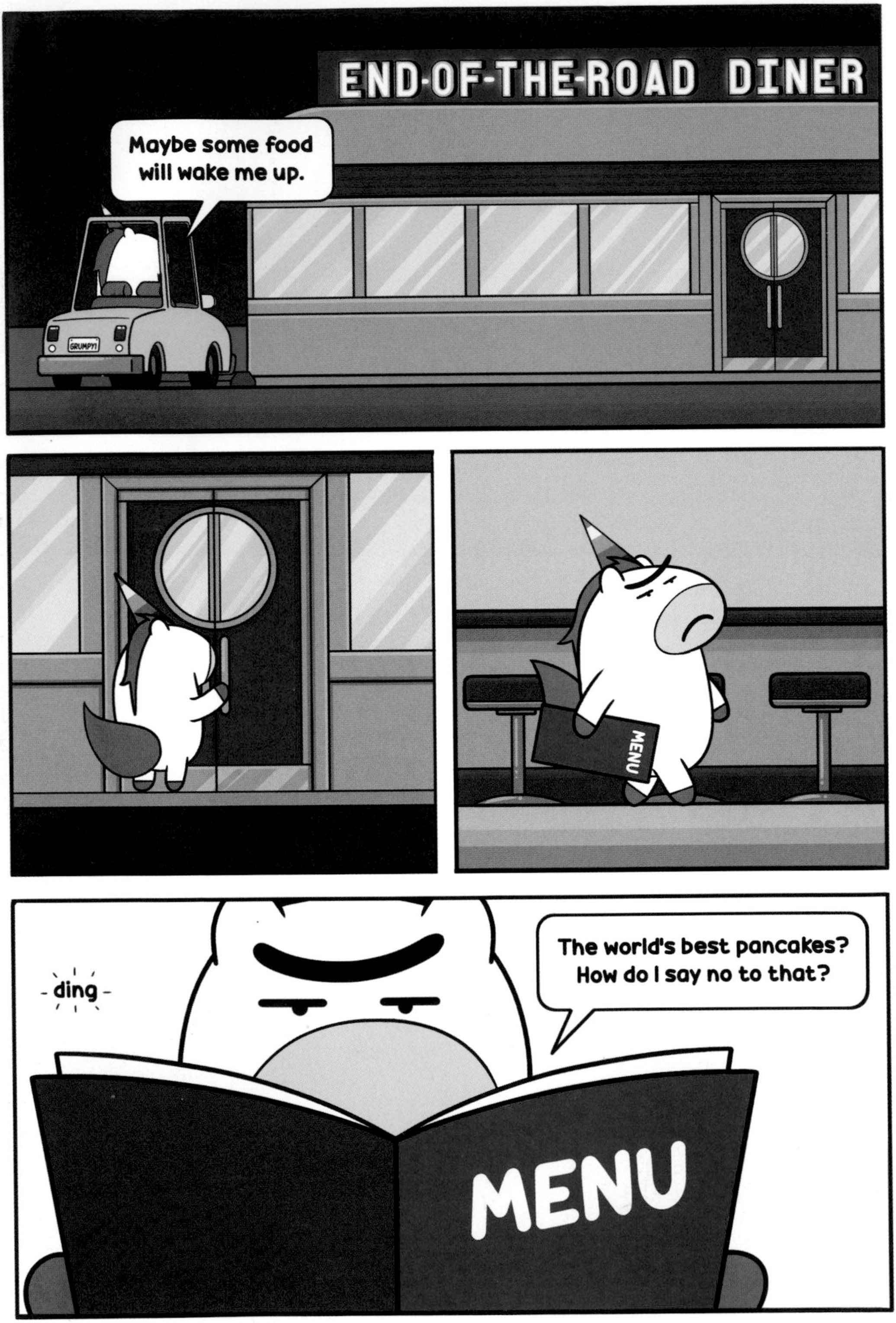
END-OF-THE-ROAD DINER
Maybe some food will wake me up.
GRUMPY!
MENU
- ding -
The world's best pancakes? How do I say no to that?
MENU

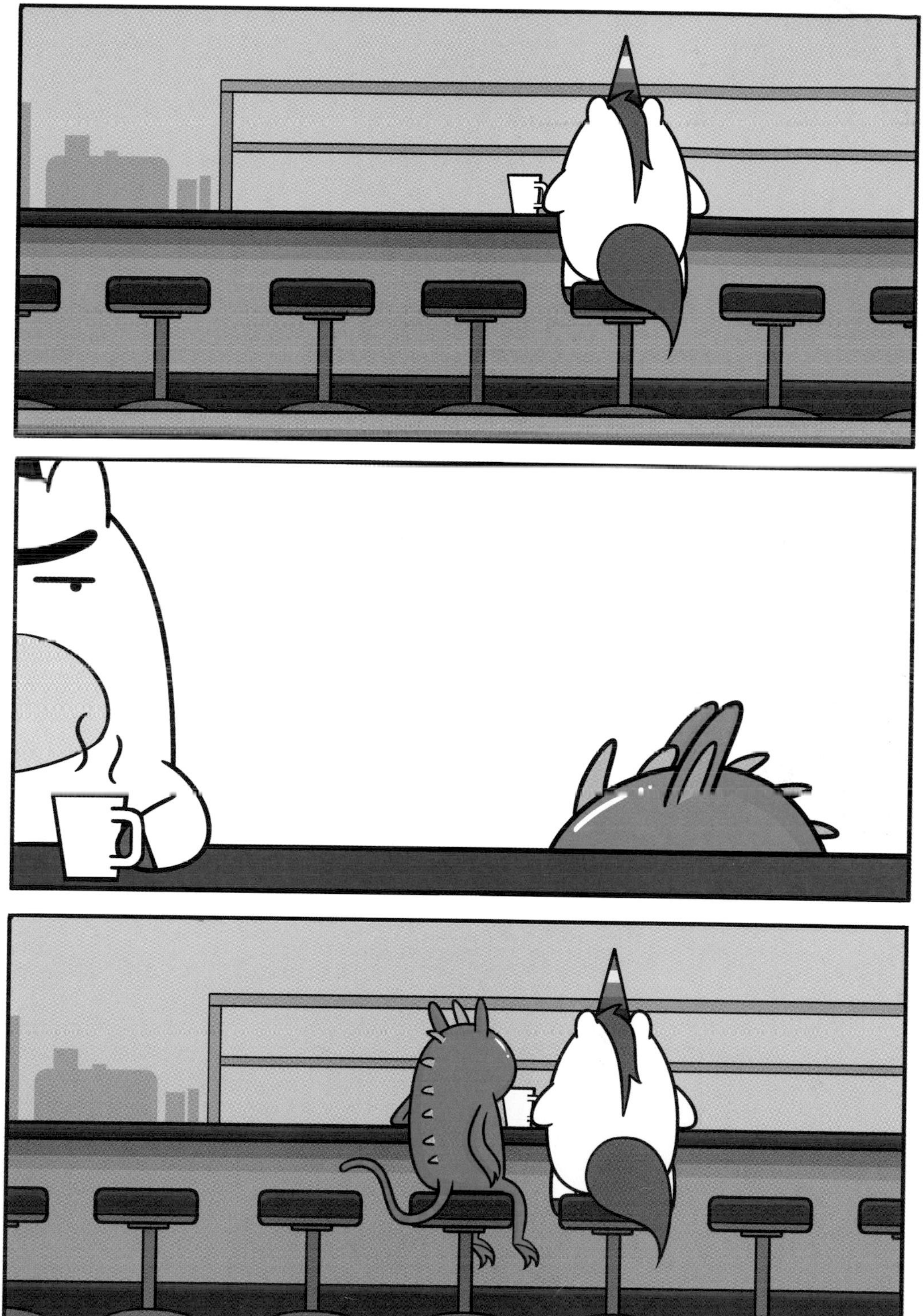

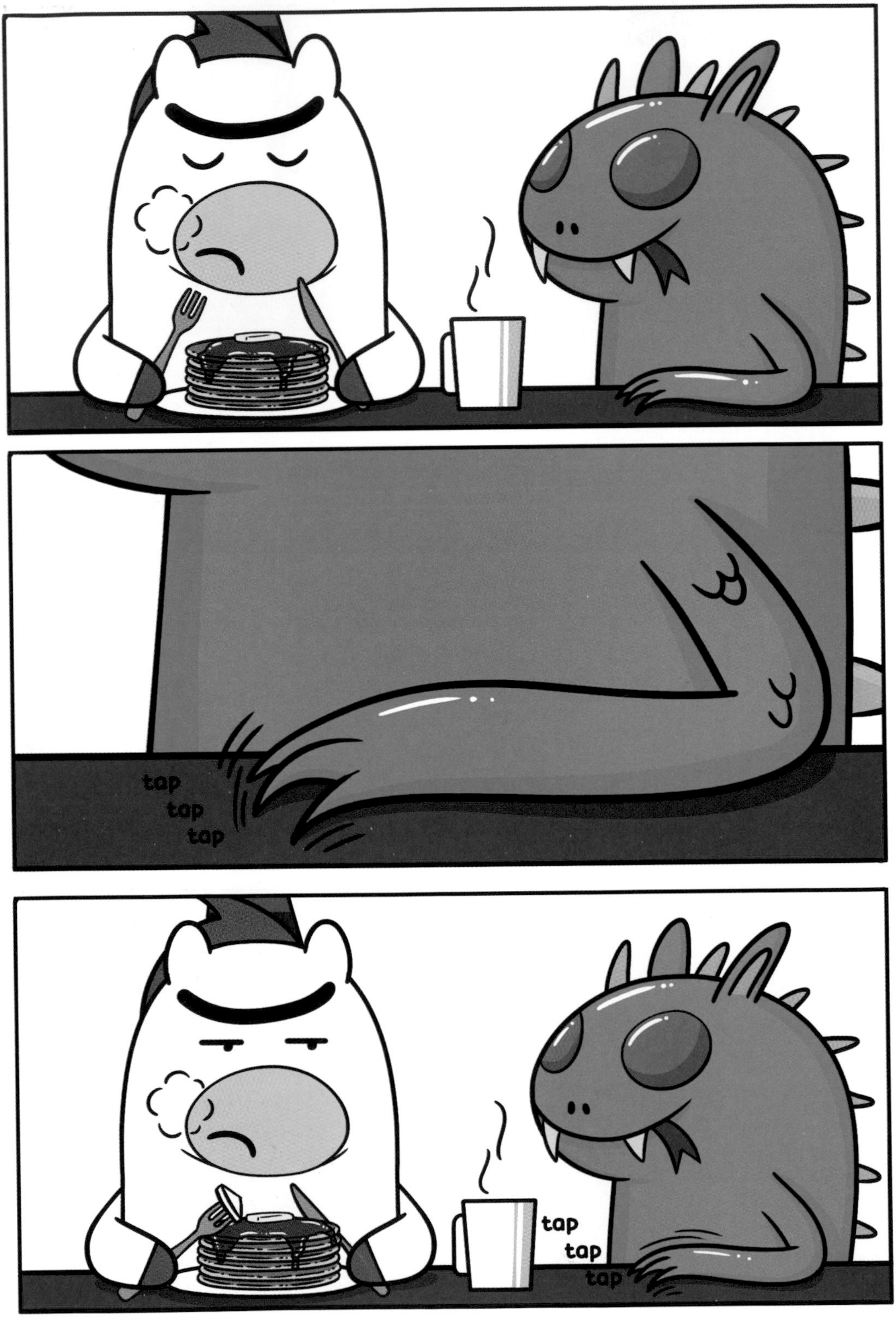
tap
tap
tap
tap
tap
tap

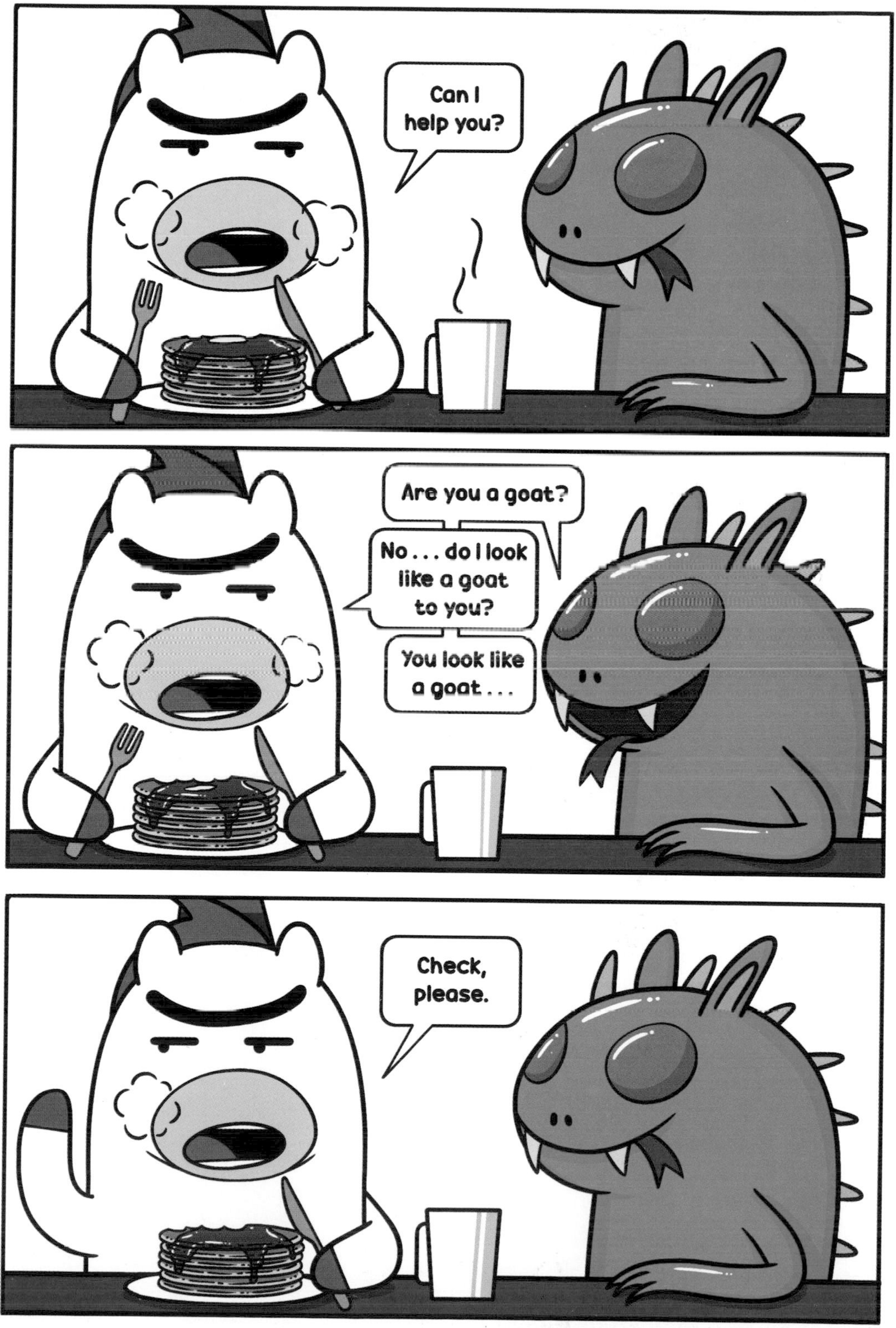
Can I help you?
Are you a goat?
No . . . do I look like a goat to you?
You look like a goat . . .
Check, please.

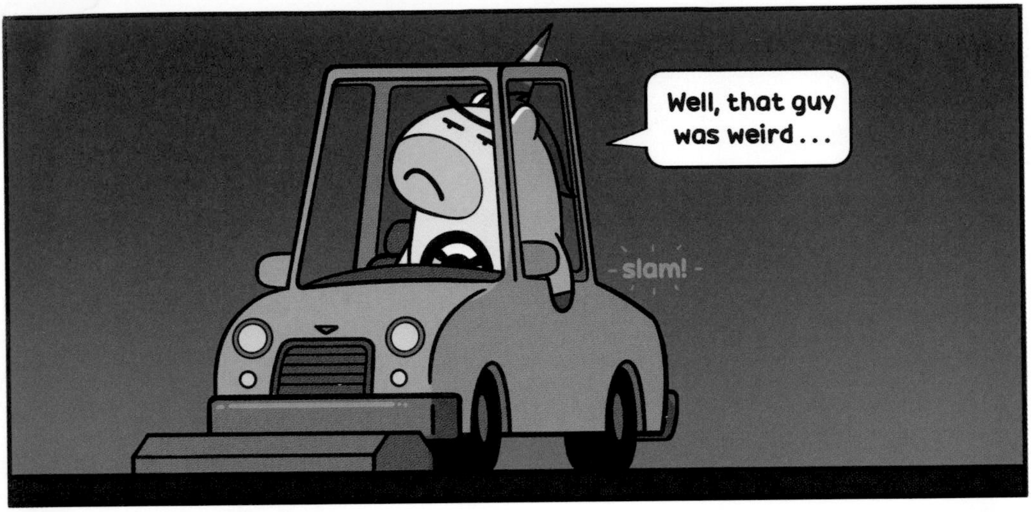
Well, that guy was weird . . .
- slam! -

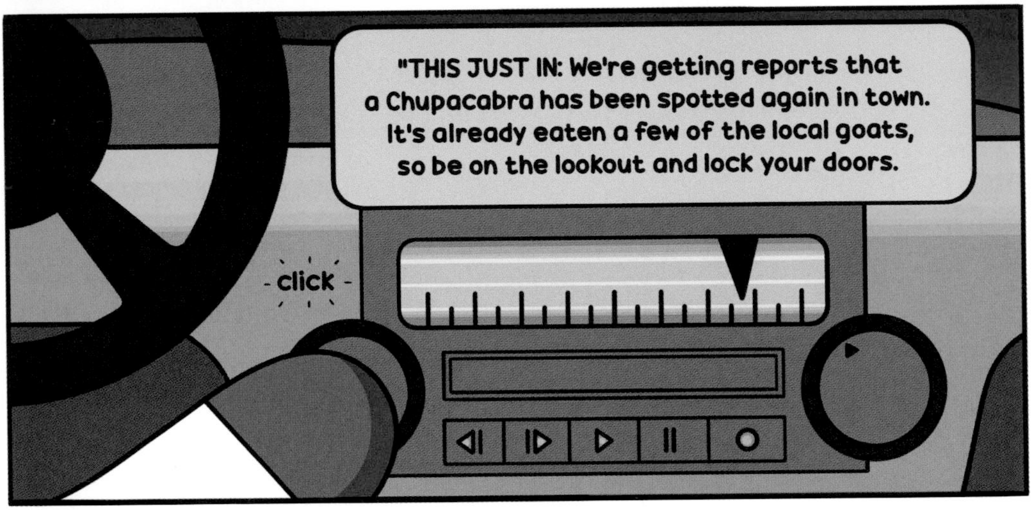
"THIS JUST IN: We're getting reports that a Chupacabra has been spotted again in town. It's already eaten a few of the local goats, so be on the lookout and lock your doors.
- click -

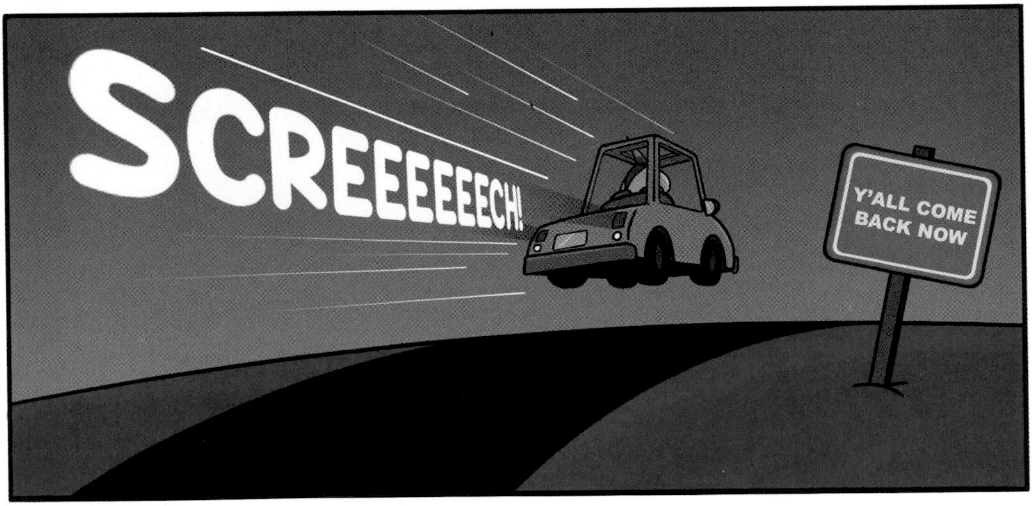
SCREEEEEECH!
Y'ALL COME BACK NOW

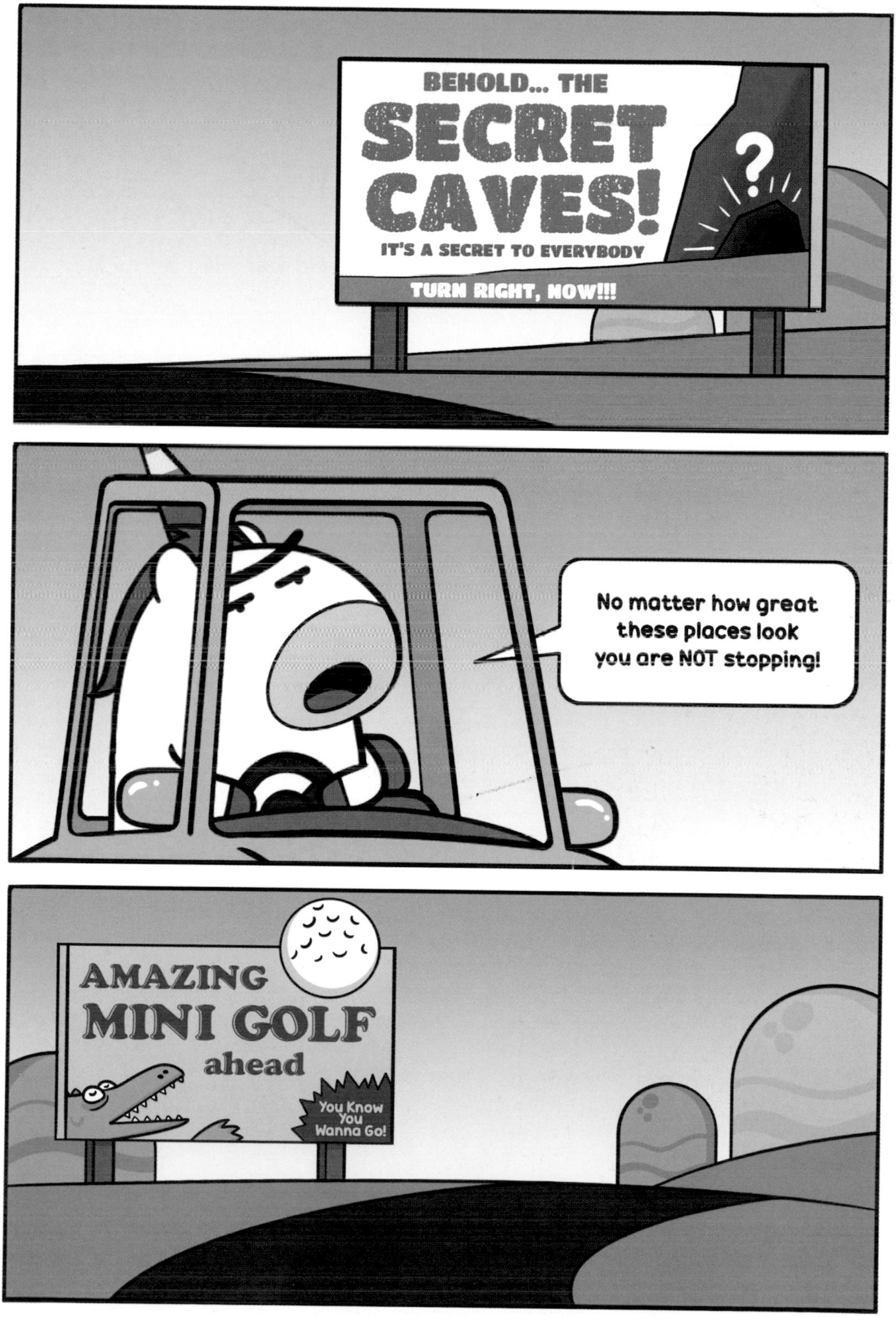
BEHOLD... THE
SECRET CAVES!
IT'S A SECRET TO EVERYBODY
TURN RIGHT, NOW!!!
No matter how great these places look you are NOT stopping!
AMAZING
MINI GOLF
ahead
You Know You Wanna Go!

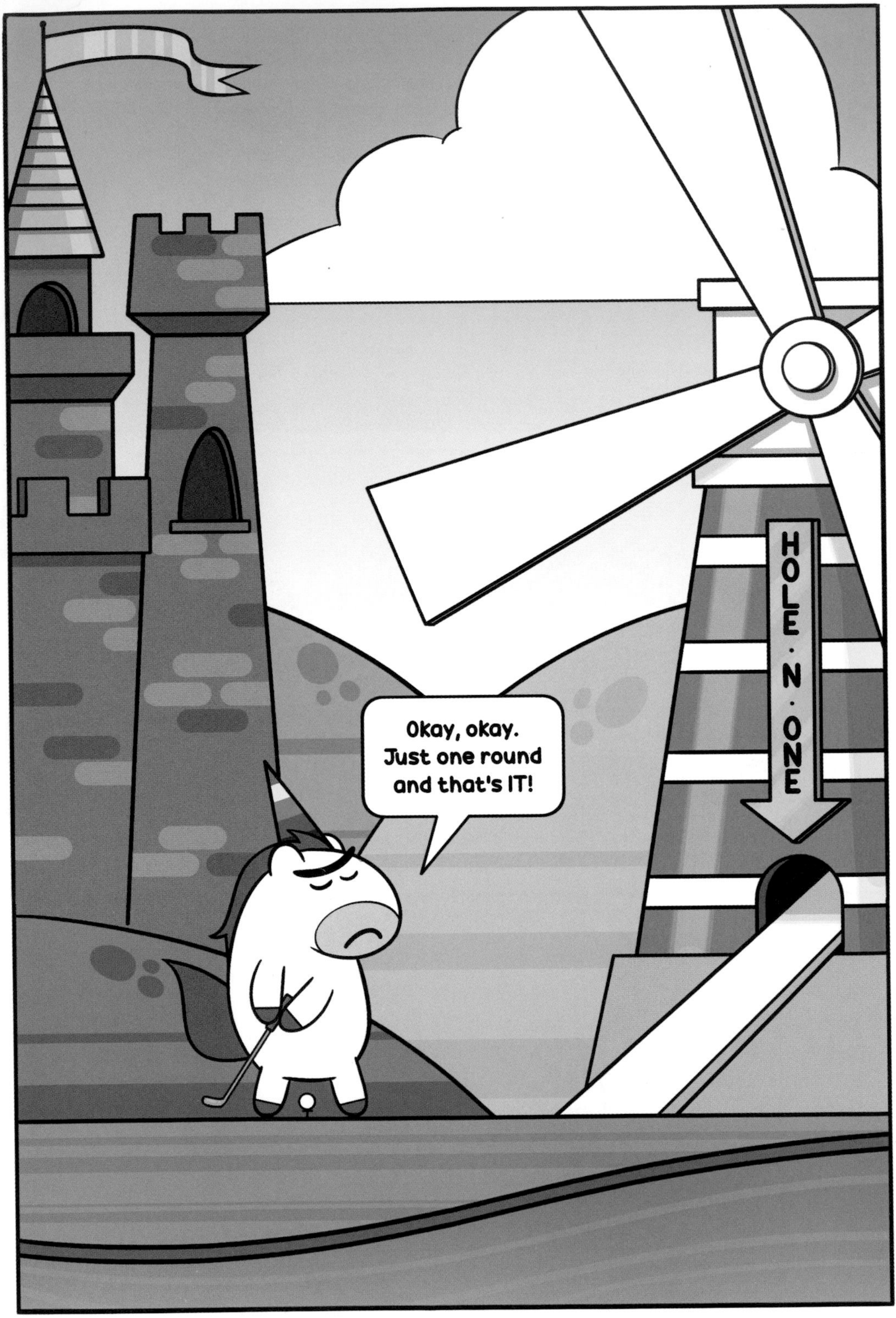
HOLE · N · ONE
Okay, okay. Just one round and that's IT!

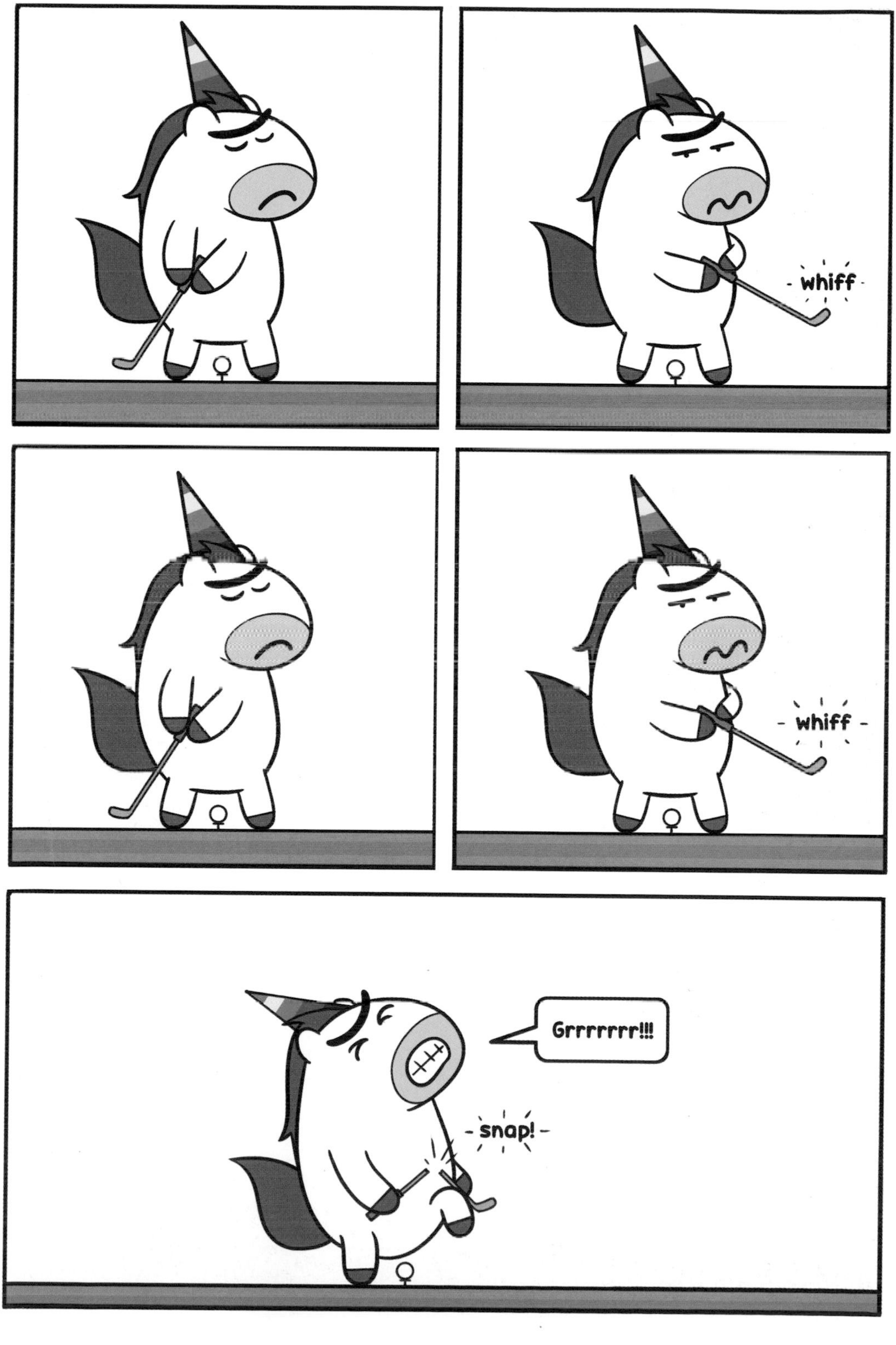
whiff
whiff
Grrrrrrr!!!
snap!

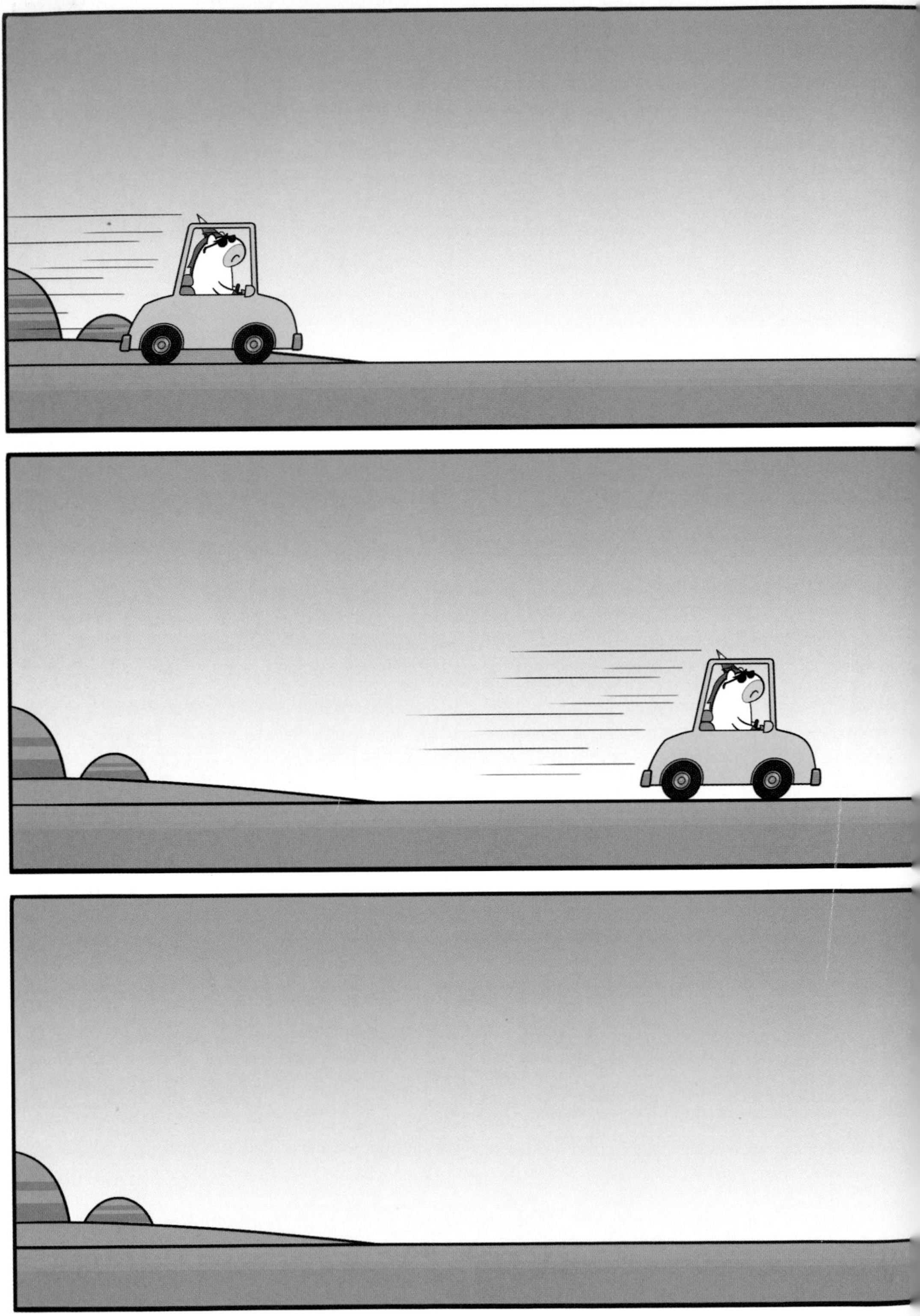

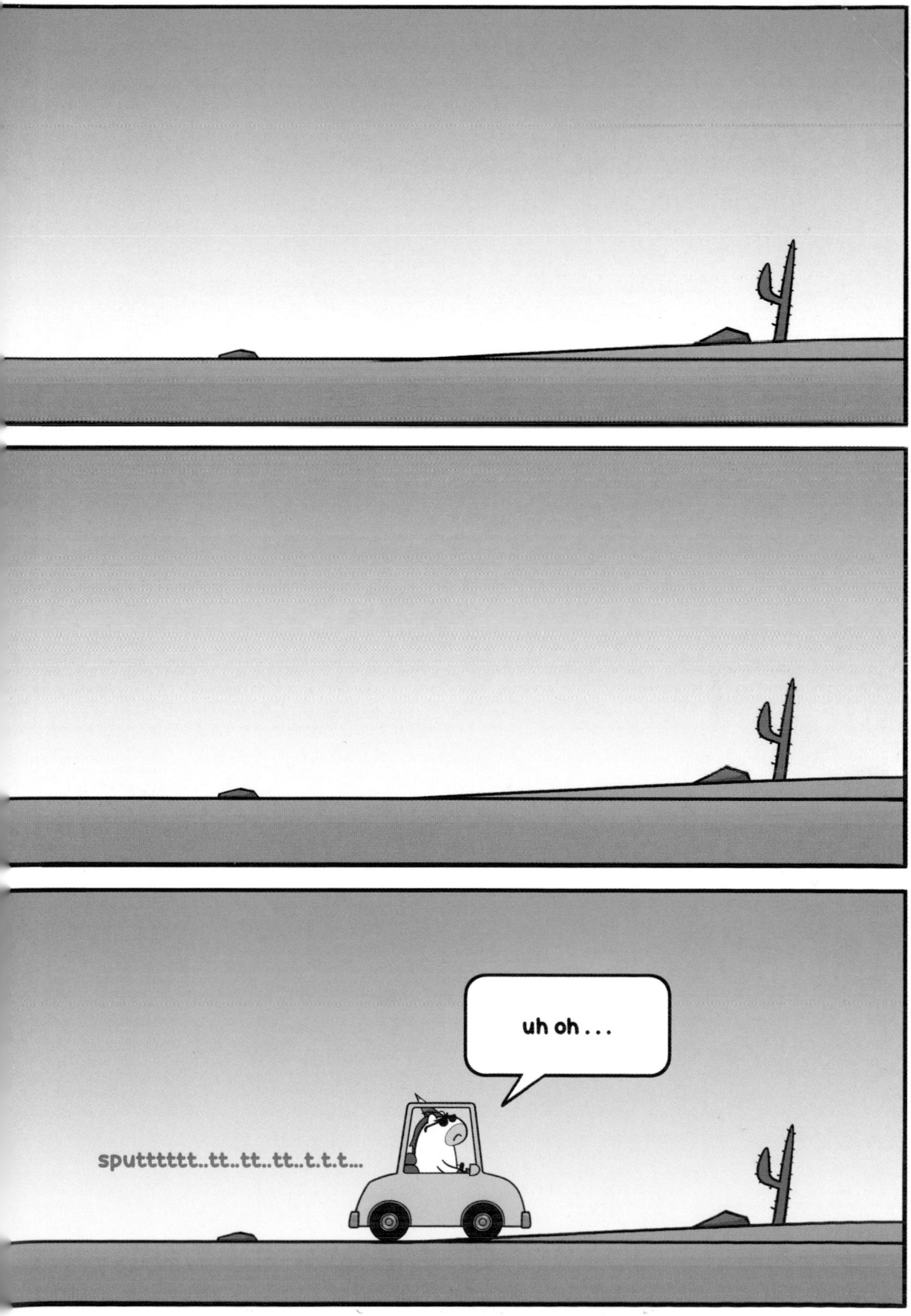
uh oh . . .
sputttttt..tt..tt..tt..t.t.t...

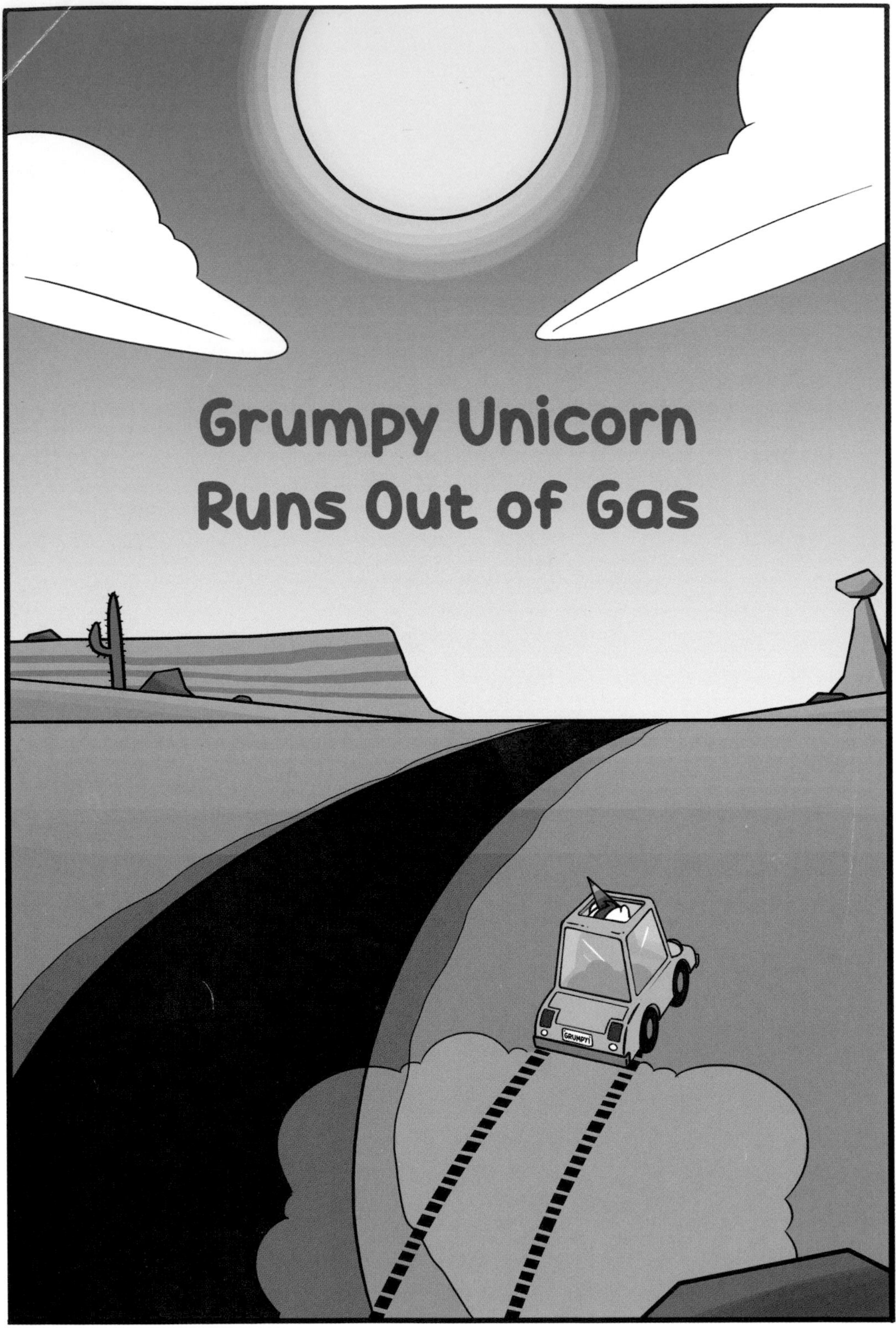
Grumpy Unicorn
Runs Out of Gas
GRUMPY!

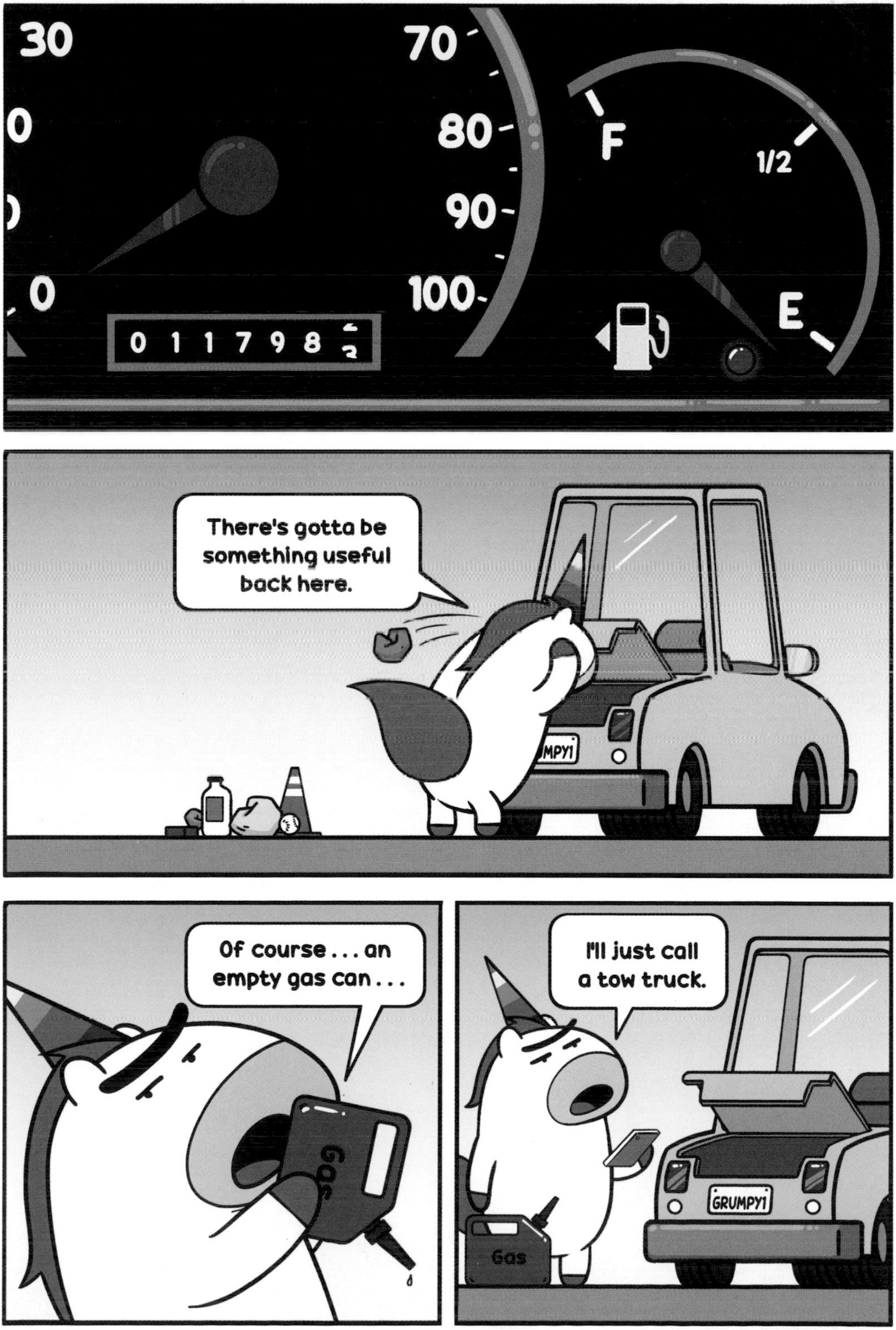
30
70
80
90
100
F
1/2
E
0 1 1 7 9 8
There's gotta be something useful back here.
GRUMPY1
Of course . . . an empty gas can . . .
Gas
I'll just call a tow truck.
GRUMPY1
Gas

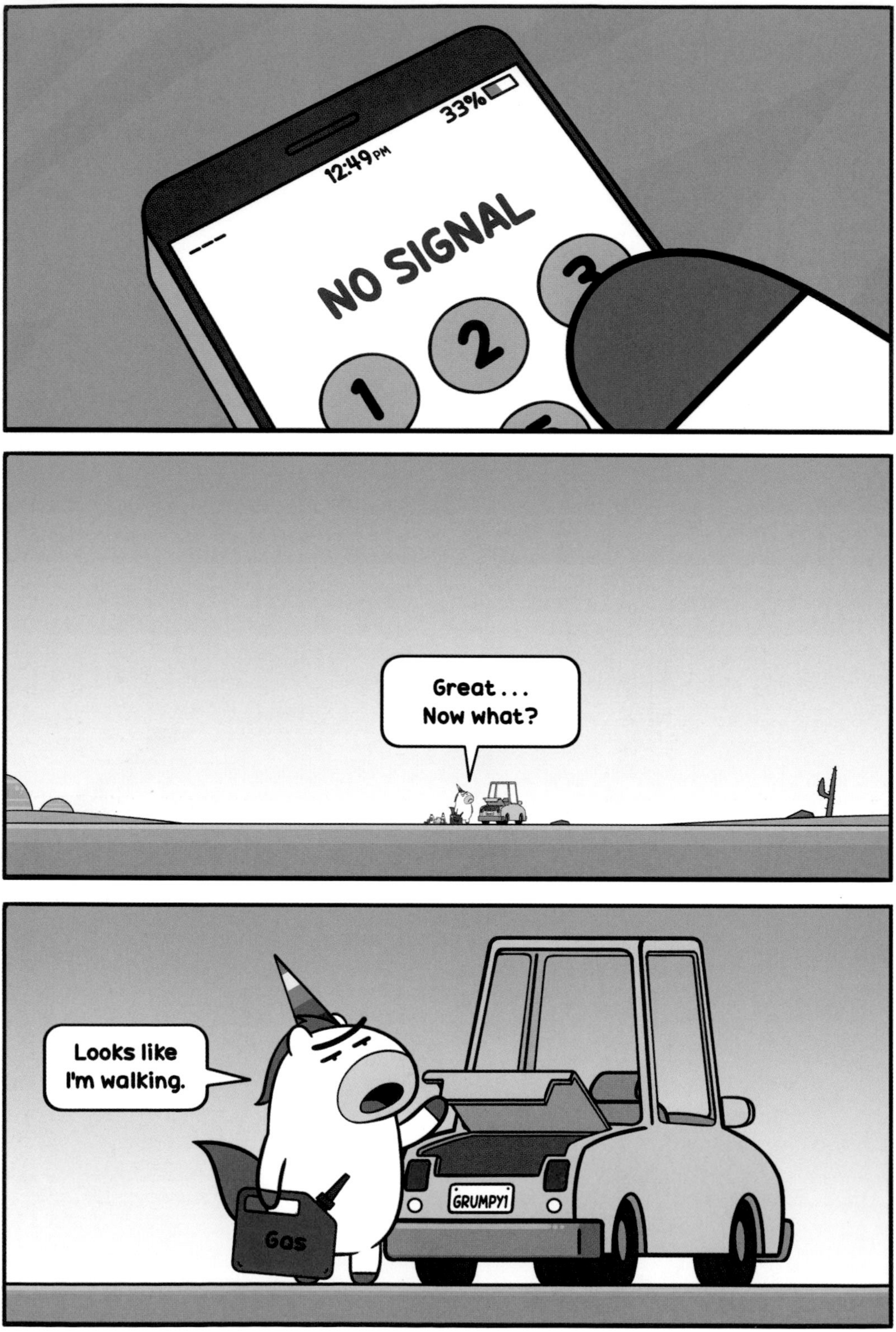
33%
12:49 PM
NO SIGNAL
1
2
3
Great . . .
Now what?
Looks like
I'm walking.
GRUMPY1
Gas

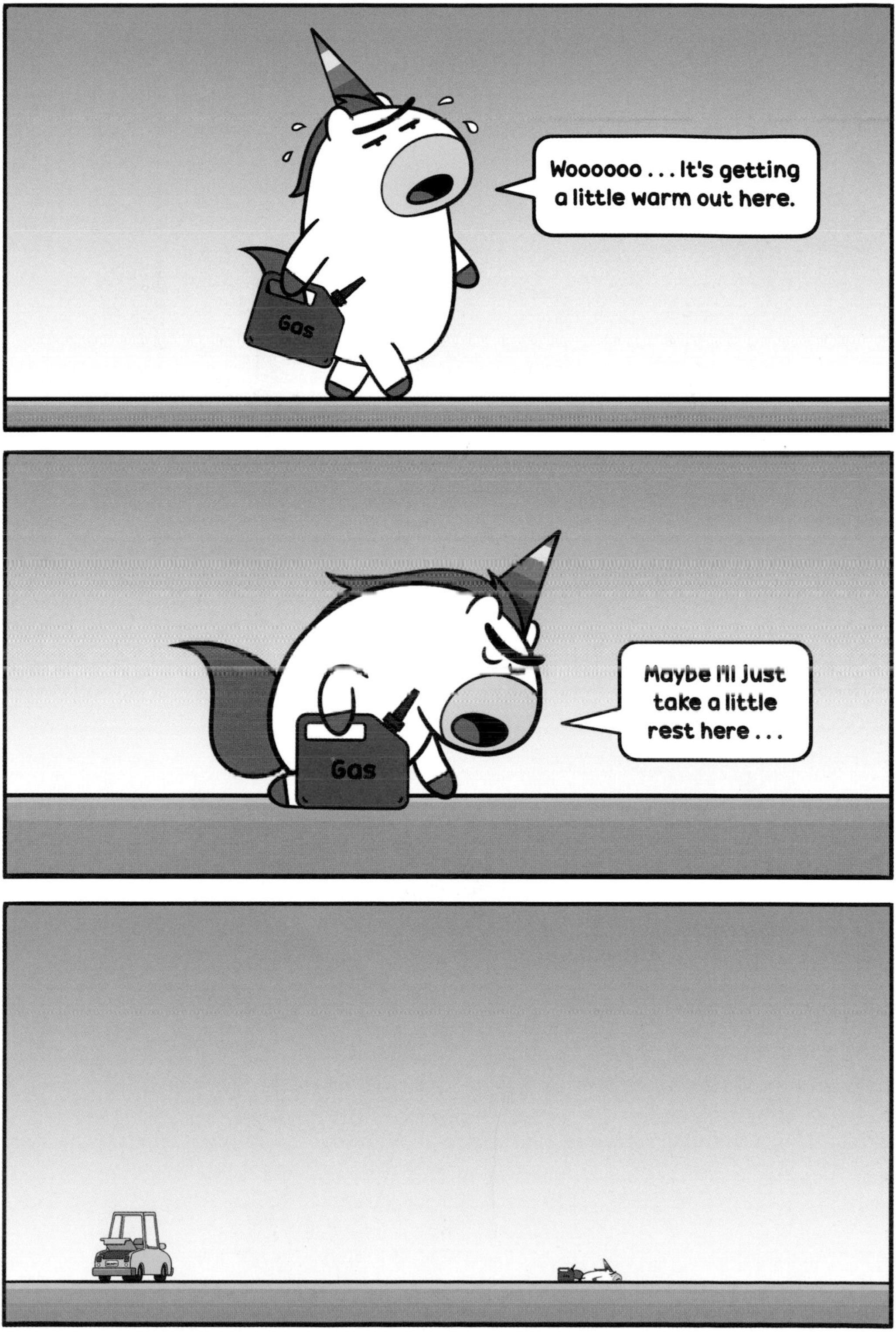
Wooooo . . . It's getting a little warm out here.
Gas
Maybe I'll just take a little rest here . . .
Gas

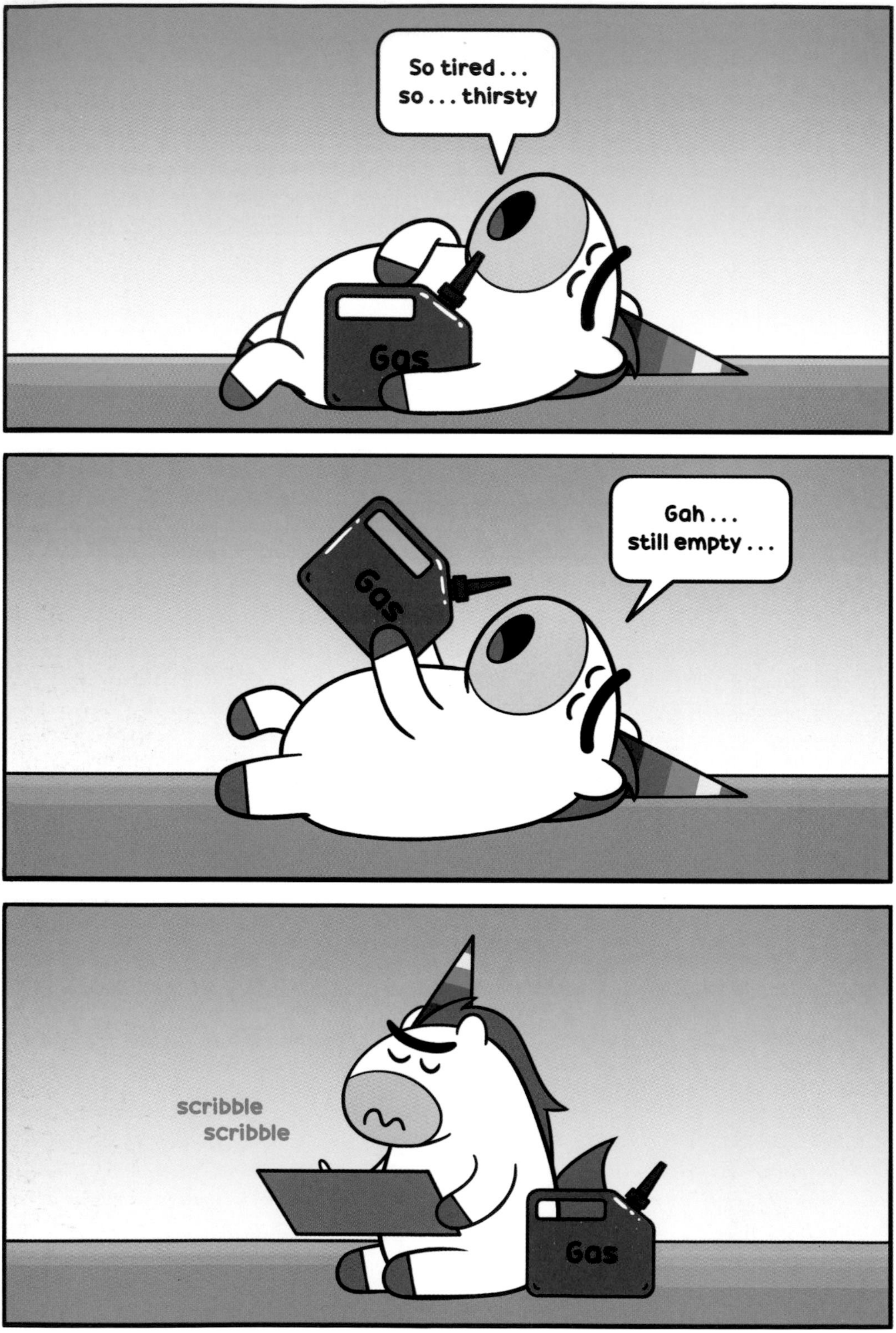
So tired . . .
so . . . thirsty
Gas
Gas
Gah . . .
still empty . . .
scribble
scribble
Gas

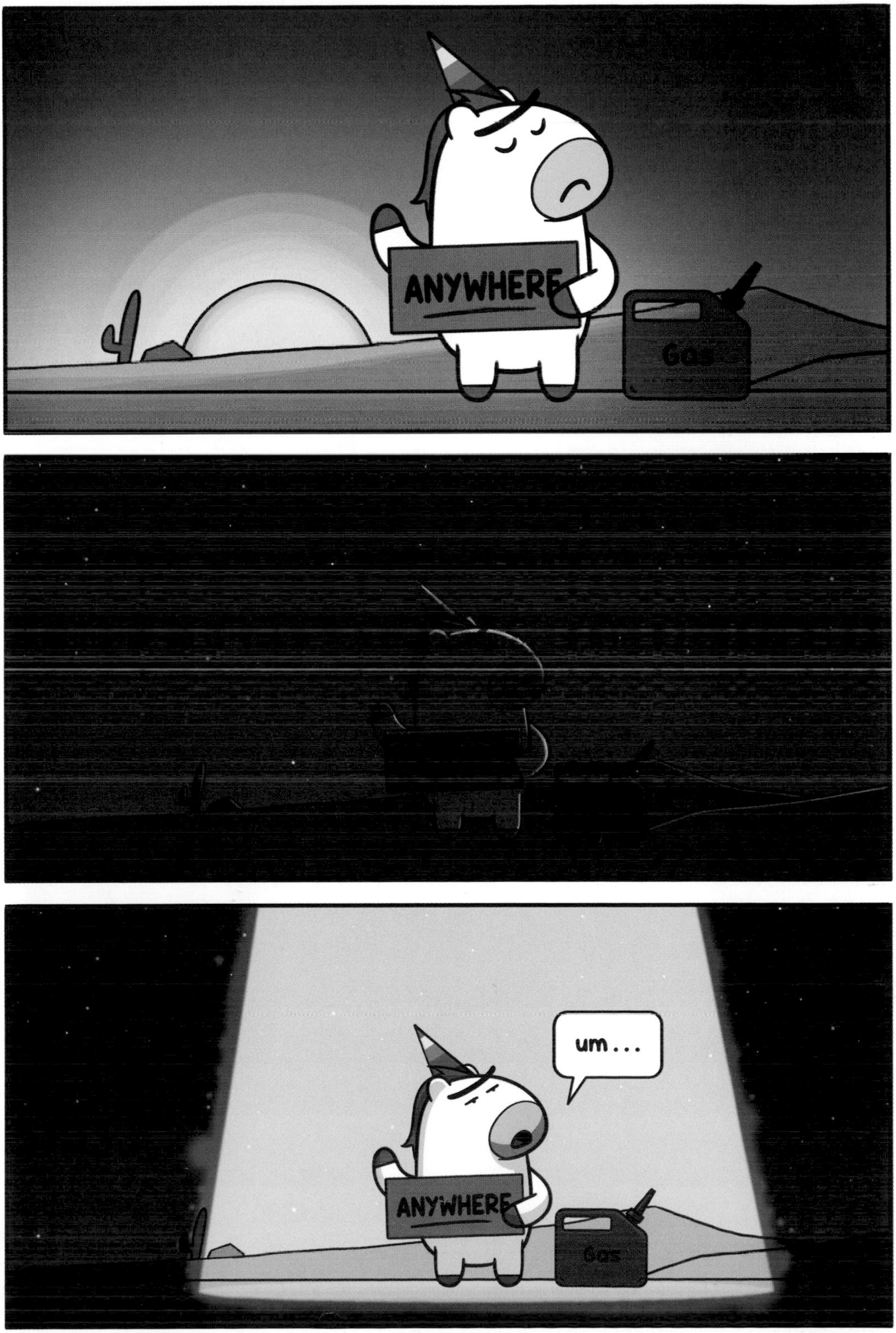
ANYWHERE
Gas
um...
ANYWHERE
Gas

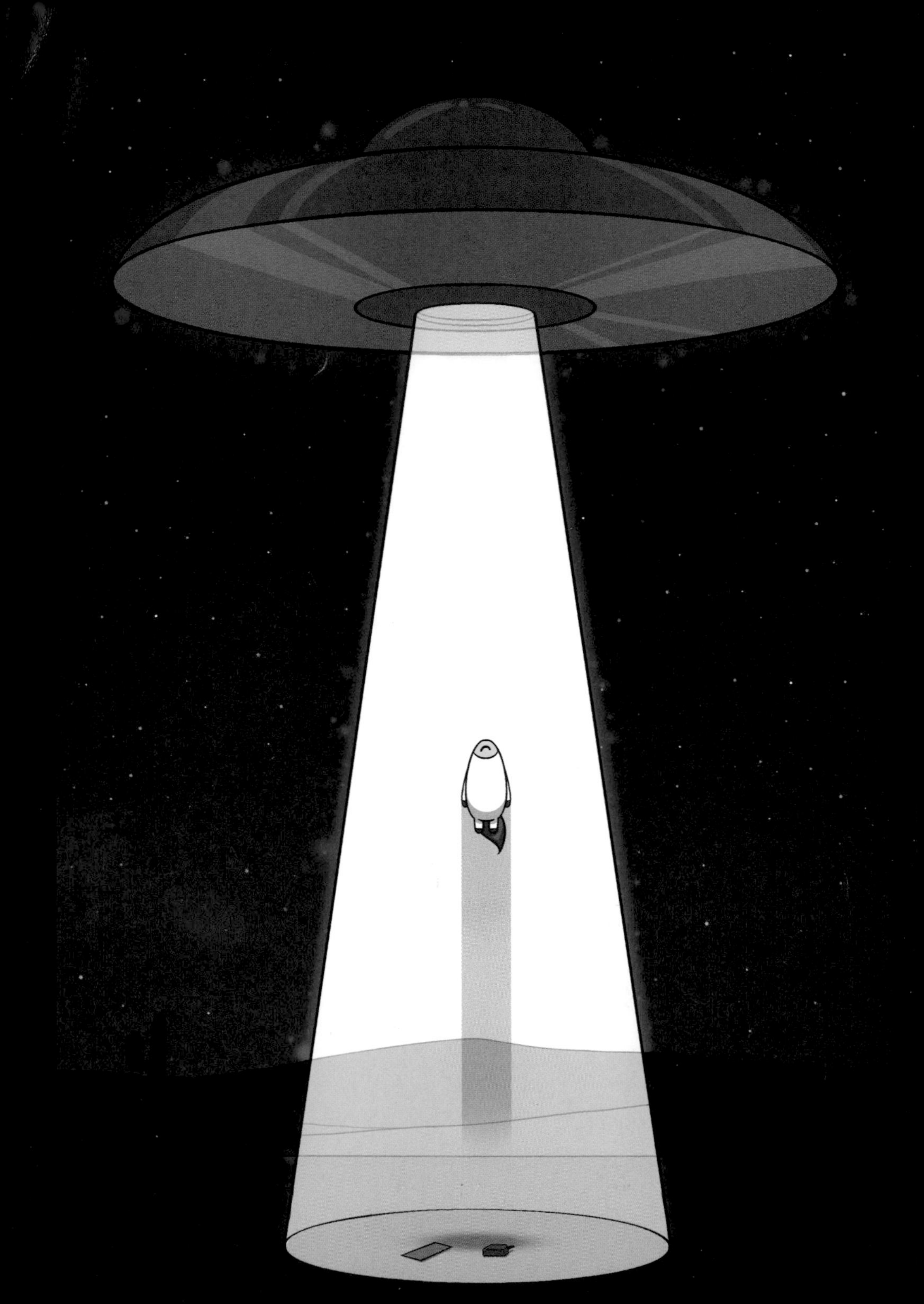

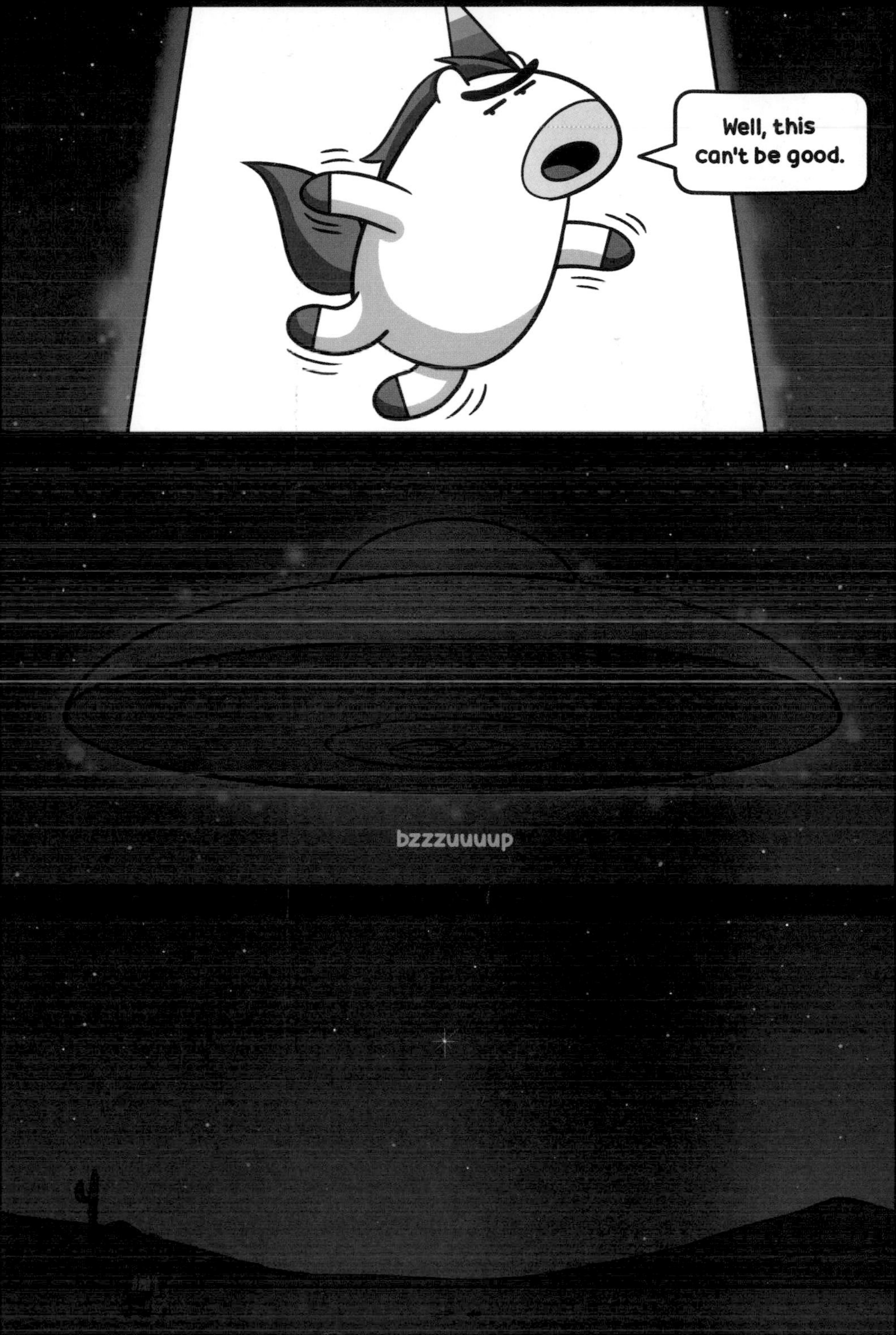
Well, this can't be good.
bzzzuuuup

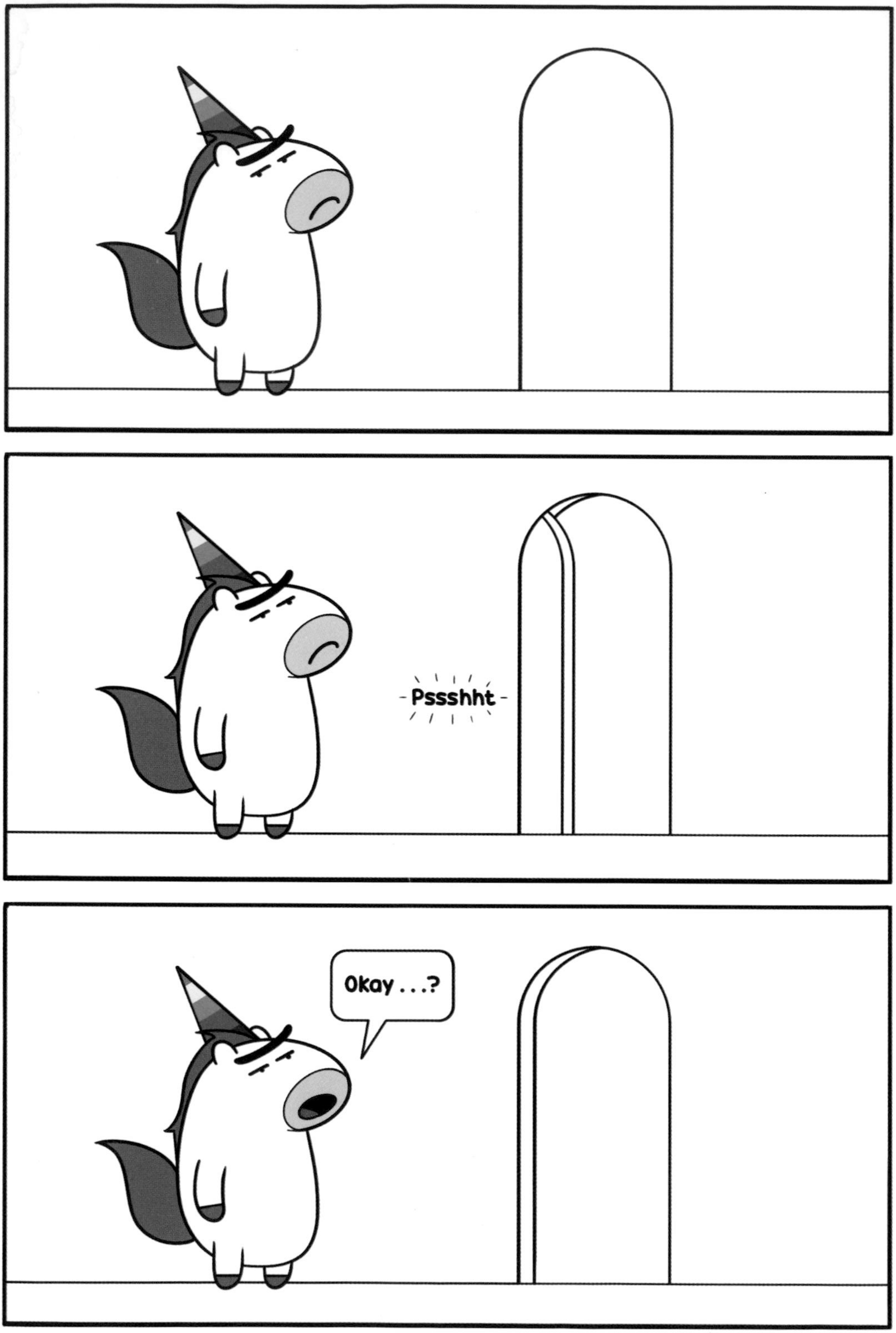
Pssshht
Okay . . .?

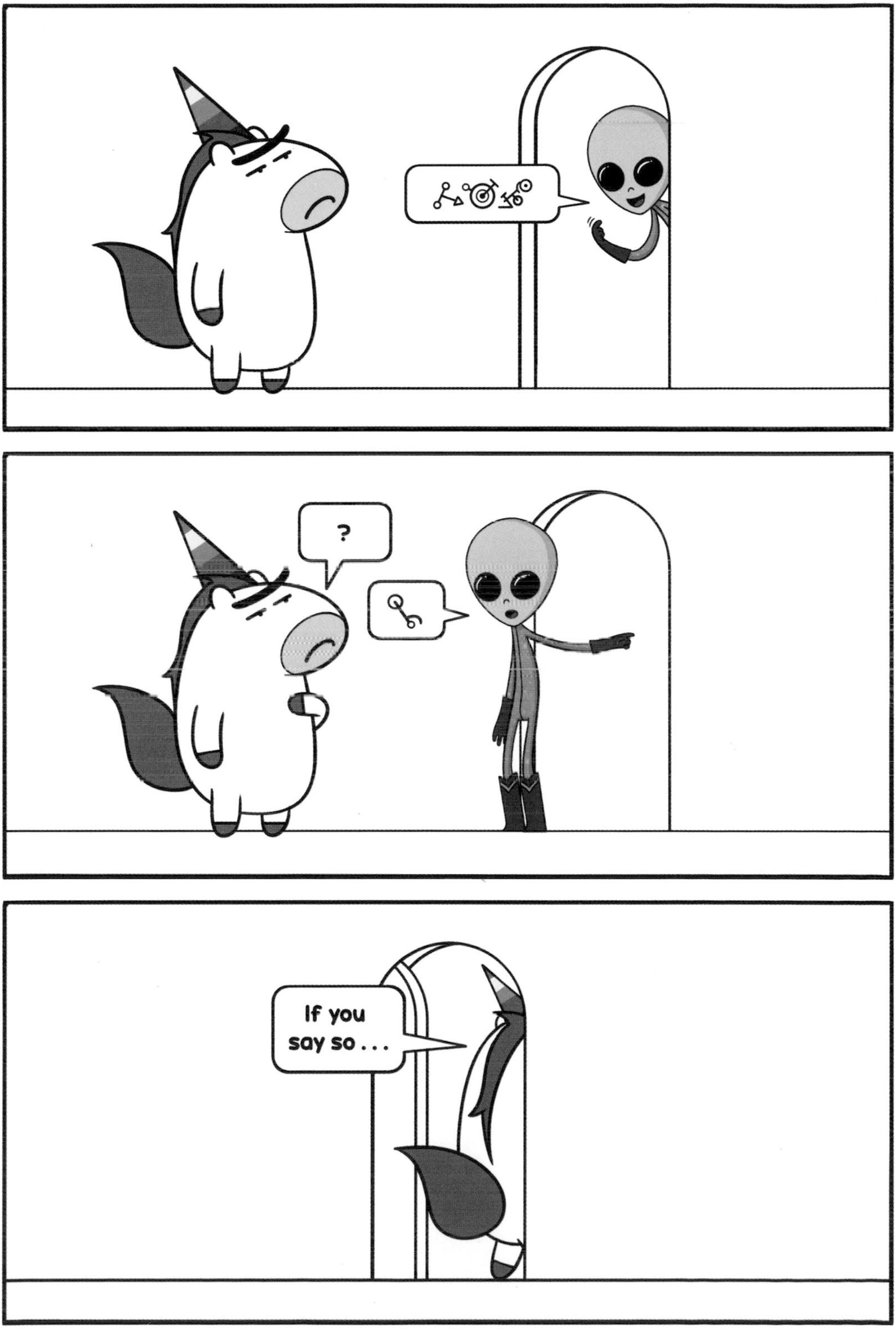
?
If you say so . . .

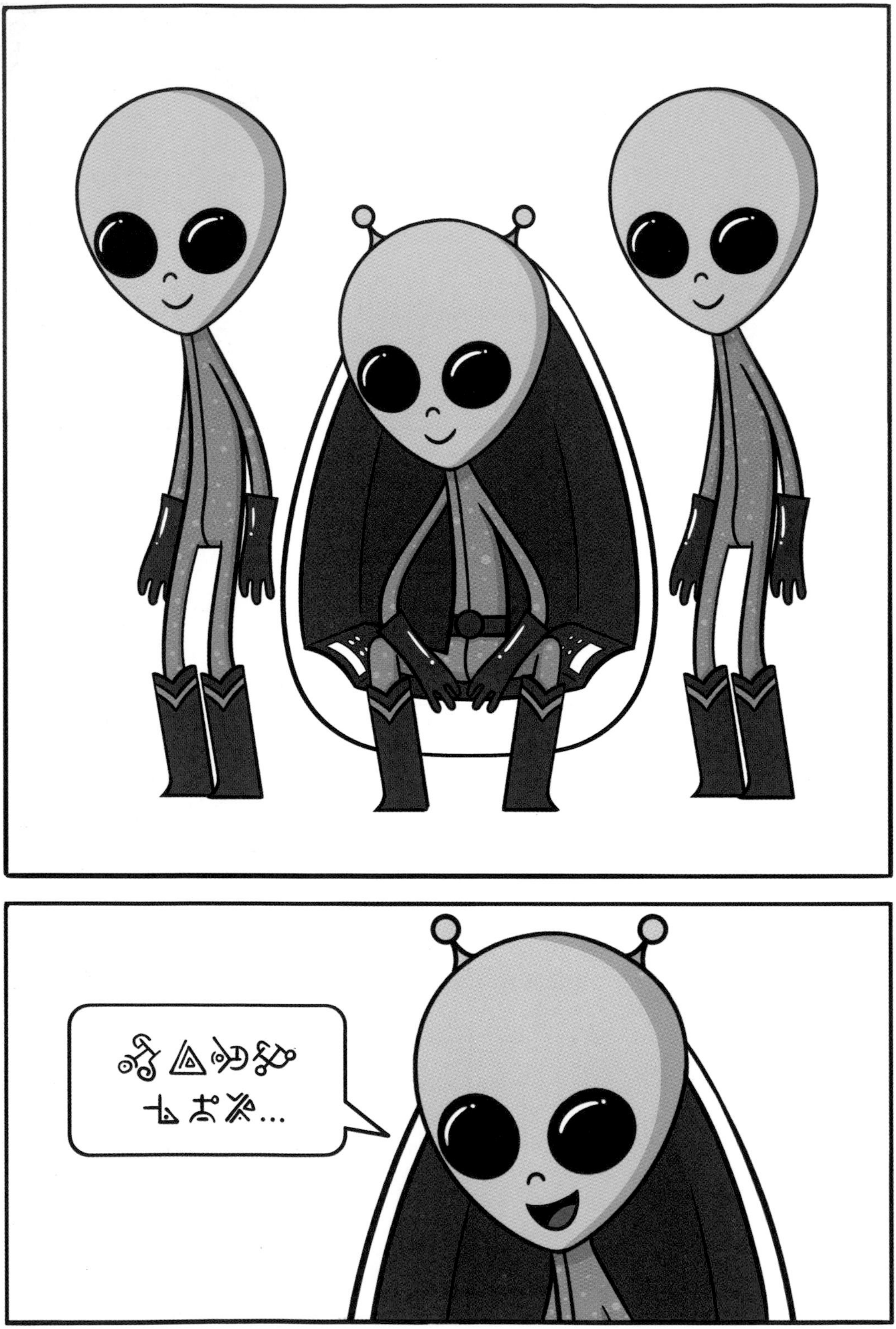

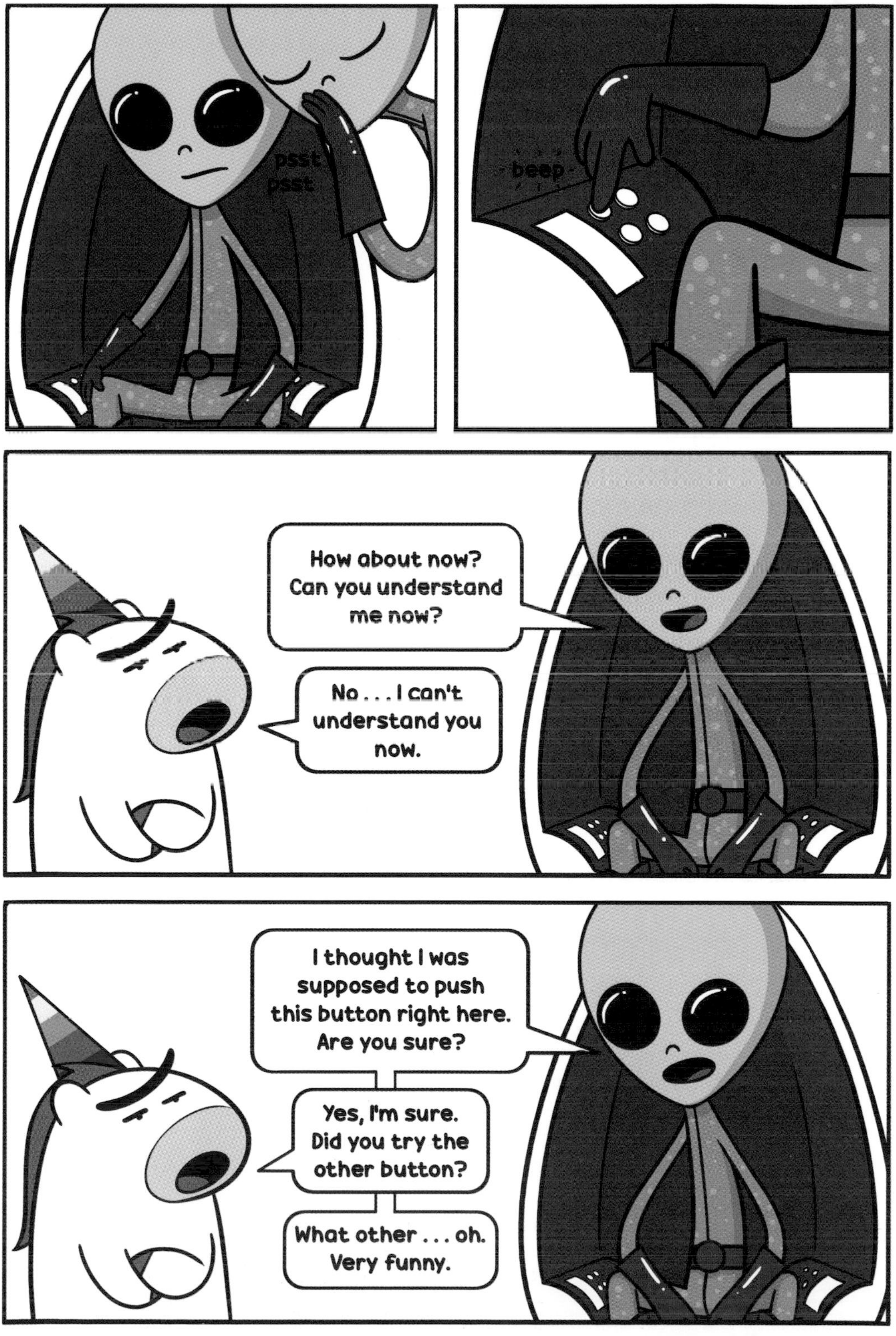
psst psst
beep
How about now? Can you understand me now?
No . . . I can't understand you now.
I thought I was supposed to push this button right here. Are you sure?
Yes, I'm sure. Did you try the other button?
What other . . . oh. Very funny.

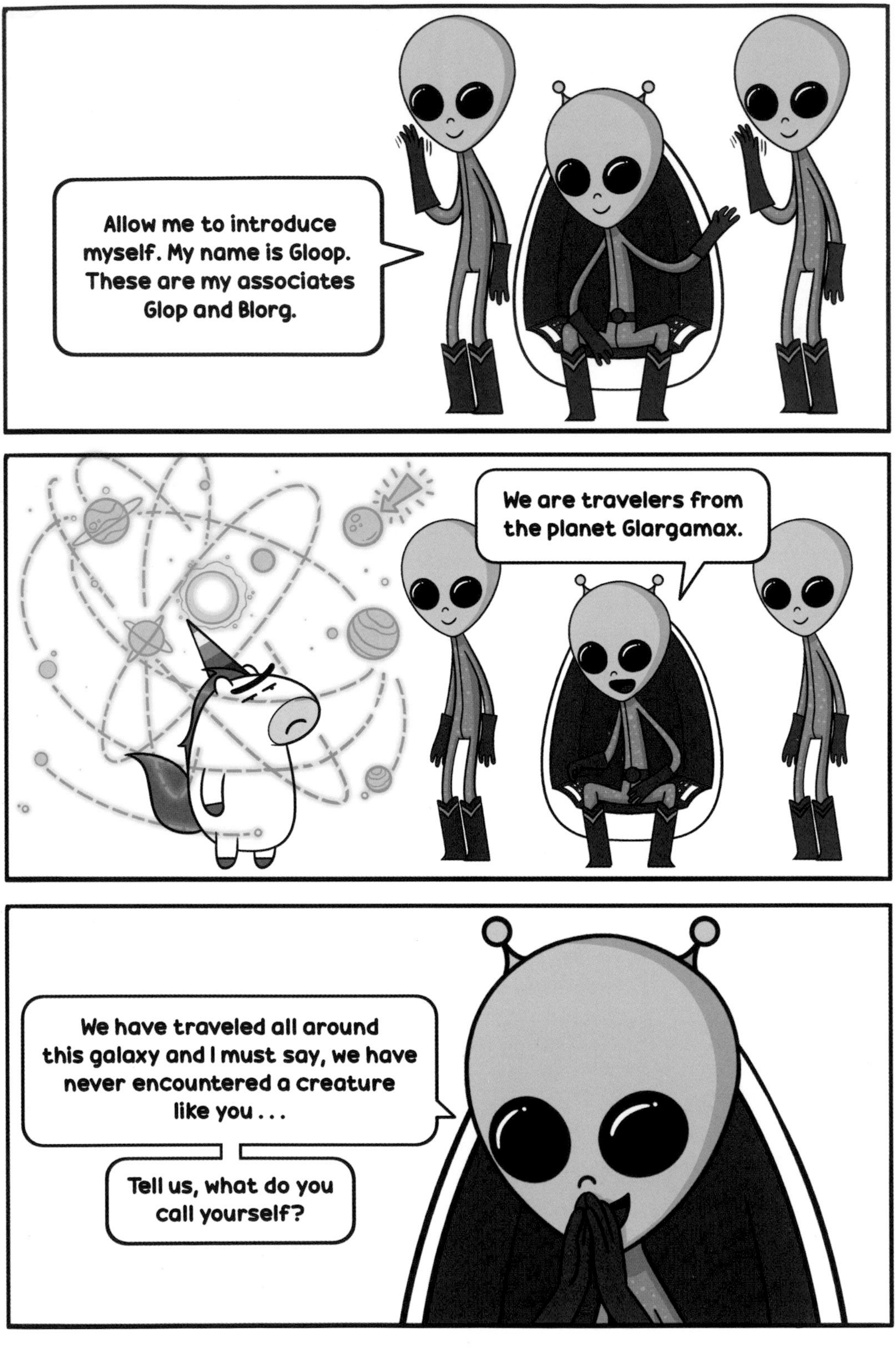
Allow me to introduce myself. My name is Gloop. These are my associates Glop and Blorg.
We are travelers from the planet Glargamax.
We have traveled all around this galaxy and I must say, we have never encountered a creature like you . . .
Tell us, what do you call yourself?

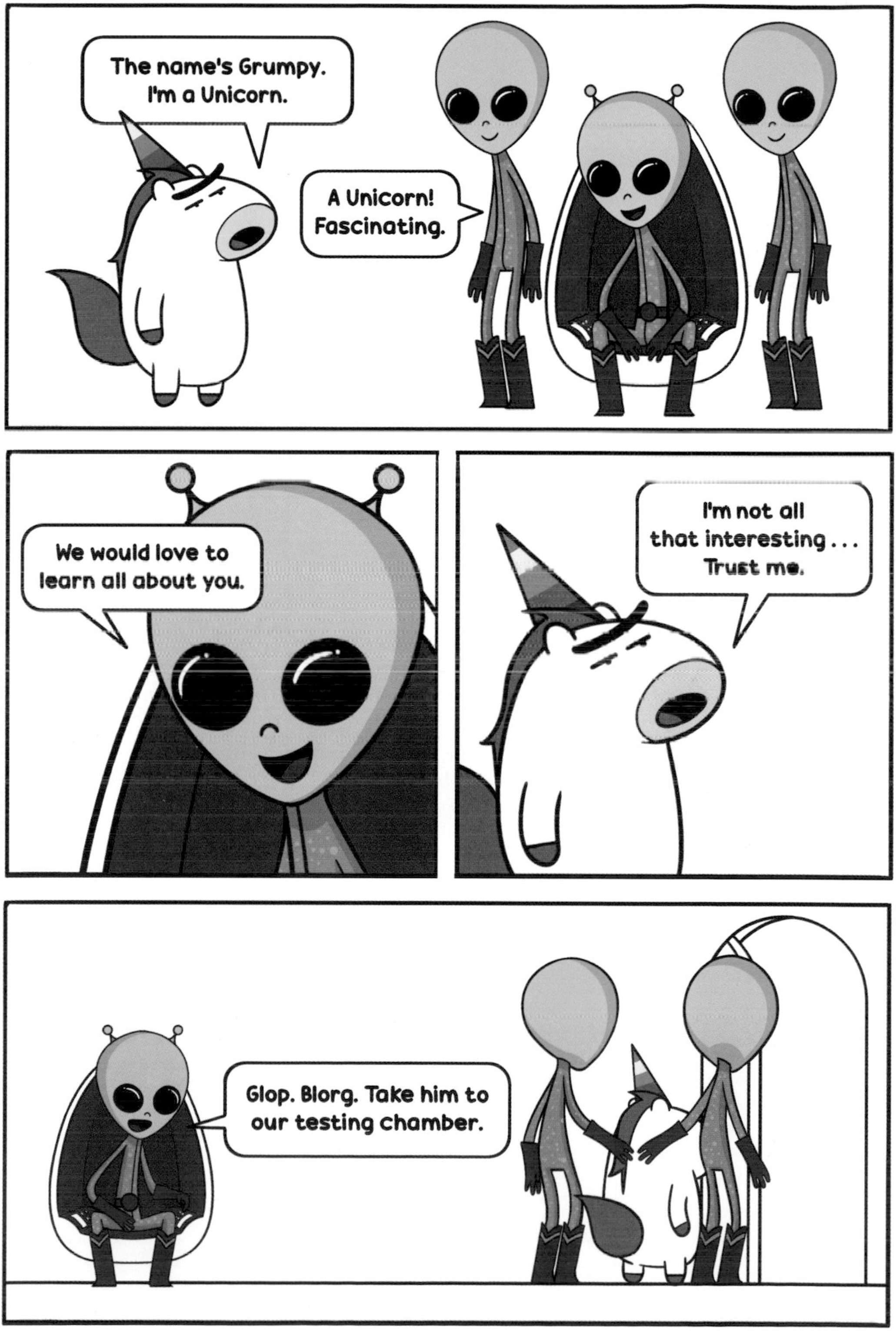
The name's Grumpy.
I'm a Unicorn.
A Unicorn!
Fascinating.
We would love to
learn all about you.
I'm not all
that interesting . . .
Trust me.
Glop. Blorg. Take him to
our testing chamber.

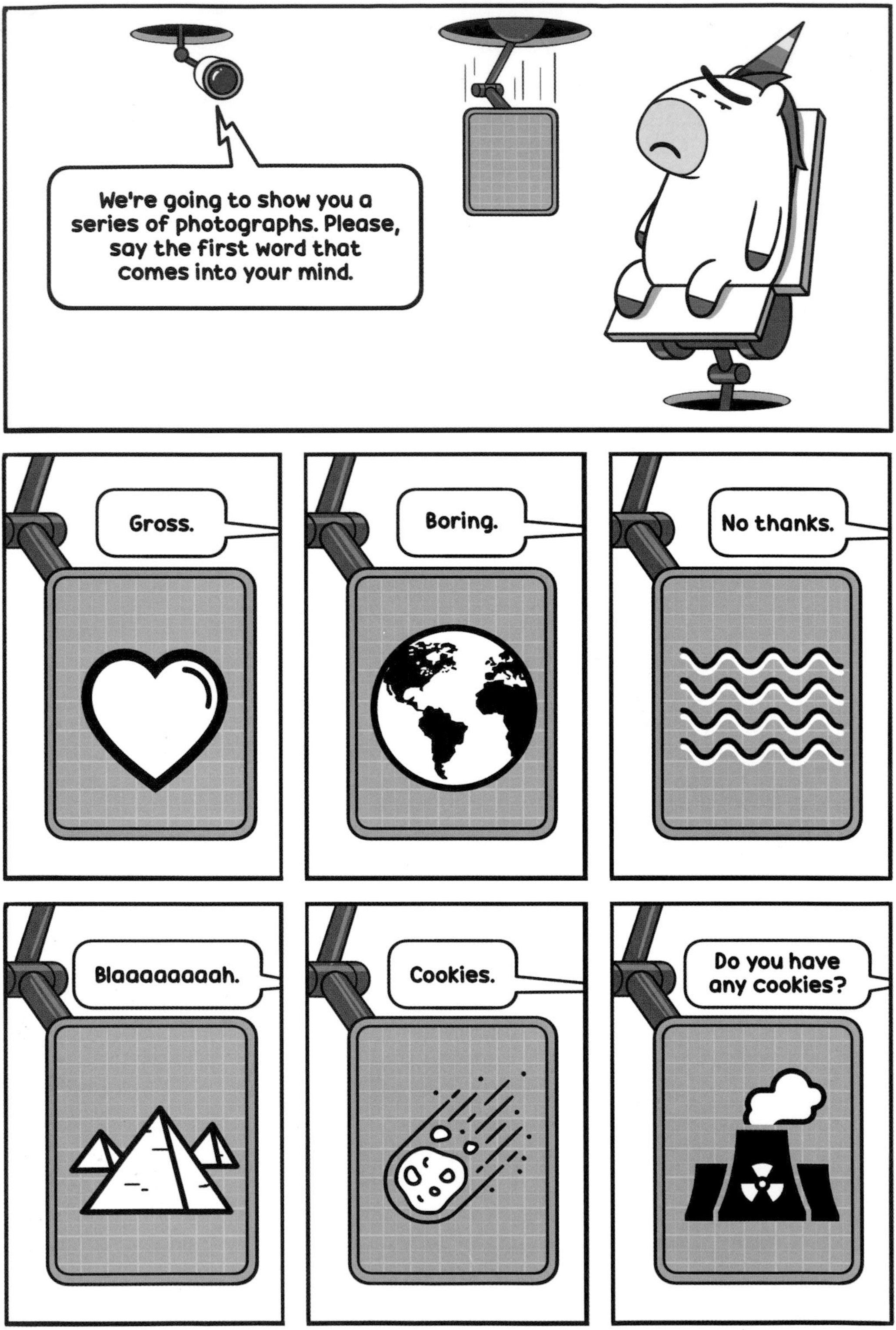
We're going to show you a series of photographs. Please, say the first word that comes into your mind.
Gross.
Boring.
No thanks.
Blaaaaaaah.
Cookies.
Do you have any cookies?

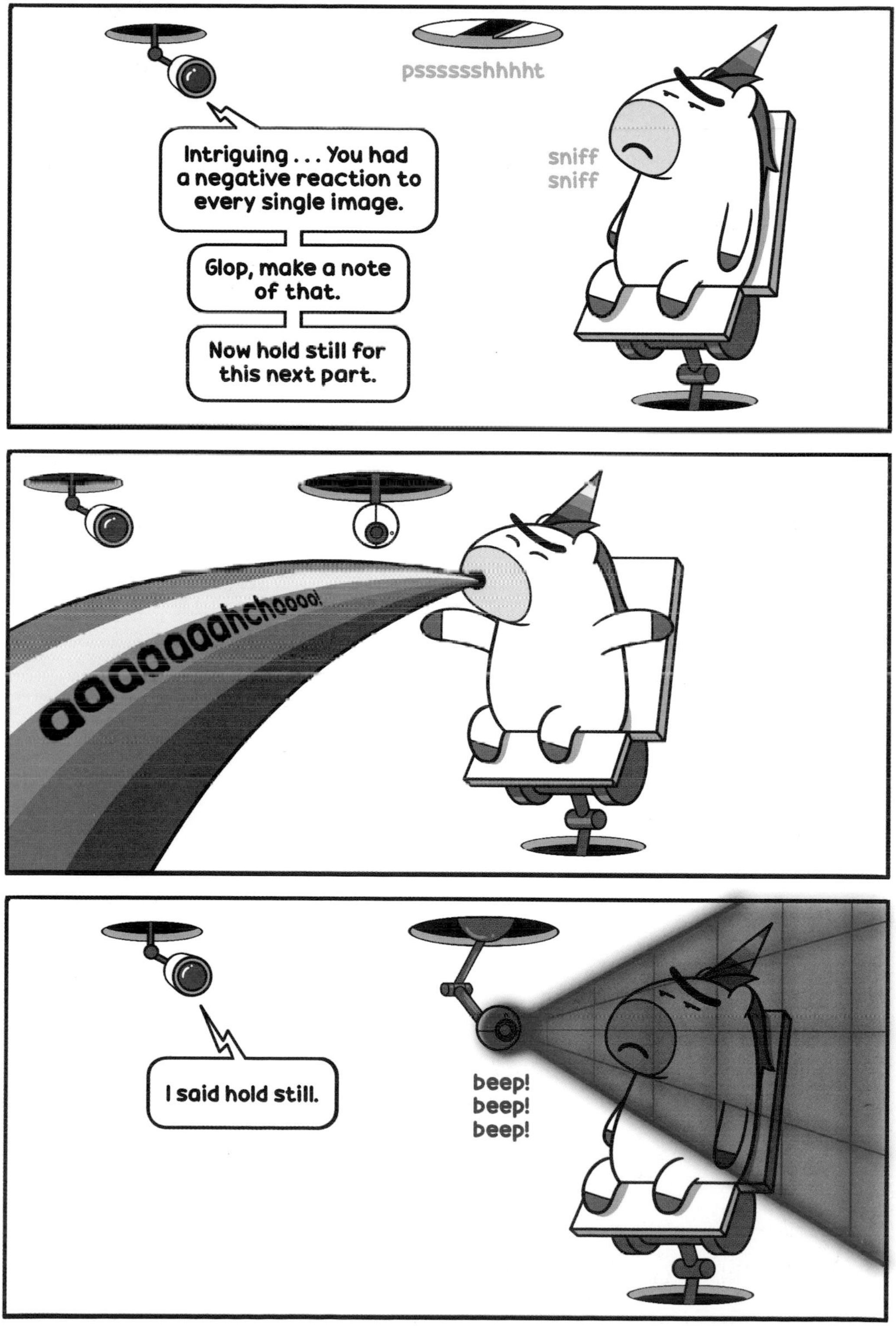
psssssshhhht
Intriguing . . . You had a negative reaction to every single image.
Glop, make a note of that.
Now hold still for this next part.
sniff
sniff
aaaaaaaahchoooo!
I said hold still.
beep!
beep!
beep!

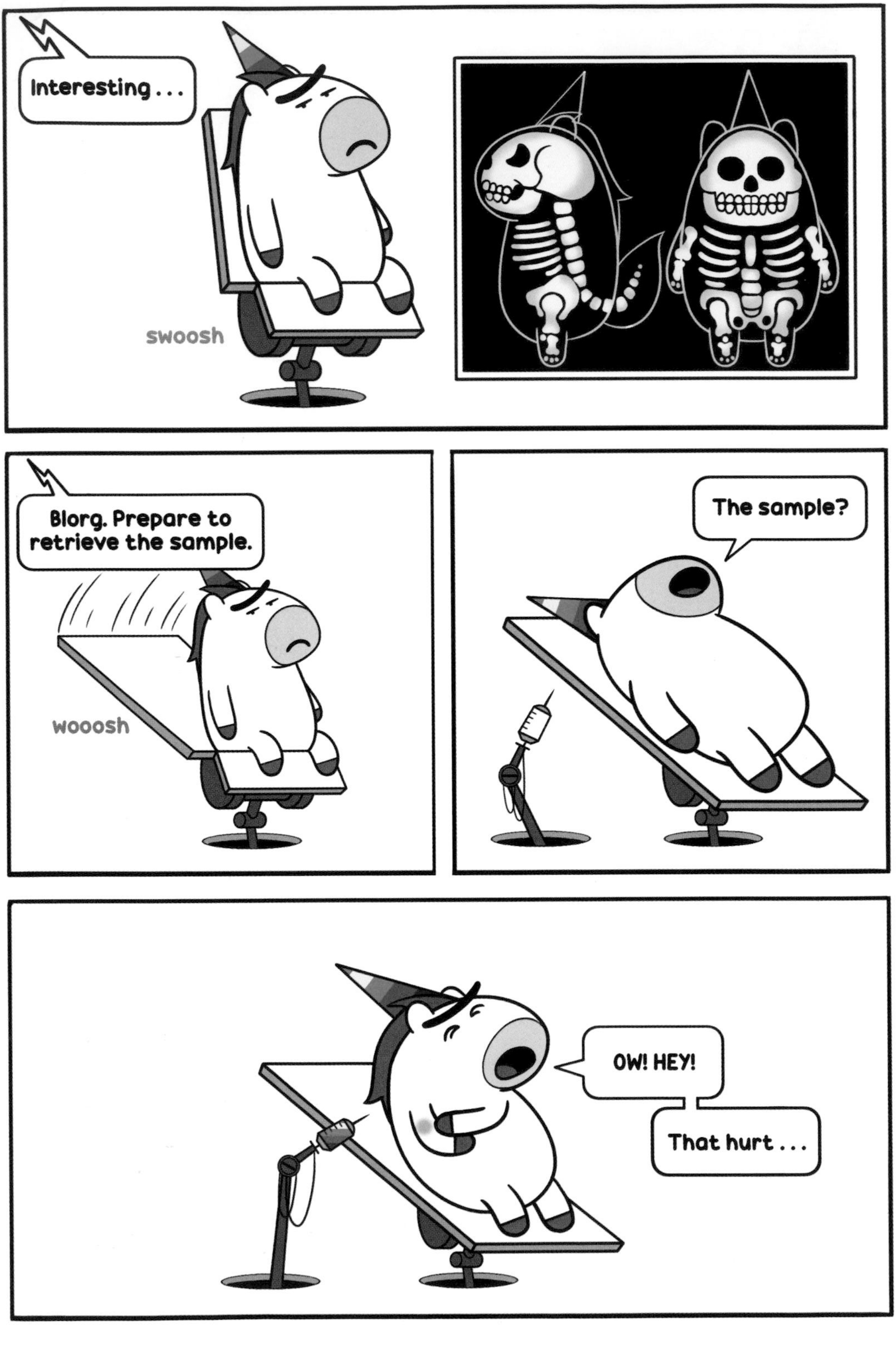
Interesting . . .
swoosh
Blorg. Prepare to retrieve the sample.
wooosh
The sample?
OW! HEY!
That hurt . . .

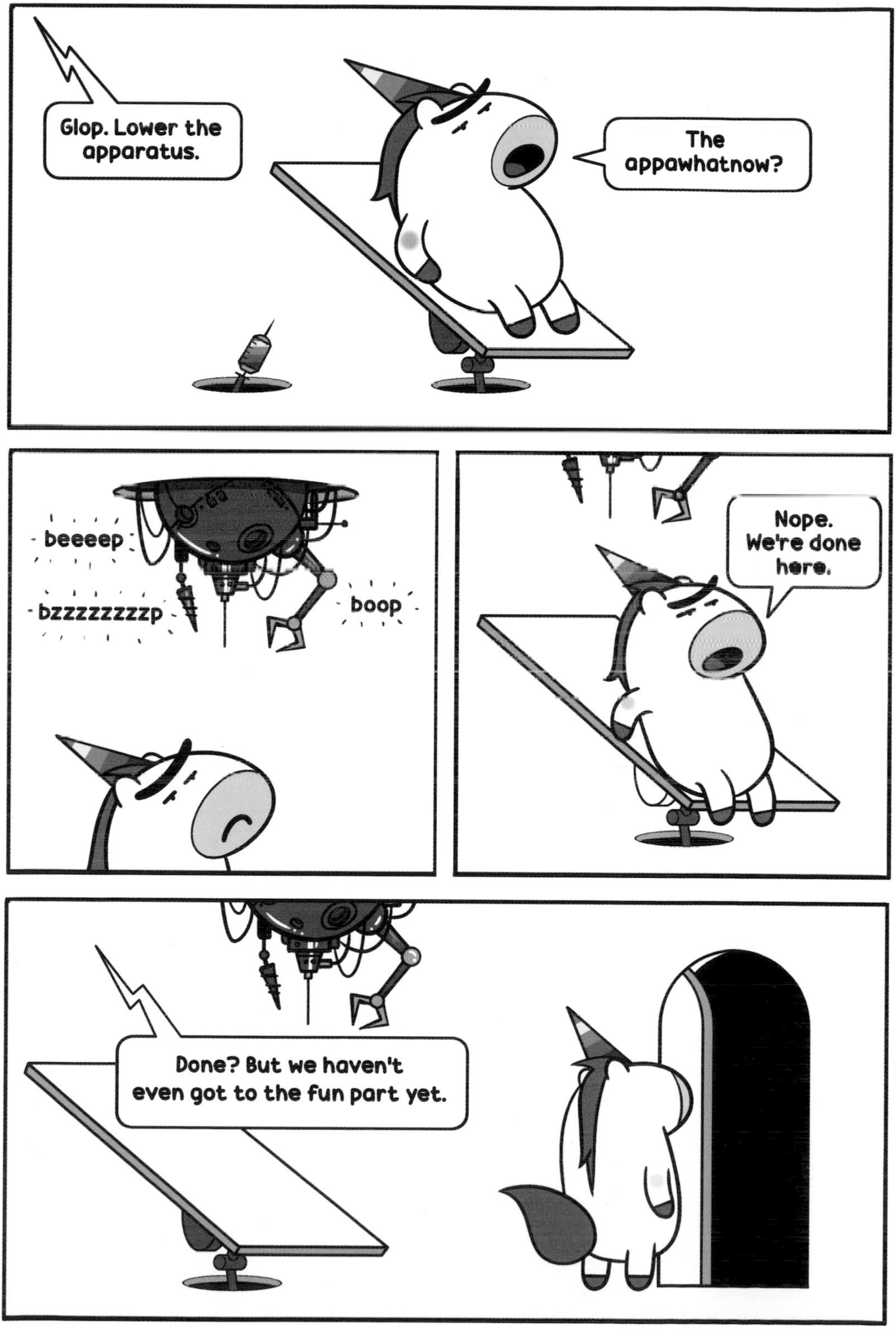
Glop. Lower the apparatus.
The appawhatnow?
beeeep
bzzzzzzzzp
boop
Nope. We're done here.
Done? But we haven't even got to the fun part yet.

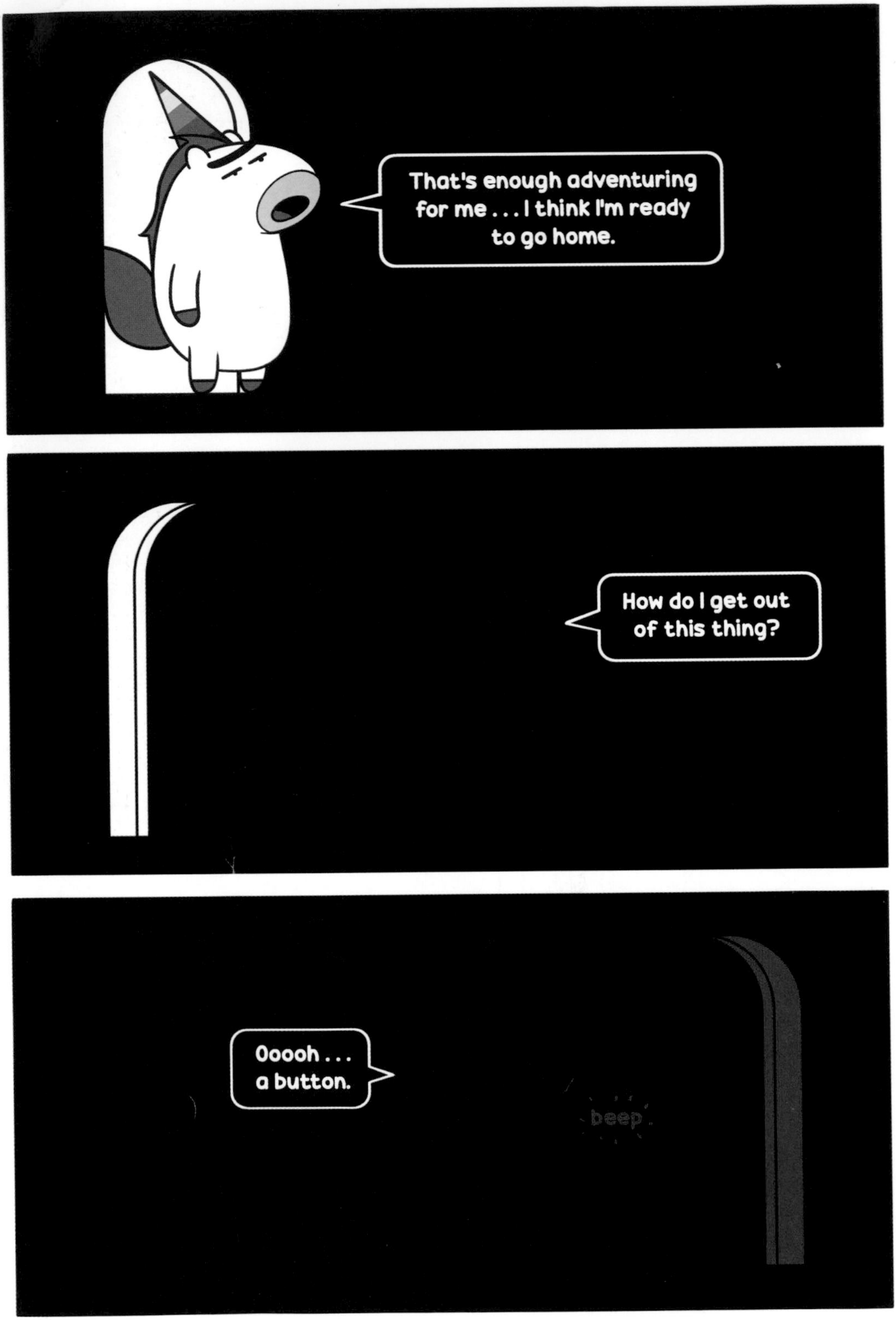
That's enough adventuring for me . . . I think I'm ready to go home.
How do I get out of this thing?
Ooooh . . . a button.
beep

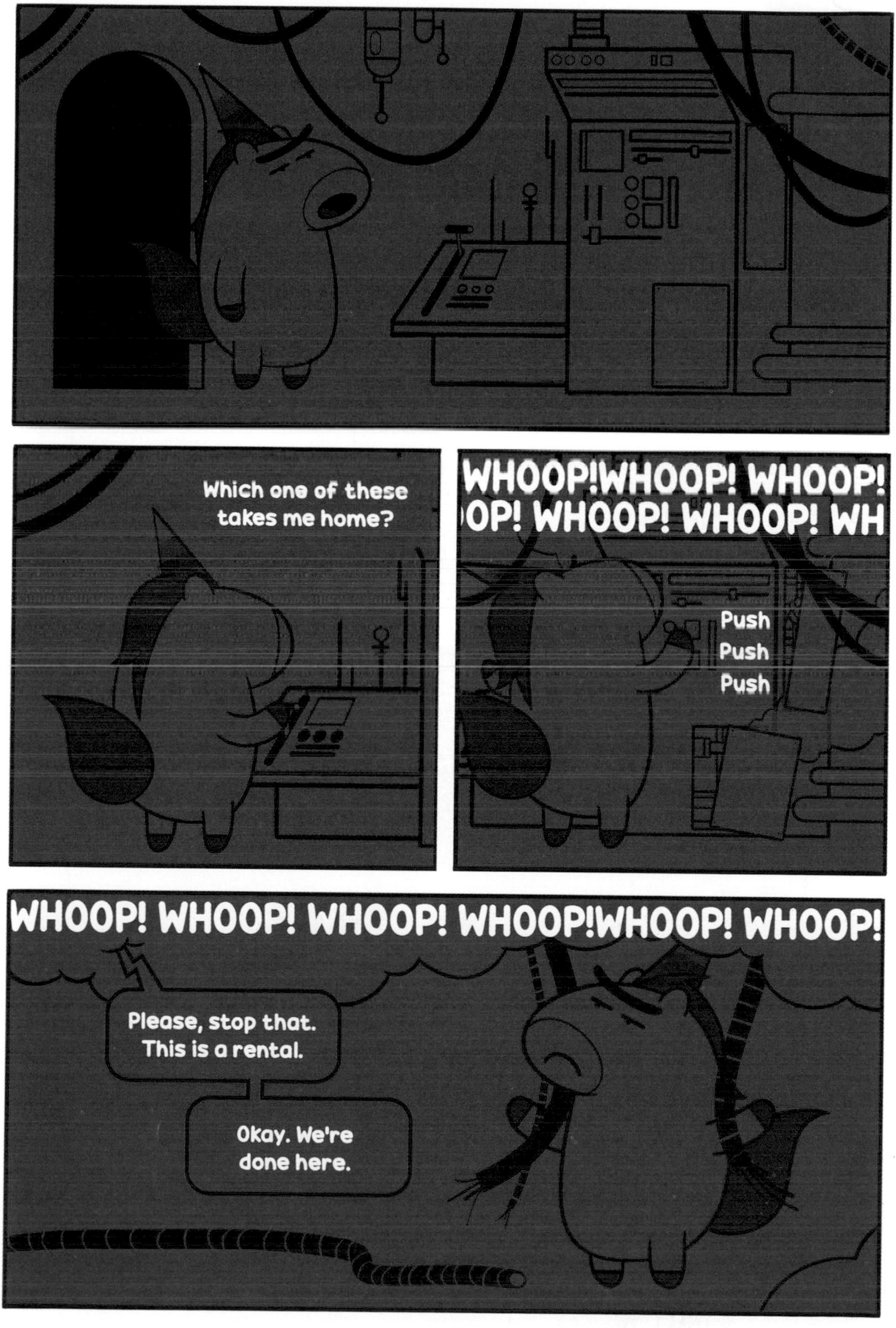
Which one of these takes me home?
WHOOP!WHOOP! WHOOP!
OP! WHOOP! WHOOP! WH
Push
Push
Push
WHOOP! WHOOP! WHOOP! WHOOP!WHOOP! WHOOP!
Please, stop that. This is a rental.
Okay. We're done here.

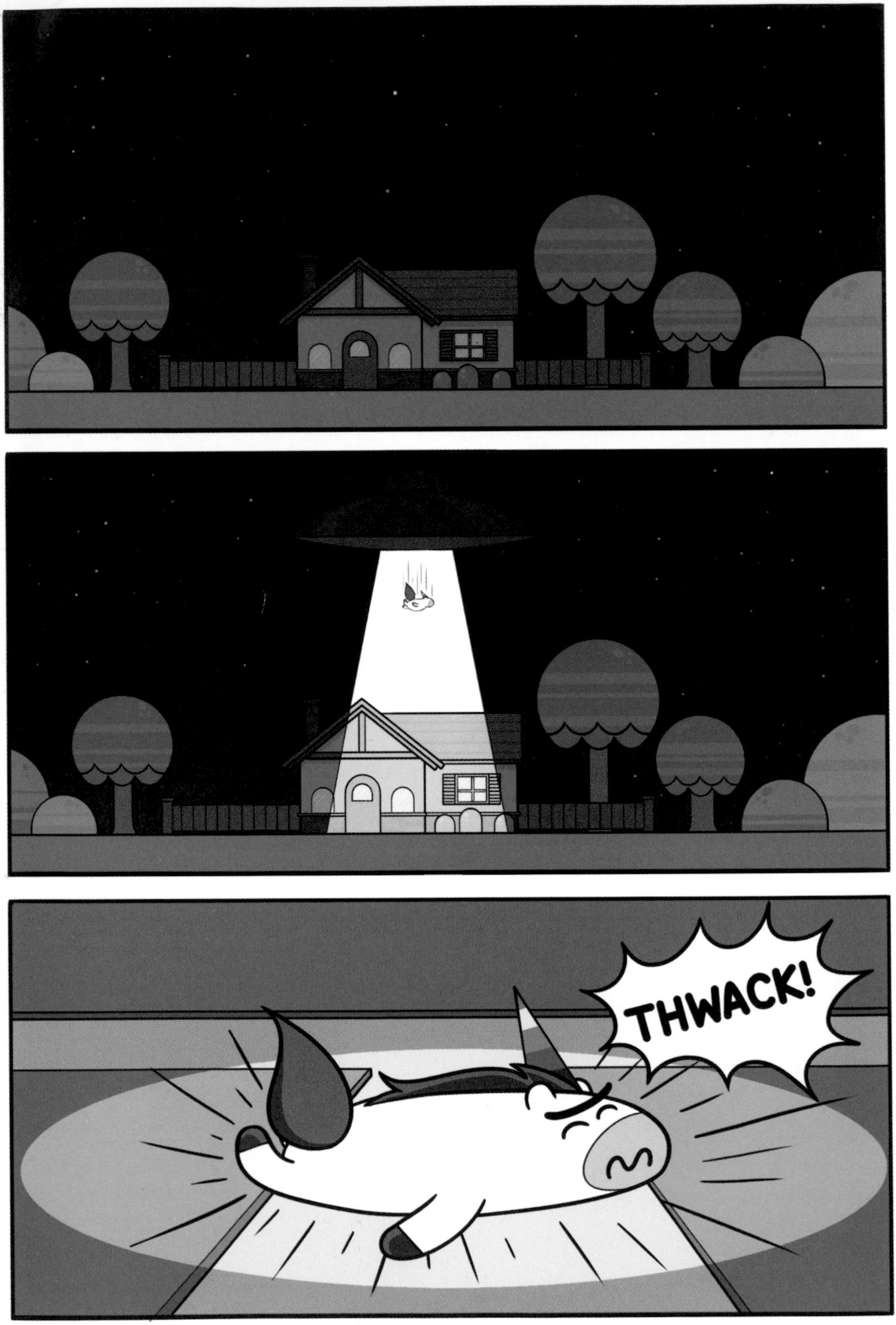
THWACK!

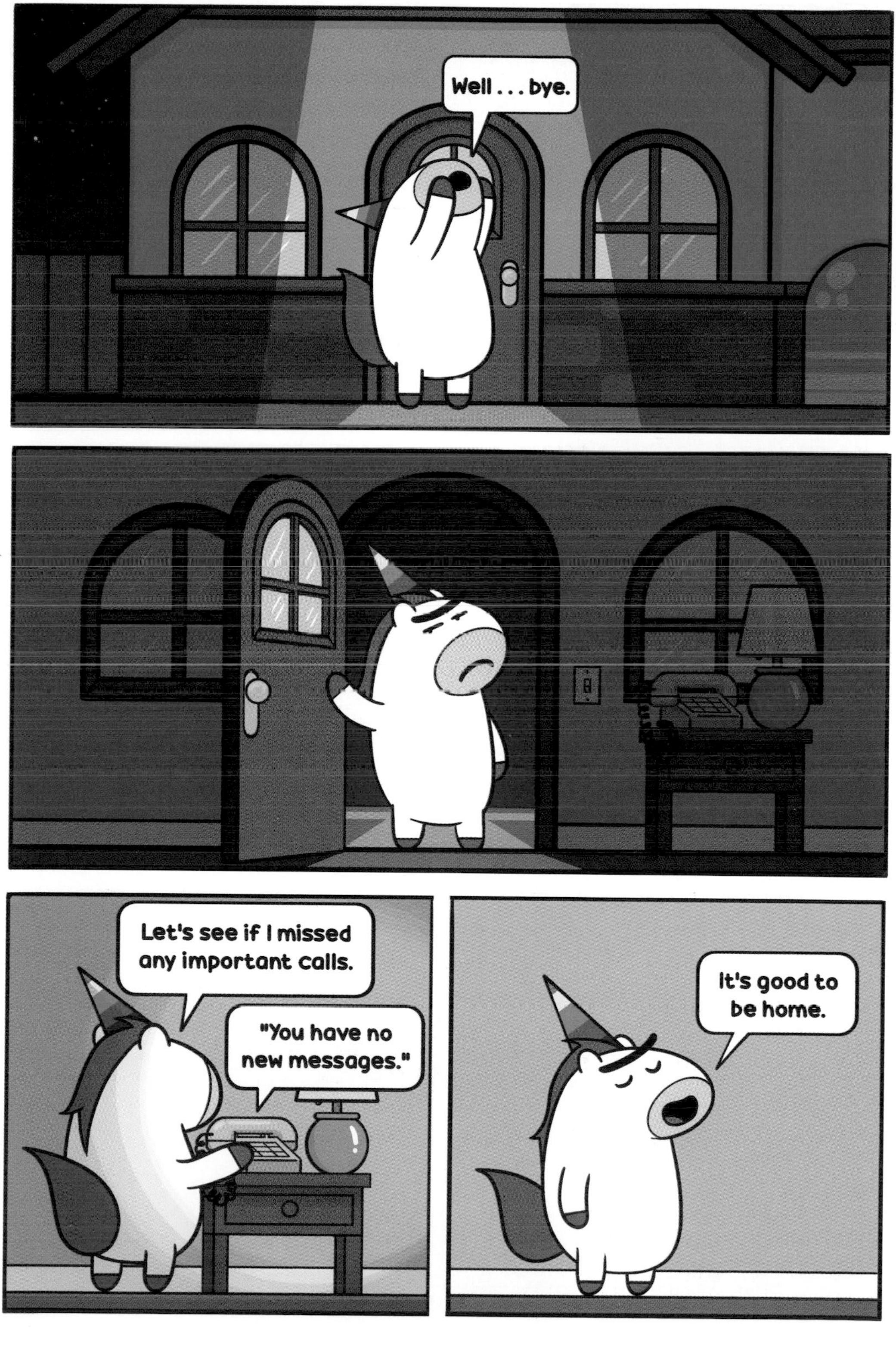
Well . . . bye.
Let's see if I missed any important calls.
"You have no new messages."
It's good to be home.

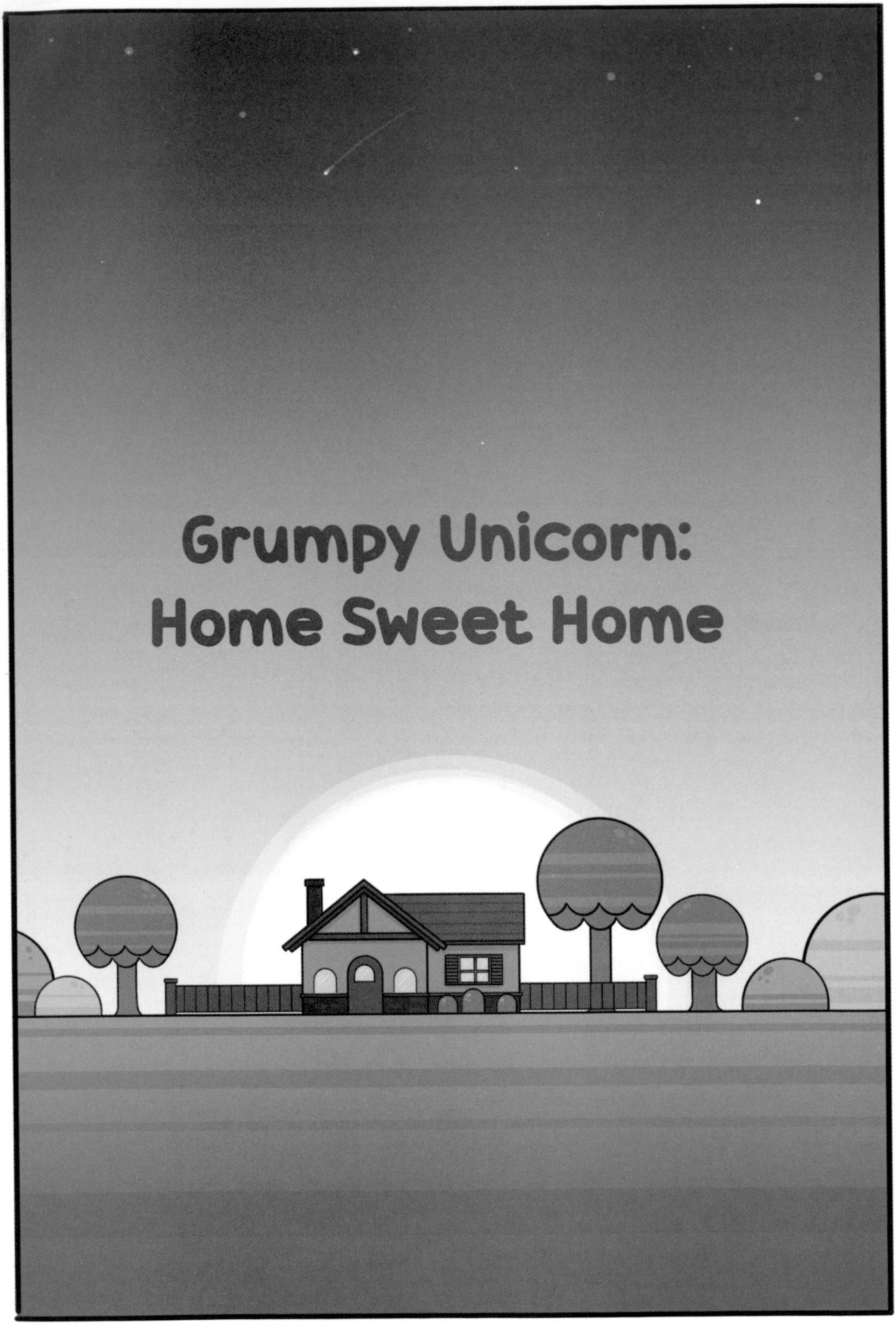
Grumpy Unicorn:
Home Sweet Home

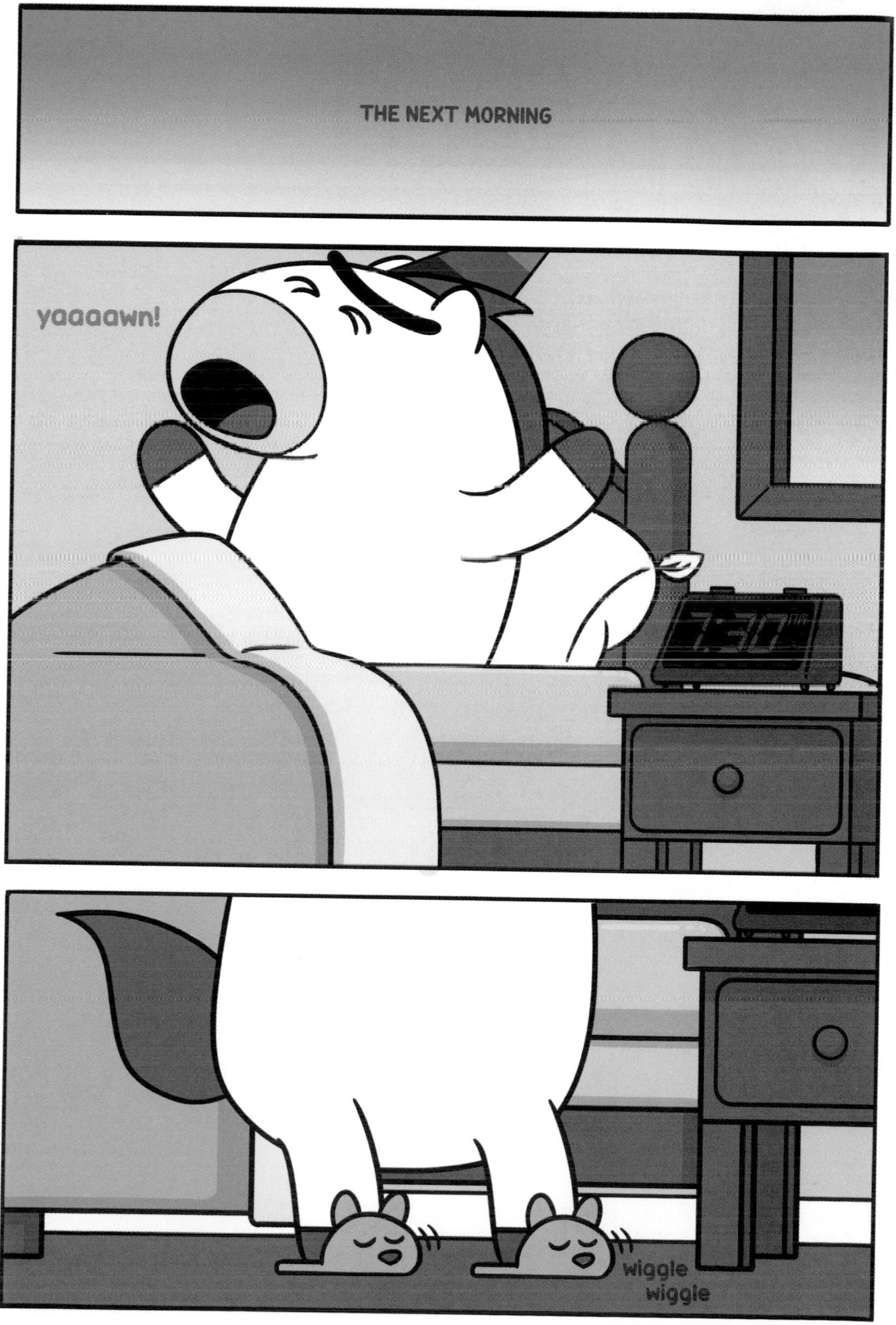
THE NEXT MORNING
yaaaawn!
wiggle
wiggle

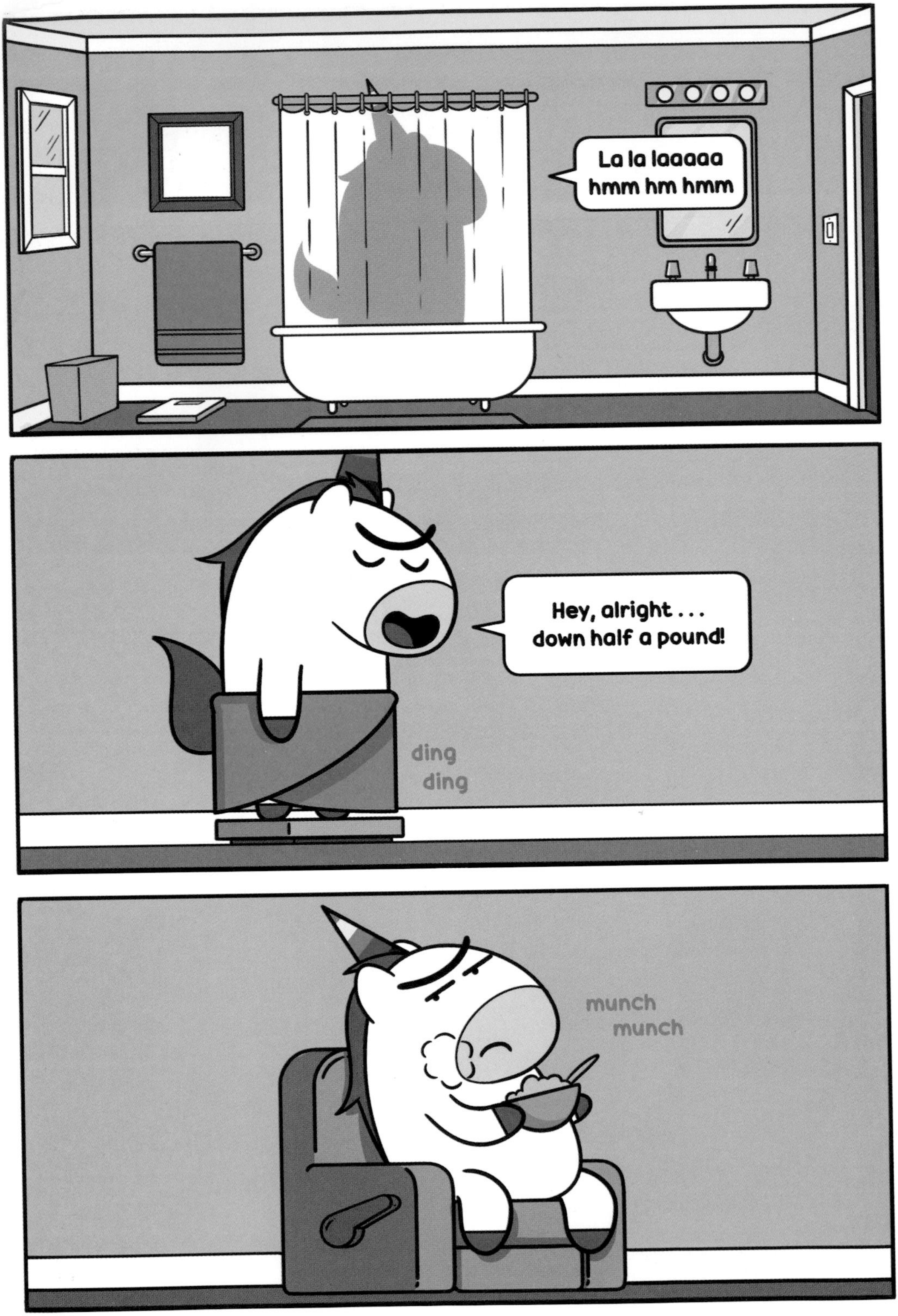
La la laaaaa hmm hm hmm
Hey, alright . . . down half a pound!
ding ding
munch munch

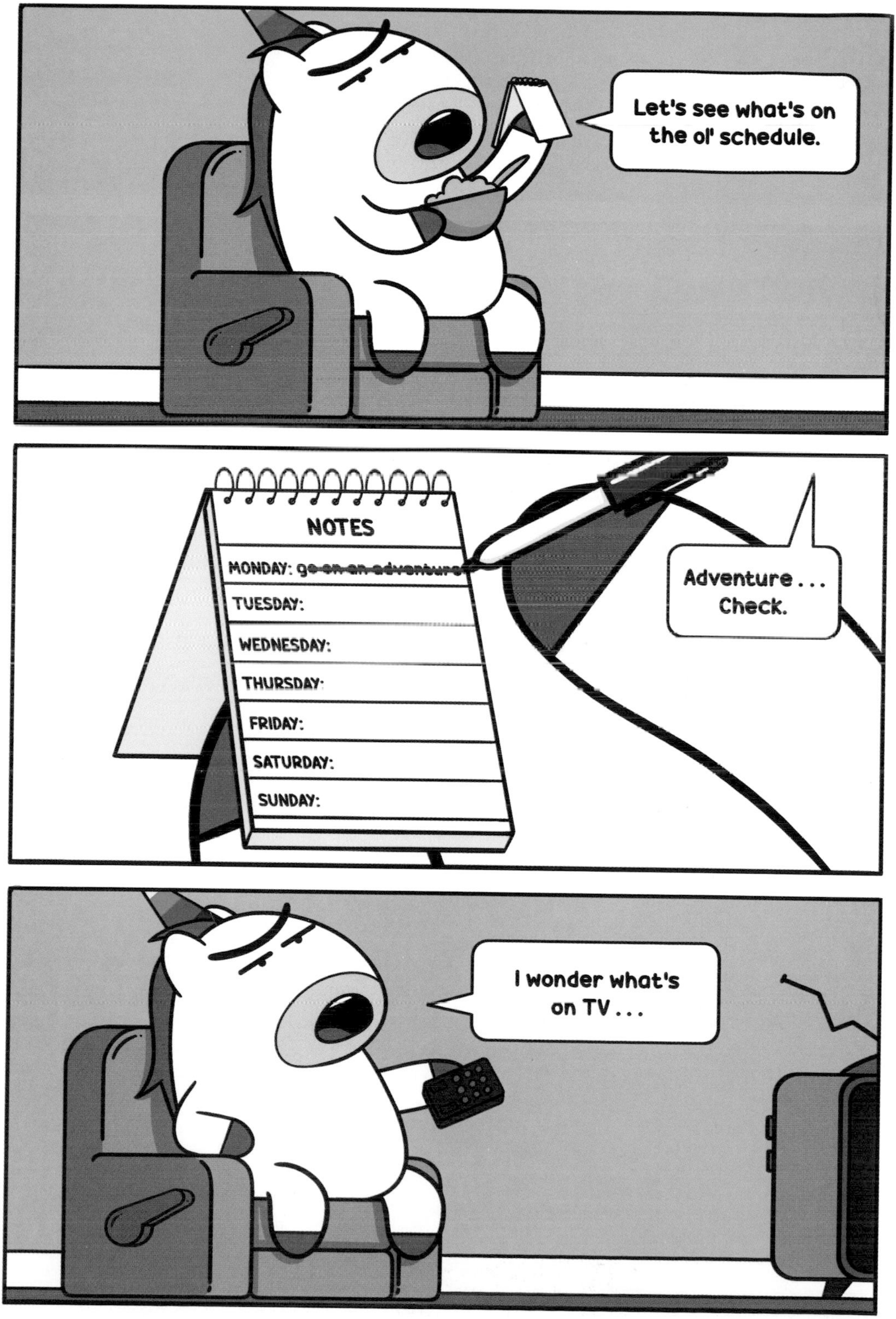
Let's see what's on the ol' schedule.
NOTES
MONDAY: go on an adventure
TUESDAY:
WEDNESDAY:
THURSDAY:
FRIDAY:
SATURDAY:
SUNDAY:
Adventure . . . Check.
I wonder what's on TV . . .

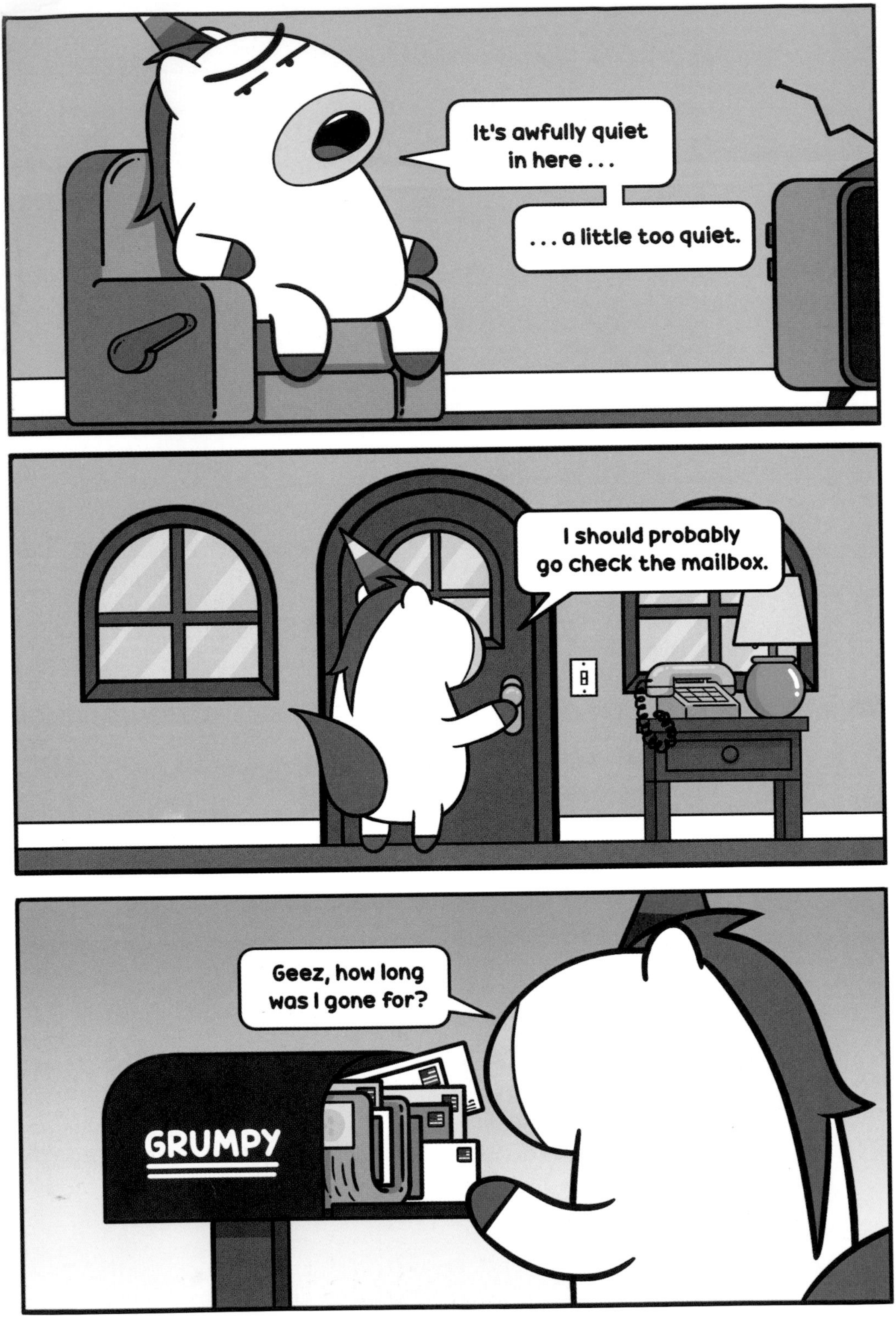
It's awfully quiet in here . . .
. . . a little too quiet.
I should probably go check the mailbox.
Geez, how long was I gone for?
GRUMPY

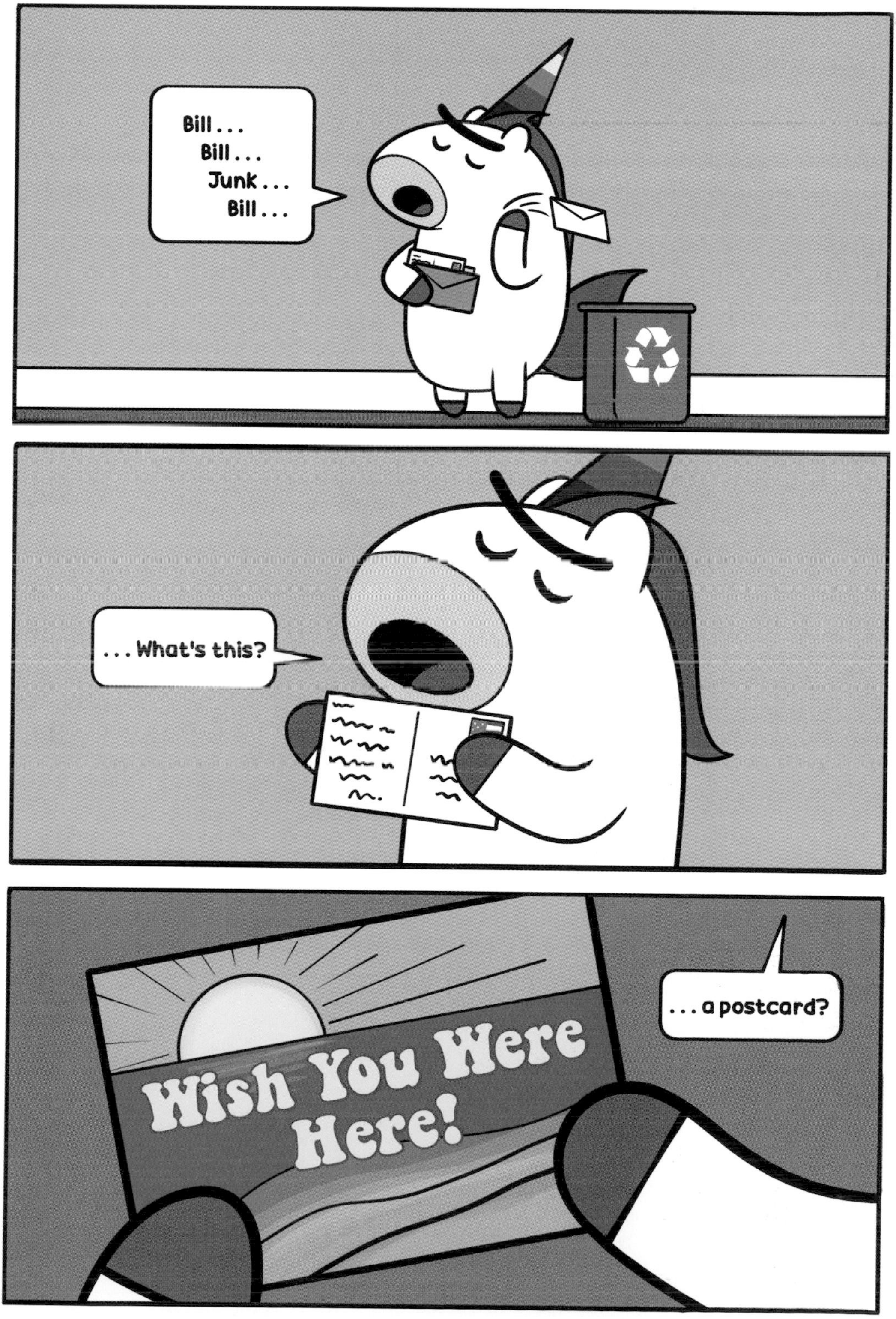
Bill . . .
Bill . . .
Junk . . .
Bill . . .
. . . What's this?
Wish You Were Here!
. . . a postcard?

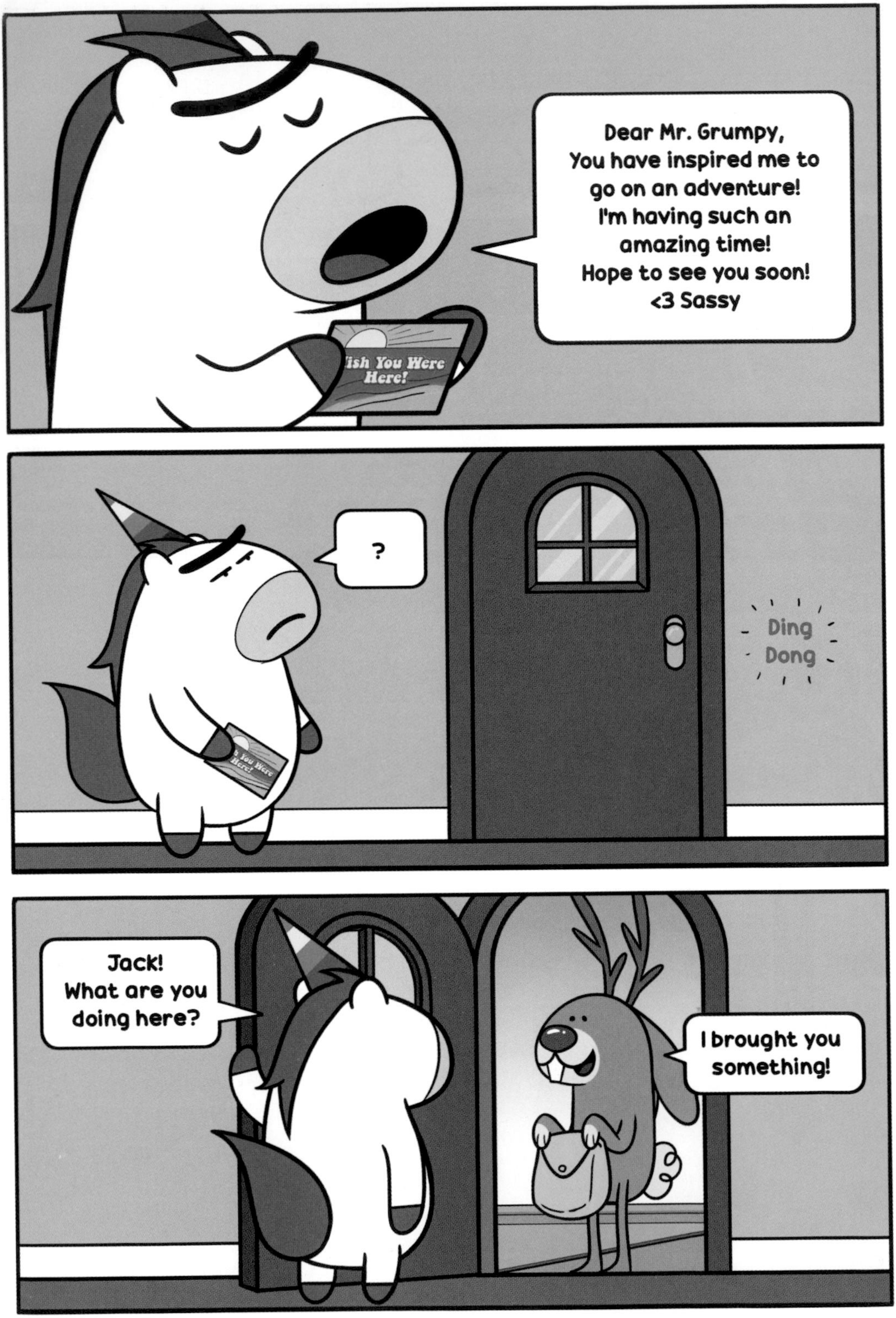
Dear Mr. Grumpy,
You have inspired me to
go on an adventure!
I'm having such an
amazing time!
Hope to see you soon!
<3 Sassy
Wish You Were Here!
?
Ding
Dong
Jack!
What are you
doing here?
I brought you
something!

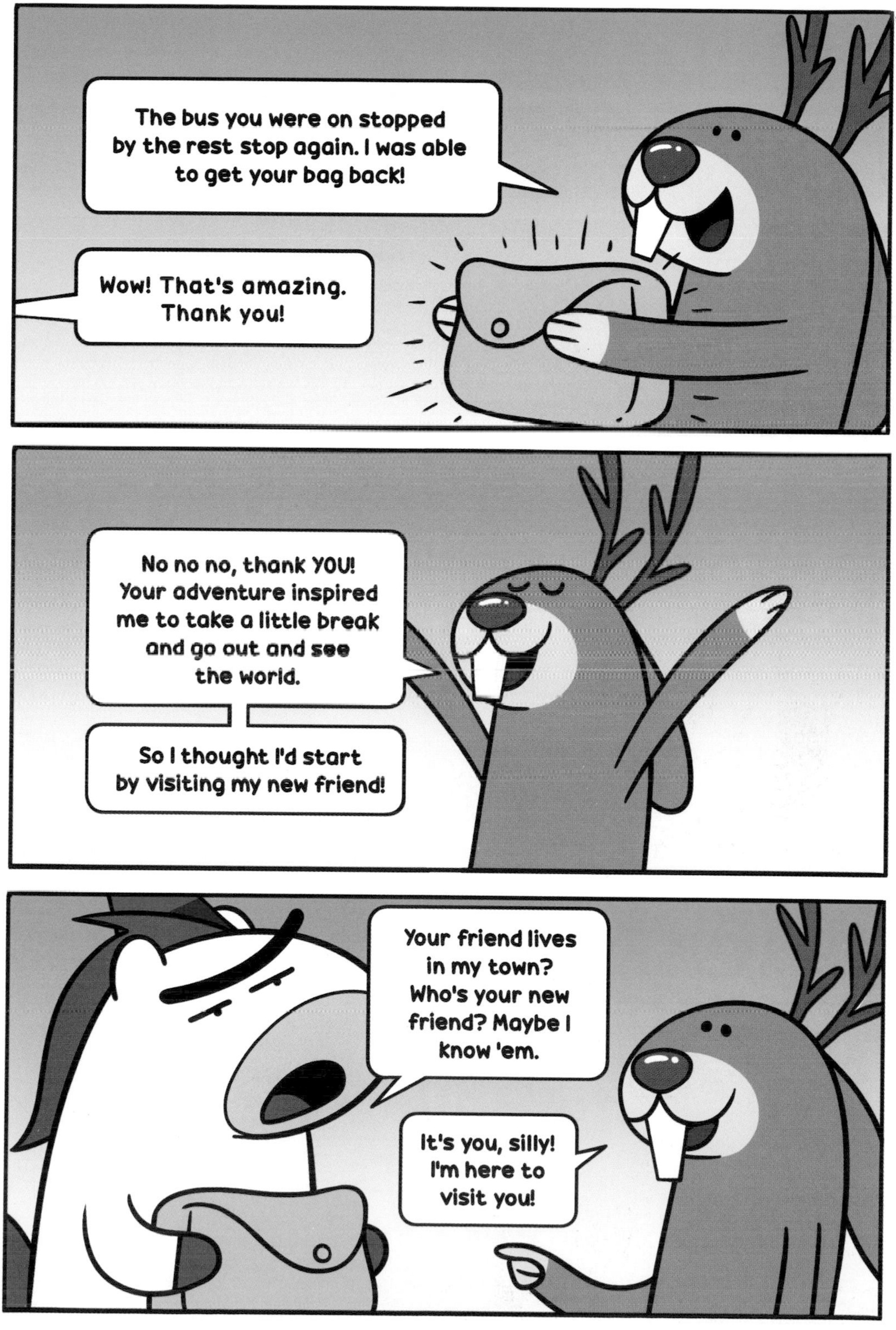
The bus you were on stopped by the rest stop again. I was able to get your bag back!
Wow! That's amazing. Thank you!
No no no, thank YOU! Your adventure inspired me to take a little break and go out and see the world.
So I thought I'd start by visiting my new friend!
Your friend lives in my town? Who's your new friend? Maybe I know 'em.
It's you, silly! I'm here to visit you!

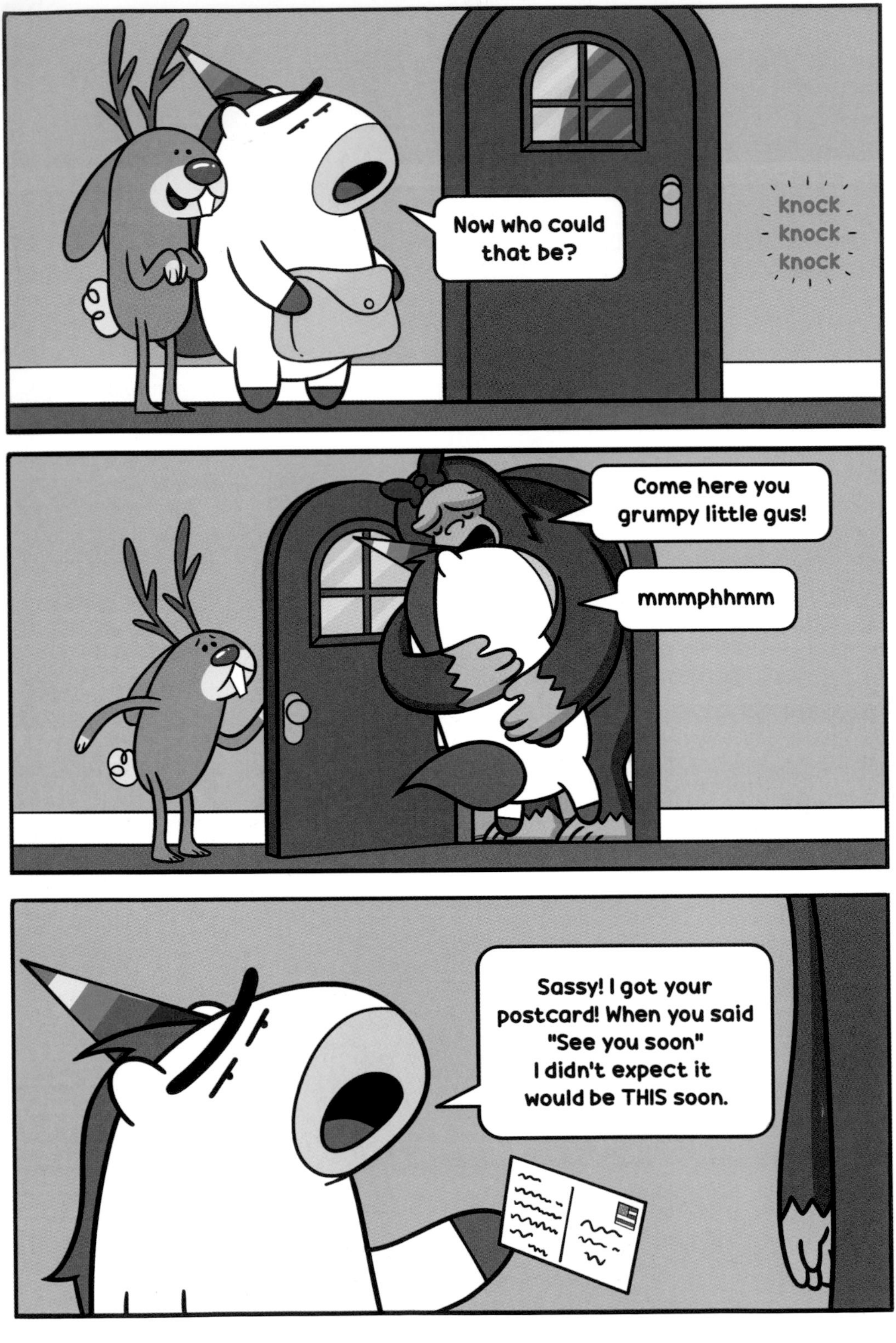
Now who could that be?
knock knock knock
Come here you grumpy little gus!
mmmphhmm
Sassy! I got your postcard! When you said "See you soon" I didn't expect it would be THIS soon.

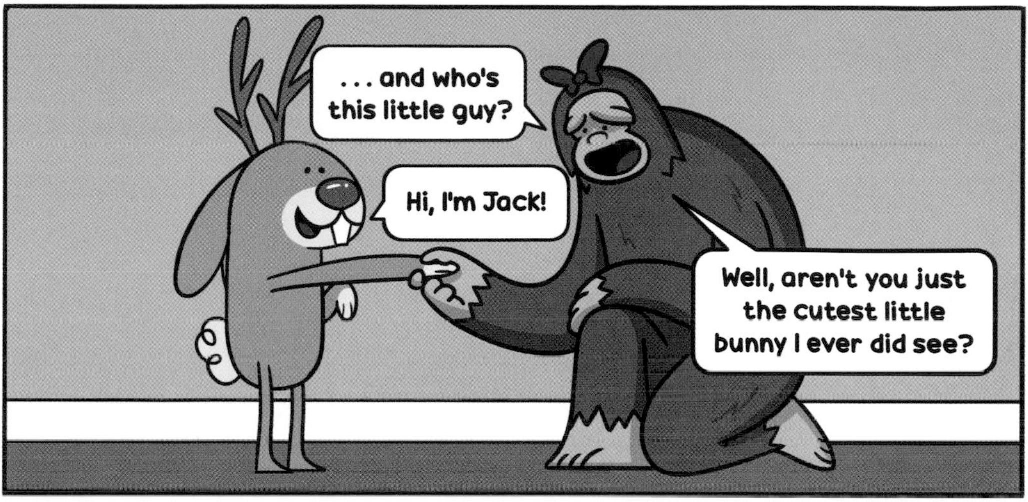
. . . and who's this little guy?
Hi, I'm Jack!
Well, aren't you just the cutest little bunny I ever did see?

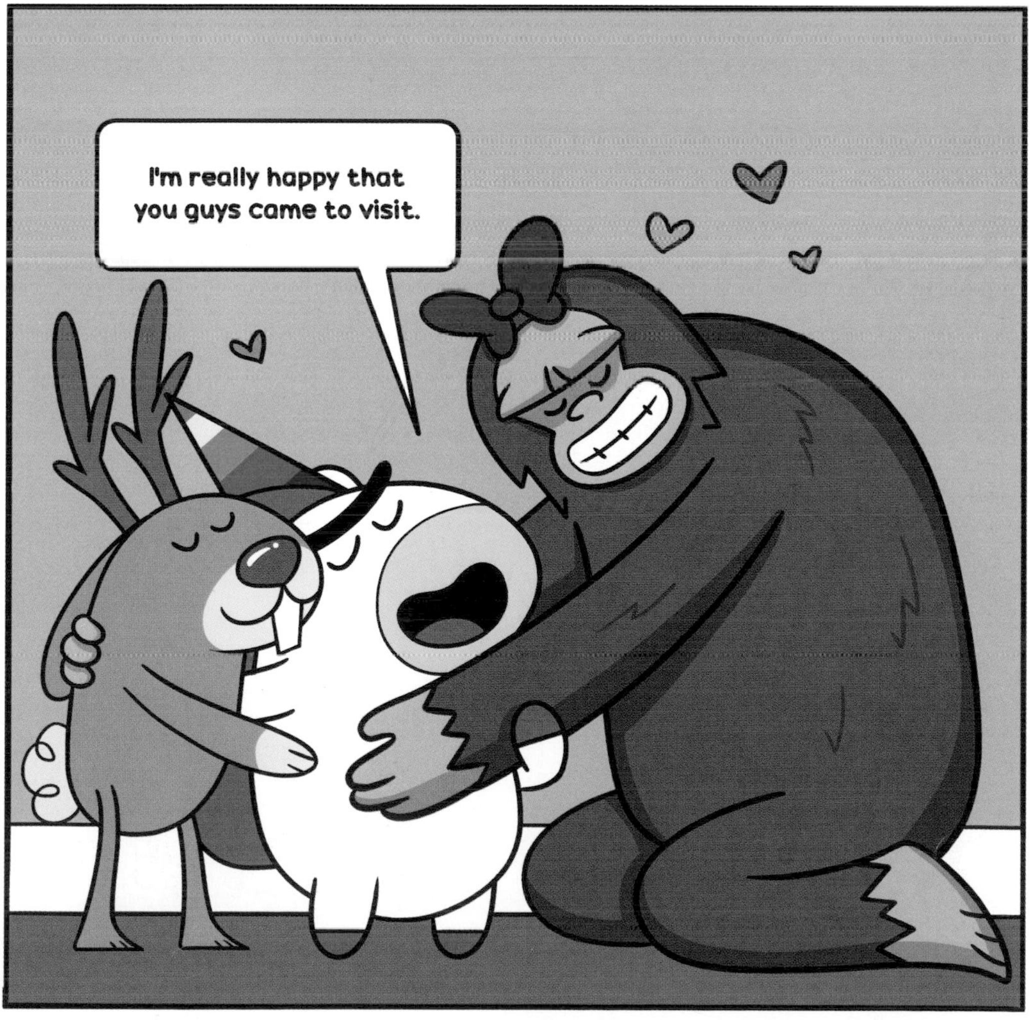
I'm really happy that you guys came to visit.

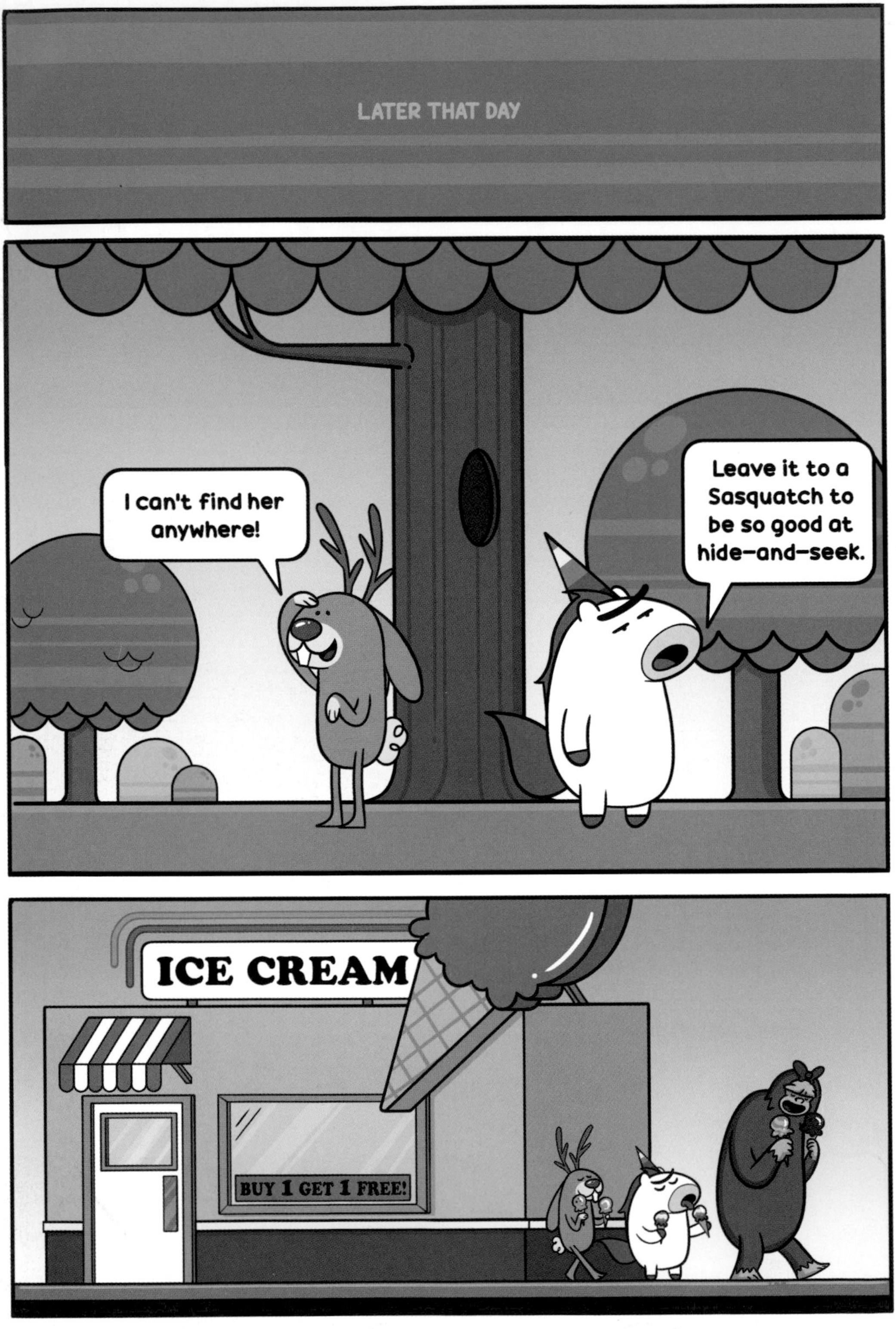
LATER THAT DAY
I can't find her anywhere!
Leave it to a Sasquatch to be so good at hide-and-seek.
ICE CREAM
BUY 1 GET 1 FREE!

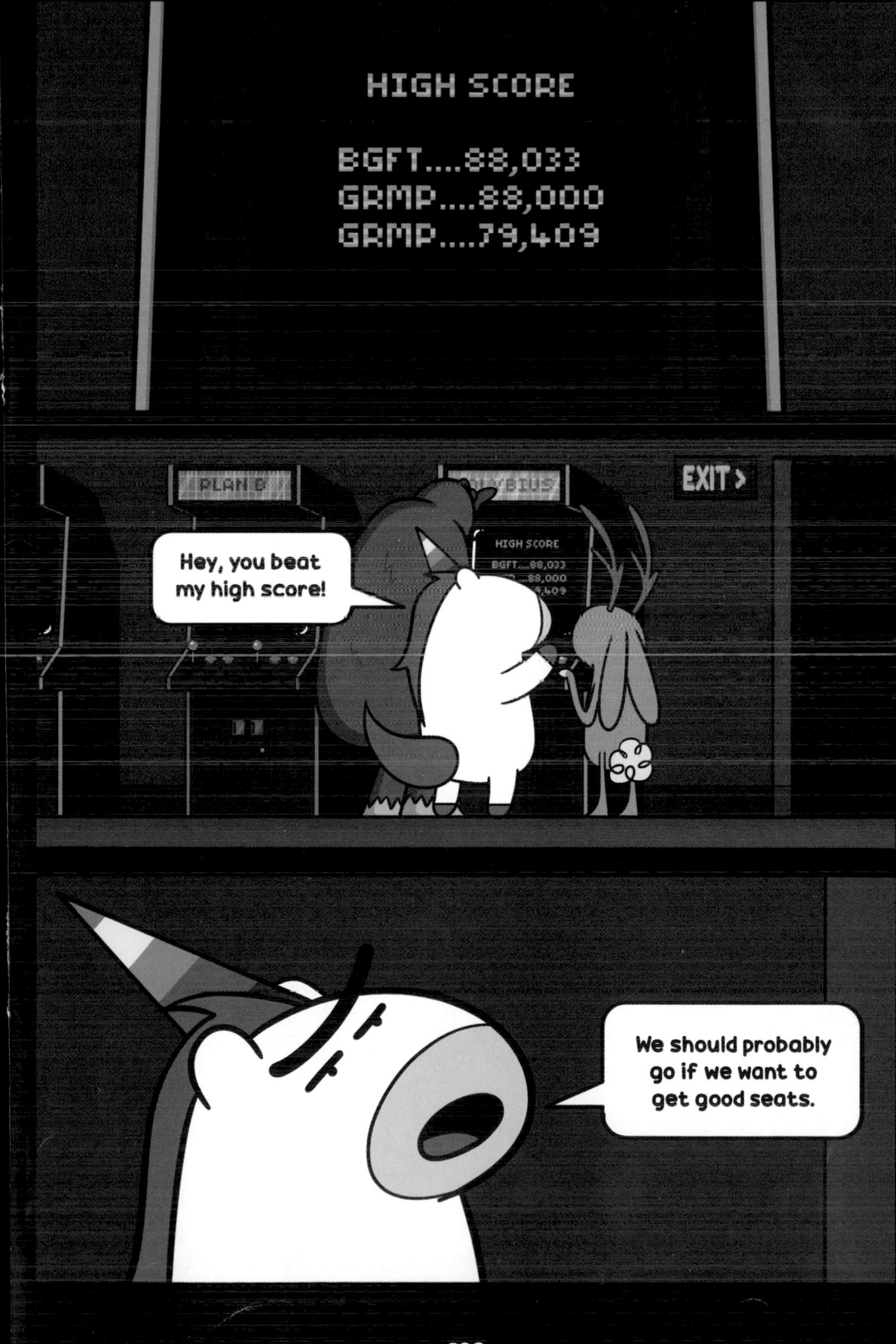
HIGH SCORE
BGFT....88,033
GRMP....88,000
GRMP....79,409
PLAN B
EXIT >
HIGH SCORE
Hey, you beat my high score!
We should probably go if we want to get good seats.

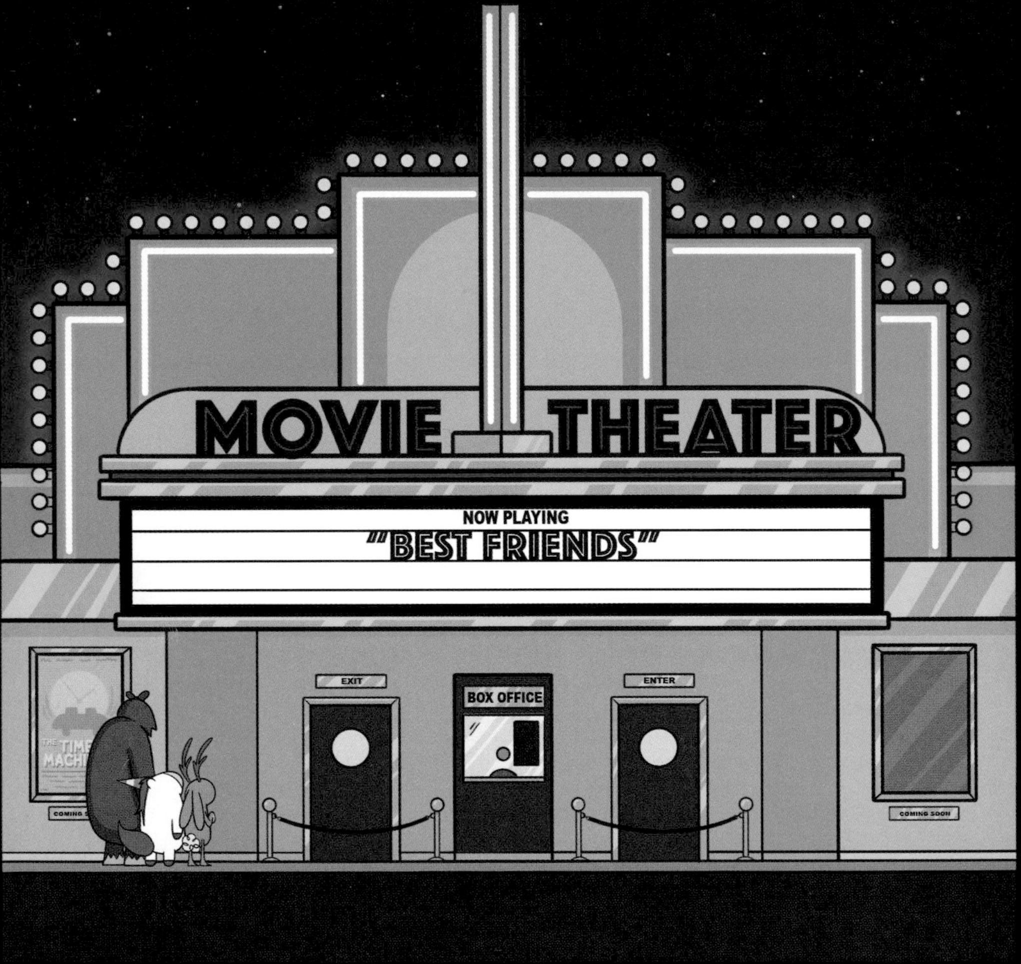
MOVIE THEATER
NOW PLAYING
"BEST FRIENDS"
EXIT
BOX OFFICE
ENTER
COMING SOON

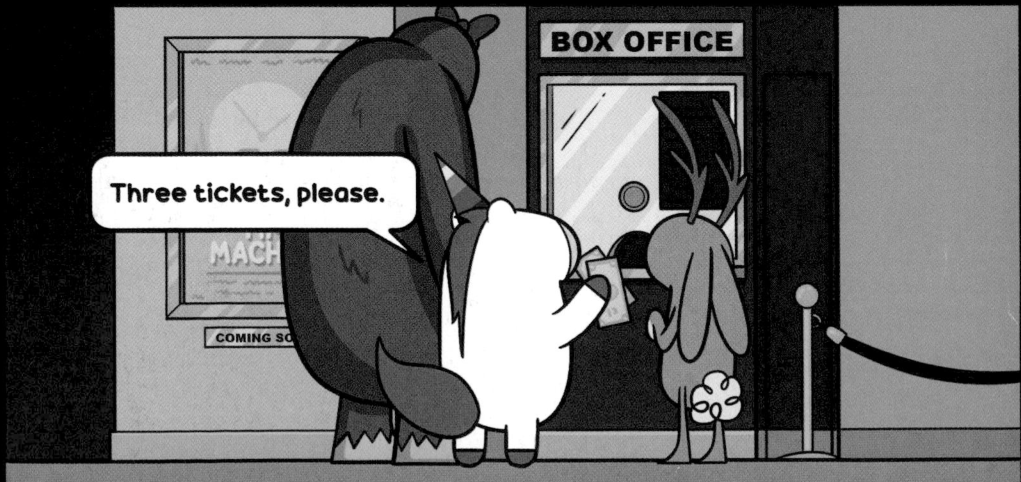
BOX OFFICE
Three tickets, please.

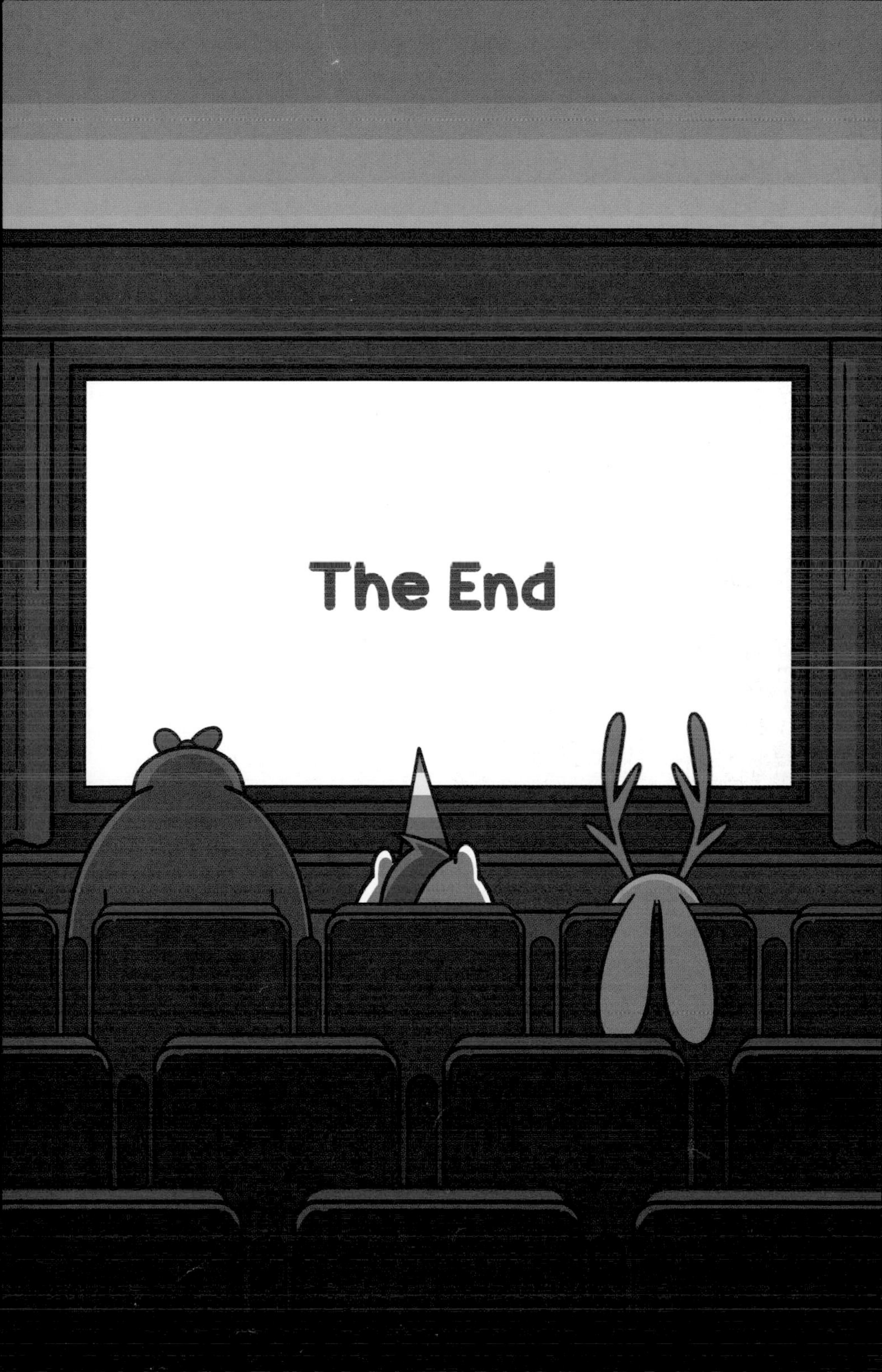
The End

# ABOUT THE AUTHOR

Joey Spiotto is an author, illustrator, and creator behind *Alien Next Door*, *Firefly: Back From the Black*, and the print series Storytime. His artwork is regularly featured at the world-famous *Gallery 1988* in Los Angeles, and he has previously worked on films, video games, clothing design, toys, and more. He lives just outside of Los Angeles with his wife and two boys, but you can visit him online at jo3bot.com.

ALSO available:

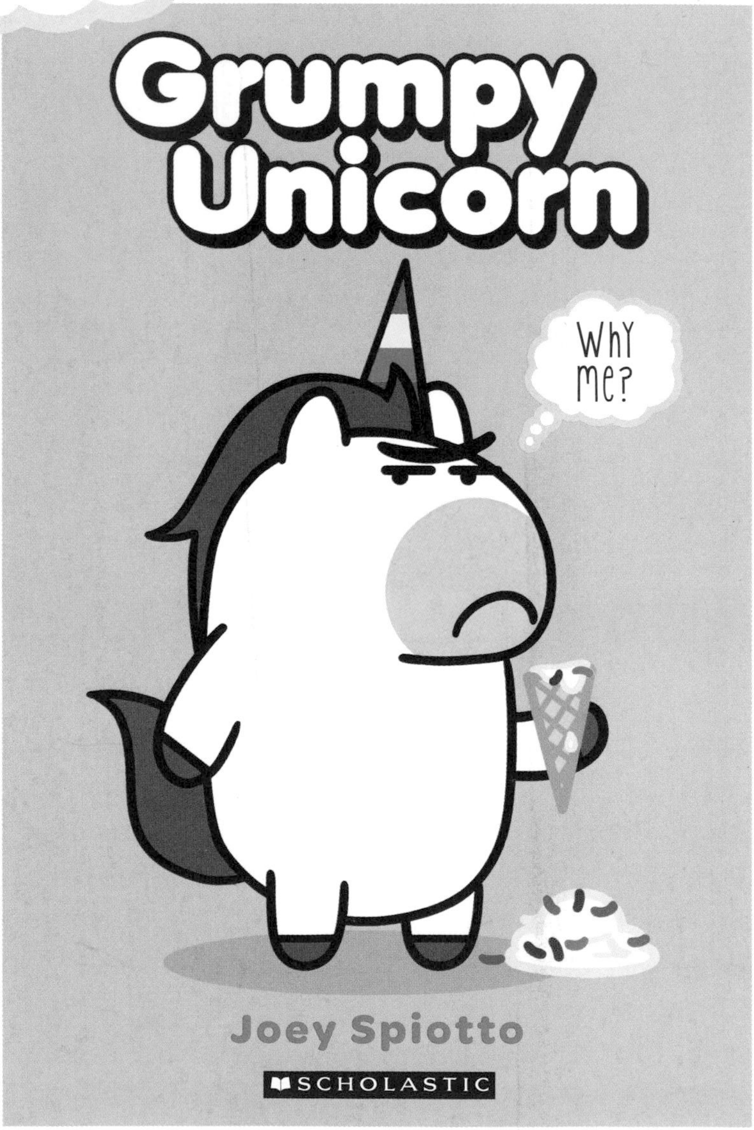

Grumpy Unicorn
Why me?
Joey Spiotto
SCHOLASTIC